HINDSIGHT

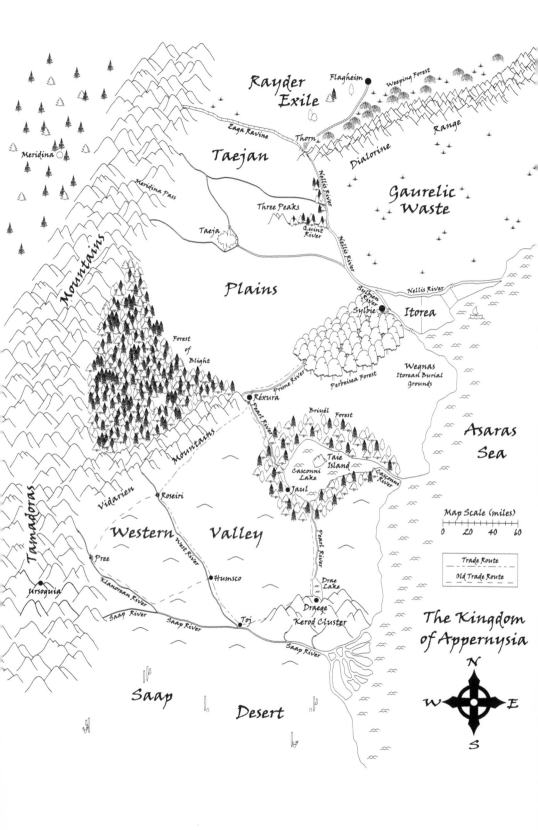

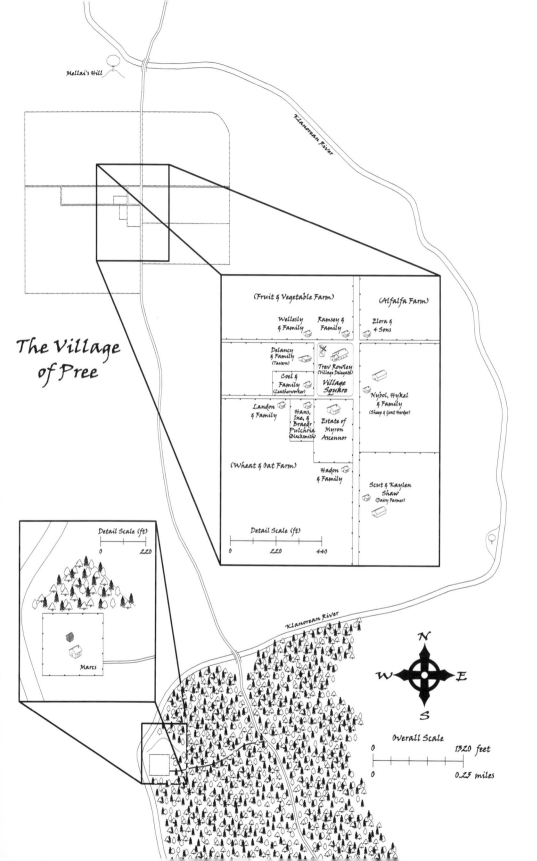

Mellai's Hill

Klanorean River

The Village
of Pree

(Fruit & Vegetable Farm)   (Alfalfa Farm)

Wellesly   Ramsey &   Elora &
& Family   Family   4 Sons

Delancy
& Family   Trev Rowley
(Tavern)   (Village Delegate)

Coel &   Village
Family   Square
(Leatherworker)   Nybol, Hykel
                                         & Family
Landon   (Sheep & Goat Herder)
& Family   Hans,
                Ine, &
                Braedr
                Pulchria   Estate of
                (Blacksmith)   Myron
                                Ascennor

(Wheat & Oat Farm)   Hadon
                        & Family

                                         Scut & Kaylen
Detail Scale (ft)   Shaw
                                         (Dairy Farmer)
0   220   440

Detail Scale (ft)

0   220

Detail Scale (ft)

0   220

Mats

Klanorean River

N
W   E
S

Overall Scale

0   1320 feet

0   0.25 miles

Gaurelic Waste

Halberd
Hook
Tip
Blade

Itorea
City of the King

Asaras Sea

Trade Route
Main Road
Canal
Aquaducts

Map Scale (miles)
0   5   10

N
W   E
S

Reed

Agricultural Lands

Nellis River

Cavalier Crook

Sythie

Sythien River

Nellis River

Prime River

Prime River

Wegnas
Itorean Burial Grounds

Perbeisea Forest

Taeja
2nd Age
of Appernysia

Three Peaks

E
N
W
S

Map Scale (miles)

0 1 2 3 4 5

Old River Path

The Swallows

Keep

North Gate

Arena

Armory & Barracks

South Gate

To my oldest son, Dallen. Your support and enthusiasm saw me through this series.

Acknowledgments

My all, my love, my own, my precious Sun Crystal.

Dallen, Dawsen, Duncan, Daxton, and Duke; the world's most amazing sons who never cease to keep me on my toes. You have selflessly sacrificed your father to Beholders for the past ten years. It's about time I return the favor.

Allen, Debbie, Angela, Mark, Connie, and Kirsten, with their never-ceasing wit and perspective. You are my truest living examples of apperception.

Scott, giving his all to redesign the books in my series. I couldn't have done this without your help.

All my editors; thank you for your enthusiasm and support.

My junior high students and their daily prodding for me to practice what I preach. It's been a long ten years with many bumps in the road, but I finally finished the series!

Prologue

Splash!

With a shudder, Reese clawed toward the surface of the freezing water. Seconds passed like decades, pounding the warmth from his body. He locked his vision on the warped glow of the yellow sun above. Only one goal filled his mind. Survival.

With a powerful kick off the riverbed and tightened fists overhead, Reese broke through the thin layer of ice. He gasped for air and threw his arms out sideways, desperately reaching for a handhold on the glasslike surface. Ice carved at the sides of his bare chest and, moments later, the current pulled him under again. Thrice more he surfaced, creating a jagged line of bloody pockets in the ice as he inched his way toward the eastern shoreline.

On his fifth attempt, Reese caught hold of a dangling tree branch that had been lowered by a layer of wet snow. With a shout, he mustered his limited reserves of strength, pulled himself above the ice, and with swinging legs, hurled himself toward the shore. The attempt was folly, but luck was on his side. The ice cracked where he fell, but held Reese's weight as his momentum carried him across the surface of the ice. He slid to a halt a foot from the bank.

Reese emptied his lungs, partially from relief, but mostly with self-disgust. He had been such a fool. No bet was worth risking his life. He weakly raised his head and searched for his three companions on the bridge upstream, but the young men had disappeared. They probably had his clothes, too, and were bragging about their prank to the girls in Roseiri.

Groaning, Reese rolled onto his hands and knees, stood, and wrapped his arms around his naked body. With a bitter shiver, he gingerly made his way up the steep riverbank, until a faint cry from the distant village stopped him midstride.

A scream—barely audible, but genuinely terrified.

The following silence worried Reese even more. He lowered himself against the snow-covered bank and peeked above the ridge, ignoring the freezing burn against his unprotected skin. Not a person or creature was in sight, but he remained frozen in place. Something was wrong.

He scanned the surrounding terrain, peering through the trees and examining the eastern trail leading up from Humsco. It was then that he noticed a fresh set of prints erratically following the shoreline from the bridge. They had stopped a few strides from his current position. He peered closer at the tracks in the snow. Wolves?

Reese shifted his attention to the bridge a hundred yards north, the bridge he had jumped from . . . the bridge where his friends had been watching . . .

Energized by a new wave of terror, Reese grabbed a thick branch from the ground for defense as he stumbled toward the bridge. The closer he drew, the more his anxieties flared.

Blood everywhere. One prostrate body. No, that's two. Wait . . . five?

It wasn't until Reese reached the bridge that he realized he had been wrong about his friends. Three mangled corpses littered the snow covered planks, barely recognizable. Two had been torn asunder. Porter and Tucker. Reese gagged and tasted bile in his mouth.

Abram's body was farther away. He had obviously fled, but even his unmatched speed couldn't save him. He never reached the opposite shore, twenty-five strides away. This wasn't the work of wolves. So who—or what—attacked them?

Reese forced himself to look away and found his clothes still hanging where he had draped them over the wooden railing. He carefully stepped through the massacre and donned his linens and boots, knowing that he was much colder than the numbness he felt. Once dressed, he eyed the opposite western shore, wondering what to do. His worries deepened when a black plume of smoke erupted farther north from the village center—right where his house was located.

"Theiss," he gasped, rubbing warmth into his limbs. He loved his family, but especially idolized his older brother. Theiss was honest, hardworking, and strong. If the village were under attack, Theiss would be leading the resistance. He was sure of it.

As Reese tried to focus on the best way to enter Roseiri, a galloping sound came from the blind side of a swell north of his position. He gripped his stout branch and summoned his courage, when Theiss's face appeared over the ridge of the hill. He was on a donkey, galloping madly down the path.

Running away?

Reese dropped his branch and sprinted toward his brother as quickly as his impaired body would allow. Their distance closed quickly, until Theiss was close enough that Reese could decipher his brother's expression. It was plagued with fear.

"Take her!" Theiss shouted. He swiveled off the donkey's back and slipped to the ground in a practiced roll. After regaining his feet, he sprinted past the slowing donkey and angled toward the grove of trees east of the trail.

"What's happening?" Reese asked, slowing to a stop.

"Go!" Theiss growled. "Warn Humsco!"

Theiss lowered his shoulders and barreled past his brother. Reese turned his head just in time to see Theiss plow headlong into the side of a hideous beast. Sharp bone spikes stuck out from its short orange fur, running along its spine from head to tip of tail. The creature hissed as Theiss tackled its enlarged wolf-like mass to the ground.

"Get out of here, Reese!" Theiss shouted, followed by a cry of pain as one of the beast's neck spikes impaled his gripping bicep.

The creature thrashed about, flailing its padded feet and snapping at Theiss's nearby face with its long, slender snout, but Theiss held firm. With his free hand, he gouged at the creature's eyes. Gurgling hisses poured from the beast's partly blocked throat. It jerked its head sideways and caught hold of Theiss's hand. Blood soaked its clenching teeth.

Reese took a step in Theiss's direction, but stopped when Theiss shook his head at him.

"Please, brother," Theiss said with eerie calm.

Realization struck Reese as intensified screaming sounded from the village. His heartbeat pounded in his ears. Roseiri was lost. No one would survive.

"Go," Theiss said. Tears poured down his cheeks.

Unable to speak, Reese mounted the bare back of the donkey and kicked its sides. They galloped south on the path leading to Humsco. He doubted he would survive the eighty-mile trip, but he had to try.

Chapter 1

Truce

An uncomfortable silence wafted through the Taejan Plains, slowly overtaking the sounds of fighting between the Appernysian and Rayder armies as they watched their Beholders. As Lon helped Tarek to his feet, he noted the intermixed ranks of soldiers. The Rayders were carefully moving into defensive clusters, while the Appernysians eyed them warily. The unspoken truce between armies wouldn't last much longer.

"Murderer," Mellai shouted at Tarek, her eyes still clouded with True Sight. "Heartless coward. Dung's dung." She pointed at Braedr's sagging head, his lifeless body still encased in dirt from the neck down. "He was completely defenseless. How could you?"

"Don't get preachy," Lon interceded. "You have no idea what he has done since joining the Rayders. Incalculable deaths, all at his hands."

"Talking about Braedr or yourself?" Mellai asked as a few plate-armored Appernysians formed a protective arc behind their Beholder. "How many deaths have you caused?"

"You want to see death?" Tarek spat as he searched about. Lon knew his friend wanted a weapon, since his sword had disappeared during the fighting. Lon had no idea how Mellai had done that. Disarming people with True Sight was one thing, but to make their weapons and armor disappear completely? He eyed the bare-chested Appernysian. Very strange.

When the commander tried to take Lon's falchion and sword from the ground, Lon stepped in front of him. "Wait a minute," Lon said quietly, then walked up to his twin sister. He ignored the shuffling armor of Appernysians moving to protect their Beholder.

"Stand down," Mellai called to them. "This is a family dispute."

Lon watched as all nearby Appernysians followed Mellai's order explicitly. "Looks like you've moved up in the world, Little Sis."

"What do you want?" she asked with derision. A cluster of men moved close behind her, no doubt her guard. One of them stepped forward and put his hand on her shoulder, his other hand gripping a drawn scimitar.

"No tricks," the man said, pointing the weapon at Lon.

Lon hadn't been sure at first, but after hearing his voice, the man's identity was unmistakable. "Kutad?"

He nodded and lowered his scimitar.

"Where's your caravan?"

"Under different management," Kutad replied. "Now get on with it."

Lon returned his attention to Mellai and spoke quietly, forcing himself to remain calm. "Let Tarek take the Rayders and set up camp a half-mile away. We both know that's where you want them, grouped together like a flock of hens."

Mellai folded her arms. "No Rayder willingly surrenders."

Lon shook his head and pushed an exasperated burst of air from his lungs. "Just let them retreat, then we'll negotiate."

Mellai examined Lon for a long time, her gaze drifting between the ranks of soldiers. With a final nod of approval from Kutad, she turned back to her brother. Lon shifted uncomfortably as she stared unblinking at him with clouded eyes.

"Very well," she finally said. "Let them go, but you stay with me."

A small commotion began south of their position, at the edge of the intermixed soldiers. Lon could see soldiers from both armies parting to make a path for a runner. Lon wanted to summon

True Sight to hear the source of the commotion, but knew Mellai wouldn't allow it.

"A messenger," he said, pointing behind his sister.

"Oh, good," Mellai replied without glancing away from Lon. "Let's do this the old-fashioned way and wait for him to reach us."

It took some time for the messenger to make his way through the ranks, but he eventually arrived, out of breath and pale. He was garbed in Appernysian armor.

Kutad moved next to the man. "What is it, Ian?"

"A message for King Drogan," Ian said, leaning forward on his thighs. "I'm sorry, Sergeant. I can't keep running."

"Beholder Mellai can deliver your message," Kutad said, placing a hand on Ian's shoulder. "Give it to me."

Ian glanced around at the nearby soldiers, then straightened and leaned close to Kutad's ear. As Ian whispered, Kutad's neutral expression dissolved into a mixture of anger and remorse. But his eyes told the most, wide with alarm.

"What is it?" Mellai asked.

"An urgent message," Kutad replied, then looked directly at Tarek. "One that concerns *all* of us. Send your soldiers away if you wish, Commander, but I suggest you keep your lieutenants behind. Quickly."

Lon looked at Tarek, who was listening carefully. Lon was grateful to see his commander recognize the magnitude of the exchange. No one could fake the anxiety on Ian's face. Immediate action was necessary.

"Mellai," Tarek called, "I need Lon to carry my message to the Rayders."

"I can do it," Mellai said. She raised her palms as her eyes clouded over, obscuring their deep brown. "Go ahead."

Lon listened with awe, having never been on the receiving end of one using True Sight. Tarek's voice swirled about as Mellai pivoted to carry his words to the entire mixture of soldiers. It was like listening to a gust of wind rushing through the trees overhead, but a wind of words. The sounds of skirmishes around the perimeter of their armies ceased as Tarek's voice filled the air.

"Rayders, withdraw from this conflict. Make camp north of the river and wait for me there. Leave the dead. We will honor them later."

After removing the earthen prison from Braedr and laying his body flat on the ground, Mellai lifted Kutad on a high pillar of hardened dirt and created a smaller platform with a staircase leading up to it.

"That looks somewhat familiar," Tarek jested as he stood next to Lon, then his expression became deathly sober. "I fear we already know the cause of this urgent war council." He held his hand forward, his armored fingers imitating a three-clawed beast.

Lon nodded as he watched Mellai climb the steps and direct a message from Kutad, no doubt directly to Drogan. "I hope we're wrong."

"You're never wrong," Tarek replied, "but that doesn't mean you have to be so submissive. Who cares if Mellai is more powerful than you? You're still a Beholder—*our* Beholder."

Lon barely heard Tarek. His mind was lost in the memory of his excursion to unblock the rivers in the Tamadoras Mountains. The attack during his journey there—strange, powerful beasts that had rushed at his squad faster than a galloping horse. His inability to stop them. The intervention of separate flying beasts. Calahein and ghraefs. Ghosts jumping off pages from Appernysia's history. It had been twelve hundred years since either had been seen, not since the end of the First Age. Had they really returned? Was it possible?

"Beholder?"

Lon blinked out of his stupor and looked at the man next to him, smiling at the long blond ponytail protruding from the base of his helm. Even in the midst of battle, it had somehow remained clean and glossy. His face and beard, however, were covered in grime and surface abrasions, the results of Mellai throwing Wade face-first into the packed snow. "I'm fine, Lieutenant. Just anxious."

"As are the rest of us," Wade replied. He and the other surviving members of Lon's squad stood behind the lieutenant, peering to the west.

Kutad's voice filled the plains, also conveyed by Mellai. "By order of King Drogan, Appernysian soldiers will allow the Rayders to retreat without resistance. Move south of our rear flank and make camp."

"By order of King Drogan?" Lon shouted sarcastically to his sister. Soldiers from both armies moved obediently in opposite directions, carefully stepping over the fallen bodies of their comrades. "I don't see him anywhere nearby. Who made Kutad his royal spokesperson?"

"He will be here soon," Mellai shouted back. Her expression had transformed to terror as she frantically searched about, validating Lon and Tarek's suspicions before Mellai used her power to whisper in Lon's ear. Lon immediately relayed the information to Tarek and his squad.

"The calahein attacked Réxura."

*　　*　　*　　*　　*

Notwithstanding their urgency, a large portion of the afternoon passed as the two armies separated. Many small skirmishes resulted as the Rayders moved between Appernysian ranks, but all were quickly quelled by Mellai, who kept watch from atop her earthen platform. Kutad had been returned to the ground, but he stood aloof from Lon with four other Appernysians. They stood around the base of Mellai's platform, with repeated glances of concern at her exposed position.

Lon focused on calming his emotions while they awaited the arrival of King Drogan. According to Kutad, the King had stayed at the opposite end of their army, *tending to other priorities* with General Astadem. Lon had scoffed at such a guarded proclamation. Drogan was just hiding behind an equal coward, a general who had fled and abandoned his troops during their previous battle. As time continued to pass, Lon doubted that either the king or general would arrive for their war council.

Lon also couldn't help but notice the way Kutad looked at him with an irritating flood of contempt. Lon hadn't seen him for over six years, not since the year Lon's family had fled from Roseiri. Still, Kutad's reaction came with little surprise. Lon didn't expect an Appernysian to understand the logic behind his choices over the past year, especially since many Rayders struggled with the same ideology, but time would show them all differently. Lon would fulfill his promise to Omar. Taeja would be preserved, and Rayders would be accepted as a part of the kingdom again—as Taejans. Lon didn't care how long it took. He would see it through; that is, if they survived this immediate threat from the calahein.

Eventually, as soldiers continued to depart, Lon noted a cluster of war horses carrying plate-armored knights toward their position. Two of the knights held vertical banners of green with white halberds stitched into the fabric. The others wielded steel halberds aimed defensively at Lon's squad. No sign of King Drogan or General Astadem, but Lon wasn't surprised. If they were even there, they would be packed safely in the center of their escort.

Not that it would do them any good if I decided to attack, Lon thought. He could kill a few people before Mellai intervened, but with her around, Lon felt about as powerful as a sapling caught in a stampede. Unable to flee. Nothing to do but wait and hope.

Mellai returned to the ground and stood in the middle of her guard. Lon didn't need to connect to her emotions to recognize something else hidden in her countenance. Plenty of apprehension, but there was something in her eyes that spoke of a deeper, immediate concern. Her gaze kept drifting between her brother and the approaching horsemen. Lon wanted to inquire, but thought better of it. Family or not, they were on enemy sides of the battlefield. The small distance between their two forces was as much a brewing danger as it was a safety precaution.

Upon their arrival, the horsemen reorganized into a solid line between their leaders and Lon's squad. Between their ranks, Lon saw three people dismount. One, obviously King Drogan, wore a helm decorated with a wrapping silver crown. He moved with the air of an entitled man while those surrounding him saluted with fists over hearts and bowed in submission.

The second man was unmistakable, not only because of the silver Lynth flower etched into his breastplate, but by his face. The same face that had forced thousands of untrained peasants into the massacre of battle; that had ordered Lon's execution during their fight for Taeja; that had fled at Lon's display of power. That same spineless face. Lon gripped his sheathed sword. If the opportunity presented itself, he would inflict his own punishment upon that pathetic excuse for a general.

The third person intrigued Lon. Her head was hidden under the hood of a thick, green cloak, but her physique was unmistakably feminine. Lon had heard stories of kings and generals bringing their servants into battle, but he had thought of them as just that—stories. Never would he have actually believed a man would risk the safety of a defenseless woman for the sake of a few extra comforts. Lon shifted to peer at the woman. He wanted to see her face—her innocent, helpless face—to justify his hatred for Drogan. King or not, this was unacceptable. But Lon never had the chance. She remained bowed in submission, hiding beneath her hood.

After a brief pause while the Appernysian leaders conversed in whispers behind their guard of knights, the protective line parted. Mellai appeared first, her moist eyes clouded with True Sight. Her shaking hands were outstretched defensively. Her guard, King Drogan, and General Astadem followed with the woman servant. She stood directly behind Mellai, her hood still low. Her shoulders shook with what Lon assumed were the same emotions that made Mellai cry.

Lon's jaw dropped slightly with realization. He couldn't believe it. This girl was Mellai's lady-in-waiting. His sister had forced her along for the ride. Abruptly, by no will of his own, Lon's gaping jaw slapped shut from an unseen force under his chin. He glared at his sister, and she returned his look in kind.

"A war council like this," Drogan began, "is usually filled with false pretenses and insulting words, but I'd like to skip past all the unpleasantries."

"Agreed," Tarek replied with surprising formality. "My name is Tarek Ascennor. I am the commander of the Rayders. Now tell me, what happened?"

"A tradesman arrived from Réxura," Kutad interceded. "I knew Rypla well; a man of his word. He revealed that the trade city has been destroyed, along with everyone living there. He barely escaped, but not before he was mortally wounded. It's a miracle he made it this far."

"And you suspect Rayders?" Tarek asked.

The response surprised Lon. He eyed his friend curiously, but Tarek maintained an unreadable expression.

"We would be fools to think otherwise," the general intervened.

"You know foolishness on a personal level," Lon spat back at the general.

Tarek grabbed Lon's breastplate and yanked him close. He spoke quickly and quietly, not allowing Lon time to respond. "This is a political discussion, one that might determine our joint survival. No personal feelings, and no insults. Think tactically, Brother. That's your greatest strength and that's what I need most right now."

Lon nodded and shifted his gaze to the Appernysians. "I apologize, General . . . ?"

"Astadem," Drogan replied. "General Kamron Astadem."

Lon also noticed Mellai. She stared at Lon warily, one eyebrow raised with the same obvious concern she had expressed many times in Pree, before Lon had mastered True Sight. Mellai's lady-in-waiting was gripping her shoulder.

"Please continue," Tarek said.

Drogan nodded. "You have spoken true, Commander Tarek. We feared that Rayders had attacked Réxura, but we identified another potential suspect—one spoken by the injured tradesman with his final breath."

"Calahein."

All eyes fell on Lon as he spoke the word.

"How could you know?" Kutad asked.

Lon thought quickly, realizing that Mellai hadn't received permission to share that information. "My squad was attacked by a vicious force a few months ago, near the Forest of Blight. We had the same suspicion. Unfortunately, no evidence has been conclusive. We haven't had any encounters since, nor have any similar beasts been spotted on the Taejan Plains."

Kutad shook his head. "But how—"

"Simple deduction, Sergeant," Lon said, flattering him with the title he had heard from the Appernysian runner. "We were attacked from the Forest of Blight. Seeing how Réxura sits on the east tip of the Vidarien Mountains, it makes sense that the invasion originated from the same force that came after us. They probably used the mountains to hide their approach to Réxura."

Silence fell on their conversation as everyone pondered Lon's logic. The silence was suddenly broken by a hard clang on Lon's steel-covered back from Tarek's gauntlet. "A regular Omar, aren't you?" he said with a fond smile and a hint of sadness over Lon's fallen mentor.

"His argument makes sense," Mellai added, giving Lon a thankful nod.

"There is only one way to be sure," Drogan said. "I would like to examine Rypla's wounds and see if his injuries support our speculation. I don't want to rush into a rash reaction without confirming the truth. General Astadem, have two of our knights—"

"Allow me, my liege," Mellai interrupted. For a second time, she climbed the earthen staircase, but this time facing south with her palms extended.

A dark spot lifted into the air at the edge of the Appernysian forces. It slowly moved closer, soon becoming recognizable as a tradesman by the bright colors of his clothing, but it wasn't until Mellai lowered the body into their midst that Lon saw the extent of Rypla's injuries. Two gaping wounds crossed his abdomen, the work of either sword or beast, but his shoulder held Lon's attention. A thin layer of flesh connected his left arm to his body, the tissue and bone surrounding it raw and decayed. One might think his shoulder had been chewed through by an animal, but no teeth marks were present. In fact, the edges of raw flesh and bone were smooth.

A member of Mellai's guard, a man with a trim physique similar to Wade's, crouched over the body. "What sort of injury is this?" he said. He ran his middle finger over the edge of an exposed tendon, his eyes focused in concentration.

"Don't touch him, Duncan!" Mellai shouted as she ran down the dirt staircase, but she was too late. Duncan's face contorted in pain as he grabbed the base of his middle finger with his other hand. An oozing blister had formed on the tip, growing in size as it crawled up his finger.

With a flash of his thick hand, another guard unsheathed a knife, took hold of Duncan's hand, and carved off Duncan's middle finger at the knuckle closest to his fingernail.

"Now bind it," the guard said as he wiped his dagger on Rypla's leg and sheathed it again.

"I like this guy," Tarek whispered to Lon with a smirk, "even if he did grab me in a chokehold."

"That was unnecessary, Ric," Mellai said as she arrived at Duncan's side. "I could have saved his finger."

"I just did, Beholder," Ric replied.

"Sorry, Lon," Tarek whispered again, this time with a broad smile, "but Ric is my new best friend."

Lon hardly heard Tarek. He was too preoccupied by Mellai's statement. *I could have saved his finger.* What did she mean by that? Did she have the power to heal? If so, how did she learn it?

This pattern of thought led Lon's mind through waves of unanswered questions. When did Mellai become a Beholder? How had she survived? Omar Brickeden had discovered the essentials of True Sight to assist Lon, but who had helped Mellai? Was it Kutad, or had she endured on her own? Had she unlocked True Sight's secrets by herself? Could she have helped Lon? Had his choice to leave Pree been unnecessary?

And why wasn't Mellai in Pree? How did she end up fighting for King Drogan? Where were their parents? Where was Kaylen? Were they safe? Had the whole world changed since he left Pree last November?

Lon dropped to one knee as he removed his steel helm and ground his left palm against his forehead. *So many questions,* he thought, *and why are they just popping into my mind now? Have I really been that preoccupied?*

A soft touch pulled Lon back into the present. Mellai stood in front of him, her two hands wrapped around his.

"Easy, Lon," she said. Her eyes were still clouded with her power, but her eyebrows were slanted back with sympathy.

Lon looked past his sister and saw Duncan examining the smooth stump of his middle finger. She can heal people. *What else can she do?*

"Let's get through this council," Mellai said, "then I'll answer your questions as best I can. About home, our parents, myself, Kaylen. Everything."

Wait, Lon thought. *How does she know . . . ?* His eyes narrowed as he stared critically at her. *Can you read my thoughts?*

A slight nod from his sister, almost unnoticeable.

Get out of my head, he demanded, overwhelmed by a sudden rush of vulnerability. He summoned True Sight, desperate to undo whatever tied their minds together. With his hazy vision, Lon saw a tendril of light connecting their two foreheads, pulsating with what he assumed must be his own thoughts.

Immediately after he witnessed the connection, it disappeared, along with the enhanced brightness that had filled his sister when she was harnessing her power. She had released True Sight.

"Alright, Lon," Mellai said, stepping back and folding her hands calmly together at her waist. "You can trust me, but how about you? Can I trust you?"

I have her, Lon thought, thrilled by the chance to overpower his sister. *One quick move and I can end this battle between our people.* But the thought was fleeting, too impractical to entertain. Mellai was his twin sister, and the threat was beyond Rayders versus Appernysians. Their people would need every man possible if they hoped to survive, and that might not even be enough.

Lon closed his eyes and sighed, releasing his power along with his pent up breath. The sight that greeted him when he reopened his unclouded eyes was unsettling. His squad gripped their sheathed swords, lips pulled tight with determination, while the mounted Appernysian knights held their halberds ready to charge. Only Tarek and King Drogan stood motionless, but obvious strain filled their faces. They were both deciding whether to give the order to attack.

"Relax," Lon said as he rose to his feet. "We worked it out."

"You sure?" Tarek replied, his eyes never leaving Drogan.

Lon stepped closer to his sister and tipped his head forward to speak quietly into her ear. "I'm warning you, Mel, if you ever do that again—"

"I won't," she replied. Her demeanor was cool and confident, but her eyes spoke sincerity. "Now give me a hug so everyone believes what you just said."

As they embraced, Lon felt a sense of love and security that he had not experienced since leaving Pree. Despite their differences and opposing forces, a hug from his twin sister felt good. One of a thousand knots in his stomach undid itself as Mellai laid her head against his breastplate and squeezed his waist.

"I've missed you," Mellai said.

Lon habitually kissed the top of her head, unable to reply. A painful lump of homesickness burned in his throat.

"Beholders?" The voice was King Drogan's. "May we continue?"

"Of course, your Majesty," Mellai said as she released Lon and moved back into the midst of her guard. Streams of tears carved paths through the filth on her face.

"Sorry to interrupt your hugs and kisses," Tarek commented with obvious impatience as Lon returned to his side, "but the calahein want to kill us all, remember?"

Lon ignored his comment. Weeks of anxiety were dispersing. He didn't have to fight Mellai anymore, and the potential of their combined power thrilled him. What could she teach him about True Sight, and would he be able to reciprocate?

"Now what, Drogan?" Tarek said.

"I hate to admit this, but we might need to extend the Beholders' truce to ourselves," the king replied. "At least for a short time."

"Well, then," Tarek replied, "let's just follow you back to Itorea and wait to be attacked. We could stay in your spare castle and polish your boots for payment."

"Excellent idea," Lon interjected, before Tarek's rant turned to a bloody conflict. "Minus the sarcasm, I think you're onto something, my Commander."

Tarek folded his thick arms across his chest. "Enlighten me."

"Itorea was built by Beholders during the First Age," Mellai said, obviously catching on to Lon's idea, "in the middle of a gruesome calahein conflict. Itorea was their fallback, a stronghold against a calahein counterattack."

"No disrespect to Rypla," Kamron said, placing a hand on Mellai's shoulder, "but you're making plans to evacuate our entire kingdom from one man's dying words, and we have yet to hear our king's opinion on the subject."

"I'm intrigued," Drogan said.

"But my liege," Kamron continued, "we need to slow down and think this through."

"I already have," Lon said, stifling his dislike for the Appernysian general. "My squad and I will travel to Réxura to confirm his claims. If we find them to be true . . ." Lon turned to Tarek with raised eyebrows, waiting for the commander to confirm his solution.

"Terrible idea," Tarek said. "Send our Beholder away and leave his sister to do with us as she pleases? While the idea has some appeal," he paused to wink at Mellai, "it's hardly in the Rayders' best interest."

"I'll go with him," Mellai said.

"We will, too," one of her guard added, a man as young as Lon.

Mellai shook her head. "Don't be ridiculous, Snoom. I can take care of myself."

"I won't have it any other way," Kutad replied. "As sergeant, it's my responsibility to ensure the safety of Appernysia's leaders. You will take your guard with you, Mellai. That's an order."

Tarek thumped his breastplate with his gauntlet to draw everyone's attention. "We still have one little problem. Rayders living in Itorea, Lon? You can't be serious."

"No one is asking you to do that yet," Lon answered. "Let us investigate. If our suspicions are true, then you won't have any other choice."

"There's always another choice," Tarek grumbled.

"Perhaps not in this case," King Drogan said, "but let's not get ahead of ourselves. Lon and Mellai will take their escorts to confirm the calahein threat in Réxura. If confirmed, we will make a decision. Itorea might be our only choice."

Tarek crossed half the distance between the two forces. "And the Rayders?"

King Drogan paused, glancing between Kamron and Kutad, before stepping forward and extending his hand to Tarek. "If I must, I will find a place for your people. You have my word."

"This is only temporary," Tarek said as he took King Drogan's hand.

The king smiled too wide. "I couldn't agree more."

Chapter 2

Divided

"He was right there," Kaylen cried, her hands trembling as she fingered the pearl necklace hidden under her gown. Lon had given it to her as an addition to her dowry. A sign of their betrothal.

"Now isn't the time," Mellai replied, tugging on her arm. "Wait until we get back, then you can talk to him."

"I'm still not sure I want to."

Mellai said nothing. She understood what Kaylen meant. Both of them were still angry at Lon—livid—but seeing him in person had momentarily diffused their hatred. He had not been nearly as savage as Mellai expected. With the exception of Braedr's murder, Lon had been fairly rational, but listening to his thoughts had been even more insightful. So many questions, and so much confusion. And what of the brutality he endured? His commander, Tarek, was a vicious and savage man, nothing like a son of Pree. Oh, Mellai would pay him back when the time was right, with something he'd never forget. A punishment much more severe than ringlets in his beard.

"Lady Prettybeard," Mellai spat as she glanced over her shoulder at Lon's retreating squad.

"Tarek lacks civility," Kaylen said, "but you have to admit—he's ruggedly handsome, isn't he?"

"I didn't notice," Mellai scoffed. "I was too busy watching him break Braedr's neck and control my brother." Mellai regretted the words as soon as they left her mouth.

Kaylen burst into another fit of crying. "Things have only become worse for Lon. I wonder how much of his fighting is his own decision, or if others are forcing his actions."

"Others like Tarek?" Mellai's words were cold and unforgiving.

Kaylen sighed.

"I can tell you this," Mellai said with a softer voice. "Lon's thoughts conflicted with his actions. Plenty of guilt, and overwhelming worry about you and our family. He doubts himself, or at least he did in that moment. I suppose that offers a ray of hope. He isn't completely lost to us."

"Perhaps not," Kaylen said with a sniff. "I wish I could come with you to Réxura."

"It's a nice idea, but your presence would only complicate the situation with Lon. Besides, you can't even ride a horse by yourself."

"I know, but still . . ."

Mellai didn't need to read Kaylen's thoughts to know her feelings. She was as confused as Lon. They had been perfect for each other, but their circumstances and perspectives forced them apart. Now opposites in two warring nations. Only time would tell whether they could work it out.

Preparations were hastily made when Mellai and her company returned to the main body of Appernysia's forces. King Drogan had sworn them all to secrecy, so it was only with concerted effort that they gathered supplies and horses for a long journey to Réxura, over one hundred miles away. The only way Mellai could deflect the many Appernysian questions was by utilizing her position as Beholder. When asked what was happening, she simply walked away without responding.

"I'm beginning to understand why so many leaders come across as pompous," Kaylen observed as another lieutenant skulked away in frustration.

Mellai crammed extra socks into her horse's saddlebag. "Not my fault. People should tend to their own fields."

"I meant nothing by it," Kaylen said quietly. She handed Mellai a wrap of cheese and bread. "I was sympathizing with you."

"I know," Mellai grumbled. "I'm just tense. Lon—" She glanced about and lowered her voice. "Lon, Rayders, the calahein. I can't handle every problem at the same time."

"Then don't," Kutad said as he approached with his horse in tow. He had exchanged his plate armor for hardened leather, similar to the garb Mellai still wore. Flexible and light, it allowed for quick movements and faster travel. Kutad gripped a light spear, and his scimitar hung at his side. Without a helm, his tangled black and silver hair flicked lightly in the chilly breeze. "That's what we're here for. Six is better than one, right?"

Mellai smiled at Kutad and the other four members of her guard, who had also swapped their armor and were loading their own supplies. Snoom, Jareth, Ric, Duncan—she was glad to have them. They were skilled fighters and men of valor. Snoom had particularly become a good friend to Kaylen.

Mellai shook her head. *Anyway,* she thought, *a friend of Kaylen's is a friend of mine.* She trusted her guard implicitly. She mounted her horse while Kaylen tightened the straps of the saddle bags.

"Please be careful," Kaylen said. "Watch out for him, please."

"If you mean don't let him do anything foolish, it's a little late for that," Mellai said with a slight chuckle. "But I will take care of him, and guide his future where he'll let me. I promise."

"Thank you," Kaylen said, then turned to Kutad, who was also sitting on his horse. "And *you* keep *her* safe."

Kutad put his right fist over his heart. "With my life."

＊　＊　＊　＊　＊

Mellai's guard met Lon and his squad between the two armies, the Rayders having followed similar protocol. They donned leather armor and sheathed swords, but rather than spears, they had glaives secured in loops on their saddles. They also had composite bows slung over their backs and a full quiver of arrows hanging on their hips, opposite their glaives. When Mellai compared their numbers— seven Rayders and six Appernysians—she felt uncomfortable, especially after watching the Rayders fight. Without Mellai to protect her guard, the Rayders would easily overpower them. She would have to remain alert and wary. Calahein threat or not, Rayders were unpredictable and violent.

Still, the bows on their backs brought Mellai a tinge of comfort. Through quick scans of their memories, Mellai had learned the Rayder arrows would come in handy. Especially from Nik, whose skill was unmatched and deadly. She reminded herself not to use the squad's names until she heard them aloud. Although she kept her promise and stayed out of Lon's head, she doubted he would appreciate her mental intrusion on the rest of his squad.

"Speaking tactically," Lon said once everyone had arrived, "it would be best for us to lead the way to Réxura. Our horses are faster and more conditioned for battle. I don't want you getting in our way."

Kutad nodded in response.

"And I might need to use True Sight," Lon continued.

Mellai chuckled. "As long as you stay where I can see you, that's fine with me."

"Sounds nice, Little Sis, but I can't promise it will stay that way. I thought you trusted me."

Mellai bit her bottom lip slightly, pondering the potential outcomes, but ultimately decided Lon was right. "Very well, but don't push me." She spoke loud and with as much authority as she could muster, meaning it as a warning for the rest of Lon's squad as much as for him.

Lon kissed the first two fingers of his right hand and brought them to the King's Cross brand on his right temple. "You have our word." His squad repeated the action. "Now let's get moving. We can give proper introductions along the way."

Mellai scanned the soldiers they were leaving behind, glad that Tarek was with them. He seemed impulsive, but he would be able to keep control of his Rayder soldiers while she was gone. Her king would be safe in her absence.

Chapter 3

Vanguard

*T*here's no better time for self-reflection than during a long
journey. Don't fear silence.

The advice had come from Kutad when Mellai and Kaylen were
traveling with his caravan from Pree to Roseiri. Kaylen had begun
the journey chirping away faster than a mad squirrel. Kutad had
responded with those words, not unkindly, but insistently. While
Kaylen didn't seem like a big advocate of the statement, Mellai
couldn't have agreed more.

Most villagers back in Pree hadn't understood Mellai's regular
need to hide away on her hill, but she didn't care. It had been there
that she found peace and knowledge, there that her jumbled thoughts
made sense. Llen, her Jaed mentor, had reaffirmed the same lesson
during her training in Roseiri, as had the oak tree which had protected her newborn mother.

Silence would always be a welcome friend to Mellai.

As she observed her brother, Mellai knew Lon had learned the
same lesson during his year with the Rayders. He rarely spoke,
and when he did, his comments were brief and usually directed to
the Rayder with the blonde ponytail—Lieutenant Wade. But what
impressed Mellai more than her brother's silence was his squad's
acceptance of it. Even when navigating around distortions in the
bleak landscape, like sagebrush or juniper trees, Lon's squad moved
with unspoken synchronization. They knew each other as well as

themselves. The thought originally increased Mellai's anxiety, until she realized it meant that if she could control Lon, she would control his squad.

As they galloped south, Mellai summoned her power and surveyed the land at regular intervals, often finding Lon to be doing the same thing. His body flared with brightness while channeling True Sight. They were following Rypla's path back to Réxura, which was easy to find through a clear trail and patches of blood.

During the first day of their journey, they found Rypla's fallen horse. Little meat remained on its ravaged carcass, but Mellai could see similar signs of Rypla's shoulder wound on the horse. Smooth lines of dissolved bone showed on its femur and pelvis, injuries Mellai directly connected to the creatures that had attacked her and her grandfather. The wolf-shaped beasts spat a wad of sticky phlegm that dissolved whatever it touched. They must have tracked the poor horse from Réxura for days, until they were close enough to spit at it and leave it to die. That must have been when Rypla was injured, too, which would explain why he was capable of making the full journey from Réxura to their battlefield. The attacking beasts must have been too close to the contending armies of Appernysia and Rayders; stealth seemed to be their highest objective, so they left him to die rather than chasing him down and finishing him off.

Mellai wanted to connect with the surrounding vegetation to confirm her suspicions, but a rescue might be necessary when they reached the city. People could still be fighting for their lives. Mellai didn't have the hours required to read memories.

Instead, Mellai relied on her intuition and Kutad's tracking abilities to support her silent theory, but doubts still filled her mind. During a short conversation with Lon, he described the calahein. Large beasts. Seven feet tall. Opposable thumbs. Fur. Spiked joints. Incredible senses. Bursts of speed. A reckless abandon for killing humans. There were too many inconsistencies between Lon's description and what had attacked her. The wolf-shaped beasts weren't calahein, so what were they?

But until she had answers, Mellai kept her information to herself. There was no reason to sow doubt. Even if calahein had not attacked Réxura, something mortally dangerous had. They needed to investigate either way.

* * * * *

Lon's goal was to travel forty miles per day, a fast pace that wouldn't completely exhaust their horses. During the second day of their ride, when civilization had disappeared in all directions and danger was at its lowest, Lon allowed himself to relax—even though they were pushing their horses to the limits of their endurance. It was then that Mellai moved her horse next to his. It was brown and small, not nearly as large as his own warhorse, but still bigger than a donkey. Perfect for his sister's size.

"Hi, Dawes," Mellai said, leaning over to rub his snout. "You been taking care of him for me?"

Dawes nickered and tossed his black mane playfully, obviously pleased with Mellai's attention.

"He remembers you," Lon said.

"Of course he does. I'm unforgettable. Ask anyone."

Lon chuckled. "I don't need to. I've already seen it."

Mellai smiled in return, then glanced around. "Can we talk privately?"

Lon breathed deeply. He had been waiting for this conversation with both dread and anticipation. After a quick nod to Wade, indicating not to follow, he gestured in front of himself. "After you, Little Sis."

They galloped ahead until they were well out of earshot. With a quick glance back, Lon noticed that Mellai's guard had moved up next to his squad.

As they should, Lon thought. *There's a huge difference between trust and foolishness.*

"That's a big scar," Mellai said.

"Yeah," Lon replied, rubbing his right temple. "Can't really hide it, even if I wanted to."

Mellai smiled weakly. "I was talking about the one on your arm."

"Ah, that." Lon lifted his right hand and flexed his forearm, stretching the scar tissue of the King's Cross he had carved into his skin. The wound had long since healed. He often forgot it was there. "Not my best engraving ever."

"*You* did that? Why?"

"A requirement of Rayben Goldhawk when I first arrived at Flagheim. He called it a test of courage."

"I'm sorry," she replied with a wince. "Where is he now?"

"Dead." Lon spoke without emotion, having never come to love his first Rayder commander. "Killed about six months ago by the Appernysians he had enslaved."

"I guess you were lucky, then?"

"If you want to call it that," Lon said, then blew out his breath. "What do you want, Mel?"

"The same thing you want from me," she replied with obvious irritation. "Explanations. I haven't had any communication from you since you left Pree. Not even a goodbye."

"That sounds more like an argument."

Mellai shifted in her saddle. "Can you blame me? Father told me your plan after you ran away. Did you forget about the part when you were supposed to come home? It nearly destroyed Kaylen when she found out you were fighting for the Rayders."

Lon hadn't seen Mellai for over a year, but he knew where this conversation was leading. Arguing with his sister at this point would be counterproductive. He kept his eyes forward and let her rant.

"And do you know who told me that you supported the Rayders?" Mellai continued. "Kaylen. Imagine how difficult that letter was to write. *Dear Mellai, My betrothed is a traitor. Your brother kills Appernysians for fun. Love, Kaylen.* I tried to keep it a secret from our parents, but Father tracked down Kutad and forced the truth out of him. Well, congratulations, Brother." Her voice oozed with mockery. "You have opened the gates into Appernysia and led the Rayders into our midst. Now the calahein aren't the only threat to our safety, and our grandparents are closer to danger than ever."

She paused to catch her breath, tears pouring from her eyes. "Rayders, Lon! After they slaughtered Myron's family and twisted his youngest son's mind to become their next commander, were you next on their list? What happened to you? What changed?"

Lon focused on his breathing to keep himself calm. He understood Mellai's pain and confusion, and he didn't expect her to understand his choices. But he wasn't the only one keeping secrets, nor was he the only one who had changed. Mellai's words were tangled with hypocrisy. However, rather than dispute their decisions, Lon sought a different focus to ease his sister's mind—a topic hidden in her rant. Where was Kaylen?

"Braedr told us that you and Kaylen left Pree with Kutad's caravan. I assume you contacted our grandparents." Lon paused, finding the next comment difficult to vocalize. He feared the conversation that would follow, knowing the pain he must have caused his betrothed. He spoke quietly, almost in a whisper. "I also heard that Braedr kidnapped Kaylen. Is she . . . well?"

Mellai wiped away her tears with the back of her hand. "You'll have to ask her yourself when we get back."

"Back where?" Lon replied. "Isn't she still with our grandparents?"

"No. I just told you that *she* wrote *me* about your choice to fight with the Rayders, remember? Why would she write me if we were living in the same house back then?" Mellai paused, staring at Lon like a mother addressing her ignorant child. "Kaylen moved on with the caravan after Kutad helped me rescue her from Braedr. She's been living in Itorea as a handmaiden. That's how she found out about you, while she was serving in the keep." Mellai opened her mouth partly, as if she wanted to add something else, but she seemed to change her mind. "When I united with King Drogan's army, Kaylen was assigned as my lady-in-waiting. I've kept her safely at my side ever since."

Realization slowly dawned on Lon as he pieced together the fragments of Mellai's story. His saliva dried up, his tongue fat in his mouth, and his body went numb. "That was her, wasn't it? In the green cloak?"

Mellai nodded, both sympathy and anger written on her face.

"Is she well?" Lon asked again, not knowing what else to say.

"When we get back," Mellai reiterated, her tightened lips halting further questions about Kaylen, but Lon refused to let her stubbornness win. Not this time.

"The least you can do is tell me how she's doing," Lon said, his frustration growing. "I'm not selfish enough to hold her to our betrothal, but I still care. I still . . . I . . . I love her."

"Is that hesitance or guilt that I hear?" Mellai snapped back. "You profess love, but show none in your actions. You know what's ironic about all of this? You abandoned us in the name of selfless sacrifice—to keep us all safe—but in the process, you pierced our hearts with a poison arrow. Everything you've done since leaving Pree has been slowly killing us. Especially Kaylen."

Lon's fury brimmed. "Don't preach to me about poisoned hearts. You have no idea what I've suffered and sacrificed as a Rayder—emotionally and physically—for the sake of everyone *but* myself. You don't know the scars I bear. And your statements about the Rayders prove your ignorance and lack of foresight. People keep referring to them as a separate nation, but I see them as something else. Something better. They aren't Rayders anymore, Mel. They're Taejans. They just don't know it yet. I had to push my relationship with Kaylen aside for a greater responsibility, something that will ultimately make this kingdom better for her. Can't you see the honor in that?"

Mellai burst into laughter. "You brought the Rayders here with the intent to unite our people? How's that going for you?"

"Better than yesterday," he said, aiming a thumb at the joined escort following them.

Mellai looked back at the line of Rayder and Appernysian soldiers, the elite fighters of both armies riding side by side behind two Beholders. Her intensity diminished. "Alright, you have me there. But seriously, Lon, how long do you think this truce will last?"

"For as long as the calahein are a threat, and hopefully longer. That's about the only thing I've been holding to this past year. Hope."

Silence overtook his sister. Her eyes clouded with True Sight as she surveyed the landscape.

"It's strange, isn't it," Lon said, "how different the world looks through our eyes?"

Mellai nodded and released her power, but said nothing.

Lon watched his sister as he carefully planned his next question, grateful for the truce between them, but anxious for answers. "When did it start?"

Mellai returned his gaze. "The same time you first used True Sight. Six years ago in Roseiri, the night we fled to Pree. Think about that windstorm, Lon. You seem to have a good handle on your power now. Could you have done that by yourself?"

He thought back to their experience playing stick-stack and what their mother had seen. Lon had been so engrossed in the game that he hadn't noticed the bale of hay obliterate over the invisible dome protecting them. *Both* of them. Realization struck Lon again, and Mellai must have seen it in his face.

"We can only manipulate what we can see," Mellai said.

"We were working together," Lon added, then habitually laughed as another thought entered his mind. "Remember how you complained that you couldn't see well that day, that dust was in your eyes?"

Mellai joined in Lon's laughter. "Well, I *did* have something in my eyes, didn't I?"

"Energy," Lon said slowly, letting the knowledge sink into his mind. "All this time and I never knew."

"Neither did I, not until True Sight killed me last July."

Lon looked at his sister, confused by her statement. "You mean *almost* killed you?"

"Not according to everyone else," Mellai said with a shrug. "Grandmother said I died for half a day. No heartbeat. No breathing. Pale as a dead fish. I don't know, though. I can't remember any of it, not after the initial pain of my transition."

Lon thought of his first time consciously using True Sight. He had pushed Mellai out of the way of a charging Rayder. Gil Baum, the first man Lon had killed. That memory still haunted him.

"What brought it on again, Mel? What forced you to use True Sight?"

Mellai's eyes glazed somewhat as she drifted into another memory, then she refocused on her brother. "My circumstance was different than yours, Lon. That's all you need to know."

"But who trained you? How did you survive?"

"I'll tell you someday, but not right now. Trust me on this."

It frustrated Lon to be kept in the dark, but perhaps the experience was too painful for her to relive. He respected that. He had his own share of memories he wished he could forget, most of which happened since becoming a Beholder.

"Someday *soon*," Lon said, and let the question go.

Mellai moved her horse closer and hugged Lon's arm. "Thank you for understanding. I've been dreading this conversation since I left Roseiri."

Lon raised his eyebrows, wanting to ask more questions about her service to King Drogan, but Mellai shook her head at him.

"That's enough questions for today," she said, squeezing his arm. She paused and squeezed his arm again methodically, smiling.

Lon pulled his arm away. "What?"

"I couldn't see it through your armor, but you've built up some muscle. Wait until Kaylen hears about this."

Lon eyed his sister, searching for an explanation. Even after refusing to discuss Kaylen's condition, Mellai had still joked about her interest in him. She had tried to laugh it off, but there was something more . . . and suddenly it connected. Kaylen still loved him.

Despite everything that should have been weighing on Lon, the thought of Kaylen's love made him giddy, a feeling he hadn't experienced since he last kissed her. His emotions must have shown on his face because Mellai smirked at him, albeit a disheartened smirk.

"Do you really still love her?" she asked.

Mellai's question surprised him, and he stuttered with his response. "I . . . well, I . . . in Pree . . ."

"It's a simple question," Mellai continued.

Lon nodded. "But the answer isn't. I . . . I don't know how to answer, Mel. When I first left Pree, Kaylen filled my every thought, was part of every decision I made. But it's been a year. I still think about her a lot, but I . . . I've changed."

"Of course you have," Mellai said, not unkindly.

"I've been wondering, and now with what you told me, could . . . could she really still be interested in me?" He paused to lick his dry lips. "I'm plagued with scars. Physical and emotional. I'm not the same person she agreed to marry. Our old future doesn't exist anymore."

"You're right," Mellai said, "but who's to say that a different future won't see you together again? You have plenty of flaws, Lon, some old and some new, but I have to give you this: you've grown up, and you don't have one foot in the grave anymore. Maybe Kaylen will love the new Lon, if he'd just come home."

Lon gripped his reins and cursed under his breath. "It always comes to that, doesn't it? *Come home, Lon. Accept the errors of your ways, Lon. Abandon the Rayders, Lon.* Why can't anyone see the vision I have for Taeja, the sacrifices I'm making for them? They are good people, Mel. They deserve better." He paused and stared at her. "Why don't *you* help *me*?"

A solid question, Lon thought to himself as he watched and felt Mellai struggle to respond. He wished he knew her past, what had driven her to join King Drogan. Was it to drive out the Rayders? To neutralize his power? Or was there something more? More than anything, he wished he could read *her* thoughts—not just a feeling in his gut, but precise, tangible thoughts. *How'd she learn to do that?*

✻　✻　✻　✻　✻

During Mellai's journey to Itorea with her grandfather, she had committed Llen's parting words to memory. They had been dense and cryptic, and she knew she would reference them repeatedly. After Lon's invitation for Mellai to join his cause, the Jaed's words filled her mind, repeating over and over.

War is coming. Appernysia is divided and unprepared. You must travel to Itorea and unite the king with his council, then lead his army in the approaching conflict. This is your purpose, Beholder. Without you, Appernysia will fall . . . Protect Appernysia. That is your primary focus.

This she had done, unless the conflict Llen referenced was the fight between humans and calahein. Either way, she fully intended to remain at the head of Appernysia's army. The next part, however, was not so clear.

Your survival is dependent upon your ability to adapt and improvise. For you, change is essential. Even the mightiest oak must adapt with the seasons.

Plenty of change had already been set in motion. Mellai was adapting as best she could and improvising when necessary. But the personal advice, that change is essential *in her.* That *she* must never be the same. What had Llen meant? Why not say everyone must never be the same? Why just her? A pure heart and pure blood supplied a Beholder with his power—her power—yet Lon had not lost his ability to wield True Sight while aiding the Rayders. Was she the blind one? Had Lon figured it out, even with the world telling him he's wrong?

It was then that Mellai finally answered the question that had been plaguing her mind for the previous six months.

Why has a Jaed never appeared to my brother?

A wave of affirmation washed over Mellai. She knew the reason undoubtedly. Lon had to figure it out on his own. *Everything.* He had to fight, struggle, and suffer through his trials without any intervention, because only a pure-hearted Beholder *experiencing* the mistreatment of Rayders would see the solution, and more importantly, *feel* the solution strongly enough to follow through.

The conviction Mellai felt in that moment overpowered any advice she had received, even from Llen—which only bolstered her understanding. If Llen had appeared to her brother and ordered him to help the Rayders, Lon's conscience would have disagreed. He would have been acting out of responsibility instead of passion, fulfilling a requirement he had believed to be wrong. In that moment, his heart would have ceased to be pure. His power would have disappeared, along with his ability to help them.

And why did Lon need to help the Rayders, to bring them into Taeja? To Lon, it was for justice long deserved, but he had discovered a deeper truth without knowing it. He needed to bring the Rayders into Taeja for their own protection—for everyone's protection—to get them into Itorea.

Mellai swallowed, her throat painfully dry.

The approaching conflict Llen spoke of would be more tragic than anyone could have imagined, and the armed forces of Appernysia and Rayders were waiting for their report. Waiting. Exposed in the Taejan Plains, but far more capable of defending themselves than Réxura and the rest of Appernysia's Western Valley.

"Quickly," Mellai shouted over her shoulder. "We're out of time."

* * * * *

Dawes easily caught up to Mellai's galloping horse, but showed obvious strain as Mellai refused to slow. Mile after mile she pushed, deaf to all inquiries from her brother.

Lon couldn't understand what had happened. His question had been pointedly blunt, but Mellai's silence afterward—how the blood had slowly drained from her face, her appearance twisted with suffering—surprised Lon as much as Mellai's order for urgency. At first, Lon thought he had struck a chord with his twin, that she was enduring a crisis of conscience as she realized Lon's vision, but not anymore. She knew something, had figured something out that pushed her to frantic action.

Hours passed. A film of sticky sweat smothered Mellai's horse. White foam dripped from his mouth. Blood drizzled out his nose. She was pushing him too hard. Dawes was well enough, having been conditioned for such exertions, but Mellai's small horse had probably spent most of his years tethered in a stable or giving rides to children. She was killing him.

Lon's protests were useless, but he refused to watch his sister ignorantly murder her mount. He summoned True Sight and erected a curving wall of earth and stone to block her path.

Mellai nearly toppled over the front of her horse as he dug his hooves into the ground. Once resettled in her saddle, Mellai turned to her brother, her eyes flaring with fury. She opened her mouth, but before she could speak, her horse collapsed.

Lon was surprised at his sister's agility. She slipped her feet out of her stirrups and swiveled her legs to her horse's upward side, her hands balanced on his neck and rump. When the horse struck the dry soil, she turned and knelt while summoning her power. Lon also dismounted and hurried to his sister, his own vision filled with the haze of True Sight.

She's going to heal him, Lon thought as he watched her vibrant essence examine the dull glowing horse, *and I'm going to see it happen.* Excitement filled him as he thought of the people he could have saved with such a skill. Omar, Riyen, Keene, Lars, Tarl, even Preton would still be alive.

Lon's excitement turned to frustration as the minutes passed. Mellai did nothing. The horse's breathing shallowed, his muscles relaxed, eyes glazed, until his essence finally shifted out and disappeared.

"Why didn't you save him?" Lon asked, releasing his power.

Tears shimmered in Mellai's brown eyes when she returned his gaze. "I can't heal a failing heart. I . . . I should have listened to you. I didn't know any better."

"What drove you to push him so hard?" Lon asked, hiding his frustration.

Mellai shook her head and turned her head to the south, toward Réxura. "Can we continue, or do the other horses need to rest?"

Lon followed her gaze, but saw nothing through the wall he had lifted in front of them. He quickly forced it down again with True Sight and peered past it at the flat horizon. "What do you see, Mel?"

"I don't see anything. I *know.*"

"Know what?"

Mellai looked at him. "Can we continue?"

Lon clenched his jaw with frustration, but digressed. After dispelling True Sight, he examined the other horses. He knew Dawes and his own squad's horses would be fine, and it looked like the mounts of Mellai's guard were sufficiently fit. How foolish of King Drogan to give Mellai such a small, unseasoned horse.

"Yes," Lon finally replied, "after a short break to eat and recover." He examined the darkening sky, void of clouds and speckled with the first stars of night. With the aid of True Sight, the two of them could travel in the dark without trouble, but the horses didn't have the same advantage. Torches weren't a safe option, either. They would have to ride slowly, leading a safe path for their companions to follow.

By unspoken agreement, Lon and Mellai returned to their escorts, who had also dismounted and separated from each other. Lon forced himself to forget about his sister and the Appernysians—for now. He had gone too long without acknowledging the presence of his own squad, yet they showed no signs of irritation. In fact, they were quieter than ever, respectfully waiting for Lon to answer their unspoken questions.

"Lieutenant," Lon said, looking at Wade, "how have you fared in the company of Appernysians?"

"Well enough, Beholder," he replied with a salute, touching his first two fingers to the King's Cross brand on his right temple. "They have been surprisingly tolerant of our presence."

"And what about our own tolerance?"

Wade shrugged. "A trial, no doubt, but one we will continue to endure as long as necessary."

"And how long will that be?" Channer said, having become more outspoken since the murder of his cousin, Keene. "What madness has possessed that girl?"

"She won't tell me," Lon replied.

"She is a Beholder," Wade intervened. "She may be Appernysian, but she must be as wise as Lon to maintain her power."

"Braedr was also wise," Thad interjected, "but sly and mutinous. This woman could be leading us to our doom."

"I would have agreed a week ago," Lon said, "but not now. Don't forget that we all share the same fear of the calahein. Regarding her urgency, I have only this to say. Mellai has discovered something beyond my comprehension. I can't blame her for keeping it a secret, though. She is still treating me with the same apprehension as she did in Pree, afraid I will lose control of my power if burdened with too much anxiety. Oh, and there's that whole enemies of warring nations thing, too."

Suddenly, Lon realized that only Wade and Tarek knew about his true past. Everyone else, including those in his own squad, still believed he had grown up as a mistreated tradesman. He searched their faces and found the same inquisitive expressions as on their journey to Three Peaks, after they had discovered Lon was a Beholder. They knew by now that he and Mellai were siblings. His disputes with Mellai would have made that obvious. But the references to Pree, the same village of Tarek's birth—where Braedr also grew up—had to concern them.

"I owe you an explanation," Lon said, once again humbled by his squad's loyalty. "I lied to Commander Rayben and the rest of you about my childhood."

"As did most of the Appernysian refugees," Wade replied. "We would have done the same to protect those we loved."

"But what about the people I have grown to love?" Lon continued. "I've been keeping the truth from the best friends ever to cross my path, yet you remain unwaveringly faithful to me. I would have expected more of you to react like Preton to my dishonesty."

"Preton's name has no place here," Channer replied, his eyes narrow, "nor does he represent our actions and commitment. He was a coward and a traitor."

"Perhaps," Lon said, "but you keep blaming him for Keene's death when you should be pointing your sword at me. Had I been honest from the beginning, things might have been different."

"Do not burden yourself with a past that cannot be changed," Wade asserted. "Use it, instead, to build a better future."

Lon smiled. "Wise words."

"As wise as their host," Wade replied. "Commander Omar gave this advice to me after your trial of weapons. I realized after you defeated me that I had misjudged you. My guilt had pushed me to the edge of self-destruction, but our commander intervened and helped me to see reason. Allow him to do the same for you."

Silence overtook their conversation as Lon digested Wade's words. "Omar was a brilliant man," he finally said, "and somehow he has found a way to keep assisting me from the grave. I will follow his advice, but that doesn't change the fact that you deserve to know the truth."

Lon briefly explained his origins. His real name, Lon Marcs, son of Aron Marcs—the same man who had defected from the Rayders. Only Channer had responded to this knowledge, and just by raised eyebrows. Lon also shared how his family had fled Roseiri when he was twelve. His experiences in Pree with Mellai, Kaylen, and Braedr. His encounter with Gil Baum's squad and the guilt following their deaths. His conflict with True Sight, and his choice to ultimately seek help from the Rayders. But he left out the details of Myron Ascennor and the rest of Tarek's family. That information belonged to their commander.

When Lon finished with his confession, Wade slowly rose to his feet. He stood proudly with his shoulders back and chin high as he saluted his Beholder. The rest of Lon's squad drew their swords and knelt to lay them at Lon's feet, bowed with an equally devout salute.

Wade stepped forward and joined his comrades upon his knees. "It takes great courage for a man with your origins to come to us for help. We are honored to serve you, Beholder. Rest assured that your tale has only increased our loyalty."

Lon kneeled and drew his own falchion, adding it to the piled swords as he fought to control his emotions. "And I pledge myself to your protection, even if it costs me my life."

✳   ✳   ✳   ✳   ✳

"It's strange to see Rayders kneeling before you," Mellai commented. She sat in front of her brother, her hands gripping the horn of Dawes's saddle while Lon held the reins. He had convinced her to ride with him on their continued journey to Réxura. "Your men obviously love you."

"It wasn't always like that," Lon replied. He shifted, seeking a more comfortable position on the two bedrolls tied behind the saddle. "Wade tried to kill me when we first met."

"Which one is Wade?" Mellai asked as she studied the line of Rayders positioned beside them. Night surrounded them, but her power would enable her to carefully eyeball each member of Lon's squad.

Lon laughed. Some things about his sister hadn't changed, like her protectiveness. "The blonde-haired lieutenant. He's changed a lot over the past year, maybe even more than me. No need to worry. He just defended you, calling you a wise Beholder. Did you know that?"

"Why would I know that?"

"I never know whose mind you're invading. Truth be known, your power scares me, Little Sis. What else can you do, and how?"

"All in due time," Mellai replied. Her voice attempted sarcasm, but Lon could hear a deeper meaning in her words.

"I've been hearing that a lot from you lately. When is that time? In the middle of an attack?"

"Perhaps."

Another one-word answer, Lon silently complained, wishing he could peer into her thoughts. *Why is she being so secretive?*

"Don't worry about the privacy of your squad's thoughts," Mellai continued. "It's a skill I only use when lives are in danger. Honestly, I'm not even concerned with what you're thinking right now. I'm just trying to figure out a way I can get us to Réxura faster with True Sight."

Lon's eyes widened at the intriguing thought. Was there some use of their power that could move them faster? Transferring energy into their horses wouldn't work, obviously. In all his experience of interacting with energy, he had never felt a rise in his own strength

or stamina. And if that had been possible, Mellai would have trans-
ferred energy into her dying horse to heal his exhaustion.

"What about flying?" Lon said aloud.

Mellai laughed. "I doubt that's a possibility, short of a ghraef's
help." When she finished speaking, her head titled back and she
examined the dark sky. Lon followed her gaze with his empowered
vision, but saw only the slow moving energy of a chilled night. As
with their surrounding terrain, the sky was void of visible animal life.

"But why?" Lon said. "Why does it have to be impossible? All
we would need is a sail connected to a vessel that could carry us."

"I've already thought of that. It seems like a good idea, but think
it through. What if we were attacked? We would be completely
defenseless until we landed safely on the ground. And what if we
were killed or knocked unconscious, or even closed our eyes? I
wouldn't want to ride in a vessel like that, jerking up and down
every time the Beholder blinked."

"I don't think blinking counts as closing our eyes," Lon said, "but
you've made your point. Flying is obviously out of the question, but
what about a land vessel, like a wagon or sled? We could even put
the sail in front of us, so we could control where we're going."

"Better," Mellai replied, "but how would we stop or steer, or keep
ourselves from flipping over?"

"Multiple sails, carefully placed. Might be a two-Beholder task,
but lucky us, we just so happen to have two Beholders here." *And
who would have ever guessed?* he thought. Two simple peasants
from a small village, twin siblings who became the most powerful
people in Appernysia in over a millennium. And one of them the
first female Beholder ever to reach the pages of history.

"That idea I'll consider," Mellai said, "but not right now. We don't
have time to experiment with ideas, and we don't have the supplies
to build a vessel large enough for our company."

Lon knew Mellai was right, but he couldn't help but search around
for trees that could be used. He thrilled at the thought, traveling

faster than a horse on a wind-powered sled or wagon. And air travel wouldn't be impractical, as long as it was done for short periods of time and close to the ground.

As he contemplated the construction of such a craft, Lon released his power and gazed at the stars again. He wished he had been better instructed in astronomy. Sure, he could find his bearings from certain constellations, but he didn't understand the timing of their rotation. Complete darkness surrounded their company. He had no idea how many hours separated them from sunrise.

They moved at a slow pace, never faster than a horse's careful walk, but every step they took reduced their distance to Réxura. Lon had originally planned to reach the city late on their third day of travel, but with their progress, they could arrive by dawn.

The thought worried Lon. He had not considered the negative outcomes of reaching Réxura in the dark. Everyone but he and Mellai would be defenseless, and he had already experienced such a night encounter with these creatures. They would be at an impractical disadvantage.

"We need to stop," Lon finally said.

"I was thinking the same thing," Mellai agreed. "Let's sleep for a few hours."

* * * * *

At sunrise, the joint company ate a quick breakfast of dried fruit and bread, then continued their long march to Réxura. The tip of the Vidarien Mountain range was visible on the southern horizon, about thirty miles away and draped with faded azure. The solitary mountain at the range's edge stood tall and proud, despite the neighboring destruction Mellai feared in Réxura. A low, dark line pushed west from its foundation, barely visible at the edge of the sloping landscape.

"The Forest of Blight," Lon said. "The most ominous place in Appernysia, if you ask me. That's where the creatures fled after they attacked my squad last summer. If the calahein have returned, I'm certain they are hiding there."

"What were they like?" Mellai asked again, still comparing the creatures she had fought in the mountains.

"Terrifying," Lon replied. "They're quick and vicious. We should have died, but . . ." Mellai felt Lon's arms tense at her sides as he faded into silence.

"But what? What did you do?"

"Not much," he finally answered. "Two flying creatures dove in from above us and chased the threat away."

"From above?" Mellai said. "Where did they come from?" Having read the memories of the oak tree Kaylen had been lashed to when she was taken by Braedr, Mellai was certain she knew what had rescued them. *Ghraefs protecting Rayders?* she wondered as she fingered the silver ghraef hanging from her neck. It was one of two pendants hidden under her leather armor, the other being her mother's King's Cross that she had found in the tree hollow. *I suppose when the Rayders have a Beholder with them, it's not completely irrational for a ghraef to intervene.*

"They must have been circling above us," Lon said. "We were in the middle of the Taejan Plains, in a barren area just like this." He paused. "This will sound insane, but I think they were ghraefs, which is probably the greatest reason the calahein attacked us. Ghraefs and the calahein detest each other. That hatred is what drove ghraefs to partner with Beholders in the First Age. Imagine it, Mel. If ghraefs are still alive, we might someday have one for ourselves."

"Beholders don't own ghraefs," Mellai said. Her mind drifted to her Beholder ceremony and the advice Llen had given her when marking her with the Beholder's eye. *Ghraefs are not pets, but powerful creatures with knowledge that in many ways surpasses our own. Should one honor you with his presence, you would be wise to join yourself with*

him as an equal companion, bound together by friendship and respect.
She shared the same counsel with her brother.

"My mistake," Lon said with a hint of defensiveness. "Those were official sounding words. Where did you read them?"

"I can't remember," Mellai lied, knowing that her interaction with a Jaed would only enrage her brother, "but I plan to live by them. If we meet a ghraef, don't demean him or take his companionship for granted. They are prideful creatures, and more intelligent than us. How else would they have gone this long hiding their existence?"

"So you believe me?" Lon said. "You think they're alive?"

"Of course."

"And from the way you're talking, it sounds like only male ghraefs unite with Beholders."

"I assume so. Male ghraefs with male Beholders—at least until I came along."

Although she couldn't see Lon's reaction, Mellai relaxed her mind and examined their unique emotional connection. Her brother was elated, like a boy opening a birthday present. Mellai's validation had a stronger impact than she had expected. He tried to hide it, but Lon was obviously intimidated by her. *As he should be,* Mellai thought. *If he wanders the wrong direction, I'll drag him back into place.*

Chapter 4

Onset

Twenty miles from Réxura, signs of a ruthless attack began to show. Trails of blood in the dirt. Limbs separated from their bodies. Carcasses so ravaged by beasts that they were barely recognizable as human. Lon watched his sister carefully examine each body they passed with a mixture of fear and apprehension, then suddenly it dawned on him. Everybody knew that Appernysia's trading caravan camped in Réxura during the winter, and Mellai had traveled with them when Kutad was their leader. They had even helped her rescue Kaylen when they had no obligation to do so. Mellai absolutely would have grown to love them.

Lon gave his sister's arm a gentle squeeze, hoping she didn't recognize any of the dead. She hadn't endured the amount of death he or the other Rayders had experienced, especially not with people she knew personally.

Lon forced Dawes to a halt on a bridge spanning the Prime River when they encountered the remains of a small child. Fortunately, the little girl's head was turned the opposite direction. Lon had seen too many dead faces, locked in time with terror or pain. He couldn't bear such an expression on this helpless victim. His eyes kept drifting to a stuffed doll still clutched in one of her tiny hands. It was stained with her blood.

Mellai sobbed openly as she slid off Dawes and carefully pulled back the girl's fingers to remove the doll. Lon sympathized with her sorrow, his own eyes wet as he surveyed the rest of their escort. All shared their anguish. Even Thad, the oldest Rayder in Lon's squad who had dealt more than his fair share of death blows, showed obvious signs of grief.

"Who could do this?" Mellai said, her head swiveling about.

Lon didn't respond. She had been speaking more to herself. Everyone already knew the answer. Calahein were the only creatures capable of such barbarism.

Mellai crossed the rest of the narrow wooden bridge, set down the doll, and raised her hands. A mound of dirt folded over the girl's body, then a column of a sand mixture sifted up through the soil. Lon watched his sister mold the sand into a ball, then somehow make it make it glow bright white. The light was intense. Lon was mesmerized by witnessing True Sight with ordinary vision. However, as the floating sphere grew brighter and brighter, Lon's curiosity got the better of him.

With the aid of his power, Lon witnessed a completely different scene. His sister's essence extended from both hands, one wrapping the glowing ball while the other penetrated the barrier to interact with the sand. Only the sand wasn't sand anymore. It had turned into liquid, its energy whipping frantically about inside the barrier.

He marveled at his sister's interaction with the sand, manipulating it with her own essence instead of utilizing other elements like fire to control it. And the piercing brightness. Was this what she was doing in Itorea when the Taejan Plains lit up with light?

"Wait," Lon said. "You'll give away our position."

"Shush," Mellai answered, her lips pulled tight in concentration.

Lon's anxieties dispersed, replaced by more bewilderment at what his sister did next. A third beam shifted out of her glowing essence. It picked up the doll and moved it toward the melted sand. With implausible skill, Mellai parted the barrier and sand, moved the doll into its midst and closed the gap again. The doll remained unscathed as Mellai calmed the surrounding energy of the molten sand. The liquid cooled and hardened, and Mellai set her creation at the head of the little girl's grave.

"Wow," Lon said unconsciously when he dismissed his power. The unharmed doll was wrapped in a glistening dome of clear glass.

"Should I remove the bloodstains?" Mellai asked as she wiped her face with the leather vambrace protecting her forearm.

"No," Wade answered before Lon could respond. "Those stains will honor this girl, along with the other victims of this sadistic attack. It is a perfect monument."

"Thank you," Mellai answered. She returned Wade's gaze, her eyes soft and sincere. "I wish I could do more."

"Maybe we can," Lon said. He patted the empty saddle in front of him. "Réxura is still a few miles away. We should hurry."

"Cautiously," Kutad spoke.

The sound of Kutad's voice shook Lon. He had been so worried about his sister's feelings, he hadn't considered the impact that Réxura's destruction would have on Kutad, who had led the trading caravan for at least fifteen years. They were family to him. While Mellai mourned the potential loss of friends, Kutad had to feel a million times worse.

"Agreed," Lon said, seeking for something to comfort Kutad. "I hope your caravan survived."

"As do I," Kutad answered, but his tone lacked hope.

Mellai slapped Lon's leg. "Get down. I can't climb up there with you sitting in the way."

Lon summoned his power, wrapped Mellai's body in air, and hoisted her onto the saddle. "There. All better."

Mellai gasped for air when Lon released True Sight, then elbowed him hard in the ribs. "Don't *ever* do that again."

✻ ✻ ✻ ✻ ✻

They entered Réxura at a light canter, having reorganized themselves to best protect the Beholders. Wade and Channer rode point with two of Mellai's guard—Kutad and Snoom—while the rest followed behind Dawes. The other Rayders were positioned in the very back, bows drawn and nocked with arrows. Kutad gripped a light spear. The other Appernysians held their drawn swords at the ready, having left their halberds behind for the long journey.

Mellai searched the city with True Sight while Lon directed their escort through the safest passages. Dead bodies littered the city, age and gender completely ignored in the merciless slaughter. Lon forced himself to look past them and stay prepared for an attack. He avoided the buildings. Even with the sun directly over their heads, an ambush could easily come from one of their shadowed rooms.

Lon knew that Kutad was a realistic man. The chance of his caravan's survival was nonexistent, especially with the injuries Rypla had received. So it didn't surprise Lon that when the caravan's razed camp came into view, Kutad rode past the scene, eyes forward and jaw tight. Obvious anger, but little surprise. Mellai, on the other hand, wept openly.

Although Lon had never previously encountered the aftermath of an attacked city, obvious signs told him that this slaughter had not come from humans. Flesh had been torn open, ragged gaping wounds uncharacteristic of a blade. Many bore the same injuries as Rypla's shoulder, with skin and muscle dissolved to the bone. And the gnawed meat of humans and livestock. Lon fought his own churning stomach. The dead had been made a meal by whatever attacked.

The thought wasn't reassuring, knowing the potential danger hiding in the nearby mountains, but Lon was still glad that a renegade battalion of Rayders didn't initiate the attack. Braedr's circle of influence had grown surprisingly large. After all, he had escaped his isolated prison in Taeja. There was no predicting his plans, and an attack on a defenseless Appernysian city wasn't beyond his reach, even from the grave.

But even with Braedr dead, Lon knew Rayder dissention still had to be quelled. Their temporary alliance with King Drogan wouldn't help matters, either.

"What happened to the trees?" Mellai spat. Her voice brimmed with unbridled anger.

Lon searched about and realized his sister was right. The scene was unnerving. Little destruction befell the buildings, but no living plants existed. Great care had been taken to uproot and destroy every living thing. Even the tiniest weeds and blades of grass were gone, torn out of their earthen home and replaced by clawed trenches.

"Strange," Wade said, leaning forward in his saddle to examine the ground. "Little farmland existed here. Why destroy the vegetation?"

"And why not just use fire to destroy it?" Snoom added.

"That much fire would have been an obvious beacon," Lon replied, "but Wade makes an excellent point. Why destroy all the plants?"

"I need to find a tree," Mellai shouted, her searching head jerking left and right.

Lon was taken aback by his sister's urgency. Tears cut through the grime covering her unwashed cheeks, polishing the blue tattoo that wrapped her left eye. He had seen that determined passion on her face before. He knew better than to argue or tease.

"Easy, Mel," he said, tapping Dawes's sides with his heels. "We'll find you a tree."

Lon moved their escort south, out of the city and toward the Prime River. He figured if a tree existed, it would be along the nearby river's shoreline. Unfortunately, the same fate had befallen the grove there. Lon gawked at the gaping holes where fully grown trees—oak, birch, aspen—had been ripped out of the soil. Splinters of wood scattered the ground. The trees had been literally torn apart. Clawed gouges smothered the remains of their trunks. Lon shook his head. Unfathomable power would have been required to do such a thing.

Mellai slid out of the saddle again as she used True Sight to expose the buried roots of the destroyed trees. Snow and dirt shifted away as she knelt at the closest root, gently touched it with her fingers, and spoke one word.

"Please."

Lon watched and waited, shifting between normal vision and his empowered sight to inspect Mellai's intents, but saw no change. Minutes passed as Mellai knelt motionless at the root.

"Mel?" Lon finally said, his impatience growing.

Mellai flicked her free hand at him. "Leave me alone. This will take a while."

It was only with great effort that Lon reluctantly complied. He hated being told what to do by his sister—he always had—but not knowing what she was doing was even more frustrating. Once again, Mellai had proven herself to be the stronger Beholder.

"Dismount," Lon called and eyed the sun. It beamed down at them from directly overhead, unobscured by the cloudless sky. He pulled some wrapped bread and a leather bladder from Dawes's saddle, then handed the reins to Elja. The rest of his squad did the same, while Mellai's guard positioned themselves on the opposite side of their Beholder. It wasn't like they trusted each other. Both groups were just trying to survive.

"What is she doing?" Wade said as he sat in the dirt beside Lon.

Lon took a bite of his bread and a swig of water from the leather bladder. "No idea." His gaze shifted from Mellai to Elja, who was watering the horses at the river. Fewer bodies existed there, which told Lon that the attack had not come from the south. While the civilians of Réxura had tried to flee north, those traveling the trade route outside the city might have survived. He hoped the killing had not followed them back to Jaul, the shipping town on the shores of Casconni Lake, nor the mining city Draege farther south. The thought was practical. Lon didn't think the calahein had much interest in precious metals.

"My head is spinning," Lon said aloud. "If this attack came from the calahein, why Réxura? And why the stealth? From the way things look around here, they could easily defeat our combined forces on the Taejan Plains. We wouldn't stand a chance."

"For the same reason they do not attack us now," Thad interceded.

"They fear you," Dovan added, absently fingering the scar on his face from their last encounter with the calahein. He and Thad were the most introverted of Lon's squad, conversing little with anyone but each other since they had become good friends during their expedition to take Three Peaks. Even so, they had obviously been calculating the answers to Lon's questions far in advance.

"Afraid," Wade echoed, his jaw raised in confidence, "as they should be."

But should we fear them even more? Lon wondered. He didn't dare speak aloud. For all he knew, calahein were still hiding in the city. They could be listening. The thought was unnerving.

"Perhaps," Lon finally replied, "but how could we ever hope to understand the calahein or their choices? They're a plague. Any arguments beyond that are just hearsay. We won't make decisions based on speculation. The only thing we should do right now is wait for my sister."

Lon gripped his bow tighter and looked impatiently at Mellai. She had moved to another root, but still knelt motionless. Lon closed his eyes and reached for their emotional connection. It burst into his consciousness like a stampede. Sadness and desperation, but even more determination. And consuming anger. Lon thought back to the night of his coming of age celebration in Pree, when Mellai had attacked Braedr with unreserved aggression. She had shown incredible prowess that day, but now with True Sight as her ally . . . perhaps Wade was correct. With Mellai around, maybe the calahein should fear them.

Lon surveyed his squad. They all emulated Wade's confidence, except Nik. He sat cross-legged with his strung bow in his lap. He stared at the ground, his lips pulled tight.

"What do you think, Nik?" Lon said.

Nik looked up at Lon. His eyes burned with rage. "It matters not who fears whom. I seek only to bury this in one of their eyes." He tapped the arrow nocked on his bowstring.

Lon nodded, not knowing what to say. Nik had grown restless since Riyen's untimely death the previous summer. Hopefully revenge would settle his mind and honor the sacrifice of his friend. And if anyone were capable of killing calahein with his bow, it was Nik.

Chapter 5

Uncovered

This is impossible, Mellai thought. She knew the roots couldn't contain memories, but she had to try. The roots were alive, but without any consciousness. Connecting with them was little different than touching one of her own appendages. Struggling life, but no mind.

The absence of life pressed upon her senses. Everything with a consciousness was dead. Even the smallest of seedlings had been destroyed. But what bothered her most were the homes and buildings that still stood. This assault had to be calculated by someone or something that knew Beholders.

And they knew she could read memories.

Who in Appernysia's history would know so much about Beholders? Only three groups were possible. Ghraefs, the calahein, and the Rayders.

Ghraefs were obviously ruled out and the calahein were already suspects, but the more Mellai examined, the more she blamed the Rayders. The calahein were strong and powerful, but she had never known them to be intelligent creatures. Besides, the clues in Réxura were *too* calahein, much too methodical and calculated. And the missing plants? Only Rayders were capable of such precision.

It made sense. Make it look like the calahein attacked, draw away Appernysia's Beholder, and slaughter the remaining forces during a feigned treaty. Mellai eyed the Rayder squad, huddled together in quiet conversation with their Beholder.

Was her brother part of the ploy?

This is one person they won't overpower, Mellai thought, rising to her feet and facing the squad. Lon's glowing form also stood and walked toward her. Mellai gratefully noted that he had not summoned True Sight. She didn't want to fight him. He might not surrender again, which would leave her only one choice.

"What's wrong?" Lon said, his left hand gripping a bow. "What did you find?"

"Stop," Mellai said, taking a step back. When the Rayders stood to follow, she trapped their legs in hardened dirt. The men gasped as she compressed the soil, purposefully causing them pain.

If Mellai had learned anything about Rayders, it was that they were resourceful and quick to action. So it came as no surprise when Nik, one of Lon's squad, loosed an arrow at her from his composite bow. As the other men drew their bows, Mellai redirected the flying arrow's steel point to Lon's neck, pressing just hard enough to draw a tiny droplet of blood. The Rayders froze, including Nik, though his fingers twitched at the feathers of another arrow in his waist-bound quiver.

"Smart choice," Mellai said with focused concentration. "Drop your weapons."

The words had barely escaped her mouth when five arrows whipped at her. She easily redirected them into the ground at her feet, but the action unnerved her. She held their Beholder at death's point. Why would they still attack?

"Stop!" Lon shouted, his chin lifted to alleviate the pressure of the arrow in his neck. "Do as she says." Surprisingly, he still had not called upon his own power.

As the six Rayders obediently tossed their swords and bows to their sides, Kutad and the other four members of Mellai's guard came to her rescue. They positioned themselves between Mellai and the Rayders, crouched defensively and ready to protect her with their lives.

"What treachery is this?" Kutad demanded. "Where is your supposed honor, cowards?"

"Ask her," Lon said with chilling calm. "She started it."

"Did I?" Mellai spat back. She sought for perfect words to condemn the Rayders and their heartless slaughter of Réxura's citizens, but all that came out was a string of curses. She finalized her rant with an energy blast at a nearby shed, old and rotten. The decayed timber blasted apart, whipping through the air hundreds of feet away from the gathered men.

"Feel better?" Lon said. He was the only one to speak, still composed, while the rest of the men stood wide-eyed and motionless.

"What do you care?" Mellai said, but Lon was right. She did feel better.

"What happened to you?" her brother continued. His words stabbed at her, spoken from the mouth of a nation who had been burdened with the same question for over twelve hundred years.

But Mellai remained undaunted. "Why? By the Jaeds, Lon, why?"

His calm morphed into confusion and defensiveness. "Have I been chewing with my mouth open? Maybe one of us sat in the snow the wrong way? Or did Elja water the horses at the wrong spot? Why *what*?"

"All your talk about the calahein," Mellai said, tears returning to her bloodshot eyes. "You almost convinced me. And now without me to protect them, King Drogan's army has as much chance of surviving as that shed."

She jabbed a finger at the building's remains to emphasize her point, then paused. Something caught her eye. Amidst the dull energy of fallen wood and tilled earth, a faint glow of life radiated from its center. Without any concern for her own safety, Mellai loosed her hold on the Rayders and sprinted to the blast's center. A tiny bud extended from the stem of a plant no more than two inches tall.

It must have been growing under the rotting floorboards, Mellai thought, falling to her knees. *Just enough sunlight and water to give it a chance.*

She openly wept as she sought to connect with the consciousness of the little miracle. It was extremely difficult. The plant was young and introverted with fear and pain. For good reasons, too. The first piece of knowledge Mellai gleaned was that this little plant was a budding aspen tree, connected to the other trees through a common root system. It had not only seen the destruction and suffering around it, but had lived it through a joint consciousness. The poor thing had died over and over again, waiting for the destructors to end its own suffering.

I'm a Beholder, Mellai repeated in her mind. *You're safe now.*

Finally, a sliver of thought, young and present, penetrated her mind. *Dead.*

From her training with the hollowed oak tree, Mellai had learned it was counterproductive to push a plant with urgency. She hid those feelings, filling her mind instead with the sadness and compassion she felt for the seedling. *I know. I'm so sorry.*

Family.

The thought was almost too much to bear. Mellai had never considered such a thought for trees and vegetation. It was suffering more than Mellai had ever experienced. Everything it knew, including its family, was dead.

Hope. The seedling continued. *You.*

I'm trying to, but I have to ask you the impossible. I need to see your memories. I need to see who killed your family.

What. The comment was not a question, but a statement.

I'm sorry?

Not who. What.

Relief and anxiety filled Mellai's mind. *Not Rayders?*

Rayders?

Mellai thought for a better word, one the seedling would understand. *Not humans?*

No.

Then what?

Tension filled the seedling's consciousness. *Look.*

The barrier disappeared. Mellai delved into its memories, desperate to find answers before the sprout locked her out again. She hurried through the days, trying to avoid the seedling's emotions, until she found what she was looking for a half-week back.

It took Mellai a moment to once again adapt to a tree's multidirectional vision. Although the sapling was hidden beneath the floorboards of the rotting shed, it saw its surroundings through colorless sensory. Its viewing distance was much smaller than the mature mountain trees, but still large enough to see beyond the walls of the abandoned shed.

Screams filled her mind, unlike anything she had ever heard, and from men and women of all ages. Indescribable responses to unseen violence that ended each of their lives. The children's cries were the most difficult to bear, piercing and terrified. Mellai's own sense of helplessness echoed the sapling's, neither of them able to save or intervene.

Mellai winced when a young girl dashed into the shed and slammed the broken door behind her. She cowered in a dark corner, hugging her knees and crying. A tiny doll was gripped in one of her trembling hands.

Please, no, Mellai thought, her chest throbbing. It was the same girl they had found on the north bridge leading out of Réxura.

A hiss outside the shed silenced the girl. She sat still, her eyes wide with terror. Mellai was certain she had the same look on her own face. She knew that sound. It belonged to the wolf-shaped beasts that had attacked her in the mountains. The same beasts that spat poisonous red phlegm from their mouths. *The same beasts that had killed Rypla,* Mellai thought, reproving herself for suspecting the

Rayders. Unless these hounds of terror were pets of the Rayders—a highly unlikely option—this attack was not orchestrated by Lon's people. Were they part of the calahein, or some other race?

Watch.

The seedlings voice brought Mellai back into its memories. While the girl shook, trapped with nowhere to run, the hissing continued. Mellai watched the beast move around the shed and at times, even above. It could have easily broken through the rotting planks, but kept stalking about, almost smiling. It was toying with the girl.

Wrath replaced Mellai's sadness as she watched the little girl glance about, trying to identify the location of her attacker. The hisses grew louder and more aggressive with time, pushing the girl to the edge of insanity.

Don't you dare, Mellai begged, guessing at the girl's erratic thoughts, until she finally stood, hugged her doll, and fled out of the shed. The terror hound leaped from the roof at the same time, sinking its sharp, narrow claws into the girl's back and knocking her to the dirt. Her face slid across the ground, rocks picking away at her smooth skin. Mellai clenched her jaw, waiting for it to end, but the terror hound surprised her. It retracted its claws and jumped back, allowing the girl to her feet. It hissed once more, the girl fled north, and it loped lazily after her—out of the tree's vision.

Emotions battered Mellai. She dug her free hand into the soil and let a howl of pain escape her lips. She felt Kutad's hand on her shoulder, but jerked away, swallowed up with her own feelings. She didn't believe such actions were possible. How cruel. How utterly merciless.

Watch.

The tree's voice filled her consciousness again, this time with more urgency. Mellai forced what little control she had left into its memories.

As the screams and hissing subsided, a different sound filled her ears. Snarls, low and deep, huffing and snorting with every breath.

These weren't growls she had heard before, not even from the ghraef. And though different than the terror hound's hissing, both sounds carried with them a message of death. Unreserved annihilation.

Mellai fell to her side, barely catching herself with her free hand when three new creatures entered the tree's vision. They stood taller than a man, covered in fur similar in length and density to the terror hounds. Their build was strange. Like a man, they had two arms and legs, but their arms were much longer, often assisting the beasts as they walked. Their hands and feet—if she could call them that—bore two fingers and an opposable thumb, each tipped with terrifying claws. While the terror hounds had spikes protruding from their spine, the spikes in these beasts stuck out of the tops of their knees and the fronts of their elbows. Much longer, too, like spear tips. Broad shoulders with powerful muscles, defined even through their fur. Ears on the sides of their heads, small and disproportionate to their flat faces and flared nostrils.

Kelsh, Mellai thought. Her body trembled with apprehension.

The three beasts stopped and faced each other in a ragged triangle. Noises did not escape their lips, and their eyes seemed glazed over, staring at nothing as if in a trance. Then without warning, they threw back their heads and let terrifying roars fly from their gaping mouths. Mellai fought the temptation to cover her own ears, knowing the sound came only through the tree's memories.

Of every attribute of these new beasts, their mouths scared Mellai the most. Jaws open wide enough to swallow a man's head. Two rows of teeth lined their mouths, sharp and plentiful, with a fat tongue bulging inside. Never before had she seen a creature so perfectly engineered with the ability to kill—and to kill humans, no less.

Stop.

The memory had been severed, replaced by this one thought from the little sapling. The word filled Mellai's mind again.

Stop.

She understood the intent of the aspen's wish. Somehow, these creatures had to be stopped. Calahein was their name and destruction was their identity. And now Mellai knew they had pets, wolf-shaped terror hounds that climbed trees and spat red phlegm. Unchecked, the calahein would sweep over Appernysia and bring about its utter ruin. Mellai didn't know if it were possible, but stopping them had become her calling in life. Her mantle.

Stop.

I will, Mellai affirmed again.

No. Halt.

Confused with the correction, Mellai habitually licked her bottom lip. The taste of blood filled her senses and dazed her mind, until she realized she had been chewing on her lip during the memory. A more careful examination revealed deep gashes that oozed blood into her mouth. She gathered the blood in her mouth and spit it onto the ground, wishing she could see inside her mouth to heal the damage. Within a day or two, those gashes would turn into painful open sores that might take weeks to fully heal.

Thank you, Mellai communicated to the tree. *I'm so sorry for your pain, little one. I wish there were something I could do to take it away. Anything at all.*

Save us.

Mellai nodded. *You have my word.*

Love and gratitude radiated from the sapling, then it abruptly withdrew its consciousness. Mellai didn't attempt to reconnect. Instead, she released her power and examined her surroundings, visualizing how the rotten shed had looked before she destroyed it with an energy blast. Where the girl had been sitting. What she must have been thinking. How the sapling had wanted to help, but was powerless to do anything.

"But not us," Mellai said with a start, rushing to her feet with new resolve. "Not me."

* * * * *

"All from a little plant?" Lon said, struggling to digest everything his sister said.

"Sapling," Mellai replied.

"Same thing," Lon grumbled.

"Actually, they're not," Mellai said, her impatience rising. "Trees are wise and observant. They think with more complexity than any other vegetation—in many ways, more than humans. They aren't just plants."

"You two can discuss the intricacies of True Sight later," Kutad inserted. "Right now, we need a plan of action." He paused to stare at Lon. "And you need to trust your sister's ability, even if you don't understand it yet. She has confirmed the calahein presence. The debate is over."

Lon returned Kutad's gaze. It wasn't a matter of trust that pushed Lon to argue. It was ignorance. Mellai had learned so much, finding answers to questions he hadn't even thought to ask. He couldn't help but be annoyed by it.

"What do you propose, Sergeant?" Wade said. The four of them stood facing each other in a tight square, encircled by the other members of Lon's squad and Mellai's guard. The outer circle stood facing away from their Beholders, eyes carefully surveying the landscape for any signs of danger.

"Our people need to be warned," Kutad replied. "We need to retreat immediately to the Taejan Plains, then make for Itorea."

"Good idea," Mellai said, "but you'll have to do it without me. I'm traveling west to Roseiri."

Kutad's eyes widened. "It's too close to the mountains."

"Exactly why I'm going."

"Me, too," Lon added, then turned to Kutad. "Our grandparents live there. We can't abandon them to die."

"And the other villages need to be warned," Mellai said. "The entire Western Valley is in mortal danger." She paused, reflecting on the memories of the little tree. "We have to save as many as we can."

Wade spoke low and intensely. "We will not leave you unprotected, Beholders."

Lon smiled softly. "I welcome your loyalty, Lieutenant. I need only one runner, and I select you." Wade's eyebrows raised in obvious protest, but Lon pressed on. "The return journey will be dangerous. I need a guarantee that Tarek will receive this message—quickly—and that he'll believe it. *You* are that guarantee. Do you accept?"

Wade's mouth twisted in obvious disagreement, but ultimately he gave the Rayder promise and retrieved his horse.

"Wait," Mellai said as Wade pulled himself into his saddle. "I am sending Kutad with you."

Kutad wasn't nearly as compliant. He put up a good fight, until Mellai finally convinced him that it was his duty as sergeant to protect King Drogan. The best way to do so would be to return to Itorea.

"What will you do?" Kutad bemoaned as he prepared his own horse. "Wander around aimlessly until you've found every last person? This is folly."

"Perhaps," Mellai answered with a tight hug around Kutad's waist, "but it's the right thing to do."

With a final salute from both runners, Wade and Kutad kicked their horses' sides and galloped away in a straight line toward the Taejan Plains. Lon watched them retreat for a short time, scanning the northern horizon with his power for signs of danger, before finally turning to his own squad.

"We should separate, as well," Thad suggested. "Beholder Mellai and her guard can visit Roseiri, but we should ride straight for Humsco. We could cover twice as much ground."

"An honorable suggestion," Lon replied, "but don't dismiss our last skirmish with the calahein. I won't leave my sister defenseless anywhere near the mountains."

"And I won't let him run off on his own," Mellai added as she signaled for her own men to pay attention, then she nudged Lon with her shoulder and spoke to him in a whisper. "Go ahead. Give 'em the speech."

Lon couldn't help but chuckle. The timing was right. Besides, he was better suited for the task. Mellai had always been a better berater than a builder. He drew in a deep breath and released it slowly, partly to calm himself, but also to signify the importance of what he had to say. It wasn't until he had everyone's full attention that he finally spoke.

"Appernysians, Rayders—brothers in arms—a solemn quest lies before us. We are but nine men and two Beholders, tasked with the preservation of life as we know it. The rescue of these villages might seem a moot point, especially to my own squad, but I promise you this. The calahein will not stop until every last one of us has been destroyed. Our chances of success are low. All of us might die. Yet, we must try anyway." He paused to glance at Mellai. "My sister and I request your help as a personal favor. Our grandparents live in Roseiri, and our parents in Pree. We need to see them safe."

"As you shall," the youngest of Mellai's guard spoke, his fist over his heart.

Mellai nodded. "Thank you, Snoom. You're a loyal friend."

"We all are," another guardsman spoke. "Please, Beholders. My own family dwells at Humsco. I'm anxious to get moving. If Roseiri has been destroyed . . ."

"Of course, Jareth," Mellai said, then turned to her brother. "Lead the way."

Chapter 6

Beholders' Guard

"And what if she attacks again?" Channer shouted to Lon with equal parts volume and intensity. "Beholder or not—your sister or not—I will not tolerate it. Has she no loyalty?"

"More than you realize," Lon replied, giving his sister a gentle squeeze on the arm. Mellai pulled her arm away and glared at Lon, nearly toppling out of Dawes's saddle in the process.

Lon shook his head and shifted his seat on the bedrolls. "What she often lacks is tact. Too often she speaks before thinking, and many times thinks too much before speaking. I will say this for her, though. With Mellai, what you see is what you get. There's no dodging into the cornfield with her."

Channer was not satisfied, and Lon knew it. But what could he say? Mellai had been interacting with Rayders for less than a week. It had taken Lon much longer to sympathize with their plight and see them as they truly were. All things considered, Mellai was reacting surprisingly well. The fact that she hadn't killed anyone in Lon's squad showed tremendous restraint. It would be so easy for her to destroy them, should she choose to.

Again, Lon's sense of worth slipped another notch as he compared himself to his twin. In her presence, he was nothing. Perhaps that was how the Rayders felt with Lon around. Maybe that's why those who hated him did it with such vehemency, conquered by their own pride and jealousy. The Rayders were living in his shadow, just as he dwelt in his sister's. There was little he could do to change their hearts, but at least he understood them better. He made a point to be more conscientious of his own attitude and actions from that moment forward. No sense in adding fuel to an already raging fire.

For the umpteenth time, he checked their ranks. His own squad formed a wedge in front of the Beholders, Channer riding point, while Mellai's guard arced at their flank. They were well spaced and gripped their weapons, eyes alert.

Good, Lon thought in response to the obvious tension. He was scared of the calahein and grateful to see that everyone else was, too.

Lon glanced at Nik, bow in hand and arrow nocked, then at each member of his squad. They had once been twelve strong, and now that number had been cut in half. Tarl to the mosquitoes, Lars at the Quint River, Riyen to the calahein, and Keene and Preton to Braedr's treachery. Now Wade was galloping madly in the opposite direction, leaving them with only six to guard against an attack from the fiercest enemy ever known to Appernysia.

✳ ✳ ✳ ✳ ✳

Over one hundred miles separated Réxura from Roseiri, along a path that frequently scraped the base of the Vidarien Mountains. The journey was hazardous for the combined escorts of Lon and Mellai, at the very least, but speed was their greatest concern and the well-worn trade route offered the clearest, most direct course to Roseiri.

For two days, they traveled without incident. Most of their time was spent in focused surveillance, with intermittent questions or directions from Lon and Mellai. But on occasion, when their path veered south from the mountains, their group relaxed and Lon sought to connect with his sister and her guard—and perhaps glean some knowledge about True Sight in the process.

"Tell me more about Kaylen," Lon prodded his sister at one point. "Who were her friends in the King's Court?"

"The only one I know of was Aely," Mellai answered.

"Is she your lady-in-waiting, too?"

"She died, Lon. Young and sprightly, and murdered while protecting your sweetheart. Stepped right in front of a throwing knife aimed at Kaylen's heart."

"Why would anyone try to kill Kaylen?" Lon felt his anger growing.

"Calm down," Mellai said, her voice split between compassion and annoyance. "The culprit is dead, so there's nothing you can do anyway. Besides, you asked the wrong question. You should be wondering who would want to kill King Drogan. Kaylen had just killed the chamberlain who had organized all the assassination attempts, so that made her a target for execution, too."

Despite how passionately Lon wanted to falsify his sister's account, he could feel in their bond that she spoke the truth. Kaylen had killed a man. She had crossed into territory that could never be fully repaired. Even though she had done it with the most honorable of intentions, she would have to fight guilt for the rest of her life. Just like him.

"What can I do?" Lon asked, not knowing what else to say.

"Nothing. You left, remember?"

Lon's lips tightened, but he held his tongue. Lashing out at his sister would do little good. He changed topics instead. "So King Drogan has enemies within his own circle, too. That's unfortunate."

"It truly is, Lon. Rayders think him to be a coward, but it has been much more complicated than that. His political hands were tied by the King's Council until Kaylen intervened. Her action alone freed King Drogan, allowing him to reign again."

"So what does that make Kaylen?" he asked, truly seeking an honest answer. "Is she an assassin posing as your lady-in-waiting?"

"You know you're talking about Kaylen, right?" Mellai scoffed. "It was a circumstantial choice made in the moment. No one ordered her to kill him."

"Good. She's too innocent, and she deserves to stay that way. The world needs people like her to keep the rest of us sane."

"But there's an important place for people like us, too. The last thing I wanted was to become a Beholder and join the fighting. I had a peaceful life ahead of me, and with a great man." Although she couldn't hide her emotions, Mellai turned her head to hide her face.

Lon sighed, wanting to ask more, but he kept his focus on Kaylen's deceased friend. "Tell me more about Aely."

"Why?" Mellai's reply was a little too guarded.

"She was a good friend to Kaylen. I wish I had known her, and I'm hoping Aely will help me learn more about Kaylen."

"You should show more respect for the dead," Mellai snapped.

"What's that supposed to mean?"

"Aely was a real person, Lon, and a good one at that. She watched over Kaylen, gave her *life* for Kaylen, while the two of us were too preoccupied with our own lives. Aely isn't a tool for you to reconnect with your old girlfriend." Again, her response was sharp, too sharp even for Mellai.

"I don't see what your—"

"Stop, Lon." Mellai was nearly shouting, glancing over her shoulder as she spoke. "Some of us still hurt too much to talk about her."

Lon followed Mellai's glance and saw Snoom with a forced smile on his face. Mellai's intensity finally made sense.

"You and Aely were . . .?" Lon started to ask Snoom, but realized he wasn't exactly sure how to finish his question.

Snoom shook his head. "She died before I had the chance to properly court her. Don't worry. You can talk about her if you'd like. Sure it hurts, but our memories are the only things that keep the dead alive." After a brief pause, he nodded his head as though he had just made up his mind. "I insist you talk about her. Please."

Mellai shrugged, her demeanor calmed. "If anyone's memories here can bring Aely to life, it's yours. All I know of her is from Kaylen."

"She was young?" Lon asked.

"Yes," Snoom replied. "Incredibly smart, but still young. When her nose wasn't stuck in a book, she was busy telling people what was on her mind."

Lon laughed. "Sounds like someone else I know." His comment earned him a sharp elbow jab in the ribs from Mellai. "What did you love about her," Lon continued, "if you don't mind me asking?"

Snoom moved his horse forward, next to Dawes. "Many things. She was beautiful. Witty. Genuine." He paused again, then added, "Her eyes captured me the most. It sounds juvenile, but when I looked into them, I felt like I was peering into a heaven wrapped in a green blanket. I felt warm. Loved."

"That's very romantic," Mellai said. "I wish she could hear you say that."

"As do I," Snoom replied with a weak smile. "How about you, Lieutenant . . . Beholder . . . umm . . ."

"Call me Lon."

"Ok, Lon. What about you? I assume from Mellai's comments that you know Kaylen? Do you love her?"

The question was innocent, but Lon suddenly wished he hadn't started the conversation in the first place. Mellai also turned and looked at him, obviously curious how he would answer.

"That's a complicated question," Lon finally said. "We were betrothed in Pree, before I left over a year ago. But so many things have changed since then. It's not practical to say I still love her, nor is it fair to expect her love in return." Lon ground his teeth, knowing that his response made him look shallow. Mellai's guard didn't know what had happened in Pree or why he *had* to leave, but Lon was in no mood to explain the situation or justify his actions. They could think whatever they wanted.

"But you plan to court her again?" Snoom said.

Lon nodded emphatically. "I hope to, but with no expectations. Whether there is any hope for us remains to be seen. In her eyes— in all of your eyes—I'm a traitorous Appernysian who has been brainwashed by the Rayders." Snoom stammered, obviously struggling with how to respond, but Lon continued. "All that matters right now is that we stay focused and work together. Rayders versus Appernysians can wait for later."

Snoom dipped his head slightly, then fell back into position behind the Beholders.

"Kaylen still loves you," Mellai said to her brother, "but don't get too excited. Her love for you makes all of . . . *this* . . . even more painful for her. You made a promise, then you broke it—in the most extreme way possible. You can't justify that away, not when it comes to matters of the heart."

Mellai's words hurt, and Lon was done talking about it. He tapped Dawes's sides with his heels and shouted for his squad to up their pace. They had wasted too much time, and he needed to stay alert.

＊　＊　＊　＊　＊

Just before sunrise on their third day of travel, when the world was still dark in slumber, the long-dreaded ambush finally came. The company was still twenty miles east of Roseiri. Mellai and Lon had been alternating night watchman shifts since their True Sight power allowed them to see clearly in the dark. However, since both were dreary eyed from sleepless nights and because they were over ten miles south of the mountains, their combined guard had convinced both Beholders to rest that evening. Thad and Jareth were on watch instead, each at opposite ends of their small camp. Thad called out a warning, having spotted a moonlit cluster of movement in the high grass, but too late for Jareth. A red glob of phlegm hit him square in the face and splattered onto his horse. Their dying screams alerted the rest of the camp.

Thad loosed an arrow into the center of the cluster, then traded the bow for his glaive as he charged forward to protect his waking company. A yelp sounded in the darkness, followed by what could best be described as wolf howls mixed with the hiss of snakes. The sound was terrifying, but Thad remained undaunted. He slid under a volley of phlegm aimed in his direction, then rose back to his feet to stab the closest hound in its open mouth. Leaving the creature to gag on his glaive, Thad drew his sword and continued his attack. Two hounds lost their heads. One spilled its innards. Thad was gaining confidence, dashing about and felling beasts with sharpened steel, until his blade lodged between the spikes protruding from a hound's spine.

With all his might, Thad used his sword to hurl the beast aside like an oversized morning star. Its bone spikes skewered another, but the effort left Thad exhausted and exposed. Three hounds leaped on him, snapping furiously. Thad grappled with equal aggression, but there was only so much he could do. His last shout, "For Taeja!" was quickly silenced as a snout found his throat.

* * * * *

Mellai jolted upright, eyes clouded with True Sight. Jareth's screams had turned to gurgling as his face dissolved under the poisonous red phlegm. Mellai rushed to his aid, but too late. Jareth's essence fled his body, as did his horse's—a welcome reprieve from excruciating pain.

"Wait," Mellai called out, hoping to interact with Jareth's essence. She had first seen this phenomenon of humans during their fighting on the Taejan Plains, but the mayhem of battle had kept her from digesting what she saw. During their journey since, however, she had oodles of time to wonder. The dead's essence exemplified many of the physical qualities of Llen. If she could talk to a Jaed, why not Jareth?

What Mellai didn't consider was the danger of her situation. It was no time to experiment with True Sight, and she was reminded of this as a glaive struck a hound midair—one that had leaped directly at her. Both glaive and beast toppled sideways, barely missing Mellai as they crashed to the ground.

Mellai shook her head with self-disgust at becoming so easily distracted and looked to the source of protection. Dovan had thrown the glaive, then joined the defensive half-circle of Mellai's guard that formed in front of her.

Channer and Elja were protecting Lon in like manner, quickly dispatching anything that came within the reach of their blades. Nik stood next to Lon, his bow drawn with nocked arrow and eyes alert. Lon was pulling energy into himself and compressing it between his hands.

He's trying to create fire, Mellai thought, realizing that Nik needed more light to effectively utilize his bow. Without waiting for Lon, she focused on a fallen pine tree twenty-five yards away and immediately engulfed it in flames, filling their surroundings with roaring light.

Lon paused and glanced at Mellai, then smiled and said something unintelligible to Nik. Lon then proceeded to fling terror hounds into the air with columns of dirt. As they flew helplessly, Nik shot them with deadly accuracy.

Mellai couldn't help but laugh with exhilaration at their ingenuity, but only temporarily because once again, she was reminded of her own mortality as Ric sliced open a hound directly in front of her.

Twice, Mellai inwardly grumbled as she turned to her own protection. Despite her power, she was a child of war—inexperienced and easily distractible. *But no more,* she affirmed as she contemplated how to end the ambush with one swift act. Her resolve solidified as she heard one of Lon's squad shout, "For Taeja!" before the hounds overwhelmed him.

They were surrounded by a large pack of hounds, at least thirty in number and scattered in formation. Mellai extended her essence among them, her left hand forming an energy shield and her right methodically grabbing every hound and tossing them into the floating prison. The hounds fought with each other inside their cell, bloodlust raging with nowhere else to spend it. When all were captured, she moved the energy shield into the burning tree and released them, taking great pleasure as she watched them burn. After they had twisted through the burning branches, they sprinted about, engulfed in flame and howling their displeasure. All had been mortally wounded and after a brief wait, their frantic dashes turned to still, sizzling masses. The threat had been eliminated.

"Next time," Lon said, a weary smirk on his face, "just crush them with that floating energy prison."

"Noted," Mellai replied.

A faint glow was growing in the east, signaling the start of a new day. Although their night's rest had been cut short, there was little point in trying to sleep. Everyone was wide awake and the danger was still very present. They needed to move. Fortunately, the trade route veered southwest for the remaining twenty miles, farther away from the mountains on its course to Roseiri.

Mellai suggested they leave immediately, but Lon refused until he had honored Thad's sacrifice. He and his four Rayders circled Thad's body, then Lon made the same pose he had been holding while trying to create fire, his hands cupped together in front of himself as though he were holding an invisible boulder. Mellai thought of offering help, but withheld. There was something ceremonial about their actions, which she finally understood when a jet of flame escaped Lon's hands and ignited their fallen comrade. She was witnessing a Rayder funeral, and Dovan seemed particularly distraught as he looked on.

"What about Jareth's body?" Snoom said. "Should we bring him back to his family?"

At first, Mellai thought it a good idea, but two points quickly changed her mind. First, Jareth had been gruesomely disfigured. No mother should see that. Secondly, carrying Jareth's body with them was unwise. Although they were travelling closer to Humsco—where his family lived—they were on an errand much more important and couldn't risk the complications of an extra load.

"I'll bury him," Mellai finally responded. Using her power, she pulled a chunk of earth from the soil, had Ric and Duncan place Jareth's body into the hole, then she lowered the earth back into the ground. She and her three guardsmen then stood awkwardly looking at the unmarked grave. "Should we say something?" Mellai asked.

"No," Snoom replied. "None of us knew him well enough to offer a proper epitaph. And I don't sing."

Mellai knew he was referring to *The Song of the Dead*, tradition-ally performed at Appernysian funerals. "But we can't just leave him here in an unmarked grave," she insisted. She looked around for something she could use for a headstone. Instead, she saw Lon standing in the distance with Thad's horse. Lon was whispering to the horse as he stroked its mane, finally stepping back and watching as the horse sauntered south into the wild of the Western Valley.

✳   ✳   ✳   ✳   ✳

Lon turned to meet Mellai's gaze and walked over to join his sister and her guard.

"What was that about?" Mellai asked.

"Rayder tradition. When a horse's master dies, we release the horse." Mellai stared inquisitively, and Lon knew his sister could see something deeper was troubling him. "It's Dovan. And Channer and Nik. All three of them have lost their dearest friends, just as I lost Omar. This pain, Mel. It'll spread across Appernysia faster than a raging storm. Everyone is going to feel this suffering."

"Not if we stop it," Mellai countered.

Lon sighed, not wanting to continue the emotional conversation. "What's happening here?"

"We need a grave marker," Snoom replied. "Mellai was contemplating solutions when she noticed you."

Lon nodded, his expression lost in a deep thought.

"What is it?" Mellai asked.

Lon didn't respond at first, but finally nodded. "I know what to do, but I'll need granite."

Mellai searched their surroundings and immediately found what Lon sought. A large granite boulder protruded from the ground under the tree she had set alight. With the aid of True Sight, she hoisted the boulder from the ground and set it at the head of Jareth's grave. It was large and round, about three feet in diameter.

"Want me to polish it for you?" Mellai asked, frowning at the black scorch marks from the tree's flames.

"No," Lon said, "but it is a little too big for my own comfort. Would you mind wrapping it with one of your energy bubbles?"

"Energy shield," Mellai said with a motherly smile, then lifted the boulder and formed a sphere around it.

Lon brought cupped hands in front of himself and pulled matter from another nearby tree to create a fireball. Once a large sphere of flame was rolling between his outstretched hands, he attempted to move the fireball into Mellai's energy shield. He struck an impenetrable barrier.

Without a cue from Lon, a section of the shield opened. He thanked his sister and moved the flame inside and around the boulder. The energy shield closed again, severing Lon's connection to the fireball. The flame immediately dispersed.

"What are you trying to do?" Mellai asked after lowering the boulder and severing her power.

"Superheat the granite until it transforms to obsidian."

Mellai stared at Lon perplexed, but the three members of her guard gaped in response.

"You can create obsidian?" Duncan asked.

"What's obsidian?" Mellai said with obvious irritation.

"I didn't know, either," Lon answered. "I was trying to melt granite so I could shape it together—like the walls in Itorea—and accidentally created a black, brittle rock."

"If you can indeed turn a boulder that size into obsidian," Duncan continued, "it would be worth enough to buy an estate in the Cavalier Crook. You'd be the wealthiest man alive."

Mellai hadn't spoken, staring at the boulder with a softened expression. "You knew this, Lon?"

He nodded. "After Wade explained it to me. We didn't grow up the wealthiest family in the world, did we?"

"That says a lot about you," Mellai continued, her eyes becoming moist, "that you'd be willing to share this secret with us and use it to create headstone for one of our fallen." She wiped away her tears and gestured at the boulder. "May I?"

"Sure," Lon said with a shrug, stifling his pride. For once, he had taught his sister something new about True Sight. Well, sort of. He had no doubt she could melt the rock without his assistance, but the end result was a new concept to her. He wished he had been able to show her—that they could work together with their power.

Mellai's eyes clouded over and the boulder raised into the air again. Lon summoned his own power to watch his twin work. She was holding the granite in an energy shield again, but she didn't create fire. Instead, she pierced her own energy shield with the essence of her opposite hand and . . . *played* with the rock. Its relaxed energy became irritated, increasing in speed and intensity.

Lon recognized the reaction. He used the same technique to create fire, but only out of combustible materials like wood, and only by pressurizing it. He hadn't thought of attempting it with something that resisted flame. The boulder buzzed with energy, a sign that it was filling with heat. It began to brighten, just as Lon had seen before.

"How hot?" Mellai asked, her face focused in concentration.

"Until it turns soft and spongy."

And indeed it did, much quicker than when Lon had used fire for the same effect back in Taeja. He thought to warn Mellai about avoiding water, but became distracted as Mellai caressed the heated granite with her essence, molding it into shape. With each stroke of her right hand, she distorted the energy shield with her left, holding the mass in shape. Soon it was a carefully crafted halberd—blade, hook, spear, and six foot shaft. It was flawlessly proportioned and seamlessly blended. One solid black stone.

When the halberd's energy had cooled to shining obsidian, the edge of the blade shimmering with dangerous sharpness, she stuck the halberd deep into the earth at the head of Jareth's grave. But Lon wasn't satisfied. "The first person who sees this will pluck it right out of the ground."

"True," Mellai said, her clouded eyes scanning their surroundings. A much larger boulder was located, over ten feet in diameter. But they didn't know this until Mellai pulled it from the ground and moved it to the head of Jareth's grave. She sunk it back into the soil, taking obvious care not to disturb the grave, until only a one foot section remained visible.

And without any signs of distress, Mellai answered Lon's confusion over how to mold stone together. She penetrated the boulder with her essence and rearranged its matter to create a small tubular hole, then moved the halberd into it. That was it. Essence interaction. A simple nudge here and tweak there, and the entire physical makeup of an object could be permanently changed. Why do the most complicated questions always seem to have the simplest answers?

Without asking for permission, Lon joined the task, extending his own essence into the combined stones. Mellai withdrew hers, letting him work alone. He gently molded the base tightly around the obsidian, sloping slightly up the thick shaft for extra strength and security. By the time he finished, nothing short of a two-handed maul would break the obsidian from its solid base.

The twins stood next to each other for a time, Lon not knowing what to say and Mellai obviously preoccupied with her own thoughts. Soon the Rayders joined them. Elja led their five remaining war horses to stand next to Snoom, who handled the Appernysian's four. The horses nickered at each other, but otherwise remained unaffected. Lon watched them with intrigue, hoping that their behavior was a sign of future interactions between Appernysians and Rayders. No, not Rayders. Taejans.

It was Mellai who finally broke the silence. "Time to move. Roseiri waits for us."

Chapter 7

Undertaking

Afta a quick glance at the glow of the southern horizon, Wade breathed in the evening dew and smiled. Kutad and his mount were miles away, having been unable to keep up with Wade's horse. Dax had been trained specifically for such long distance races, and although he hadn't been pushed to this extreme since rushing from Three Peaks to Thorn, he easily outpaced their Appernysian company.

Wade's smile widened as he patted Dax on his neck with one hand and pulled the reins with his other. "Ease up, friend. Appernysians would not take kindly to a lone Rayder galloping into their camp. Like it or not, Kutad is our shield against an ugly skirmish."

Dax slowed to a casual walk while Wade surveyed the northern landscape. The sun was setting, revealing hundreds of cooking fires that spotted the land. The entirety of Appernysia's army lie before him, blocking Wade's path to his own commander farther north. But once Kutad overtook their position, he would lead Wade safely through the Appernysian ranks.

When Kutad was only a couple hundred yards away, Wade's pride gave way to impatience. Kutad halted his advance and dismounted. For thirty minutes he sat in the dirt, until the rising darkness turned him into nothing more than a shadowy outline. Just when Wade had decided to ride back and drag his traveling companion to their destination, Kutad finally mounted his own horse and continued forward.

The two men said nothing to each other, but Wade noticed a folded piece of parchment in Kutad's hand as the sergeant rode past and led the way toward their armies. The note only increased Wade's irritation. Why waste time writing a message that Kutad would be delivering himself?

Before they were within bow range, Kutad retrieved a torch from his bundle and ignited it with flint and steel. In spite of his annoyance, Wade nodded gratefully. The light would show they had no intention for stealth and thus ease the Appernysian watchmen's minds.

Or so he had hoped.

The man on watch must have been entertaining his own anxieties for too long, because at first sight of Wade and Kutad, the watchman loosed bolt after bolt from his crossbow. They were too far for a warning or call for identification, and Wade could not retaliate. Even kicking Dax into a gallop would draw negative attention. All he and Kutad could do was count the time between bolts, and relocate their cantering horses accordingly. Luckily, the watchman was not a talented crossbowman. No bolts found their mark while they closed the distance.

"Hold," Kutad shouted when they drew close enough, "by order of Sergeant Kutad Leshim!"

His order came just in time. Three other watchmen had just joined the first and added their own bolts to another volley. One nicked Dax's turned head, drawing a pained whinny from the horse.

The four watchmen dropped their crossbows, but stood firm with their halberds extended. Wade pulled on his horse's reins, bringing Dax behind Kutad. He was no fan of submission, but he wasn't a fool. If someone were to get stabbed, he would graciously let Kutad fill that role.

No such luck.

Kutad slowed to allow the watchmen to view his face, then led Wade through the Appernysian forces until they reached a tent camp. A week had passed since their two groups set out to investigate Réxura, so Wade was pleased to see the passive arrangement of housing rather than more blood splattered across the snow. Kutad disappeared into the largest tent for a brief moment, leaving Wade under a circled guard of pikemen, until the sergeant reemerged to escort Wade through the rest of Appernysia's forces.

"King Drogan requests a private war council with your commander," Kutad said once they passed into neutral territory. "He will meet my king between our forces at dawn, unarmed and without escort."

"As long as Drogan comes in kind," Wade replied, then kicked Dax into a gallop toward the Rayders.

✳ ✳ ✳ ✳ ✳

Tarek glanced over his plate-armored shoulder at Wade, their distance from each other increasing. "An abandoned puppy without his Beholder," Tarek mused, but his heart wasn't in the jest. Wade's report had been far too unnerving, especially Lon's decision to plunge deeper into danger. "Fool," Tarek spat, turning his attention forward and gauging a halfway point between the two armies. Without a Beholder to protect them, no one would survive a full calahein attack. Roseiri and Pree weren't worth the risk.

Tarek knew complaints were pointless, but it was a hard habit to break. His people's future now rested in his hands, contingent upon the delicate politics he was about to discuss with Appernysia's king.

"And where is he?" Tarek growled, having stopped his horse without any signs of an approaching Appernysian. But he knew the answer to that question, too. King Drogan was waiting for him, making sure Tarek was alone and without weapons. "Not that I'd need any to break his scrawny neck."

Eventually an armored man moved out of Appernysia's front line. "About time," Tarek mumbled, raking his thick beard with a gloved hand. The ringlets Mellai created had left permanent crimps in his red facial hair. "Lady Prettybeard," Tarek said aloud, followed by hearty laughter. The act had been growing on him, a masterfully inappropriate response in such a deadly standoff. Just the kind of thing he would do. There was no doubt about it; Mellai would make a great Rayder. "And maybe even a wife," Tarek said, followed by more belly laughs.

About this time, Tarek sobered when he confirmed that the approaching man was King Drogan. Tarek sat tall in his saddle, his hands calmly gripping the reins in front of him. He wasn't afraid of being attacked—Drogan would be a fool to act so rashly. What concerned Tarek was the potential outcome of their war council. No matter their decision, more Rayders would despise Tarek after this day. He'd have to take even more precautions for his own safety.

"Hail, Commander Tarek," Drogan called, his hand raised in an unoffending gesture of peace.

"And I for . . . to you, King Drogan," Tarek replied awkwardly. "Bah. I've never had a talent for formal speech. How about I speak normally and you take no offense by it?"

"Fine by me," Drogan said with an unreadable smile. "I assume your man has shared our Beholders' findings?"

"He has. The calahein threat has been confirmed. What are your solutions?"

Drogan eyed him curiously. "Do you wish to stay in Taeja?"

Straight for the throat, Tarek thought begrudgingly. To say yes would be to sentence the Rayders to death. To say no would place himself in a position of debt and servitude to Drogan. But he had no choice. "Of course I do. But I can't stand by and watch my people's extermination. We've already established that Itorea is the safest place for everyone."

"Indeed it is," Drogan continued. "What do you request?"

"Let us accompany you back to the Fortress Island. Together, our forces will protect humanity."

Drogan paused to lean back and breathe in the crisp morning air, then a dark smile formed on his face as he reconnected his gaze with Tarek. "Say please."

Tarek's first instinct was to rush at him, knock him out of his saddle, and sit on the king's head until the man suffocated against the snow. What brazen pride. Outright degradation. Their lives were in the balance, and he had the gall to demand a please?

"Surely, the least you can do is develop good manners," Drogan continued.

Tarek knew his body language exemplified how he felt, but it took every ounce of his self-control not to flatten the Appernysian king. He didn't care if Drogan knew he hated him. In fact, he preferred it. Tarek had to comply, and Drogan knew it. A little hatred was perfectly appropriate.

"Please bring my people into Itorea," Tarek spat between clenched teeth.

"Very well," Drogan replied, "but only under strict criteria. Have you contemplated the reverse—how difficult it would be for you to bring *our* people into *your* city? It's not just about resources and space. Imagine how your Rayders would react if our entire nation showed up on their doorstep, unannounced and expecting free food and lodging?"

"Rayders have not had the luxury of experiencing anything for free," Tarek countered, "nor do we expect it now. We offer you our protection. We will repay your hospitality with our lives."

Drogan shook his head. "Tsk, tsk. It sounds nice, but I can't think of a greater way to ensure chaos than to integrate armed Rayders into the guard of our capital. Surely you can understand my simple logic."

Tarek's anger was dissipating, with annoyance quickly taking its place. Appernysians could complain all they want about Rayder totalitarianism, but he could think of few things more torturous than sitting in an Appernysian council of nobles talking this way to each other for weeks on end. Even his father's stories of simple town councils sounded arduous, and Myron was a level-headed delegate of a small village. No, quick and decisive action was Tarek's way, even if it came from a man other than himself.

"Enough of these games," Tarek said flatly, his arms folded across his chest. "What do you have planned for us?"

Drogan's joviality also disappeared as he gripped his saddle horn with one hand. "You will bring your men into our midst and surrender yourselves as prisoners. We will allow you to keep your weapons, but if you draw them even an inch, we will slaughter you like cattle."

"Oh, is that all?" Tarek replied. "How about the hair off my chest, too?"

"Those are my terms."

Tarek clenched his jaw, grinding his teeth with frustration. The Rayders wouldn't be happy about this, but what choice did they have? He eventually forced himself to accept.

Drogan smiled. "Very well. Then we will escort you under armed guard through Itorea. Once you have been safely moved east of Itorea's keep, your independence will be returned to you. We do not ask for, nor do we require your assistance protecting Itorea from the calahein. Stay safely out of our way, and we will gift you with our city's protection and supplies. Cross us, and we will leave you to die."

Deliberations had ended; Tarek could read the finality upon the king's face. Even though it infuriated the commander, he had expected such a response, since he, too, would have demanded the same terms. Drogan was not completely unreasonable in his request, but unfortunately, many of the Rayders would not see it the same way. Neither would the Appernysians, for that matter. Drogan would be under the same scrutiny as himself. Humility wasn't one of Tarek's strongest characteristics, but if it could bring the preservation of his people, it was a trait he would gladly develop.

"And what of my civilians still in Taeja?" Tarek said.

"Send a dispatch to escort them to Itorea's west gate and we will treat them in like manner."

Tarek moved his horse forward to the Appernysian king. Drogan showed obvious concern over the close proximity, but Tarek continued until he was within arm's reach. "Where I come from, a handshake is stronger than stone, holding men of honor to their word." Tarek extended his right arm, palm upward. "Do I have your word, king of Appernysia?"

Drogan glanced over his shoulder at his own men, then returned his gaze to Tarek. "By my honor," Drogan replied as he took Tarek's hand.

"Very good," Tarek continued, squeezing Drogan's hand hard enough to draw a grimace from the middle-aged king. "Violate your word, and I will see to your punishment myself. That is *my* promise."

✳   ✳   ✳   ✳   ✳

Wade sat upon Dax, watching his commander and brothers-in-arms move themselves into the center of Appernysia's one hundred thousand men. He knew the full details of the war council arrangement, his commander having confided in him so Wade would know what to expect when he reached Itorea with the rest of their population. To eliminate as much resistance as possible, the rest of the Rayder soldiers would be notified of their imprisonment once surrounded and with no hope of escape.

"I have a critically important task for you," Tarek had told Wade in private before departing. "Bringing our people to Itorea is essential, yes, but I fear it'll be more difficult than we expect. From what Braedr told us, he left quite a mess in Taeja during his rescue. For all we know, Braedr's followers may have taken full control of the city. You need to eliminate the resistance first, by whatever means necessary, then bring our people to Itorea."

"What if some of them refuse to depart?" Wade had asked in response.

Tarek had paused and heaved a weighty sigh. "Then leave them to their own fate. We don't have time to convince them, and you won't have the manpower to force them. Just save as many as you can."

Knowing many supply wagons would be necessary for the civilians' journey to Itorea, Tarek had assigned Bryst—overseer of supplies—to help Wade in Taeja, along with ten other soldiers. Bryst sat in the coach seat of one empty wagon, pulled by a team of two large draft horses. Bryst was a veteran complainer, so it had caught Wade off guard when Bryst complied with their commander's assignment without resistance. Yet, it didn't surprise Wade too much. He had learned to trust few with his safety or secrets. He would just keep constant watch over Bryst and the ten Rayders, as he did with everyone else.

"Come," Wade said as he turned Dax toward Three Peaks. "We have no time to spare."

By the end of that day, they had crossed the South River that Lon had opened, then traveled along its northern banks toward Taeja. When they were thirty miles from the silhouette of Three Peaks, Wade ordered the ten Rayders to carry the calahein news to the mountain watchtowers. Lieutenant Thennek still controlled the mountain, much to Wade's liking. Lieutenant Thennek was one of the only Rayders that Wade fully trusted, a responsible man that had displayed fervent loyalty to Beholder Lon. The entirety of the Taejan Plains could be viewed from Three Peaks. As long as those peaks remained void of fire or smoke, the Rayders were still capable of being saved.

Wade had also sent the men away because that meant ten less men that he had to beware.

Another day of travel brought Wade and Bryst to the joining fork of the North and South Rivers, three miles east of Taeja's perimeter wall of dirt. Wade squinted into the sunset, reflecting brightly off the windswept snow. Drifts had covered the wide tracks their soldiers and wagons had made through the snow when they left Taeja two weeks earlier. Despite its undisturbed beauty, Wade also recognized the danger surrounding him. Every track, including those who might have deserted from their army, or calahein who could have passed through during the night, had been swept away. Threats could literally come from any direction.

Wade explained the calahein threat to Bryst, emphasizing that they needed each other's protection during the night.

"Why don't we just move into Taeja?" Bryst asked. "We could be safely behind her walls in an hour or two."

"I would like a full day to work with our civilians and prep them for our journey to Itorea, and we could both use the rest before such an arduous task."

Bryst reluctantly consented, and Wade gave him the first watch of the night. With practiced perfection from time spent guarding his Beholder, Wade mimicked a deep slumber and listened as Bryst stole away through the snow toward Taeja, leaving his wagon and draft horses behind.

Night had fully enveloped the Taejan plains, darkened by a layer of clouds that overcast the sky. No moon or stars shone through the thick blanket, providing Wade with the opportunity for stealth that he desired.

"Thank the Jaeds," Wade whispered as he, too, made his way toward their homeland. But he turned north, whereas Bryst's tracks showed he was headed straight toward the south gate into the city. The snow was soft, but dangerously deep in many places. Wade made sure not to travel anywhere higher than Dax's knees as they aimed for the northern blade of Taeja—where Appernysian refugees had made their home before becoming branded as Rayders themselves. The journey was three times farther than Bryst's, but it would offer the safest point of entry into the city.

Wade wondered over Bryst's behavior as he traveled. His flight could have been driven purely by anxiety, but that was doubtful. Bryst had endured worse encounters in the middle of battle, yet been more worried about the security of his supplies than his own safety. No, Bryst had to have been in league with Braedr, and rushed ahead to warn the city that Lieutenant Wade Arneson was approaching. Even without an army to back him up, Wade was a man not to be trifled with. The dissenters were right to be afraid, for he would show them no mercy.

Two hours later and with an incredible amount of good fortune, Wade discovered a bridge into the city. Snow drifts had filled a portion of the wide trench surrounding Taeja and piled against the perimeter wall of dirt, at a slope gentle enough for Dax to climb. And climb it they did, right into the northern blade of Taeja.

The Swallows had not been idle. Their night watchers discovered Wade as he crested the hill of dirt and immediately surrounded him with glaives when he descended into their territory. Wade did not fight back, hoping that someone would recognize his face and associate it with Lon and Tarek, men who had been committed to their safety and survival.

"Any final words before we slice you in half?" one Appernysian said as he gripped his glaive. A young boy stood behind him with a drawn dagger.

"That was Beholder Lon's glaive, was it not?" Wade said as he dismounted. "I was with him the night he gave it to you, along with the brands on you and your son's temples."

"Lieutenant Wade?" the man said, his glaive lowering as he spoke. "Is Beholder Lon with you?"

"I am afraid not, but I have sworn to Commander Tarek that I will protect you and lead you to safety. What is your name, Rayder?"

The man paused with a sidelong glance at those surrounding him. "I . . . my name is Quinten. Quinten Witkowski. Sorry, Lieutenant. We're just not used to being called Rayders."

"It is I who must apologize," Wade replied, "for your mistreatment and abandonment. Braedr Pulchria has been executed, but that doesn't make up for your losses. Tell me, how many men did you lose guarding his prison?"

More whispers surrounded Wade. "I don't know," Quinten finally replied. "A lot, I guess, but it didn't stop there. They freed all the other prisoners, too, and we've been repeatedly attacked since then."

Wade nodded. "The persecution stops now. Tell me, who is leading? Who directs the north blade of Taeja?"

Quinten looked around, as did everyone else in Wade's presence—an assortment of men, women, and children. No one seemed to know the answer to his question. They were leaderless as a whole; just small bands of resistance doing their best to survive in their own spheres of influence.

"I see," Wade continued. "Spread the word among your brothers. I have taken control of the north blade, and I will answer all attacks tenfold upon those who commit them. By order of Commander Tarek Ascennor, everyone in Taeja now answers to me."

"Thank you, Lieutenant," Quinten said with a broad smile. He picked up his son and sprinted north, disappearing into the darkness.

Word quickly spread of Wade's presence and many Swallows flocked to his command. Fearing a preemptive attack from Bryst, Wade put aside sleep to organize a group of one hundred men into a militia. He reminded them of Tarek's training with weaponry, and instructed them on basic commands and formations. If he had any hope of controlling the civil disputes in Taeja, he needed to stop them by force. His band would need to make a name for themselves and earn the respect they deserved.

As they trained, his militia made their way to the south end of the north blade and took shifts guarding their borders. Only then did Wade dare to rest, and with only a couple hours left of night.

Chapter 8

Retreat

"Slowly," Kaylen spoke as she helped an injured Rayder to his feet. She had been one of only a few Appernysians to volunteer their services in behalf of the Rayders. Kaylen was no healer, but many injured Rayders were in dire need of medical attention after their battle on the Taejan Plains. Kaylen had spent every waking moment tending to the wounded Rayders since the day Lon and Mellai departed.

Many of the injuries she cared for had occurred after the truce. When Tarek ordered his men to surrender, a surprising number of Rayders had resisted. More skirmishes ensued, mostly just between the Rayders—those loyal to Tarek and those who refused to obey. It took a few hours, but Tarek's command was finally enforced and all Rayder soldiers sheathed their weapons.

For two days now they had traveled as one company toward Sylbie, following the new river the Rayders claimed Lon had opened from the mountains. Their progress was slow, though, and it would be over a week before they finished the hundred-mile trek. Kaylen was in no hurry, suspecting that once they reached Sylbie, the Rayders would cross the west bridge into Itorea and into King Drogan's imprisonment indefinitely.

"One step at a time," Kaylen continued, bracing the Rayder soldier with his arm over her shoulder. "Does it hurt?"

"No more than a hammered thumb," the Rayder replied with a smile, then collapsed to the earth when he placed too much pressure on his injured foot.

Kaylen squatted down and lifted the Rayder onto his strong leg. "It must be broken," she said, helping him back into the medical wagon. "No amount of willpower will fix that. You need to rest and let it heal."

"As you wish," the Rayder replied, touching his King's Cross brand with two fingers on his right hand. "Thank you for your assistance."

Kaylen nodded and wandered away, not exactly sure of her destination. Two days earlier, she had thought the Rayders savage and violent. But their will to fight had diminished, replaced instead by a loyal courtesy that she and the other Appernysian volunteers received. These Rayders lived a high standard, exemplifying honor and integrity at levels she had not thought possible. From a nation known to be ruthlessly cruel, she now saw nothing but overwhelming kindness and appreciation. Had they always been like this, or had Lon's leadership been influencing their behavior over the previous year?

Yet, she wasn't ignorant of the opposite perspective. She had also helped gather and bury dead Appernysian soldiers into a mass grave. She had seen their mortal injuries, fatal strokes from a deadly nation of Rayders who knew how to kill with the least amount of effort. She had smelled the charred flesh of their men caught in the explosion—Lon's explosion.

Kaylen stopped, too preoccupied with her thoughts to move her feet. It wasn't until many minutes later that she realized the Rayders were stepping around her on their journey east, many uttering soft offerings of assistance in her behalf. Tears filled her eyes and she broke into a stumbling run directly north, desperate to escape their confusing company. At one point, she cut too closely in front of a Rayder and tripped over his tree-branch crutch, landing face-first in the snow. She felt a gentle tug at her arm and turned her head to see the Rayder trying to help her to her feet.

"My apolog—"

His words were cut short by a crossbow bolt, which had struck him in the back and protruded out the front of his breastplate. The Rayder glanced down at the injury, gave a heart-wrenching frown, then tightened his grip on Kaylen's arm and hoisted her up. Only after Kaylen was standing firmly on her feet did the Rayder fall sideways into the snow.

"Who shot him?" Kaylen cried, her eyes searching for the offender. It was then that she noticed Kutad galloping toward her. "Who shot him, Kutad?" she cried again, but the sergeant didn't answer. He simply lifted her into his saddle and carried her out of the Rayder army.

*   *   *   *   *

"What were you thinking?" Kutad said. "I didn't want you helping the Rayders, Kaylen, but I let you continue, hoping it would be a good allocation of your big heart. You have to be smarter than this. Keep your distance from them, especially when you feel the safest. It might seem like it was all an accident, but given another minute, that Rayder could have done any number of things to you."

"He was trying to help me stand up!" Kaylen shouted. "He was apologizing, and you shot him!"

"I told you before," Kutad replied, "it wasn't me."

"Prove it."

Kutad shrugged. "You're safe, Kaylen, and that's all that matters."

"No, Kutad. It's not all that matters. That Rayder deserved life as much as either of us, but we stole it from him. We can't give it back. He'll never get it back."

Kutad sighed as Kaylen fell forward onto the neck of his horse and sobbed. She had become so distant, so emotional since Lon's return. Kutad fingered the parchment letter folded in his pocket, missing yet another opportunity to give it to her. It seemed that every passing day made it more and more difficult to tell Kaylen how he really felt, how deeply he loved her. Once again, the letter would have to wait for another time.

Chapter 9

Devastated

"Jaeds save us," Dovan whispered, echoing the apprehension that filled Lon's mind. Even from a mile away, the noonday sun revealed that Roseiri had been completely destroyed. Unlike the caution the calahein had taken in Réxura to remain unnoticed, this village had been decimated with fire. Black rubble replaced many aged houses.

Lon wrapped his arm around his sister, who sat physically shaking in front of him. "Remember, Mel," he counseled with a gentle hug, "we have to be careful, now more than ever. No rushing into anything, and heads always on a swivel. Tree memories can wait for later. Got it?"

"You should have given me Thad's horse," she complained with a half-nod.

Lon moved his hands back to Dawes's reins. He had the same opinion as his sister, although Jareth's horse would have been a better option if it hadn't died in the attack. Lon turned to address the rest of their company in a low voice. "Stay away from narrow paths and blind corners. Let's not make this easier for the calahein."

Fists pounded hardened leather vests and fingers touched brands. Without further instruction, their joint guard formed a protective wedge in front of their Beholders, with the exception of Nik and Elja, who were positioned in the rear with strung bows and nocked arrows.

"Forward," Lon ordered, and they continued west on the main trade route into Roseiri. He had not seen any signs of life, human or calahein, but they still had to search, hoping against all odds for their grandparents' survival.

"What's his name again?" Lon asked his sister.

"Theiss," Mellai replied, a tremor in her voice. "Theiss Arbogast."

"And Reese is his younger brother, right?"

Again, Mellai only managed a slight nod.

Lon ground his teeth with frustration. If Theiss had somehow managed to escape the slaughter, Lon would still make him pay for hurting his sister. It wasn't her fault that she was given True Sight, and she had done nothing to deserve his venom. What quality of love shatters so easily when presented with a complication? *None worth holding to,* Lon thought. He had already shared the same opinion with Mellai when she had finally divulged her broken betrothal. The closer they drew to Roseiri, the more Lon had seen the same pain, the same hopelessness in Mellai's eyes that he had experienced himself. Only Mellai's heartache wasn't of her own doing. Theiss had chosen to abandon her when Mellai needed him the most.

But the closer they drew to Roseiri, the more Lon's focus shifted away from Theiss. He had expected the same scene at Réxura—mangled corpses littered across the snow—but none were to be found. Plenty of blood, but no bodies.

Maybe they were taken captive, Lon thought, but he pushed the failed logic away as quickly as it had entered his mind. His life in the Rayder Exile had taught him differently—Rayben Goldhawk had shown him the efficiency of ruling by fear, and the calahein had used the same tactic in Réxura. They had purposefully left bodies scattered across the trade city to create terror, thereby weakening Appernysia's confidence. But Roseiri had been handled differently. There was no need to send a message to travelers who happened upon this village. It had served a different purpose.

"No," Lon spat through clenched teeth.

"No, what?" Mellai replied, her head jerking back and forth as she scanned their surroundings.

"This village was a meal." The words came not from Lon, but from Channer, and they escaped his lips without emotion. "We will not find survivors here."

"He's right," Ric inserted, "and staying will only add us to the platter."

They halted at the east banks of the West River, directly in front of the open field where tradesmen and Roseiri's villagers used to celebrate every year. But both had been slaughtered. They would not meet again in this life.

Lon followed Mellai's gaze as she looked north, staring at the party tree where they had first synchronized their power in a game of stick-stack. Six years had passed since then, but Lon's mind didn't wander into that memory. He focused instead on the tears pouring down Mellai's cheeks. Despite his own trials, Lon knew his sister had suffered much the past year. Above all else, Lon knew he had caused her the worst pain when he fled Pree. Because of his choice, Mellai had toiled through the helpless, even hopeless marsh of ambiguity for nearly a year. Never again. Lon would make sure she had closure, even if it came at the risk of his own life.

He eyed the opposite bank of the river, a mere hundred yards away. Houses lined both sides of the river, but destruction had been far more severe on the western shore. It looked ominous and full of threats. *No matter,* Lon thought, his mind made up. They would cross the bridge and travel to his grandparents' property three houses north. Any sign of their deaths would be better than nothing at all.

Lon cleared his throat and spoke confidently, commanding obedience from their company. "I'm taking my sister across the river, and we're traveling there on our own."

His own squad nodded their assent, but Mellai's guard tried to reason with him. Snoom was the most vocal of the bunch.

"What use are the two of you dead?" Snoom said. "Our kingdom needs your protection. Would you risk legions of lives for the sake of such a trivial matter?"

"Trivial?" Lon countered. "Since when would an Appernysian underst—"

Mellai ripped the reins from Lon's hands and kicked Dawes on his sides, silencing Lon's speech and sending them galloping toward the river. Ric tried to grab Mellai as they thundered past, but she tossed him out of his saddle with a flick of her hand. Lon turned back to see Snoom and Duncan galloping after them, but none of their horses matched Dawes's speed. In just a few seconds, they had reached the stout bridge spanning the West River and were thundering across at a dangerous pace.

His own anxieties flaring, Lon shouted for Mellai to slow down. She turned her head to argue just as four calahein ground troops burst from the rubble of the two closest houses. The kelsh, fur colored dark orange and red, would be on top of them within seconds.

Lon froze, unable to respond or summon his power.

Mellai was facing the wrong way. She didn't even realize the threat. They were going to die.

In that moment, when time seemed to freeze and halt any physical reaction from the two Beholders, an eternity of thought flooded his mind. Lon reflected on his previous year since leaving Pree. Of everything he had done, the many deaths and lives spared at his own hand, one regret towered above them all.

Kaylen.

If Lon could only see her face one more time, he would make sure she knew. He never forgot her. He always planned to return to her. He loved her.

Kaylen.

A shadow had fallen over them. Lon did not fear death. His suffering would finally come to an end. No more impossible decisions.

No more constant threat of death. No more Braedrs. No more drama. Only peace.

But what about Appernysia? If Lon and his sister died, the entire kingdom would be destroyed. Everyone would die, including Kaylen.

Lon blinked himself out of his stupor and realized the shadow had been real, cast from two enormous beasts that had skimmed over the top of their heads to intercept the attacking kelsh. Mellai must have seen them first, because her gaze followed the beasts' flight toward the threat. Lon didn't need to look twice to know they were ghraefs, renowned for their size and power, yet the calahein didn't back down. Two kelsh leaped high into the air at the Beholders' protectors, while the other two charged underneath with the apparent intention to flank the superior ghraefs.

But the ghraefs were ready for them.

The shaggy black-haired ghraef smashed the skull of the kelsh below with its armored tail. At the same time, it locked the leaping kelsh in its jaws and, after a lethal crunch, swallowed it whole.

The short-haired brown ghraef was more slender and agile. It buffeted the other sprinting kelsh with its feathered wings, toppling it off the road and down the riverbank. In the act, the ghraef had twirled in the air to catch the other leaping kelsh with its four paws. With a sickening shriek, the kelsh was ripped in half and tossed aside, before the ghraef performed an aerial loop and charged headfirst into the river. It tackled the tumbling kelsh and pinned it under the water, standing waist deep and growling menacingly as it slowly drowned the thrashing beast. Only after the kelsh stopped moving did the ghraef hoist the dead calahein out of the river, toss it backwards, and swing its armored tail with perfect accuracy. The bone sphere on the tip of the ghraef's tail connected directly with the kelsh's core, knocking it out of the river and beyond the northern limits of the village.

Everyone had pulled back on their reins, bringing their horses to a cautionary halt. Lon also gladly recognized that no one had been foolish enough to draw their weapons.

The shaggy ghraef landed, blocking the old trade route leading west out of Roseiri, while the brown-hair clawed up the west bank of the river to join his . . . tribe? pack? brother?

Lon shuddered, realizing how little he knew about these powerful creatures before him, even less than he knew about the calahein. The ghraefs were huge, easily as big as one of the village's quaint houses. Their forelegs were thicker than Tarek's broad-shouldered body and just as long, while the hind legs were even broader. *Probably for leaping into the air,* Lon thought as he gazed at their wings. Folded against their bodies, the feathers blended into their like-colored hair.

Another low growl escaped the brown-hair's muzzle, which was similar to the snouts of the dogs they kept in Pree. Teeth, lips, tongue, nose, ears, eyes—no, not the eyes. Even from a distance, Lon could see that these ghraefs held an uncanny amount of wisdom as they skulked about on padded paws, quiet as a fox. Their armored tails— with tufts of hair jutting between the many bone segments—coiled into the air like a scorpion, the weighty-bone tip dangling above their rumps as they sniffed the ground cautiously.

"They're hunting," Lon whispered to Mellai, which could mean only one thing. There were more calahein about.

Lon finally summoned his power and noticed a partially obscured figure still hidden under the charred timbers of a destroyed house. Although Lon hadn't seen it with his naked eyes, True Sight revealed the creature's bright essence flaring out of the rubble. Without a second thought, Lon captured its essence in an air pocket and hoisted it up. Another kelsh.

Mellai's essence flared bright as she summoned her own power. A tendril of light shot from her to grab one of the timbers and stab the suspended kelsh through the chest. Its pained howl was terrifying, yet the two ghraefs only cocked their heads to one side as they watched it die. While the humans trembled with fear, the ghraefs radiated curiosity.

Once the kelsh's essence had shifted out of its body and disappeared, Lon finally dropped the dead beast to the ground. He was about to release his power, when he noticed another string of light extend from his sister. This time, it aimed at the head of the black-haired ghraef and connected with his skull.

A rumbling roar shot from the ghraef as he swatted in front of his face, then he dropped low as if ready to pounce. He snarled and looked directly at Mellai. It had somehow felt the Beholder's power and obviously despised the interaction. Mellai was smart enough to immediately recall her essence and dismiss True Sight altogether.

"What were you thinking?" Lon said, knowing his sister had just tried to read the ghraef's mind. As a sign of peace, Lon released True Sight, too, but he forgot his question as soon as he asked it. Out of the ghraef's thick mat of black hair were staring large blue eyes. Lon remembered a similar vision, north of Roseiri on his journey to the Exile a year earlier. This had to be the same ghraef that had watched him and Dawes from the shadows of the Vidarien Mountains.

The black-hair pushed off its front legs to stand on its back two, its tail methodically coiled across the ground for support. It towered into the air, at least two stories high, and inhaled with closed eyes. A few seconds later, it blew the air out, fluttering through its lips like a horse, and lowered onto four paws again. Both ghraefs visibly relaxed after this signal.

"That must've been its way of letting us know we're safe," Lon said.

"I know him," Mellai replied as she slid out of Dawes's saddle. "He saved Kaylen from Braedr."

"This thing cut off Braedr's arm?" Lon said, earning another sharp growl from the shaggy ghraef.

Mellai glared at her twin. "He's not a thing, Lon. Remember what I told you about ghraefs? They're smarter than us."

Strange noises came from the brown-hair. A mixture of snorts and coughs escaped its—his—snout and his tongue dangled out the front of his mouth. He seemed amused by Mellai's comment, almost as if he were laughing. *And why not?* Lon thought. If ghraefs were wiser than humans, laughter seemed only natural. But wait . . . if he was laughing, that meant he understood what Mellai had said.

"Can they speak our language?" Lon asked his sister.

Mellai shrugged. "I have no idea."

The twins had stopped at the west edge of the bridge, and Mellai gingerly stepped off of its wood planks in the direction of the blue-eyed ghraef.

"Wait, Mel," Lon cautioned, realizing what she was about to do. "You just made him angry."

"I *know* him," Mellai retorted with another few steps.

The ghraef remained surprisingly passive as Mellai closed the distance between them. He only watched her curiously, unlike Lon, who was screaming inside, hoping his sister didn't do anything else to anger the beast. Lon glanced back at their escorts, seeing the same frozen stares of apprehension written on their faces.

As Mellai continued to inch her way forward, the only fact that maintained what little was left of Lon's confidence was the Beholders' aged relationship with ghraefs. As Mellai had said, they used to work together in partnerships. Beholders had not existed since the First Age—not until this past year—so it couldn't be coincidence that ghraefs also now appeared. And this wasn't the first time they had intervened on his behalf. These must have been the same two who saved his squad's lives on the Taejan Plains. They had to be.

But how were those partnerships formed? Lon thought, hoping Mellai knew more about the subject.

* * * * *

Mellai placed one foot in front of the other, her entire focus on remaining calm and confident. *They saved us,* she kept telling herself. *They want to help.*

When only a few feet separated her from the massive snout of the blue-eyed ghraef, Mellai brought her right fist to her heart and bowed low. "Thank you. For everything. Kaylen is my best friend, and her life means the world to me."

As the last phrase escaped Mellai's lips, the possible deaths of her grandparents and Theiss struck home. Tears filled her eyes. Her heart throbbed. Where had these ghraefs been during Roseiri's destruction? Why hadn't they saved the village? Both of her arms hung limp from lowered shoulders when she realized the truth. Her real pain came from the fact that she could have saved the village herself. Why did Llen send her to Itorea? He had to know that the calahein were approaching, but the Jaed forced her to leave Roseiri defenseless.

"I could have saved them," Mellai said, her voice a faint whisper.

The ghraef seemed to understand Mellai's torment. He returned Mellai's gesture with his own apologetic nod, then used his snout to motion to the other ghraef.

Mellai wiped away her tears and glanced at the short-hair ghraef and his brown eyes, confused. Kaylen had been sure her rescuing ghraef had blue eyes, and Mellai also had seen shaggy hair in the tree's memories of the rescue. "He helped save Kaylen, too?"

The black-hair ghraef rolled his eyes and stepped over Mellai, his belly easily clearing her five feet. With a few massive strides, he moved directly in front of Lon and sat on his haunches.

Mellai stared at the shaggy ghraef for a moment, then moved her focus to the short-haired ghraef, who had ceased smiling. His eyes spoke the pain Mellai felt in her heart.

"I don't understand," Mellai said, half a statement and half a question.

After gently touching his snout to Mellai's forehead, the brown ghraef lowered himself onto his belly, his head lying on his left paw. His right paw lifted into the air and, after making a fist with one claw extended, tapped the ground in front of himself.

And it all came together in Mellai's head. The short-haired ghraef was to be her companion. The shaggy one, on the other hand, had to have been focused on Lon since before Kaylen's kidnapping, even watching him struggle with True Sight in Pree. It's the only explanation for why he would intervene to rescue Kaylen—he was taking care of his Beholder, even to the extent of saving Lon's sweetheart. Mellai looked in Lon's direction again, unable to see him on the opposite side of the black-haired ghraef, then returned her attention to the nearby ghraef and walked in front of him.

"My name is Mellai," she said, dipping her head respectfully. "What's yours?"

The ghraef lifted his head ever so slightly, licked his chops, then opened his mouth wide. Mellai was taken aback by the huge canine teeth filling his mouth as she imagined the power behind a full-force ghraef bite. She was glad the ghraef appeared to be on her side. A strange sound emitted from his throat, undoubtedly spoken in the language of ghraefs, but nearly indecipherable to Mellai's ears. "HWWYUURRK."

Mellai winced cautiously, not wanting to offend the ghraef. "I heard Huirk. Is that right?"

The ghraef returned his head to his paw and shrugged his shoulders, kindness emanating from his eyes. He didn't seem to mind her attempt, so she would stick with it. "Very well, Huirk. Pleased to meet you."

A moment later, the other ghraef gave what must have been his name, sounding like a noise a bear would make. "BWWRROOHHMMAAWWKSS."

"Bromax?" Mellai asked Huirk, gesturing to the other. Huirk puffed air out his nose, his eyes still smiling, then swiveled perpendicular to Mellai. Still looking at her, Huirk tapped between his shoulder blades with the tip of his curved tail.

Mellai tried to swallow, her throat painfully dry. "Are you asking me to ride you?"

Huirk nodded.

Mellai faltered, taking in the enormity of Huirk's size. He was so powerful, and she such a tiny thing. Even when lying flat on the ground, his spine rose well above her head. And what about those air maneuvers? She would have toppled off his back repeatedly in those few seconds of battling the calahein, falling to her death or drowning in the river.

"I'm afraid," Mellai whispered as she stepped forward and placed her hand on Huirk's foreleg. His short hair was tough and coarse, the strands so densely packed she could barely make out his leathered skin hidden underneath.

Huirk only tapped between his shoulder blades again.

Warily, Mellai reached up and grabbed handfuls of hair, pulling herself up while using Huirk's foreleg as a foothold. It was difficult, but she finally managed to take her place at the base of Huirk's neck. Then without warning, the ghraef stood and walked toward the bridge. Mellai squeaked and dropped low, but she had little to fear. She sat waist-deep in a padded blanket of hair, and the ghraef floated across the ground, nothing like the jostling gait of a trotting horse. Huirk would not let her fall, even without a saddle.

Mellai was so equally fascinated and terrified by the experience that it wasn't until Huirk laid next to Bromax that she realized Lon hadn't moved. In fact, he was arguing with the other ghraef.

"It's a matter of loyalty. Of friendship." Lon patted the neck of Dawes, who stood wide-eyed in such close proximity to the ghraef. "Dawes has been with me for over a year and saved my life many times. There's no greater horse in Appernysia and I won't casually cast him aside."

An awkward silence followed as Lon and Bromax stared at each other, not disrespectfully, but stubbornly. Mellai looked to their guard, but they seemed to take little notice of Lon's conversation with Bromax, more interested in watching her on the back of Huirk. Mellai couldn't help but smile as she smoothed Huirk's hair in front of herself. It had to be an awe-inspiring sight, to see a Beholder sitting on the back of a ghraef, both beings of unmatched power working together for the first time in Appernysia's Second Age. As a partnership, as friends, they would be capable of miraculous feats. Had they been present during Réxura's or Roseiri's invasions, they would have stopped the calahein, maybe even scared them from attacking in the first place. But there were still cities and villages left to protect. Places like Pree.

"Don't," Mellai said to her brother. "Don't leave Dawes, I mean. Who else in Appernysia loves him, probably even more than you?"

"Flora," Lon replied, pointing north, "but she's on the other side of these mountains. How would I get Dawes to her?"

"Flora?" Mellai repeated, not caring who this girl was that fell in love with Lon's horse. "No, Lon. Turn your brain on. Who else?"

Lon's eyes widened, then he glanced down in obvious contemplation before addressing Bromax. "Will you follow us to Pree, so I can deliver Dawes to my mother?"

Without a moment's hesitation, Bromax insistently shook his head. And there they were again, Lon and Bromax stubbornly staring each other down.

A terrible thought entered Mellai's mind. She leaned forward, speaking quietly for only Huirk to hear. "Is Pree destroyed?"

Huirk didn't answer. Bromax silenced any potential response from Mellai's ghraef with a half-second grunt-growl. Bromax was obviously the alpha male and growing impatient.

"Well is it?" Mellai said louder, her own impatience growing. "Are our parents dead?"

Bromax didn't look at her, but his long claws dug into the snow with obvious frustration. At first, Mellai thought this physical response confirmed her worries—that Aron and Shalán had been killed, along with the rest of the village—but the longer she watched Bromax, the more she began to understand these creatures. It wasn't that Pree had been destroyed; this was a matter of pride and honor for Bromax. He was putting Lon on the spot, forcing him to immediately prioritize between his horse or a ghraef. A ghraef was the obvious choice, but Mellai also understood Lon's perspective. How could she convince him to give up Dawes, and to do it now?

It was Elja who finally offered the solution. "Allow me, Beholder. I will escort Dawes to your mother."

"I'll make sure they get there safely," Snoom continued, a quick nod at Mellai.

"And we will make sure your family stays safe," Channer added. A hint of sadness accompanied his proclamation, but coupled with devoted determination. Channer had recently lost his cousin, Keene, to the calahein. His body language spoke that he would do everything in his power to keep the same pain from reaching Lon.

Lon turned to address their men. "Everyone in Pree is like family to me. Would you risk your lives to protect every villager, people you don't even know?"

Ric pounded his leather-covered chest with his right fist. "All of us will."

Mellai was honored by their loyalty, but as she looked over the mixture of Rayder and Appernysian men, she couldn't help but wonder how the people of Pree would react to such a diverse and dangerous group entering their village.

"Can we at least fly ahead to notify them?" Mellai asked Huirk, who directed the question to Bromax with his eyes.

Lon jumped in. "Not only would we warn them, but we would also inspire hope. Let us reveal ourselves to Appernysia. They need to know Beholders and ghraefs are fighting together again. Our people need to believe they'll survive."

Mellai spoke when Bromax's eyes narrowed. "How about we just start with Pree? Appearing before a handful of villagers won't hurt, right?" Mellai focused on Lon. He had such grand visions of a reunited Appernysia with Beholders and ghraefs . . . What he lacked was patience. *All in due time, Brother,* she thought, pleading with her eyes for Lon to back down.

Lon nodded his assent, then leaned back in his saddle to address the ghraef towering above him. "I will leave Dawes to Elja's care, but I have a couple of deman—uh, I mean requests."

Mellai watched anxiously, but Bromax's eyes softened with a hint of amusement.

"Thank you," Lon continued. "Mellai and I would like to search Roseiri, not just for survivors, but for explanations as well. A half-day is all we ask, then we can continue on to Pree, then . . ." Lon paused, unsure of what would follow.

Huirk finally joined the conversation. Mellai squeaked and threw herself against his neck again as he stood. With exaggerated movements of one foreleg, Huirk first pointed to the ground in front of himself, then at Lon, and finally at his own chest.

Lon tilted his head in confusion. "Here are Beholders and ghraefs?"

Huirk shook his head and thumped the snow-covered ground with his tail. Once more, he pointed at Lon, then at the ground.

"You want me over there?"

The ghraef rolled his eyes and rattled off a stream of growls and grunts at Bromax. The larger ghraef turned his head to lock eyes with Mellai.

Mellai sat up. "I'm listening."

Bromax carved a picture in the snow of what looked like the outline of a house, then pointed at Mellai and back at the picture.

"My house?"

The ghraef nodded, then pointed at himself and the picture.

"Oh. My home, then your home," she shouted, a little too excited to see the ghraefs' nest. What was their society like? Were there other living ghraefs? Did Huirk and Bromax have mates, or maybe even little baby ghraeflings?

Bromax clicked his teeth together, then turned back to Lon.

"Agreed," Lon said as he dismounted Dawes. Mellai could see by Lon's slow movements that he was pained to leave the black horse behind. After an over-thorough examination of his supplies, Lon finally turned to Bromax again. "I'll leave my glaive behind, but what of the remainder of our tack? Will you carry our food and bedrolls for us?"

Bromax turned his head sideways and stuck his snout in the air like a spoiled child. Huirk laughed again.

"It's alright," Mellai interceded. "We can hunt and build shelters with True Sight. We don't need supplies."

Bromax huffed air out of his nose, emphasizing Mellai's observation.

Chapter 10

Manifestation

L on stepped in front of Dawes and placed his forehead against the horse's snout. A lump had formed in his throat, making it painful to breathe. November was coming to a close. Dawes and Lon had left Pree in that same month a year earlier, when the snow had just begun to fall. So much had happened since then. Adventures, trials, rescues, battles—Dawes had carried Lon through them all, physically and emotionally. They had grown to become close friends, relying implicitly upon each other for survival. To pass Dawes off felt so wrong, yet the choice had already been made. Lon tried to take solace in the fact that his mother would eagerly inherit his horse.

But is she alive? Lon thought. *And even if she is, will she listen to me? Will she see reason?* For the sake of Dawes, Lon was certain that Shalán would hear him out, but what about Aron? Would his father accept the change that had befallen his only son, a son who had worked tirelessly to eliminate the cruelty and conflict that had driven his father to defect from the Rayders? Would he understand?

He'd be a fool not to, Lon thought. Mellai and Lon would be together and, even if just for a moment, finally fulfilling Lon's promise. He would return home. *And not just as a simple peasant, either,* Lon mused, taking Dawes's bridle and walking him across the bridge, weaving between Mellai's guard. *I will return as a Beholder,*

First Lieutenant of Taeja, and Mellai as Appernysia's Beholder. Not to mention Bromax and Huirk.

As Elja took the lead rope and secured it to his own horse's saddle, Lon paused to say one final goodbye to Dawes.

"Farewell, my friend," he said, stroking Dawes's neck and admiring, perhaps for the last time, his shining black hair and powerful muscles. "Protect my parents as you have protected me."

Dawes nickered and tossed his mane playfully, but then something happened that Lon would remember for the rest of his life. Dawes paused, watching Lon intently, then moisture filled the horse's eye and a tear trickled down his cheek.

Lon wanted to give in, to throw his arms around his horse and weep, but he was afraid he'd never let go. He simply wiped the tear, kissed Dawes on his nose, and walked way.

Bromax was now prostrate with his head on the snow. Lon compared the two ghraefs, noting that even without his shaggy black hair, Bromax was significantly larger and broader than Huirk. Lon assumed the size difference was because of age, since Huirk behaved younger and answered to Bromax.

Although he couldn't see Mellai, Lon knew his sister was hidden somewhere behind Huirk's massive head. Odds were, Huirk didn't realize he was blocking her view, either. After all, it was probably the first time the ghraefs had ever carried humans. The vast beasts would have to make adjustments along with Lon and Mellai.

As a practiced rider, Lon scaled Bromax's enormity more easily than Mellai had. He was soon buried in the hair at the ghraef's neck. Lon shuffled his legs uncomfortably. If Bromax decided to turn upside down while flying, Lon would undoubtedly fall to his death. Huirk appeared to be the more acrobatic of the two. He was a good fit for Mellai, who had always had a better sense of balance and coordination than her twin brother.

With Bromax's head still lying on the snow, Lon had an unobstructed view of his squad. He sat up straight and brought his right two fingers to his King's Cross, crisply saluting his brothers-in-arms. The Rayders returned the gesture with a unified shout, "For Taeja!"

"For Appernysia," Lon returned, then drew his sword and pointed it at Channer. "Lieutenant Channer, I leave you in charge of our combined Beholders' guard. I'm relying on you. Don't be caught unaware. We can't afford further losses."

Channer drew his sword and kissed the etched pommel, signifying that he accepted his promoted role as lieutenant, then slid it back into his scabbard and saluted again.

"Once you reach Pree," Lon continued, "escort my parents and the rest of the villagers east across the Western Valley. Use the southern trade route and visit every population, gathering as many people as you can. You must reach Itorea. Making a stand there is our only hope for survival."

Lon sheathed his sword and turned to Mellai, offering her a chance for a final speech to her men. "Lieutenant Channer is in charge," she said without looking away from Lon. Her eyes were sincere and respectful.

Lon breathed a sigh of relief, grateful for his sister's compromise. "Lead the way, Little Sis. Let's find out what happened."

✳   ✳   ✳   ✳   ✳

Lon held his sister, unsure of what to say as she buried her face against his arm. He could feel the sleeve of his tunic becoming damp, soaking up Mellai's agonized tears. At their feet was the motionless body of Theiss Arbogast, partially buried in a snow bank off the trade route. Puncture wounds peppered his body, signs of his final duel with the dead terror hound they had discovered farther up the road, near the south bridge of Roseiri.

Lieutenant Channer had left immediately with the Beholders' guard, traveling west along the old trade route toward Pree while the Beholders stayed behind. Mellai had asked Huirk to first take them to their grandparents' house at the north end of the village, where she relived the first moments of the calahein attack from a partially burned birch tree. With a shaky voice, Mellai had told Lon that Dhargon and Allegna were the first to die, consumed by a pack of terror hounds while two kelsh set fire to their home. The terror hounds had also died in the flames, too absorbed in their feeding frenzy to flee the danger before the entire house collapsed on top of them.

What had held Mellai together, lending her enough composure to share the experience with Lon, was the conversation that had happened just before the attack. Dhargon had seen the calahein rushing in from the north, allowing him enough time to convince Theiss to gallop south on their donkey.

"Someone has to warn our village," Dhargon had argued, "along with the people in Humsco. We're old, but you still have your whole life ahead of you. Now ride, Theiss, and save as many as you can!"

When Mellai had immediately ordered Huirk to the south bridge, in the same direction that Theiss had fled, Lon agreed. He wanted to scout the village for possible survivors, and Mellai could read the memories of a tree at the south end of Roseiri to see if Theiss had survived.

With terrifying power, both ghraefs had leaped into the air and coasted over the village with their great wings. Once Lon overcame his impulse to decorate Bromax's hair with vomit, he had peered over the sides of the ghraef. The destruction below had been unnerving. No houses stood on either side of the river, having been reduced to blackened timbers. Lon hoped more terror hounds, maybe even kelsh, had died in those fires, too.

Lon had also scanned the terrain for any glowing essences, but no signs of life existed. Even the wildlife had abandoned the village—that, or been consumed along with everyone else in Roseiri.

At the south bridge, they had found the scattered remains of three boys, along with the dead body of a terror hound. Huirk had lapped up the terror hound and swallowed it. Lon couldn't tell if it was out of spite or hunger.

Mellai's spirits had lifted when they found human and donkey footprints leading away from the dead bodies. "Find him," Mellai had whispered to Huirk, then the ghraef sprinted along the trade route. Splashes of blood eventually led them to Theiss's body, two or three hundred yards farther south, and the donkey prints had continued on alone.

Even before they found the body, Lon didn't need to be able to read tree memories to know that Theiss hadn't survived. The destruction of Roseiri appeared to have been absolute, as it had been in Réxura.

"How do we fight this?" Lon finally asked, half to Mellai and half to himself as he soothingly stroked his sister's hair. They were standing halfway between the two ghraefs, where Lon had caught Mellai after she slid off Huirk's back and stumbled along with no particular destination. "What hope do we have of winning?"

Bromax clicked his teeth in response. When Lon looked at him, the ghraef pulled back his lips to flash a deadly set of incisors and stomped his hairy black paw on the frozen ground.

"You make a good argument," Lon said, half smiling. "With both of you around, our odds are much higher."

Bromax nodded, then laid in the snow. Once again, he tapped between his own shoulder blades, indicating for Lon to climb aboard. Huirk did the same, following the alpha's lead.

"We need to bury Theiss first," Lon said. When Bromax flared his paw to reveal twelve-inch claws, Lon continued. "Wait. I'm sure Mellai wants to do it herself. Right, Sis?"

Mellai shuddered with an intake of air, her body trying to stem the overpowering grief that pressed down on her. "I don't even know what I'm so upset about," she finally said, pushing her brother away as she shifted from sorrow to anger. "Theiss gave up on me the minute he found out I was a Beholder. He wanted nothing to do with me." She turned to the ghraefs, her gaze moving back and forth between them. "Is that why you didn't save Theiss like you did Kaylen? Theiss didn't love me anymore?"

The ghraefs only returned her stare with steady gazes. Lon didn't respond, either, knowing his sister's words were hollow. The damage surrounding them showed obvious signs that there had been too many calahein in Roseiri for the ghraefs to fight on their own. And Theiss . . . Lon didn't know the exact circumstance of Mellai's parting conversation with him, but Theiss would have welcomed Mellai with open arms if she had been around during the attack on Roseiri. Mellai would have shown her true power and why she was such a benefit to their kingdom. *Yes,* Lon thought, watching Mellai wield True Sight so effortlessly to bury Theiss deep in the frozen ground, *Theiss would have understood.*

"Do you want to check any other tree memories?" Lon asked after Mellai had finished.

"I can't," she replied, her voice still shaking. "I can't watch anyone else die. Not today."

"But maybe someone was riding that donkey," Lon continued, pointing at the tracks leading south.

Mellai still shook her head, until Huirk stepped forward and nudged her with one of his claws. "Fine," she spat, glaring at the ghraef as she walked farther down the trade route, "but not here."

A few minutes later, when they were far away from Theiss's grave, Lon watched his sister summon her power and touch a large birch tree. He wondered over how she did it, pulling memories from humans and vegetation. "Was it difficult learning how to do that?"

"Took me two days," Mellai replied. "Now be quiet. I need to focus."

Lon wanted to try it himself, to test his abilities against his sister's, but they had no time. Pree still waited, along with the ghraef's home. *And how long will that take?* Lon thought, wondering over the purpose of the latter. Appernysia's whole kingdom was amassing in Itorea; it was there where the Beholders were needed most, so why make a domestic visit to a ghraef nest? And where did the ghraefs live? Somewhere near Pree? Is that why Bromax had agreed to stop by their village on the way?

"It was Reese," Mellai said, stepping away from the tree and wiping fresh tears from her eyes. "Reese was riding the donkey."

"Was he hurt?" Lon asked. Theiss must have passed the donkey on to his little brother, then grappled with the terror hound while Reese escaped.

Mellai shrugged. "Maybe. His tunic was bloody; but nothing has followed him. I searched the tree's memories afterward, up until today."

"That's good, Mel," Lon said, looking south. "I'm sure he made it to Humsco."

"He didn't have any supplies, Lon. Eighty miles is a long way to travel without an extra cloak or bedroll. It would take a miracle." Mellai paused, looking at Huirk and pointing south. "Can we?"

Huirk's eyes softened, but he shook his head as he pointed at Mellai, then himself. Bromax huffed in confirmation.

"I get it," Mellai said, looking down the trade route. "Our home, your home."

Lon knew that more reasons than Reese pulled his sister toward Humsco. Jareth's family lived there, and they should know that he died fighting to save Appernysia. But they would find out. Their Beholders' guard would carry the message to Humsco after they evacuated Pree.

Lon climbed onto Bromax and sat himself at the ghraef's neck. "Time to go."

*　*　*　*　*

Huirk and Bromax flew at an unfathomable rate. Half the day had passed while they had investigated at Roseiri, yet they were already approaching their Beholder' guard after less than thirty minutes of flight. Mellai couldn't see their men—the ghraefs were far too high for her eyes to recognize anything but large hills and rivers. Huirk nudged Mellai with his tail, a warning before he tipped forward, his wings pulled tighter against his body. They dove so fast that Mellai could barely see, her squinted eyes blurred with protective tears against the rushing wind. Mellai gripped Huirk's hair with every ounce of her strength, terrified of being ripped from his back.

Thirty seconds later, Huirk flared out his wings to slow their descent, the force great enough to slam Mellai's face into his hairy back. After regaining her senses, Mellai realized they were only fifty feet from the ground, her guard traveling directly to their left. The men were shouting enthusiastically, swords drawn and brandished above their heads.

Once again, Mellai thought how exhilarating the experience must have been to someone watching from the ground, and she decided to capitalize on their guard's enthusiasm. With True Sight, she pulled a large sphere of snow from the ground and, as she had done with King Drogan in Itorea, dispersed the snow into a flurry that fell up on the guards' heads. The men whooped and hollered.

Huirk also became caught up in the excitement. With a few strokes of his massive wings, the ghraef increased his speed at an alarming rate as he arced upward. Mellai felt herself slipping from his back with every flap, so in a desperate attempt to stay alive, she used her power to braid Huirk's short hair around the full length of her legs and thick knots around both of her feet. She yanked the hair tight, drawing an uncomfortable snarl from Huirk, but she wasn't about to stop. "If you fly like this," she shouted at the ghraef, "you can deal with the pain."

With a huff, Huirk continued to beat his wings, increasing his angle upwards until he finally locked his wings and arched back. Mellai screamed with combined terror and elation. For just a moment, Huirk was upside down and she had an unobstructed view of the land below, then the ghraef finished his loop and leveled out again.

Mellai breathed hard, her blood pumping frantically. "That was amazing!" she shouted at Huirk, who responded with another trademark laugh. The ghraef began flapping his wings again, more slowly this time in a casual ascent to rejoin Lon and Bromax. They were still high above, beyond Mellai's sight.

Mellai closed her eyes and leaned her head back. The rushing air was bitter cold, biting at her face as they flew, but it felt good. Mind-numbing, even; a welcome experience after the destruction of Roseiri. Reese had been the only survivor, if he had even made it to Humsco.

"Wait," Mellai shouted at Huirk. "They need to know about Reese."

Huirk nodded and angled down again, circling the Beholders' guard two times to slow his speed before landing softly in the snow. Mellai relayed the news to her guard, specifically instructing Channer to find Reese in Humsco, then Huirk leaped into the air.

Bromax seemed to endure Huirk's joviality like a tolerant father. The two ghraefs flew next to each other, the tips of their wings occasionally touching as Mellai and Lon shouted to each other.

"Our guard knows about Reese."

"I'm glad you survived to tell them," Lon shouted back, then pointed at the brown ghraef hair weaved around his sister's legs. "Good idea. Think Bromax will let me do that?"

Mellai knew her brother was half-teasing, worry still written on his face. But the joke didn't sit well with Bromax, who had flown expertly, taking great pains not to jostle Lon or let him fall. In response, the ghraef whipped sideways and Lon rolled off his back, barely missing the bone tip of Bromax's armored tail.

Mellai panicked and called upon her power, intent on grabbing Lon with her essence, but Huirk turned sharply, placing Lon directly behind them. Mellai turned, desperate to save her brother, so Huirk dropped into a steep dive to block her view again.

"What are you doing?" Mellai screamed, doubting that the ghraef could hear her as the wind whipped past her face. But apparently he did, because Huirk responded with an emphatic shake of his head.

"I should just let Lon fall to his death?"

Again, Huirk shook his head, this time leveling out to give her a view of Bromax. The ghraef was also in a steep dive, flying next to Lon's flailing body. Her brother was obviously shouting at the ghraef with animated body language, but every gesticulation sent him tumbling in a new direction.

Mellai couldn't help but laugh, realizing that Bromax was teaching her stubborn brother a lesson. Trust, flight, patience, respect—whatever it was, Lon was not catching on. But her laughter stopped when her clouded vision revealed that Lon had also summoned his power, his essence flaring brightly as he fought to control the air surrounding himself. His efforts were foolhardy, every attempted air pocket or gust of wind creating a barrier that would send him toppling out of control again.

Lon became more and more furious, until a sphere of energy formed in his hands and burst outward at Bromax. The energy blast should have been invisible to a ghraef's naked eye, but clouds were displaced as the sphere moved toward the ghraef, warning Bromax to maneuver out of the way. The energy blast continued past, losing its potency as Lon's distance from it increased, until it eventually fizzled and joined with the surrounding air.

When Mellai returned her attention to her brother, she realized that Bromax had grabbed Lon in his paw. Lon's arms were pinned at his sides, but he seemed to accept the temporary prison. His fighting had stopped, although he still maintained his power as they continued toward the ground.

Bromax didn't stop his dive until the last moment, flaring out his wings and soaring over the surface before he tilted his wings back a little more and alighted on the snow. Huirk and Mellai were a few seconds behind, and had just landed themselves when Bromax lifted his paw and flicked Lon aside. With a quick glance around, Mellai gratefully confirmed that they had moved out of their guards' viewing distance. Whatever was about to unfold would not be good for Appernysia's morale.

Lon slowly dragged himself out of the snow and stood facing Bromax. Mellai feared for both of them, knowing the harm they could cause each other, but she forced herself to trust in Huirk's judgment. This was between Lon and Bromax, and they needed to work this out. Any physical intervention on her part would only cause more harm. But that didn't mean she couldn't yell at her twin.

"You disrespected him, Lon," she shouted at her brother. "Apologize."

He didn't reply, a bad indicator of his state of mind. She didn't need to connect with their emotional bond to know Lon was furious beyond reason. Mellai used her power to unweave the hair capturing her legs, then dismissed True Sight and sat sideways on Huirk's back. Worry filled her mind, which is why she couldn't watch this with True Sight. She wouldn't be able to stop herself from getting involved.

Bromax was on all fours, his normally coiled tail resting flat on the ground. He returned Lon's furious gaze with his own uncanny calm. Mellai wondered how old the ghraef must be, how much wisdom and experience was necessary to maintain such calm. Bromax wasn't angry, but still insistent that Lon learn his lesson. This was the only explanation Mellai could supply when Bromax swept his left paw over the ground, sending a wave of snow at Lon.

Lon raised a dirt wall to block the snow, then slammed the dirt back into the ground over-animatedly.

"Is he trying to make Lon mad?" Mellai asked Huirk, but the ghraef didn't respond. He was lying flat on the ground, watching intently with his head resting on his right paw.

Again, Bromax threw snow at Lon and, again, the Beholder blocked it, this time with an air dome that redirected the flurry to his sides.

He's trying to make Lon lash out, Mellai realized, surprised that although raging with obvious fury, Lon had maintained his own calm responses. Their father had used the same tactic during their sparring sessions, eliciting an emotional response out of Lon every time. But not now. Her brother's self-control had grown significantly since he left Pree.

Bromax stood on his hind legs, as he had done in Roseiri, but rather than sniffing the air, he opened his muzzle and uttered a terrifying growl, much like an angry bear. It lasted many seconds, then Bromax jumped forward to charge at Lon, who had obviously been planning his own defense strategy. He shot a column of dirt out of the ground, throwing the ghraef into the air. Bromax caught himself with his wings and dove at Lon. His tail dangled straight behind, until just before he landed, when the bone tip curved to one side.

Mellai realized what Bromax was doing too late to warn her brother. The ghraef landed on all fours and used his momentum to swing his tail full-force at the Beholder. Lon dropped to his belly, barely escaping the death blow, then leaped to his feet and began forming a dirt prison to encase Bromax's hind legs.

In response, the ghraef buffeted Lon with a wing, sending him tumbling through the snow and stopping just a few feet from Mellai and Huirk.

"Give up," Mellai counseled, "before you get seriously hurt."

"You don't get it, do you?" Lon shouted back, then used his left hand's power to push a man-sized hole into the snow-covered soil. He dove into the tunnel just before Bromax's leaping body landed, escaping the ghraef's jaws. Bromax tore at the hole with his claws, snarling and snapping, too distracted to notice when Lon pushed out of the soil behind the ghraef, having tunneled underground to flank him.

Lon formed a sphere of stone and hurled it just below the ghraef's raised tail, earning a pained howl from the massive beast, before drawing his falchion and escaping back into his underground tunnel.

The ghraef smashed the tunnel opening with its bone tip and leaped into the air, turning mid-flight to face his opponent.

Mellai had to fight the temptation to summon her power. This contest had become deadly, and in a moment of cruel irony, it was the ghraef who had lost control. One miscalculated move on Lon's part would surely get him killed.

Suddenly, huge boulders began flying out of the ground towards Bromax. He dodged some, smashed others with his tail, and even caught a couple with his front paws and hurled them back at the ground. Once again, Mellai was reminded of the ghraefs' formidable power, and Lon was just making him angrier.

During a volley of three boulders from one side that required Bromax's full attention, Lon suddenly emerged from the soil on a rising pillar of dirt directly below the ghraef. The Beholder held his sword directly above his head.

Mellai knew Lon had the element of surprise, that Bromax didn't see him coming. Huirk had obviously come to the same realization as he raised his head with increased interest. If Lon aimed the sword just right, it would mean a death blow to the ghraef.

Lon's aim was true, but just as the tip of his sword pierced Bromax's neck, he stopped his advance and directed his attention upward with his right hand. Bromax's body became rigid, obviously caught in an air prison created by the Beholder, but the ghraef's strength overpowered Lon. Bromax broke free and bashed the dirt pillar with his tail, sending Lon toppling over the side.

Beholder and ghraef were at least a hundred yards in the air, and Mellai screamed as she watched her brother fall. Lon's falchion had escaped his grip, and he rolled himself in the air until his belly faced downward, his arms and legs flared to maintain control. Just when Mellai thought it would be too late, Bromax swooped underneath her brother. Lon grabbed hold of Bromax's black hair and pulled himself close, while the ghraef leveled out and landed safely in the snow next to Huirk.

Mellai opened her mouth to berate them both for their foolishness, but her words caught in her throat when Lon leaped off Bromax's back and moved to stand directly in front of the ghraef. Bromax flashed his teeth, but only for a brief moment before dropping onto his belly and dipping his head before Lon.

"You beat him?" Mellai said, stunned at Bromax's submission.

"No," Lon countered, bringing his hand forward to rub Bromax on his snout. "We both won. This wasn't an alpha-male competition, Mel. It was a battle for respect. I didn't trust Bromax, and he didn't think I'd keep him safe in a fight against the calahein—that I was too weak. We have proven each other wrong."

Bromax clicked his teeth together and nodded.

Mellai's jaw dropped and she stared at her brother, confused and unsure of what to say.

Lon turned and, after seeing her face, winked at his sister. "It's a male thing."

"I don't care," Mellai finally responded. "That was stupid and dangerous. You could've killed each other."

"But we didn't," Lon answered. "The risk was worth the reward. I don't expect you to understand, but it was through this same kind of experience that Wade became so loyal to me." Lon untied the cords on the right side of his hardened leather armor, then lifted his tunic. On his right side, from his armpit down past his belt line, was an ugly scar. It was fully healed, but thick and pink.

Mellai gasped. In addition to the brand on his face and the King's Cross carving on his right forearm, Lon had this reminder of his life with the Rayders. She wondered what other scars covered his body, signs of the suffering he had experienced.

"I had to fight Wade when I first reached the Exile," Lon continued as he dropped his tunic and retied his leather armor. "He was intent on killing me, but I won by slapping him upside his head with a True-Sight-charged sword."

"I think I remember that day," Mellai said. "I woke up about a month after you left Pree, knowing you had been seriously hurt. Scared Grandmother half to death with my screaming, too."

Mellai's face fell at the memory. She missed her grandmother terribly, but refused to think back on the way her grandparents had been killed. It was too much to bear, and there were other tasks that needed her focus. Her parents. Kaylen's father, Scut. Trev Rowley, village delegate of Pree. These were good people that she could still help.

"It's time we finally return to Pree," Mellai said, swiveling to straddle Huirk's neck.

"Agreed," Lon replied, moving to mount Bromax's back.

As Mellai secured her legs with the ghraef's braided hair, she leaned forward and whispered at Huirk. "Don't even think about getting into a fight like that with me."

The ghraef only laughed.

Chapter 11

Full Circle

Afer a quick search by Huirk—he found the falchion, along with a handful of Lon's arrows that had fallen from his quiver—the four of them took to the air again. Pree was over seventy-five miles southwest of Roseiri, a journey that would take the Beholders' guard three days to traverse in the snow. Yet, while flying on ghraefs, they reached the village after only two hours in the air. Of course there had been delays that slowed their progress, like investigating Roseiri and the duel between Lon and Bromax, but the village still came into view before dusk.

Everything in Pree appeared as normal, even though the tiny village dwelt in the shadow of the colossal Tamadoras Mountains, towering only five miles to the west. Plumes of smoke escaped the scattered chimneys as families prepared their evening meals. A few children played in the snow surrounding the village square. Scut's cows lazily wandered around his snow-covered grazing fields. No one was looking skyward. They had no reason to.

Without instructions from Lon, Bromax led them a mile and a half south of the village, on the other side of the wrapping Klanorean River. This was the Marcs property, where Lon and Mellai had spent over five years of their childhood after the stick-stack incident at Roseiri. It was here where their parents, Aron and Shalán, should still live. Lon gratefully noted smoke rising from the chimney of their two-story frame house.

It came as no surprise that without instruction, Bromax still knew exactly where they had lived. He and Huirk landed in dense foliage at the summit of the large hill abutting the west side of their property. Lon absently licked his lips, remembering the countless hours of training with his father and the taste of metal every time True Sight had overwhelmed him. So much had happened since then, when he had considered True Sight to be a curse. Now he knew differently, and the power he and Mellai wielded could be the defining factor between Appernysia's survival or utter destruction.

Mellai and Lon slowly descended the hill, but their ghraefs stayed behind. The twins had decided they should unveil everything slowly to their parents. It wasn't that their parents couldn't handle the shock of two ghraefs standing in their front yard. Inversely, it would be an amazing discovery to them, along with the news that Mellai was a Beholder. But both points would also distract from the most important family conflict behind their visit. One that needed to be resolved quickly.

Lon was a Rayder and had helped them kill thousands of Appernysians.

When Lon opened the front gate for Mellai, as he had done a year earlier when they were fleeing from Gil Baum and his Rayder squad, his resolve faltered. After everything Lon had experienced, there he stood again. Back where the death had all started; where Appernysia's fate was waiting for two Beholders to realize their power.

And my sister wonders why I'm so worried about this reunion, Lon thought bitterly.

Mellai took Lon's hand and gave it a gentle squeeze. "Pretend to have a good time," she said, offering the same counsel Lon had given her that fateful night. "Will you do that for me, please?"

Lon paused and looked at his sister. Her brown eyes were obscured by the summoned power of True Sight connecting to his forehead. *Have you been digging around in my mind?* he thought.

Mellai shrugged apologetically, then dismissed her gift and spoke softly. "Only because I care."

With an understanding nod, Lon returned the hand squeeze—albeit a little aggressively—then together they took the final steps of their separate round-trip journeys.

✳   ✳   ✳   ✳   ✳

Aron looked up from his cup of steaming herbal tea, a little startled by the soft knock at their door. "Are we expecting company?"

"Not today," Shalán called as she bustled about the kitchen. "Maybe it's Trev?"

"Since when does Trev journey south of the river?" Aron replied as he set aside his tea and stood. An unexpected, soft knock at their door at this time of night would only come from one person—Theiss Arbogast, and it was about time. Months had passed since they last received word from their daughter. Aron smiled, hoping Theiss had finally mustered the courage to propose to Mellai. He was a good man and would make a great husband and father.

"It's been far too long," Aron began as he swung the door open, but the heavy wood escaped his grasp and crashed into the wall. On his doorstep stood his two children, both dressed in leather armor and Lon equipped with an array of weapons. They looked weary and travel-worn.

Mellai rushed forward and wrapped Aron with her arms. "Hello, Father. Sorry for knocking. I didn't want to startle you."

Aron returned the hug, but half-heartedly as he continued to stare at Lon. His son was staring at the ground, his head turned just enough to reveal the King's Cross brand on his right temple.

Aron absently rubbed the scar on the right side of his own face, then reached his arm forward. "Welcome home, Son."

Lon crossed the threshold and joined the group hug, followed quickly by Shalán, who had run out of the kitchen to see the reunion. She kissed her twins' heads as she squeezed them.

"Oh, my babies!" she cried. "I was beginning to doubt this day would ever come."

An eternity passed as they held each other. No one spoke, either unwilling to end the solemn reunion or too afraid to begin explanations. As for Aron, he didn't care what his son had done or what brought either of his children to Pree. Questions and answers could wait. All that mattered in that instant was that Lon and Mellai had returned home safely. They were a family again.

It was Shalán who finally broke the silence. "You're just in time for dinner. Seat yourselves at the table and I'll bring you a royal helping." She paused and stared at her daughter. "What did you do to your face?"

Aron also looked at Mellai, surprised he hadn't noticed the blue marking that wrapped her left eye. Although his wife didn't recognize it, Aron had learned during his education in the Rayder Exile that the tattoo was the mark of a Beholder. But he said nothing, watching curiously as Lon and Mellai exchanged a silent glance, then Mellai nodded and turned to them, her dark brown eyes paled with True Sight.

"You, too?" Aron whispered as he held Mellai by her shoulders. "Is this what brought you both together? Is Lon training you? Did he tattoo you?"

Mellai shook her head with a half-hearted smile and the haze in her eyes disappeared. "The Jaeds have chosen us to protect Appernysia." She paused, licking her dry lips. She looked conflicted as she, too, hung her head forward to stare at the floor. "Bah! Forget it, Lon. There's no easy way to do this. Better to get it all on the table at once."

"What is it?" Aron asked, his eyes full of concern.

Mellai sighed and looked up at her father. "The calahein have returned. Réxura and Roseiri lie in ruins. Grandmother and Grandfather are dead, along with Theiss and everyone else who fell victim to the assaults." Her breathing quivered. "I'm so sorry."

Shalán collapsed to her knees at the news of her parents' deaths. Mellai knelt in front of her and pulled the ghraef pendant from around her neck, placing it in her mother's hand. Shalán looked up and smiled weakly at her daughter, then gripped the pendant tight and began crying. Mellai held her, adding her own tears to Shalán's.

"We were too late to save them," Lon continued. Aron noted that his voice had changed. His son spoke with authority, his emotions controlled with layers of experience. "And time continues to work against us. Our Beholders' guard is traveling here from Roseiri. They'll arrive in no more than two days and Pree must be ready to evacuate. We need to get everyone in Appernysia to the Fortress Island as quickly as possible."

Aron was dumbfounded at the thought of evacuating their entire kingdom. Itorea was big enough to hold their full population while under siege, but it would indeed take a desperate situation to warrant such a thing. "Were any other cities attacked?" he finally asked.

"Not to our knowledge."

"And what of the Rayders?" Aron continued, trying to hide his disgust. "Will they stay in Taeja?"

"No," Lon replied emotionlessly. "Tarek should be leading them into Itorea as we speak."

"Myron's son?" Aron said, taken aback. "You found Tarek Ascennor?"

Lon nodded. "He's my best friend, and the new Rayder commander."

Aron turned and helped his wife to her feet, then sat at the table, picked up his tea, and resumed sipping it. "What happened to Rayben Goldhawk?"

Lon and Mellai joined their father at the table, while Shalán returned to the kitchen. "Rayben died on the way to Taeja, murdered by the Appernysians he had enslaved."

Aron paused and looked at Lon. "Were you part of that group? One of the enslaved?"

"No, Father. I defeated my opponent at my first weapons trial, earning my place among the Rayders."

Aron glanced at Mellai, who seemed just as intrigued by the conversation. At least part of this was new information to her ears, too. "And what of Omar Brickeden? Did you find him?"

Lon winced, pain in his eyes. "I did. Omar is the only reason I mastered True Sight. He took me under his wing, educating and protecting me whenever possible. He took Rayben's place as acting commander, but he was murdered before a tournament could be held." A tear finally crept into Lon's eye and he paused to wipe it away. "Actually, that's not true. It was me who should have been murdered, but Omar threw himself in front of the javelin." Lon paused again. "It should have been me."

As Aron watched his son toil over his experiences with the Rayders, all remaining anger fled his consciousness. Lon was no Rayder, if for no other reason than the tears in his eyes. He cared too much to be counted among them.

"I'm sorry, Father," Lon continued with a shaking voice. "I know Omar raised you, and I should have done more to protect him, for both our sakes. So many people have died, either because of me or in spite of my efforts. Of the twelve men in my squad, only half of us still live. Mellai has already lost one of her guard, too. Beholders are not as all-powerful as everyone thinks."

"Nobody knows what to think of Beholders," Mellai cut in, "especially since I joined the ranks."

Aron turned his attention away from Lon, allowing his son a reprieve. "And what about that, Mellai? When did the Jaeds favor you with this curse?"

"The same night as Lon, during our game of stick-stack in Roseiri. But the full realization of my power didn't return until about five months ago, when Llen forced the full weight of True Sight upon me in late July."

"Who's Llen?" Lon asked. Aron could see that his son had guessed already.

Mellai's countenance fell. "The Jaed who's been training me."

Aron set down his tea, his instincts returning as he expected an explosive response from Lon. Aron didn't like the thought, but he would continue to incapacitate his son if Lon lost control of his power.

To Aron's surprise, Lon began laughing. A full-bellied, hearty laugh. "It really has been a long time since I left, hasn't it?" He paused, hiding his smile behind his left hand. "Don't worry, Father. I'm in full control of myself. You'll never have to knock me unconscious again."

Mellai also smiled. "It's true. In fact, I'd like to see you two duel again. Lon is one of the most deadly swordsman I've ever seen, and a master of True Sight. He has become so talented, he even defeated his ghraef in a spar on the way here."

Dishes clattered, dropped out of Shalán's startled hands. "Ghraefs still live?"

Mellai stood and helped her mother clean up. "There are two sitting on your hill right now, waiting to take us to their home."

Aron didn't need a mirror to know that his own eyes were wide with amazement. So much had happened in their kingdom over the previous year. Two Beholders—his twin children, and one of them the first female Beholder in Appernysia's history—and their ghraefs, joined to battle the calahein just as during the First Age. The Rayders had also returned. Aron hated to admit it, but they would make an invaluable contribution to Itorea's defenses. Where others might flee, Rayders would stand and fight to the last man. And the Jaeds were indeed real, and communicating with Aron's daughter.

"We need to hurry," Lon said. "Can you gather the village, preferably before dark?"

"Not until you eat," Shalán said as she stood and served them heaping plates of hot potatoes and roasted chicken. "I'm glad I made extras. It was intended for Elora's four sons. They're struggling this winter and need the extra help. But no matter. I'll make more once we're finished."

"There won't be time," Mellai replied. "Everyone will have to be satisfied with cold produce and salted meats for awhile, especially after you reach Itorea. With the Rayders around, our kingdom's supplies are going to be stretched thin through the winter."

"They'll bring their own food," Lon interjected. "Tarek will make sure of that."

*　*　*　*　*

Aron enjoyed the hush that ensued while his family ate, and he couldn't help but smirk when Mellai finally spoke. She was never one for awkward silences.

"Any news from Pree?" she asked.

"Not much has changed," Shalán replied. "Oh, except for Hykel. Do you remember her family? Scut's neighbors?"

"Of course."

"Well, Hykel died of brain fever last spring. Nybol's been doing alright though, raising his three daughters and Tragan by himself. In fact, one of them is being courted by Tirk."

"Ramsey's son?" Lon asked.

"That's right," Shalán continued. "He's a good boy. I knew it even before he reported Braedr's assault of Mellai."

"Braedr is dead," Mellai said casually, "and he deserved it, too. After abducting Kaylen and dragging her into the mountains for two days, he joined the Rayders and finally died in battle."

"Oh, my goodness," Shalán said, cupping her hand over her mouth.

"He was responsible for Omar's death, too," Lon added. "I even lost two of my squad because of him."

"Then indeed he deserved his death," Aron said. "But what of Kaylen? Is she well?"

Mellai nodded. "She survived the abduction, if that's what you're asking. In a strange way, I'm actually grateful that the whole thing happened. It led me to a sacred clearing in the Vidarien Mountains, where I met Llen and learned . . ." She paused, glancing at Shalán. ". . . where I learned some other important things."

"So a Jaed really has been training you?" Lon asked, a hint of spite hidden in his voice.

"Yes. Before you freak out, though, know that Llen couldn't help you. You had to figure it out on your own."

Lon shook his head and continued eating. "Of course I did."

"Where is Kaylen now?" Aron said, wanting to maintain the peace between his family.

"With King Drogan in Itorea. When I was tattooed as Appernysia's Beholder, Kaylen was assigned as my lady-in-waiting. She joined me at our latest battle, but I made her stay behind when Lon and I left to investigate the calahein threat."

"Another battle?" Aron brought a contemplative finger to his lips, his thumb hooked under his chin. "Sounds like you are Beholders of opposing nations, yet you travel together?"

Lon answered. "We were in the middle of fighting each other when a messenger from Réxura arrived. The two of us leaving together was the only way to maintain the peace."

"You were fighting against each other?" Shalán asked, her voice panicked. "Are you still enemies? Has this visit just been a charade?"

"Not at all," Mellai replied, shaking her head vehemently. "A lot has changed over the past week. Lon's squad and my guard have joined together, and the two of us met Huirk and Bromax, our ghraefs."

"I'm glad your small group worked through your differences," Aron said, "but King Drogan is bringing a nation of Rayders into Itorea. That is incredibly dangerous."

Aron fell into a vein of musing. Just as the strength of Rayders could offer invaluable assistance in Itorea, it could also sow destruction, especially if their whole kingdom was being gathered into that city. The Rayders would be reliable if they gave their word to protect the city, but without such a promise, Appernysia would be in mortal danger from within and from without.

"Maybe," Lon said, with nothing more than a shrug of his shoulders. "All we can do is hope our commander and king establish peace. It's out of our hands."

Aron dropped his utensils and stood. He had so many questions, yet no time to ask them. With Rayders present, Itorea would need every loyal Appernysian available to keep the peace. He crossed the room and entered his bedroom to retrieve his sword. When he left the Rayders, he had hoped never to use the falchion again. With the exception of the confrontation a year earlier when the Rayder squad attacked his family, Aron had thus far been successful at maintaining that hope.

"Time flows in a circle," Aron said aloud as he belted the three-foot sword around his waist. This had been Omar's parting knowledge decades earlier and, as usual, was proving itself true. Although Aron had abandoned the Rayders for a better life, here he was, prepping to team up with them again. He glanced through the doorway, watching his twin children at the table and wondering what cryptic advice Omar had given his son. Like himself, Lon had become quiet and guarded, undoubtedly from ineradicable experiences that had burned themselves into his memories. They both now understood that where time could not heal, silence offered a shield. But silence couldn't protect them anymore. Time called for action.

"Let's have at it," Aron said, stepping from his bedroom. His hand rested on the pommel of his sword as he crossed the room.

"A duel?" Mellai asked excitedly.

"Don't be so naive," Aron replied. "Time to warn Pree."

*   *   *   *   *

Shalán walked hand in hand with her husband, quickly traversing the mile-and-a-half distance to the village center. The sun had dropped behind the Tamadoras Mountains, but light still poured from behind the peaks. They had at least two hours before full darkness fell on the village.

After a brief conversation with her children, Shalán had convinced the twins to stay behind with their ghraefs and wait until the moment was right. Pree's villagers were hardworking and loyal, but stubborn to a fault. It would take a dramatic entrance to convince everyone of the reality of their situation. Even Shalán was still trying to process everything she had just learned. Mellai was a Beholder. Ghraefs were alive and partnered with her own children. The calahein had survived and become an even greater threat to Appernysia than in the First Age. Too many things, all at once.

To distract herself, Shalán gave Aron's free hand a reassuring squeeze. "What will you say?"

"Whatever I must," Aron replied, his eyes cheerless. "It's not our safety that matters anymore."

As with many of their conversations, it ended as abruptly as it had begun and Shalán was forced to fill in the blanks. But she had developed quite the skill at reading her husband, especially when he was in Rayder mode. She glanced at his face, the scar still obvious through the flaring wrinkles off his right eye. His uncut hair fluttered as the wind rushed past his lips, which were pulled tight—his standard response to serious situations. Not much to read there, but Aron's left hand gave him away. With every step they took, his fingers gripped the sword pommel a little tighter. It wasn't his past as a Rayder that worried him, though; he wasn't trying to hide the

King's Cross etched in the falchion's pommel. It was their mortal danger, the threat looming to the north that truly concerned him. He would do everything in his power, even die if necessary, to protect the villagers.

As they crossed in front of Scut Shaw's property at the south end of Pree, Shalán's hand drifted to the ghraef pendant hanging around her neck. "Do you remember the day you gave this to my father?"

"Of course," Aron replied without looking. "Dhargon didn't quite know what to think, did he?"

Shalán laughed. "Not at all. No man had received a bribe for their daughter before."

"It was a gift," Aron said, "not a bribe." A slight smile formed on one corner of his mouth.

"And a handsome one at that," Shalán added, touching the shining pearl tip on the ghraef's tail. "I never understood why Mother and Father so easily agreed with our engagement." Her face fell. They had never explained themselves, nor would they be able to again.

"They were great Appernysians," Aron replied, this time turning to look at his wife, "and the two most understanding people I've ever met. Your existence is proof of that." He released his wife's hand and placed his arm around her back, hugging her waist. "I hurt, too, Shalán, and I promise time for both of us to grieve once we see this through."

Shalán leaned into Aron as they walked, her hands wringing the leather strap of her healing satchel. Just as Aron donned his sword, her bag of herbs would be her tool of war. "Maybe I could have saved them," she said half-heartedly.

Aron kissed the top of her head. "We can save *these* people. Stay strong, Shalán. Pree needs to know we're confident."

"Are you?"

"As I'll ever be."

Shalán nodded. With their two children keeping watch, she had to agree.

Within a few minutes, they had passed Myron's estate and entered the square. Without speaking first to Trev Rowley—the village delegate—Aron entered the meeting hall and sounded the warning bell suspended at the top of its steeple. The bell clanged loudly as he pulled the thick rope, and the villagers immediately responded.

Trev was the first to arrive, half stumbling out of Delancy Reed's tavern with a bar stool in his hands. "What's the meaning of this? Who rang that bell?"

"I did," Aron replied, "and I'll save my explanation for the whole village."

A silly stand-off ensued. Shalán chuckled as the village delegate sized up her husband, taking extra notice of the sword at his side. "Very well," Trev finally said, lowering his stool, "but it better be something significant."

All twelve families appeared with children in tow, huddled together with pitchforks, knives, sharpened walking sticks, lit torches, and a few bows. The square was flooded with as many questions as villagers, and they congregated in front of Aron when they learned he had sounded the alarm. Although closer to the square than most, Hans and Ine Pulchria were the last to arrive. Both were armored in tanned leather aprons and adorned with nearly every blacksmith tool in his collection.

One by one, the villagers became quiet as they also noticed Aron's sword, its exposed crossguard shimmering in the flickering torch light. Shalán knew most of the children had not seen an actual sword before, with the exception of a few lucky glances at those hidden beneath the tradesmen's winter cloaks. But Aron had no cloak, despite the failing light and snow on the ground, and none had suspected he owned such a dangerous tool of war, let alone would wear it so openly.

Shalán smiled at her husband. He stood proudly atop a table, his chin up and shoulders back, with his left hand still covering the etched pommel of his sword. It wasn't until he had the full attention of every villager that he spoke.

"Grave news has reached our ears. Death has fallen upon Appernysia—not from the Rayders, but from an enemy far more terrible. The calahein have returned, and already sow death across our kingdom."

As Shalán expected, immediate outbursts interrupted Aron's speech.

"What are you plotting at?" Elora shouted. "My sons fear the darkness enough without their father alive to protect them. They don't need your stories fanning the flame."

"Neither do my daughters," Nybol added, although he eyed the dark mountains to the west as he spoke. His only son, Tragan, put on his bravest face for a nine-year-old.

"And don't forget my Sonela," Delancy Reed added, hugging a small cask of his best brewed mead. "She's enough of an emotional wreck as it is." Sonela only burst into tears.

Aron stood firm, neither arguing nor denying his words, until Scut finally asked the question Shalán knew her husband awaited. "What's yer proof? Where are these rumors comin' from?"

Shalán smiled and looked up at the sky, signaling her children. Just as they had planned, two dark shapes appeared far above, descending fast. The flying shadows increased in size until two vast beasts took shape and landed in the nearby snow. The black beast, the one carrying Lon, hit the ground hard and slammed his bone-tipped tail into the snow for emphasis. Mellai's light brown ghraef, on the other hand, had circled the villagers, his wing tip just touching the snow, before pulling up and alighting next to the meeting hall behind Aron. Even as the smaller of both ghraefs, it was still nearly as large as the building—so it was with ease that he lifted his armored tail and tapped it against the steeple's warning bell.

Shalán reeled to see her children atop ghraefs, and the ghraefs themselves. Inspiring! Scut's words captured her own thoughts exactly.

"I'm convinced," Scut said, "and the rest of you'd be fools to be thinkin' anything to the contrary."

One by one, each villager lowered their weapons, pacified by the ghraefs. Every man in their midst had been to Itorea and seen the aqueduct statues. They knew what stood before them, and had undoubtedly shared the stories with their families.

Aron drew his sword, no longer covering the Rayder-marked pommel. "Roseiri and Réxura lie in ruins, their civilians murdered." He pointed the sword toward his wife. "Shalán's parents were among the victims, along with Mellai's betrothed."

"But not your daughter?" Trev asked.

The ghraef behind Aron dropped to his belly and lowered his head. Mellai emerged, gracefully sliding down the prostrate foreleg.

"I wasn't there," Mellai called, stopping below her father. Her blue tattoo showed easily under the torch light. "I was with King Drogan's army, fighting the Rayders in the Taejan Plains." Mellai's eyes hazed and she created a fireball above her right hand.

An audible gasp filled the square, the villagers' eyes wide with amazement. They knew a Beholder stood before them, and not just any Beholder. A female Beholder, the first of her gender.

Scut stepped forward to face Mellai. "Is my Kaylen safe?"

Mellai nodded. "As safe as anyone can be right now. My father speaks the truth. The calahein have returned, but the Jaeds foresaw their coming. They prepared two Beholders to protect this kingdom. Appernysia will survive."

All eyes shifted to the larger ghraef behind them, waiting to see who was hidden behind the thick mat of black hair. The ghraef stood motionless upon on all four legs, his tail raised like a scorpion. Moments passed, long enough that Shalán worried Lon had lost his courage. Finally, a pillar of dirt rose out of the snow next to the ghraef. Lon leaped off the ghraef's back and landed on the column, which then lowered back into the ground. Lon stood straight, neither proud nor intimidated as he walked. The villagers parted before him with a different wave of gasps and whispers. They had a full view of the brand on his right temple, along with the multiple weapons and leather armor he wore. Rayders had never been welcome in Pree, and little had changed.

"What is this madness?" Delancy said, hiding behind his daughter when Lon reached the front. Others reached for their weapons.

"This is Lon," Mellai pleaded, but louder than any human could speak. Shalán's ears rung and her head pounded under the shockwave of noise. At the same instant, every weapon except Aron's falchion flew toward Mellai, retracted by her outstretched left hand, while the flames of their torches flew into the sphere above her right. Shalán gaped at what her daughter could do, then Hans drew her attention. A hammer had caught in his apron, pulling him forward a few feet before snapping the leather strap and joining the other crude weapons.

"Catch," Mellai called to her brother, extending her right hand. Lon's eyes also clouded over and the flame flew to his left hand. More gasps from the villagers.

"These weapons are useless against the calahein," Mellai continued, "but we will craft you better ones. Our Beholders' guard is just two days north, traveling here to protect you and your children. You are our family—every last one of you." She placed the collection of various tools on the snow in front of herself. "Please try to see reason. King Drogan and the Rayders have joined forces in Itorea, and the rest of our kingdom has been summoned to join them. No more Appernysians or Rayders. Only humanity. We fight together, or we die alone."

"And the Jaeds have not left us defenseless," Aron called. "They have selected my twin children, barely eighteen years old, to secure the future of this world. With the ghraefs to assist them, their power is unmatched. We must rally behind them and answer King Drogan's call."

Everyone watched as the fireball flared brightly. Whether by the hypnotic dance of the fire or by the preoccupation of their own thoughts, silence fell on the villagers. They did not speak as they watched the flames with distant eyes. As for Shalán, she thought of the fate of her kingdom. Her family had spoken accurately. Fire and death would spread to its furthest corners, including Pree. Retreating to Itorea was the obvious solution.

Shalán dropped to her knee, showing her humility and loyalty. Even with bowed head, she knew others were joining her by the crunch of the surrounding snow, but she didn't care. All that mattered in that instant was the unity of her family. Finally, after a year of heartache and doubt, they were together in body and intent.

She looked up. Aron had stepped down from his platform to kneel beside his children. Mellai had taken back the fireball and was redistributing it to the torches while Lon calmly looked at Mellai manipulating a glowing mass of iron on the ground. Shalán couldn't help but wonder why he stood by and let his sister perform all the tasks of True Sight. Was it humility, or was he intimidated by her abilities?

Two people had not kneeled before the Beholders—Delancy and his reluctant daughter. "I've worked too hard tilling my fields and brewing my crops to simply abandon them," he shouted. "As soon as we leave, a band of thieves will move into Pree and assume management. We'll never get our village back."

"You might be right," Lon replied calmly, "but there's a greater chance that there won't be any village left to take back. You haven't seen what we've seen—the destruction that the calahein are capable of."

Delancy spat on the ground. "Nor do I intend to. You can lead everyone else away to their deaths, Rayder, but I'm staying right here."

"You are in worse danger here," Mellai replied.

"Says you. What are you going to do? Make me go with you?"

Mellai reached out her hand. "I could."

"But she won't," Lon cut in, scowling at his twin. "You can make your own decisions, Master Delancy."

With a quick glance around and a grumpy harrumph, Delancy grabbed Sonela by the arm and marched his sixteen-year-old daughter away. Shalán worried over the daughter and her innocence, wondering how Lon and Mellai might react, but the twins let her go.

"They've made their choice," Aron said, standing to clasp his hand on Lon's shoulder, "as have the rest of us. Pack your essentials. We travel for Itorea at first light."

Chapter 12

Ursoguia

"Two days?" Aron growled. "After a speech like that, you expect us to wait two days?"

"If we don't leave immediately," Shalán added, "more people will change their minds. There's not a choice here. Your guard will have to catch up to us on the road to Humsco."

Lon hated to admit it, but they were right. His men would be able to make up the distance easily enough, but the difficulty would be convincing Bromax and Huirk that they need to backtrack and notify them. He glanced at the two ghraefs. They were both lying in the snow, allowing the torch-bearing villagers to walk around and admire them. Huirk, ever the playful one, kept swishing waves of snow at the children, who responded with squeals of delight.

Bromax was not amused. Coel's youngest daughter, only four years old, had grabbed hold of Bromax's hair, pulled herself onto his paw, and was precariously ascending his foreleg. Fortunately, Bromax only rolled his eyes and huffed out his nose. Coel, on the other hand, ripped his daughter from the ghraef's leg and stomped away into the darkness, shouting reprimands.

"Looks like I'm not the only one who struggles with self-control," Lon mused, elbowing his sisteras he pointed at Coel.

"Funny," Mellai replied dryly, "but you actually bring up a good point." She turned and stared at Aron. "Now the burden passes to you, Father. There will be a few Rayders in our guard, good men who will die to keep the villagers safe. Can *you* control yourself?"

Aron didn't respond. In typical fashion, he ignored the question and walked away with Shalán, back toward their house.

"Wait," Mellai called as she ran over to Huirk. Aron turned and waited impatiently while she leaned close and whispered to the ghraef. After a quick glance at Bromax, Huirk nodded to Mellai.

Mellai beamed and addressed her parents. "Would you like Huirk to fly you home?"

* * * * *

"May the Jaeds watch over you," Mellai called into the darkness, projecting her voice to her parents below as Huirk circled their house one last time. Only with the aid of True Sight was she able to see that Shalán still held a basket full of food, which Lon had politely declined, and rightly so. Mellai knew that Pree would need the supplies far more than she or her brother would. If everything went as planned, Aron would lead them through every southern civilization of Appernysia to warn and gather people on their way to Itorea. A journey like that would take at least five weeks to make in the snow, growing ever longer as more people joined their party. And that was without any additional complications, which was also highly unlikely with the calahein prowling about.

This is why Mellai had complied when Lon asked her to extract iron ore from the ground and use her power to forge weapons for the villagers. The process had been tedious, using up another two hours of their time, but now a huge collection of weapons were piled inside the Marcs home. Arming swords, javelins, spear and arrow heads—Mellai had created all manner of steel weapons, while Lon had used True Sight to expertly craft the spear and arrow shafts out of solid timber. That left only lashings and feathers to the villagers, a task they could easily complete as they walked. Aron would distribute all weapons, both complete and needing assembly, as the villagers moved south out of Pree. Aron also planned to train them in weaponry, but Mellai doubted he'd succeed. The villagers would never allow Aron to beat on them as he had Lon.

Under Lon's instructions, Mellai had also crafted a beautiful glaive forged of pure steel. Lon repeatedly tested her work, swinging the glaive about and having her tweak here and adjust there. The final product was a perfectly balanced glaive, finer and sturdier than any weapon owned by the Rayders. Lon had taken the glaive and knelt in front of Aron.

"For your training and patience," he had said, raising the gift up to his father. Aron had reluctantly accepted the Rayder weapon, but his hesitance quickly disappeared once he, too, had begun flailing it about. Neither Mellai nor Lon had needed a thank you. The light in their father's eyes had been enough.

"Now to our guard," Mellai said to Huirk, who relayed the request to Bromax in ghraef language. His speech was low and guttural, no more intelligible than a bear roar mixed with the fluctuating tones of a dog—minus the high-pitched whining. Mellai peered at the other partnership, smiling at the hair woven around Lon's legs. It had taken some convincing on her part, but Lon finally conceded that it was a good idea. Already, he looked more confident on Bromax's back.

Mellai closed her eyes, breathing the frigid air and thinking of the combined Beholders' guard. From the way Lon talked, his squad knew Appernysia's paths and warning signs better than anyone. Mellai had no choice but to trust that the Rayders' stealth would see them safely to Pree, despite how much she wanted to escort them.

From her nightly trainings with Llen, Mellai had become talented at keeping time and direction by use of the ever-changing stars, so she knew that about ninety minutes had passed when they reached their guard. Mellai projected a call down to them, warning them of the ghraefs' descent, then Bromax and Huirk dove to the earth. By the time they landed, all men were awake and standing at the ready.

Lon gave quick instructions to Channer, but loud enough for all to hear. Pree was safe. The villagers would leave first thing in the morning, so Channer needed to make up time in order to reach them before Humsco. The Beholders' father, Aron Marcs, was responsible for navigation and recruitment, whereas Channer should focus solely on escort. Their objective was to keep everyone safe and obey Aron's requests.

It pleased Mellai to see the dutiful devotion that the four Rayders gave to Lon's demands. Surely they knew Aron Marcs by name—that he had deserted the Rayders decades ago—yet none of them even so much as flinched at the mention. They only kissed their fingers and touched the King's Cross brands on their temples, their heads respectfully dipped at Lon. Snoom, Ric, and Duncan added their own fist-over-heart salute, then Bromax and Huirk leaped into the air again. As the ghraefs carried Mellai and Lon away, each member of their guard slowly slipped back into their bedrolls until only one was left keeping watch.

Mellai noticed that Bromax had turned southwest, back in the direction of her parents. "Is there something wrong?" she shouted into the wind.

Huirk shook his head and extended his left paw to point at himself.

"Your home," Mellai echoed. "Is it near Pree?"

Huirk did not answer.

Despite her excitement to see the ghraefs' home, and although the rushing wind bit through her clothes, exhaustion overpowered Mellai. For over a week, she had been constantly under threat, and riding horses had proved to be strangely exhausting. Her fitful sleep had offered little reprieve, and Mellai felt the fatigue aching in her bones. Now, though, flying miles above the ground on the back of Appernysia's most powerful creation, life wrapped the Beholder in a warm blanket of security. She nuzzled into the thick brown hair covering Huirk's neck and closed her eyes. The ghraef's body radiated heat into the Beholder and soon she wafted into a deep, restful slumber.

*　　*　　*　　*　　*

In darkness Mellai had fallen asleep, and in darkness she awoke again. She forced herself to sit up, the skin on her face worn sensitive from Huirk's coarse hair.

"Are we close?" she asked the ghraef, hands stretched high above her head, but Huirk didn't reply. His rumbling breath was slow and . . . echoing. Mellai blinked, realizing that they weren't flying, nor were there stars overhead. Just as in Itorea, she felt a crushing weight from the oppressive black and summoned True Sight for reprieve.

Her jaw dropped at her surroundings.

They were undoubtedly in a cave, only it was much larger than any cave Mellai had seen, and furnished for human comforts. In fact, it was even larger than the royal chambers of King Drogan. Shelves lined the opposite wall from the floor to the cave's dome, over three stories above, and each shelf was packed with aged books and scrolls. A dusty divan had been placed to the side of the shelving, while at the other side was a squared stone table and stuffed high-back chair. The table was clear, except for a feather quill in a dried ink vial.

Between Mellai and the bookshelf was a massive rug, woven with innumerable patterns of shapes that spiraled out from its center. Each was unique in design and hue, yet every shape complimented the overall beauty of the rug. It reminded Mellai of Itorea's perimeter wall, covered in ornate crystals. Then it hit her. They were the *exact* shapes as those at Itorea. Somehow, this rug and the Fortress City's designs were connected.

"Where am I?" Mellai whispered as she unraveled Huirk's hair and slid off his back. "Is this some sort of Beholder room?"

"Most likely," Lon answered. He was sitting on the floor in front of Huirk's snout, watching the ghraef sleep.

"Where's Bromax?" Mellai asked, glancing around.

"Not sure," Lon answered, pointing to the opposite end of the cave. "He disappeared through that passage a while ago."

Mellai slipped off her boots and walked barefoot across the rug. "Not nearly as soft as it looks," she complained, twisting the tight weave with the ball of her foot. "Hey, what time is it?"

Lon only shrugged his shoulders, but Mellai understood why. Only two passageways led into the cave, and both were as black as obsidian. It was impossible to keep time in perfect darkness.

"How'd we get in here?" Mellai asked, mostly to herself as she pivoted toward the passages. The tunnels were large enough for the ghraefs to easily fit through, one sloping down and the other—where Bromax left—sloping up.

"My guess is the upward passage," Lon said, "but I'm not about to wander into either of them. I don't want to stumble into a sacred nest or something."

"Smart idea." Even with the aid of her power, Mellai could only see a short distance into either tunnel before they angled out of sight. "So you fell asleep, too, huh?"

"Indeed," Lon answered, rising to his feet, "and it's the best rest I've had in a long time. There's something inexplicable about being around Bromax and Huirk. I haven't felt calm like this in years, since before we fled Roseiri with our parents."

"I know what you mean," Mellai answered, frowning as she thought back to the village's destruction. So much had changed for her there, even before the attack. It was as if the calahein knew her ties to the village and had sought to cause her personal harm.

"Listen," she continued, crossing the room to the divan. A cloud of dust filled the air when she dropped onto its aged cushions. "I have a few things I need to tell you, Lon."

"Allow me," an ethereal voice spoke as Llen appeared in the center of the rug. The glow of his shadow-formed essence filled every dark corner of the cave with penetrating light.

"Good . . . uh, whatever time of day it is," Mellai greeted the Jaed, squinting as she watched her brother's reaction. His hands were up in front of his face, guarding his eyes. Mellai leaned back into the sofa and folded her arms across her waist, remembering her first experience seeing Llen.

"I am Llen Drayden," he said to Lon, "the first Beholder of Appernysia and supreme Jaed of this world. I bring news and training for both of you."

"Lon first," Mellai answered. "He's been in the dark far too long."

"And why is that?" Lon asked, cold and poignant as he lowered his hand to stare at the Jaed. "Where have you been the past six years?"

Mellai listened as the Jaed calmly gave the same explanation she had received months earlier, while Lon listened stone-faced. Sacred knowledge known only to Beholders—the necessity of a pure Taejan bloodline and two generations of pure hearts to be worthy of True Sight. Had Lon been ordered to join the Rayders, his heart would have ceased to be pure. He needed to learn for himself that the Rayders were a people worth saving. The true origins of Shalán's birth, and her adoption by Dhargon and Allegna. Mellai's role for Appernysia, a compassionate beacon who would show mercy to the Rayders, just as Lon had done for the Appernysians in their previous battle.

"And now you both fully understand why Beholders have returned to Appernysia," Llen added, "not only because of your purity, but because of necessity. Without your partnership with each other and the ghraefs, this world will be destroyed."

"So why are we here instead of fighting the calahein?" Mellai asked. "And where is here, anyway?"

"You are in Ursoguia, hidden deep in the bowels of the Tamadoras Mountains," Llen answered. "Above you lies the ghraef civilization you must impress, before you the knowledge you must obtain, and below you the quest you must complete. Every Beholder has resided in this room while they mastered True Sight. It is a sacred dwelling where only wielders of True Sight and the highest honored ghraefs may enter. Tradition is of the utmost importance while you are here, where time no longer matters. Not even I can rush this process without offending the ghraefs."

Llen floated across the floor to the three-story bookcase. "This cave holds every journal of the Beholders, saved from destruction by the ghraefs while Bors Rayder led his rebellion in the First Age. Many ghraefs and Beholders died to protect this sacred property, along with the knowledge of its existence. Do not take it lightly, nor the loyalty of ghraefs to humanity. For centuries they have been watching for a Beholder to return, and Bromax is their current liaison. He has sacrificed everything to protect you."

Lon quietly crossed the room, placing his hand on the nearest scroll. "Omar would have loved this place."

"Undoubtedly," Llen replied, "for his collection was vastly incomplete. But do you understand, Beholder, that this wealth of knowledge must never come to anyone but a Beholder? Not even to someone as stalwart as Omar Brickeden."

Mellai saw the pain written in Lon's eyes as his hand fell. She wanted to soothe him, to jump up and squish the happiness back into his boyish face, but such times had passed. They had both grown and experienced far too much for simple fixes.

"Just like Omar, your message was coded," Lon said, facing the Jaed. "Where can we find the knowledge required to complete our quest and impress the ghraefs?"

Llen's eyes flared bright with satisfaction. "While Mellai excels in the raw use of True Sight, your strength has always been your intuition. Do not undervalue this gift, Beholder."

Lon nodded, not-so-patiently waiting for the Jaed to answer his question.

"In the First Age," Llen said as he gestured across the cave, "Beholders in training would read every record in this room. The knowledge and experience of Beholders who existed before you outweigh any direct instruction I can give." He paused speaking until he had moved directly in front of Mellai's brother. "Much like yourself, Lon Marcs, my mortal journey was to unveil the secrets of True Sight on my own. I also befriended the ghraefs and established the beginnings of our companionships. Find my record, and you will know exactly what is expected of you."

"That's it?" Mellai cut in. "It's that simple? No surprises?"

The light pouring from the Jaed's eye sockets slanted with a hint of amusement. "You have not paid attention if you believe this process to be simple. I would explain more, but again, this is a matter of honor to the ghraefs and something you must discover for yourselves."

Llen signaled for Mellai to join her brother. "I do not doubt your dedication, Mellai, but you will undoubtedly struggle with your priorities." The Jaed's eyes flared bright again. "Know this. Despite your worries or frustrations, neither of you may leave this cave until you have found my record and followed its instructions. Do you understand?"

Mellai nodded, while Lon gave the Rayder sign of compliance. Mellai rolled her eyes, partly irritated with Lon's formality but mostly annoyed with her own stubborn independence. She had not adopted any of Appernysia's formal expressions of loyalty. *But maybe it's time to change that about myself,* she thought. Mellai looked up at the Jaed. He was nodding slowly to her, affirming her hidden thoughts, so Mellai dropped to one knee and brought her right fist over her heart. "We understand, Llen."

Llen's eyes softened as he floated away. "Do not despair, Beholders. I will appear to you again before you leave Ursoguia. Together, you are stronger than anyone has thought possible, and you must physically realize this before you return to your people." With those final words, the Jaed disappeared, leaving them in darkness only True Sight could pierce.

"So that's a Jaed?" Lon finally said. "Not quite what I had imagined."

Mellai stood. "Really? What did you expect?"

Lon shrugged. "I don't know. Maybe wings or something, but definitely different than the essences that appear when people die."

Mellai examined her brother, his own essence glowing brighter while he channeled his power. So brightly, in fact, that his physical form had disappeared behind the glow. "He *is* different, though. I didn't realize it, but he looks the same as you do right now."

Lon nodded, returning her gaze. "Makes sense I guess, if only Beholders become Jaeds." He paused, looking up and down the shelves. "It's tempting to be angry that this was my first visit from a Jaed, but I get it, considering the whole *pure heart* thing. It's a little intimidating, isn't it, knowing that our ability to use True Sight is completely dependent on the condition of our hearts?"

"Which is why we can't tell anyone about it," Mellai replied. "Llen said that just knowing the requirement would destroy people's ability to have a pure heart in the first place."

"I heard him," Lon said as he crossed the room to the shelves. "Who else might qualify? The Rayders are changing, Mel. Slowly, but they really are. My people aren't who they used to be. Take Wade, for example. He even has a pure bloodline—at least that's what he bragged about during our first duel."

Mellai followed him to the shelves. "I don't know, Lon. Maybe with time we'll see more Beholders in Appernysia, but that's only if we survive the calahein. From the way Llen talks, I'm certain we're on our own for this fight." She grabbed a parchment roll. "If I understood Llen correctly, we *could* read all of these papers, but we only *need* to read his. Is that what you heard?"

"Indeed," Lon replied, grabbing a scroll for himself. "So let's start with the oldest looking ones."

Chapter 13

Reclamation

W ade reached for his sword, startled out of sleep. Quinten stood nearby with the butt end of his glaive a few inches from the lieutenant, a trick Tarek had taught them to use when waking a deadly Rayder—someone like Wade.

"Sorry to wake you, Lieutenant," Quinten said, "but I'm not sure what to do with all these people. It's getting a little crowded."

Wade flung his blanket aside and stood from his bedroll. Quinten was right to fret. Thousands of men surrounded them, all having answered Wade's summons.

"How long have I been asleep?" Wade asked, wondering how so many men had gathered so quickly.

"A day and a night," Quinten replied. He stepped back with nervous eyes. Dawn had been hours earlier—the sun was already a quarter of the way across the sky.

Wade cursed under his breath, knowing he should have given instruction to be woken earlier. Yet, many months had passed since he last felt this rejuvenated. Rest had not been his ally since he swore to protect Beholder Lon.

A quick glance at the fresh brands of the gathered Rayders told Wade that they were Swallows, but it made no difference. Under his direction, they would overwhelm the dissension in Taeja and restore order.

"Gather the leaders of each resistance group," Wade ordered.

"We're all here," Quinten replied, pointing to a small group of nineteen men huddled next to him.

"Well done, Cadet," Wade replied, then turned to the other men. "Gather closely, Rayders. We have much to do."

Wade knew that the deadliest opposition would come from two places, and both presented their own complications. The south blade held Taeja's armory, so any defectors would guard it aggressively. And the leader of the renegades would undoubtedly be in the keep—the most fortified structure in Taeja—and surrounded by his most loyal men. Wade had enough men to attack both simultaneously, but that didn't solve the greatest complication of all—casualties. Itorea needed as many survivors as possible to defend its walls from the calahein. They could ill afford a civil war.

The one advantage that Wade held, the only option that could be used to preserve lives, was surprise. Bryst undoubtedly warned the dissenters of his approach, but they would be looking outside their walls. Even with small skirmishes taking place between certain extremists and the Swallows, none would suspect Wade to be leading the next attack. Nonetheless, lives would still have to be sacrificed on both sides before complete order could be restored.

Three thousand men had rallied with glaives and shields, providing a company of one hundred and fifty soldiers to each of the twenty cadets. Wade gave concise instructions to each cadet. Battalion one—composed of seven companies—would march directly south, about two miles east of the keep. Battalion two—containing another twelve companies—would swing west through the arena where Tarek Ascennor had earned his rank as commander and Braedr had been held prisoner. While the battalions surrounded the keep, the last company, under the leadership of Quinten, would follow Wade directly toward the keep's center. Once the Rayder majority had been drawn out, Wade's squad would slip in and eliminate their leaders. Everyone would then converge on the armory and south gate. If Wade's presence and a display of their dead rulers didn't bring submission from the Rayder dissenters, then an overwhelming display of force would.

Unfortunately, organizing the Swallows into ranks was a tedious and time-leeching process. Petty disputes regularly surfaced—friends who refused to serve in separate companies, enemies who refused to fight together, and a few who demanded companies of their own. Wade's appearance squished every contention like an annoying bug, but as soon as he moved on, more would surface.

With little time or patience to spare, Wade mounted Dax and drew his sword. If they would not conform to reason, they would cower with fear. He galloped into the middle of each company and shouted the same life-threatening speech. "By the Jaeds, if one more squabble reaches my ears, I will trample over your company until I reach the offender and remove his head with my own sword. You are Rayders, and you will obey without question or complaint."

Only once did someone scoff, and Wade immediately made good on his threat. Six men fell under Dax's iron-shod hooves until Wade decapitated the smirking man and swapped sword for glaive. "Any other comments?" He twisted Dax in a circle, knocking more men into the snow, furiously driven to quell their malcontent. No one dared move or speak.

Wade slammed the glaive into the iron rings on Dax's saddle. "Control your men, Cadet."

Quinten saluted. "Yes, Lieutenant."

An entire day had been exhausted, but Wade did not let them rest. Under the cover of night, the two battalions moved out. Wade knew the arena path would be relatively clear of dissenters, which is why he had sent the majority of his men in that direction. Plenty of Rayder civilians would lie in their path, but the Swallows had been given strict instructions not to harm the innocent. "And always announce your company under my leadership," Wade had added, a tactic to subdue questions of authority.

Quinten's company stayed behind with Wade, giving time for the battalions to engage in battle. The keep was only three miles to the south, so they didn't have to wait long. Surprisingly, their journey was free of fighting. Wade made a quick assessment: enemy Rayder scouts must have seen his two battalions split to surround the keep, so the scouts had withdrawn to warn their mutinous leaders, resulting in all rebel Rayders retreating before capture. Wade's forces made it to the keep's northern doorstep before Wade called a halt to their progress.

"An ambush awaits us," Wade whispered to Quinten. Unlike the rests of Taeja, which was covered in comfortable darkness, torches lined all sides of the brick keep. It was narrower than the surrounding domes Beholder Lon had created, but taller and twice as thick.

Wade squinted into the darkness, searching for moving shadows on top of the keep or signs in the terrain. But the snow had been trampled flat, obscuring anything Wade might track, and the dome's peak was too high for the torchlight to reach. He calculated his options, wishing for a ballista or Beholder Lon to crumble the protective dome. Superior numbers would do little good against such a defense. A narrow entrance, no more than two men wide, dipped under the wall and into the keep. Even his superior fighting skill would not protect him in that approach. Attacking the wall itself would also be pointless. It was at least four feet thick, and undoubtedly protected by archers above.

After half-heartedly contemplating whether to send a few sacrificial Swallows to identify the defensive strengths, Wade decided there was only one practical option. He must tread into the circle of light alone and signal for parlay. He doubted he would survive— what dissenters ever abided by rules of war?—yet he still had to try.

"I go alone," he said to Quinten, "and you will not follow me, Cadet. If I do not survive, rally the two battalions and surround this location. Starve them out."

Quinten nodded and touched his brand. "Yes, Lieutenant."

Wade handed his glaive to the young cadet, then grabbed him by the breastplate and pulled him closer. "Listen to me very carefully, Quentin. More is at stake than you know. Our entire kingdom is under threat. All people, both Appernysian and Rayder, are being evacuated to Itorea as one combined force. It is the only place where we can hope to survive this attack." He altered his voice to a poignant whisper. "Have you heard of the calahein?"

Quentin's eyes grew wide as he nodded in response.

"Good," Wade continued. "Our ancestors believed the calahein exterminated, but they were wrong. Beholder Lon and I have battled directly with the kelsh. We have also seen the destruction that comes to any community that is not protected by a Beholder. Réxura has been obliterated, as will all other civilizations that choose to resist. We *must* join the Appernysians in Itorea. Do you understand?"

After receiving another somber nod from the cadet, Wade stood and slowly trod forward. His strung composite bow draped over his shoulder and an arming sword was sheathed at his hip, opposite his quiver of arrows. He extended his arms to his sides, palms upwards in a sign of peace. With every step he took, his heart rate increased, but Wade maintained a practiced calm. He did not speak as he looked upwards, staring into the darkness where archers would be watching him.

Even when the keep was only twenty yards away, there was no lethal response. Wade was baffled, even annoyed at the lack of action. He had always been precise at reading people, knowing their intentions and how they would act.

At five yards from the entrance, Wade finally spoke. "Lieutenant Wade Arneson seeks parlay with the leader of this rebellion."

No response.

Wade's hand slipped to his sword. "If I must enter your keep, I come sword drawn. I will not be taken by surprise."

Still no answer.

"Very well," Wade called, ripping his sword from its scabbard. "I enter." He yanked a torch out of its sconce and threw it into the passage under the outer wall of the keep, then retrieved another torch and sprinted into death's gate.

The keep had been abandoned, an acre of dry soil with furniture and bedding in disarray. Only one person waited for the lieutenant, a woman lying on the ground with hands and feet lashed behind her back and a gag wrapping her head. She was facing the opposite direction, lying precariously close to the deep trench which had once surrounded Braedr's prison.

"Are you conscious?" Wade asked, inching closer with the torch still in his hand.

The woman nodded in response.

"Are you alone?"

Another nod.

Even so, Wade still pivoted around the perimeter until he was at the hut Beholder Lon had constructed for Flora Baum and her three children. It was empty, too, and Wade finally had a view of the woman's face.

She was Flora, and tears streaked her face.

After one more glance at the dome's smoke vent sixty feet overhead, Wade sheathed his sword and moved to Flora's aid. "Are you hurt?" he asked after removing the gag.

"No," Flora answered, "but please hurry. They might have my children."

Wade pulled out his dagger and cut the bonds. "Who might?"

"Bryst Grayson," she said, sitting up and rubbing the raw flesh around her wrists, "and that red-headed woman who tried to kill Commander Tarek."

"Elie Swasey?" Wade asked, offering a hand to Flora.

Flora took Wade's hand and stood. "And about fifty other men. They tied me up, just moments after I had sent my children away."

"Why would they do such a thing?"

Flora leaned her head against Wade's chest. "For collateral."

Wade understood his mistake as soon as the words left Flora's mouth, but he was too late. At least he would have been, had he not been wearing leather armor under his cloak. A dagger penetrated his stomach, but barely pierced the skin before the armor stopped its progress.

Faster than a snake, Wade twisted his body and retrieved the dagger, stepping behind Flora and touching the blade's edge to her exposed neck. "Collateral to kill me?"

Flora's eyes flashed panic, then determination. "They are returning north, back to Flag—"

An arrow whizzed through the air, striking Flora in the top of her left shoulder and penetrating deep into her heart. She collapsed in the lieutenant's arms.

Whether or not the arrow was intended for Wade was a moot point. Either way, Flora was beyond saving, but not without retribution. Wade lowered Flora and dropped the torch, then ran toward the keep's exit. Two more arrows struck the ground behind him, barely missing their mark as he made his escape.

Once outside, Wade sprinted around the keep just in time to see a man sliding down the opposite wall. His shadowed figure struck the snow in a practiced roll and took off into the darkness, with Wade ten steps behind him.

Wade cursed, wishing he had Dax with him, then realized he still had his bow. Five seconds later, his arrow struck the fleeing Rayder in his right thigh, dropping him to the ground. Without a pause, Wade tossed his bow aside and tackled the man, and not a moment too soon. The man had drawn a dagger and was aiming it for his own throat.

A moment of chaotic grappling followed, both fighting for control of the dagger, until Wade finally broke his opponent's elbow and kneed his face into the packed snow.

"Your name," Wade shouted, pulling the dropped dagger from the snow. When the man didn't respond, Wade used the dagger to carve into the man's exposed ear.

Through the cries of pain, the man also laughed. "Run me through, Lieutenant. Go ahead. Help the calahein."

Wade halted, recognizing the voice of their old siege weapons master. He had been imprisoned during the tournament for assisting in the plot to kill Commander Tarek. "Warley Chatterton. I had wished never to hear your voice again."

"Then silence it," Warley spat, struggling under Wade's knee. "We are all dead anyway."

"Who told you of the calahein? Was it Bryst?"

Warley laughed again. "Your deductive skills astound me, Lieutenant. Now kill me. I would rather die by your hand than under the imprisonment of Appernysians. Tarek is a fool. He leads our people to their deaths."

"And you think Flagheim can save you?" Wade growled. "If we fall at Itorea, Flagheim will follow. You will be swept aside like a fishing boat caught in a hurricane."

"But on my terms," Warley argued. "Not as a prisoner."

Wade cursed again. The conversation was leading nowhere, and doing nothing to help Flora's offspring. "The children, Warley. Do you have them?"

Warley became deathly calm.

"How many?" Wade asked. "How many hostages?"

"I am done speaking."

And Wade believed him. A quick jerk of Wade's hand thrust the dagger where Warley had originally aimed it, permanently silencing the traitor.

How many? Wade thought again as he stood and searched the northern darkness. How large was Bryst's company, and how many children did they take? Was it just Flora's? Warley had been a sacrificial scout, left behind only to make sure Flora followed through—and it had been pure luck that she had died instead of Wade. The rest of Braedr's cult had already fled, too far away to pursue with no more than inexperienced Swallows to aid him. And an even higher priority tugged at Wade's will. It was a damnable decision, but he had no choice. He could still save the rest of Taeja.

Gratefully, Taeja's citizens calmly accepted Wade's return. A few complaints emerged when the civilians discovered that he had organized Appernysian Rayders to retake the city, but none lead to bloodshed.

And there were no more signs of dissenters. Wade met the two battalions of Swallows at the south blade of Taeja, but needlessly. The armory had been abandoned, along with the watch atop the perimeter wall. From what Wade could gather from the civilians, Bryst's group was far smaller than he had anticipated—no more than fifty men. They had plotted their escape carefully, killing anyone who had tried to stop them.

After sending the two battalions to man the southern perimeter wall, Wade and Quinten's company began the arduous task of preparing the city for departure. They moved quickly, gathering supplies and weapons from the armory, but without a Beholder to spread his proclamation, Wade had to communicate the calahein threat with small groups of civilians at a time.

Fortunately, the news spread like wildfire and most Rayders took the danger seriously. Bryst had already sown rumors during his short return, so Wade's proclamation reaffirmed what they had originally hoped was mere propaganda. Also, in the mayhem of evacuation, Flora's three children appeared under the care of an elderly Rayder widow. Wade thanked her profusely, then took charge of the children and escorted them to the body of their deceased mother.

Unfortunately, many civilians still refused to leave their dome dwellings, either because they had sacrificed too much to retake Taeja or because they would not side with Appernysia. Wade fought his desire to force their submission. Time remained their greatest enemy, and Commander Tarek had been very clear. He must save who he could and leave the rest behind.

Three days later, all Swallows and ninety percent of the Rayders followed Wade out of the city. Enough supplies had been left behind to keep the others alive through the winter, but Wade had little hope Taeja would avoid the calahein threat for that long.

Wade pulled Dax's reins and moved next to the wagon holding Flora's body and her three orphaned children. No other youth had been reported missing, but that would make little difference to Beholder Lon. He would still demand an explanation for Flora's death, and Wade would assume full responsibility.

Chapter 14

Languished

"Looks like they finally found us," Aron said, looking up from his cup of cold tea.

Shalán stepped back from the donkey-drawn wagon and followed his gaze west. A small group of men had just crested a hill on horseback and in a wedge formation. Even from two hundred yards, she could see they were disciplined and deadly. Leather armor and swords flashed under their assorted cloaks, and what looked like glaives were secured to the saddles of those wearing blue.

One of the men in blue, positioned at the left flank of their formation, lead another horse behind him. The riderless horse was large and muscular, his black hair shimmering under the bright sun.

"They *did* bring Dawes," Shalán proclaimed, a broad smile on her face. Caught up in the excitement of her returning children and ghraefs, Shalán had forgotten about Lon's horse until after they left Pree. She had hoped Dawes was still alive, and reeled to see him again.

"Undoubtedly for you," Aron responded, "or they would have released him after Bromax took his place."

"Who's Dawes?"

Shalán turned to see Scut Shaw, his long arms folded across his chest.

"Lon's horse," Aron answered. "He took it from the Rayder who tried to kill our family."

Scut snorted. "I thought Myron did the killin', or so you say. What claim did Lon have on it?"

"One survived Myron's attack," Shalán said gently. "He tried to kill Mellai, but Lon protected her."

"My son killed him," Aron continued, "so the horse belongs to him."

"Beholders or not, ghraefs or not," Scut said, his hand shifting to the buckle of his leather belt, "your family's still been livin' a lie. And brought my Kaylen into the middle of it, too. I ought to pull out my sword and serve a little justice myself."

Aron turned to face him, his eyes narrow. "Then get it over with, Master Scut."

"I know better than to cross swords with a *Rayder*." He spit out the last word and stomped away.

Shalán sighed. During their six days of travel, each villager had taken a turn to let the Marcs know exactly how they felt. None of the comments had been kind, but Scut had been especially abrasive, and on a daily basis.

Aron and Shalán had answered each question and attack with absolute truth. The village now knew why they had fled to Pree, and how they had come to settle in Roseiri in the first place. Knowing Aron used to be a Rayder was the hardest truth for them to accept, despite everything the Marcs had done for Pree and even though their two children were now the only hope for Appernysia's survival.

None had allowed Aron to train them in the proper use of their weaponry.

Shalán watched her husband, his fist gripping the pommel of his sheathed sword. His patience was worn thin, and now four armed Rayders would be joining their caravan.

"Jaeds protect us," Shalán whispered and turned to watch the approaching guard.

*   *   *   *   *

"Because of *that*," Aron said, handing his spyglass to Channer and pointing east.

Atop his horse, Channer was afforded a clear view over the heads of the surrounding villagers. Five miles to the east was Humsco. Although Channer had never visited the village, he could see it had been defensively prepared for a siege. Anything and everything had been used to create a perimeter; wagons tipped on their sides, fallen trees, logs, beams, planks of timber, barrels, crates, boulders, sharpened staffs, and even heaps of dirt. The defensive line ran tightly at the village center, abandoning the dismantled homes and fences spotting Humsco's outer borders.

"If this much has been done to protect their borders," Channer said, returning the spyglass, "the villagers will be armed and prepared to defend themselves. Well done, Aron Marcs. You were wise to wait for us here."

"But who warned them?" asked delegate Trev Rowley, his arm protectively around his wife, Anice. He watched the Rayders carefully, but spoke respectfully enough.

Channer had been surprised at first to see that every of-age villager from Pree wore a leather belt—gifted from their leatherworker, Coel—with an arming sword slid underneath it. Most gripped a spear or javelin, too, while the younger children held bows ready with nocked arrows. Channer had immediately recognized the swords as Beholder work, along with their javelins and spears. The steel shone differently than their own weapons, brighter and more pure. It was an impressive display, but he doubted whether the villagers knew how to use such weapons.

"Reese must have survived," Snoom said. "It's the only explanation."

"And he wasn't followed by the calahein," Ric added. "This wall of theirs wouldn't hold up against an attack. The terror hounds alone would have leaped over it with ease."

Channer nodded. "But I respect them for trying, and I believe their defenses are not meant only to protect against the calahein.

With the entire kingdom running for their lives, bandits will take advantage of the weak and defenseless."

"Just like Rayders do," Scut spat.

Channer did not answer. He had recognized the tall man immediately from Lon's description of his betrothed and her father.

"*Did*," Elja responded. "Our people are changing, father of Kaylen."

"Don't you dare be speakin' my daughter's name!" Scut lowered his spear at Elja. "Dirtyin' it with your filth!"

Channer moved his horse between the two and kicked Scut's spear out of his hand. "A fool's errand, Scut Shaw. We are not your enemies."

Scut's chest heaved with fury as he withdrew into the middle of Pree's villagers. He left the spear lying on the packed snow.

"I made the same observations," Aron continued, undeterred by Scut's disruption. "That's why I'm crossing these last five miles alone and unarmed. I know a few people in Humsco, and I watched Reese grow up. If I'm lucky, they'll recognize me. If not . . ." he turned to address the villagers, "then they'd be doing you all a favor by killing me, right?"

"Aron—" Shalán began, but Aron silenced her with a raised hand. "I've made up my mind. I only waited for our children's guard so they can keep the peace while I'm away."

Shalán let go of Dawes's lead rope and took her husband's hand. "And I've made up my mind, too. I'm coming with you."

"So will Anice and I," Trev added. "I know their delegate, Nadjor. We have dined together in Itorea on a few occasions."

*   *   *   *   *

True to Aron's word, they left everything threatening behind. Trev and Anice had placed their weapons in a wagon. Aron had entrusted his falchion and glaive to Channer's care, and Shalán had left Dawes with Elja.

"For just another few hours," Shalán had said, stroking the horse's face. Dawes had nickered in response.

They were now a half-mile away from Humsco's barricade, having just crossed a simple bridge over the West River. They passed between the disassembled remains of many outskirt dwellings. Each had been completely stripped, leaving only foundations of buried timbers and broken fence posts in the frozen ground. Everything had been taken to strengthen the new wall—except the planks off the bridge, but perhaps they thought it might provide a retreat if the calahein attacked from the north. The village livestock had also been moved inside.

Shalán squinted forward. "I wish you had your spyglass."

"Then Channer wouldn't know whether or not this village is capable of being rescued," Aron answered. "Relax. We'll be fine."

"But what if we won't?"

Aron leaned over and kissed Shalán on the cheek. "We will be."

His actions didn't match his mind, though. Aron was scanning the wall for any sign of movement. With the sun setting behind them, their approach would be partially obscured to Humsco—a good and bad thing. If someone became a little too nervous at their unrecognizable faces, they might shoot an arrow at them. Or a volley of arrows.

Aron extended his arms outwards, palms up, the Rayder sign for peace. Despite the threat to their lives, his heart pumped with anticipation over the next ten minutes of their journey. In a way, he felt the excitement of a young Rayder sneaking into a village for the first time. He tried to swallow, but his mouth was dry.

What Aron had not told Channer was that he had only associated with Humsco while his family was living in Roseiri. Surely the rumors of Lon and Mellai's magic trick would have reached this village, too. They would distrust him as much as anyone from Roseiri would have, had they survived. But Aron refused to trust

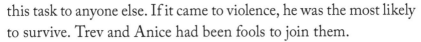

this task to anyone else. If it came to violence, he was the most likely to survive. Trev and Anice had been fools to join them.

Aron glanced at his wife. Shalán acted brave, but her face gave her away, drained of blood. She understood the same danger that might await them in Humsco. *Why did you have to come?* Aron thought, along with a string of unspoken curse words.

With less than a hundred yards remaining, the first arrow leaped from the barricade. Aron caught sight of it at once and stepped protectively in front of his wife. Trev and Anice just froze. The arrow landed thirty feet to their right.

Shalán tugged at the back of his shirt. "Did they miss on purpose?"

Aron shrugged and shouted as loudly as possible. "We carry a message from King Drogan."

Another arrow shot from the wall and disappeared into the snow, closer than the previous.

"Please," Aron shouted, "your lives are at risk. The calahein have returned."

Silence followed, then two figures appeared, having slipped through a hidden passage in the barricade. They both held bows and began walking toward them.

Aron breathed a sigh of relief, his arms still extended from his sides. He knew that Humsco, too, was probably watching Pree's camp with a spyglass. They would have seen a well-armed population and seven horsemen, making anything Aron said less believable. Fortunately, Pree's villagers had come from the west, opposite the direction of Appernysia's main population and a likely attack from criminals. And foolish or not, Trev's presence might possibly quell bloodshed.

"Be careful what you say," Aron counseled Trev, who had regained his nerve and moved next to Aron. "They probably saw your face and will want to speak with you."

"Which is why I came," Trev answered. "It is my responsibility to protect our village. *My* duty."

Aron nodded and stepped back with Shalán, acknowledging Trev's authority. But not too far back.

The two men from Humsco stopped twenty feet away, arrows nocked on their bowstrings. Aron recognized Nadjor, but couldn't identify the younger man with him, though he had a hint of familiarity about him.

"I am Nadjor Eddi," the older man spoke, "delegate of Humsco. You are trespassing on our land."

"When have visitors from Pree ever deserved your suspicion?" Trev replied. "We come peacefully to offer our protection and escort your village to Itorea."

"Itorea?" Nadjor repeated. "That's conveniently far away from here. How do we know you don't seek to lead us out of our homes and take command of our defenses?"

Aron stopped listening to the two delegates, bored with their petty politics and more interested in the younger man. His eyes were locked on Shalán, his expression screwed up like he were solving a difficult farming problem. For at least a minute he watched her, until his eyes popped wide with surprise.

"Shalán?" the young man called, interrupting the two delegates. "Shalán Marcs?"

Shalán stepped clear of her husband and reached out toward the young man. Her voice was shaky and full of emotion. "I'm so sorry, Reese."

Reese dropped his bow and sprinted across the snow until he had wrapped his arms around Shalán and buried his face in her dress. He wept hard and openly, and Shalán answered his tears with her own.

"They're all dead," Reese cried. "Theiss. My parents. Everyone."

Shalán didn't answer. Aron could see that she was grieving her own loss. She, too, had lost her parents in Roseiri, and the display tugged at Aron's heart strings. In front of him stood the last two survivors of Roseiri's blood ancestry, one an orphaned boy no older than fourteen.

Aron waited patiently for them, as did the other three adults looking on. Eventually, Shalán regained enough control to step back and hold the young man's face in her hands. "Look at me, Reese. Not all hope is lost. Two Beholders are protecting us, and ghraefs have joined them for the fight. You even know one of them."

Reese looked up at her, his breath stuttering with shallow hiccups. "Who?"

"My daughter, Mellai. She has joined King Drogan's army and is destroying every calahein she encounters."

Reese's face morphed from pained to fuming. "Good," he muttered between clenched teeth. "I hope she kills them all."

"As do we," Aron said, placing a hand on Reese's shoulder, "but there is little good we can do here to help her." He turned, pointing west. "See those men on horses back there?"

"Yes," Reese answered. "They look like Rayders."

"Some of them are," Aron answered, "but not the kind of Rayders we hear about. They are more like the Taejans who used to protect our kingdom. They are elite fighters, and they have joined Appernysia's best soldiers to form the Beholders' guard."

"If Rayders have joined our forces," Nadjor cut in, still shouting from twenty feet away, "that can mean only one thing. The other Beholder is from the Rayders, isn't he?"

"Yes," Shalán answered, letting go of Reese to address Humsco's delegate. "He is our son, Lon, and a preserver of lives—regardless of the rumors you've heard."

"Everything they've said is true," Trev added, "even about the Beholders' partnership with ghraefs. I saw all four of them with my own eyes. They came to personally warn us in Pree."

Nadjor lowered his bow, but his hand still gripped the nocked arrow. "And where are they now, these Beholders? Too important for Humsco?"

Aron paused. The truthful answer would only anger Nadjor, that the ghraefs had taken them to their home in the Tamadoras

Mountains—at least that is where Aron assumed the ghraefs lived, since they had flown away in that direction.

"Preparing to defend Itorea," Trev answered. "Forget your pride, Nadjor. Lon and Mellai sent their entire guard to protect you. That alone is an honorable sacrifice."

"And what about *his* family?" Nadjor said, pointing at Aron. "They've been hiding in Pree for the last six years, after scaring Roseiri half to death."

"And we gladly welcomed them," Trev answered again. Aron couldn't help but smile. Trev was speaking in politics again, smoothing concern with his partial truths.

"Something amuses you?" Nadjor said to Aron, his patience wearing thinner.

Aron nodded. "I find it hysterical that you are standing here bickering over the insignificant details of the past when it is our future that really matters. It all comes down to one thing, Nadjor, and you know it. Do you want to live or die?"

Silence ensued, everyone waiting as Nadjor battled within himself, until the delegate finally withdrew his arrow and stowed it. "You've made your point, but I still have a village to protect. I must speak with the Beholders' guard before I allow you any closer to Humsco."

Trev turned to Pree's camp, held seven fingers in the air, then waived them forward. "As you wish."

While they waited for the horsemen to cross the five miles to their position, Shalán had her own interrogation to conduct. "While we're asking questions, Nadjor, I have one for you." Her hands moved to her hips and chin lifted into the air. The ghraef pendant swung loosely from her neck as she spoke.

Aron smiled again. He had been the recipient of similar lectures that began with that posture. Not one was pleasant.

"If you suspected us as dangerous," Shalán continued, "what in the world prompted you to bring Reese out here with you? Hasn't he risked enough? Suffered enough?"

Any man in his right mind would look at Aron's wife and know better than to refuse an answer, and Nadjor was no fool. "He grew up with your family, and I wanted him here to verify your identities." He paused, glancing over his shoulder at the barricade surrounding Humsco before finally closing the distance between himself and Pree's representatives. He spoke in a low voice, revealing his true answer. "Our village suffers. It's because of your explanation that I brought Reese out here, even before my own wife and daughter. Discord has filled my people, Shalán, and my control over them is slipping. I feared for Reese's safety in my absence."

"Then it is good we've come," Aron answered. "Like it or not, fear is the quickest way to quell rebellion. Give me and the Beholders' guard responsibility to keep the peace. You may not like our methods, but you will welcome our results."

Trev took Nadjor's hand in a firm grip. "I still speak for my village—as will you, my friend—but these men have been tasked with safely escorting us to Itorea."

"How can you trust them?" Nadjor replied, returning the handshake. "What reassurance do you have that they aren't leading us to our doom?"

"The promise of my children," Shalán answered, her arm lovingly around Reese. "Their word alone is enough for me, but as Beholders, their guarantees are indisputable."

After another brief pause, Nadjor nodded. "Very well."

✳   ✳   ✳   ✳   ✳

Introductions ended quickly. Trev signaled for the rest of Pree to follow after them, then Nadjor led the small group toward the barricade. Trev and Anice were first in line behind Nadjor, followed by Aron and Shalán leading Dawes with Reese on his back. The guard brought up the rear, flared out in their usual wedge formation.

Shalán was ever armed with her healing satchel slung over her shoulder and Channer had returned Aron's falchion and glaive. Trev and Anice, on the other hand, would have to wait for Pree to bring their wagon before they could rearm themselves.

Not that weapons would do them much good, Aron thought again, still frustrated that the villagers had not allowed him to train them. He held his glaive upright, using it as a walking stick, and his left hand rested on the pommel of his sheathed sword.

Ten feet from the barricade, when other members of their group would be preoccupied with finding the hidden entrance into Humsco, Aron knew their danger was at its highest. The villagers of Humsco now had a full view of their company, including the Rayder brands on four of the horsemen.

No matter what Aron or the guard did, there would always be those who refused to trust them, so it came as no surprise when another arrow shot out from farther down the barricade, aimed at Channer. He flinched and the arrow narrowly whipped past his face to land harmlessly in the snow, but only because of an amateur archer. Had the aim been truer, Channer would have been counted among the dead.

While the rest of the guard slid off their saddles, Nik immediately responded with an arrow of his own. Aron heard a grunt when Nik's arrow pierced the barricade, then nothing more as the Rayder nocked another arrow. He remained in his saddle, his eyes daring someone else to attack.

"Halt!" Nadjor shouted. "These men are our allies, sent here by King Drogan to escort us to Itorea."

Aron stepped in front of Shalán again and focused his attention on the wall. A small protrusion revealed a stout door into the barricade, hidden from view unless looking from the side. The door opened and Nadjor stepped inside.

"Allow me," Aron said, gripping his glaive as he forced past Trev and into the doorway. If an ambush waited for them, he would thwart the attempt.

But his anxieties were unnecessary. Humsco's outward display feigned their lack of preparation inside. Only men stood behind the wall with pole weapons ranging from rusty war scythes to rotting pitchforks. A few of the young men, no older than Reese, held only rocks in their hands and an unfortunate few gripped hunting bows with quivers half empty. None were armed appropriately for war. Farther down the line, Aron caught sight of the man who had attacked them. He was middle-aged and lying flat on his back with the feathered end of an arrow jutting from his eye. But no one seemed to notice, their limited energy fully focused on the Rayders.

"Where are your women and children?" Trev asked, having entered behind Aron.

"My wife, Laecha, is looking after them in that barn," Nadjor said, pointing to the only building still standing. He sighed. "Now you understand my caution. In our haste to prepare this wall the past three weeks, I fear we've made our situation worse." He removed his woolly cap and placed it over his heart. "Thank you for coming."

Chapter 15

Forefront

"There's something I never expected to see," Tarek said aloud, staring wide-eyed at the abandoned city down the hill. He had always longed to see Sylbie, the city where his father had earned the Lynth pendant for intervening during a tavern fight. Even without experiencing it himself, Tarek had always smiled at the memory. One part of his bloodline would always link him to Myron. They both never backed down from a fight.

"See what, my Commander?" the man next to him asked.

"All of it," Tarek answered, sweeping his hand across the horizon. "This abandoned trade city. Itorea's massive wall. The Perbeisea Forest and its huge trees. All of Appernysia's wonders, Lio, caught in one grand vision."

Lio nodded. "Itorea's wall is reassuring, my Commander, but I worry its protection will not be for us."

Tarek rolled his eyes. As the head of Tarek's escort, Lio Cope was an inescapable whirlwind of annoyance. But his logic was sound and paranoia supreme, making him a perfect candidate for such a position. "What this time, Lieutenant?"

"If our roles were reversed, where would you place your Appernysian prisoners, my Commander?"

"In Sylbie," Tarek answered, scowling with realization. "I hate it when you're right, Lio."

"Thank you, my Commander," Lio said, saluting. "Placing our people there would supply a perfect prison and a buffer of protection for Itorea."

"Drogan intends to sacrifice us," Tarek growled. Sylbie was wedged between the Prime and Sylbien Rivers, and guarded the only access across the half-mile bridge to Itorea's west gate. If the Rayders were stationed there, they would be cut off without any route of escape, except across the bridge and into the Fortress Island. But what if Drogan wouldn't let them enter? They'd be mercilessly slaughtered by the calahein.

Appernysia's army of one hundred thousand men was already filtering into Itorea. Tarek had been told it was to organize an impenetrable escort through the city—just in case—until they reached the hook east of the keep. There the Rayders would live, or so Tarek had understood, until the calahein threat had been eliminated.

This is why the Rayders had been allowed to keep their weapons; not as a sign of trust and respect from Drogan, but because the Rayders would need them to kill off as many calahein as possible before they were finally overrun.

In his confidence, Drogan had not yet joined his men across the river. He sat upon his horse in the midst of his own plate-armored escort no more than fifty yards away. Tarek intended to make full use of the opportunity.

"Follow my lead," Tarek said to Lio, then turned his horse toward Appernysia's king. Lio tapped his own horse's sides with his heels and signaled for the commander's guard to follow.

They rode casually, hands away from their weapons, right up to Drogan's circle of knights. The Appernysians brought their horses together in two rows, blocking Tarek's access to their king.

"What can I do for you, Commander Tarek?" Drogan asked without looking.

"We shook hands in agreement," Tarek replied coolly, "yet I see a perfect opportunity here for you to tarnish your honor. How do you answer?"

"King Drogan does not answer to you," General Astadem replied from beside the king. "In truth, you owe him your allegiance, child of Pree."

Tarek remained calm. "Answer my question, Drogan. Will you keep your oath?"

"Tell me, Tarek," Drogan answered, still not looking. "What oath have I given you?"

"Safe passage through Itorea. *Through*, not *to*. You will not sacrifice my people for your own protection by deserting us in Sylbie."

Drogan's eyes brightened and he finally turned to look at the Rayder commander. "A tempting offer, Tarek, but no. I am a man of my word. We will provide safe passage through Itorea, for Rayders and for my people. Feel free to move your men into Sylbie for the night, if you wish, and I will meet you at Itorea's west gate in the morning to escort you through myself." He kicked the sides of his horse and rode away with his escort.

"Remember my promise," Tarek called over the clanking plate armor, "If you're lying, I'll kill you myself."

✳　✳　✳　✳　✳

The comforts of Sylbie were too tempting to ignore. Tarek's men slipped peacefully into the unlocked homes and inns. The buildings had been depleted of food and bedding, but most were still stocked with hay-stuffed mattresses—a luxury his men had not enjoyed in many months. Tarek chose a two-story inn close to Itorea's bridge, and he set his men on watch at the bridge's west edge to prevent Appernysians from sneaking into the city that night.

Not in the mood for company, Tarek retired early to his chambers. He laid on his bed, fully clothed with his drawn sword leaning against the straw mattress, and stared at the ceiling for hours.

The role of commander was miserable, with constant death threats from his own people, but now that Appernysia's politics were mixed in, the responsibility was nigh unbearable. And underlying it all was Tarek's self-doubt and worry for the safety of the Rayders. His people were spread precariously thin, and it all began when he led his army out of Taeja for war. Now Lon's squad was traveling somewhere in the Western Valley of Appernysia, a month's journey away, and Wade was undoubtedly cleaning up a bloody mess in Taeja.

Had Tarek made the right choice, going to war a second time? Had Commander Rayben Goldhawk calculated wisely when he first chose to lead their people out of the Rayder Exile? At least in Flagheim, they would be living an established lifestyle of relative comfort and protection. They wouldn't be consorting with 'Nysians for their survival.

But if the calahein had attacked the Exile while the entire Rayder civilization lived there . . . *No*, Tarek thought, pushing the idea aside. He refused to think that way. He had learned through sore experience that despair was the quickest path to defeat and death.

Tarek scolded himself. *So what am I doing?* He knew he couldn't change the past, so why fret? He had made every decision as best he could, in the best interest of his people at that time. All he could do now was secure their future. His options were few, but he still maintained control of them.

At the forefront was the city looming to the east. Was entering Itorea the best choice? It had sounded nice during their war council, but that was with Lon and his squad present. It had made sense, retreating to a city built by Beholders so that Beholders could defend it.

But where were Lon and Mellai?

Chapter 16

Research

"L isten to this," Mellai called from the divan, a dusty scroll open on her lap. Although the room was so utterly dark that she wouldn't be able to see Lon's finger if he poked her in the eye, everything was perfectly visible with the aid of her power. *'Having manifested True Sight for the first time, the council banished me from Taeja on a quest to master my gift. We all knew this to be the journey every training Beholder must endure, but I had no idea what the Jaeds held in store for me.'* Sound familiar?"

"Like every other scroll we've read so far," Lon answered, his voice full of annoyance.

"I'm talking about you, dimwit. The way this man phrased it, it sounds exactly like what you've endured."

"But that's not Llen's record. *'They all knew it'* means there had been Beholders before."

"You still don't get it," Mellai said, standing and crossing the floor to her twin brother. He was sitting at the table on the other side of the Beholders library, and she laid the scroll down in front of him. "This person understood what you had to go through. He suffered like you did."

"His experience was nothing like mine," Lon said, pushing the parchment to the side.

"Oh, no? Keep listening." She picked up the scroll and paced in front of Lon. *"'I journeyed south, following the path of my predecessors into the Forest of Blight'*—or in your case, Rayder Exile—*'with only my horse, my sword, and a small pack of supplies to stay alive. It was in the forest that I met Pak, although not in the way I had imagined. He swooped down from the sky, knocking me out of my saddle before climbing into the air again, my mount gripped in his paws. As the ghraef circled overhead, I wept while I watched him eat my horse.'"*

"I don't know what I was thinking," Lon interrupted. "That's exactly what happened to me."

Mellai rolled her clouded eyes. "Keep listening. *'After consuming his meal, Pak turned on me again. He dove repeatedly in an attempt to grab or crush me under his bone tail. I barely escaped each death blow by diving out of the way, but Pak was getting wise. Each of my escapes became narrower as time passed. I knew Pak was going to kill me. I tried summoning my power, failing in every effort, until Pak finally grabbed my leg and took to the air. At first I thought he would eat me, until I realized he had let go and I was falling hundreds of feet to my death. I became desperate, and finally my power manifested itself. I pulled the world's energy into my body, but knew not how to release it. More and more energy poured into my essence, until I was unable to contain it. In a blinding flash of light, my . . .'* uh, never mind."

Lon stood. "What, Mel? What did he do?"

"I thought this would end differently," Mellai replied. "I was just fascinated that his ghraef let him fall like Bromax did to you."

"I've already read dozens of accounts like that. Now finish his record. What happened?"

Mellai sighed. "*'In a blinding flash of light, my mortal body combusted in an explosion too vast to describe. I hadn't realized that Pak was beside me, intent on rescuing me if I couldn't save myself. I killed us both, and destroyed ten miles of forest in the process. I failed my quest, the ghraefs, and all of Appernysia.'"*

Lon leaned forward, his hands flat on the table. "Omar told me about that story. It's a little different, though, hearing it described directly from the record."

"It says the account was written posthumously by Beholder Llen Drayden." Mellai rolled the scroll and used her power to return it to its place on a high shelf. "If Llen gave that account, it has to mean he was watching it happen. Why didn't he do something to save them?"

"What could he do, Mel? Llen must have been too far away to remove the Beholder's eyes, and you've shown me the only other way to intervene is with an energy shield. But Llen wouldn't have been able to contain the blast. It would have killed him, too."

"We're lucky that never happened to you," Mellai said, sitting down on the cave's floor and leaning against the shelves. "Remember what you did to Father? That could have been a lot worse."

"You said that before," Lon answered. "Speaking of, did you notice he's not limping? That's a good thing, I guess."

Mellai pounded the back of her head into the shelves with frustration. "What are we doing, Lon? We've been stuck in here for who knows how long, and for what? Our parents might already be dead, along with half the kingdom. We don't have time for this."

"But Llen said—"

"Maybe Llen's not as all-knowing as we think he is. You want to know what I think? I think I hate this prison of a cave." She stood, her anger growing. "I think I hate these scrolls." She tipped a shelf, sending it crashing to the ground in a shattering burst of parchment and timber.

Huirk had been quietly watching the Beholders from across the cave, but now he was on his feet, rushing to intercept Mellai before she destroyed everything the ghraefs had worked so hard to preserve.

Mellai saw his approach. "And I hate this rug!" She whipped the woven collection of stitched crystal designs into the air and flung it at the ghraef. It wrapped around Huirk and sent him crashing into the wall.

"Look!" Lon called. Diagrams and illustrations were etched into the cave floor, along with an embedded crystal design exactly like the red cube stitched in the rug that used to cover it. Lon began walking around the illustrations, his brow furrowed in concentration. "What is this?"

Before Mellai could give the floor any consideration, Bromax appeared at the mouth of the upward tunnel, his energy bristling with anger. He glanced at Huirk, unconscious and wrapped in the rug, then redirected his attention to Mellai. A rumbling growl echoed from deep within the ghraef and he flashed his teeth at her.

Lon stepped back and lounged on the divan, a broad smile on his face. "Your turn, Little Sis."

"I don't think this is a fight for respect, Lon. He looks genuinely angry."

"Wouldn't you be? Look what you did to his stuff."

Mellai raised her hands in submission. "I'm sorry, Bromax. I'll clean it up right now."

Bromax clicked his teeth, then flashed them again at her.

"That means *now!*" Lon said, laughing.

Mellai extended her essence to Huirk, carefully unwrapping the rug and grateful it wasn't notably damaged. She moved Huirk onto his nest of dry leaves and dark soil, then rolled the rug and set it gently against the far wall.

Bromax took a step forward, motioning with his snout toward the broken shelving and scattered parchment.

"Exactly how you found it," Lon said, still chuckling.

*　　*　　*　　*　　*

An hour or so later—it was impossible for Lon to accurately keep track of time while in constant darkness—Mellai completed the arduous task of repairing the shelving and placing hundreds of scrolls and manuscripts exactly where they had been. After Bromax disappeared up the tunnel again, she crossed the cave and spoke softly to Huirk. The ghraef had regained consciousness long before, but had stayed on his nest while Bromax disciplined Mellai. Now Huirk ignored her, looking the other direction whenever she stepped in front of him.

Lon smiled, thinking back through the previous hour. Aside from the entertainment of watching his sister squirm, he had learned much while watching her. Wooden beams had shattered and parchment had torn, so Mellai had to stitch them back together. At least that's how she described it, though it looked more like blending to Lon. Eventually, though, the shelf had been fully repaired with every scroll back in its proper place. Bromax had seen to that, snapping at Mellai every time she mislocated something.

Lon had also spent some time studying the newly revealed record on the floor. It consisted of the crafted cube crystal, two diagrams, and a sequence of illustrations. The illustrations were very clear. They depicted a quest deep into the downward tunnel, until the Beholder found a room of crystals. Lon and Mellai would each select a crystal, bring it back to the Beholder's cave, then Bromax and Huirk would lead them out of the mountain. A ceremony would follow in front of many ghraefs—perhaps the whole population. Bromax and Huirk would bite the bone tips from their tails, then Lon and Mellai would attach the crystals in their place. With a little training from his sister, Lon was certain he'd be able to complete the task.

The two diagrams on the cave floor, however, were not that simple.

The first showed a hand and crystal connected by a line, and a shattered hammer touching the crystal's edge.

In the second diagram, two hands held a crystal wrapped around the sun.

Laughter from Huirk signaled his forgiveness of Mellai. Lon looked up to see them playing. The ghraef was repeatedly dropping his bone-tipped tail in front of his head, while Mellai jumped around trying to dodge it. Huirk eventually pinned Mellai to the ground with his tail, but she used her power to flick the bone tip aside. It ricocheted off Huirk's forehead and struck against the stone wall with a resonating crack. Both of them laughed again.

"Come look at this, you two," Lon called. Mellai climbed onto Huirk's back and he carried her across the room to stand at Lon's side.

"What do you think?" Lon said, pointing at the diagrams.

"The second one is obvious," Mellai answered immediately. "I saw sun crystals like that in Itorea's keep. Queen Cyra wears one around her neck. The other one was enormous. It hung from the ceiling of the great hall like a chandelier."

"Sun crystals?"

Mellai nodded. "They hold light that never ceases to glow."

Lon pointed at the first diagram. "And what about that one?"

His sister studied it for a few minutes. "I'm not sure. Maybe a way of using steel to craft a crystal?"

Huirk snorted and stepped away, returning moments later with two rocks in his mouth. He placed them both on the ground, then twisted sideways and smashed one with his bone tail. Mellai created an energy shield at the last second, blocking a few of the projectiles from hitting her and the ghraef, but Lon had to duck out of the way.

After another fit of laughter at Lon, Huirk shifted his weight and swung his tail at the second stone, only he didn't crush it. He merely tapped it with his tail, then whipped his tail at it another time, barely touching it again. He repeated the action a few times, then dropped down and grabbed his tail in mock pain.

"Brilliant!" Mellai shouted, sliding off his back to kiss Huirk on his feigned injury. "It's a way to create indestructible crystals, isn't it?"

The ghraef stood again and stepped forward, touching the last story illustration with his claw. It was the picture of the Beholder attaching a crystal to the ghraef's tail.

"I get it," Lon said, fascinated and terrified at the same time. "The crystals we choose for you and Bromax have to be impervious to damage."

Huirk nodded, then touched his claw sideways to his lips.

"A secret?" Lon asked, understanding the shush gesture. "Who would we tell, Huirk?"

The ghraef pointed at the tunnel where Bromax had exited.

"Oh," Mellai said in a whisper. "We were supposed to figure this out on our own, weren't we?"

After a subtle huff out his nose, Huirk returned to his nest and laid down.

"And this cube design," Mellai observed, moving to the collection of crystals buried in the floor. "It's the center symbol of that rug, which could only mean one thing."

"We found Llen's record."

"And this must be the shape that was on Llen's ghraef," Mellai continued. "I'll bet you it's dark purple." She pulled a pile of dry leaves and branches from Huirk's nest and laid them next to the design, then ignited them. Her essence dimmed dramatically when she released her power. "Take a look," she said, pointing at the flat cube.

Lon closed his eyes to sever his connection with True Sight, then reopened them with regular vision. The small fire lit a portion of the room, casting its light into the design, where it reflected deep purple flickers across the cave. Lon nodded with understanding. While viewing the shape with his power, Lon had only been able to see a dull washed-out purple, void of any true density of color.

Mellai sat down on the divan. "These monuments cover Itorea's wall, Lon. If we ever have the time, we'll have to add Bromax and Huirk's crystals to the collection. The rug, too."

Lon doubted that day would ever come. The more he read from the Beholders' journals, the more he realized he knew nothing about True Sight. The First Age Beholders were capable of exponentially more tasks with their power, yet they barely fended off the cala-hein. How could he and his sister alone expect to defeat them, let alone find time to spend what must be weeks sculpting a crystal into Itorea's wall?

"So what do we do now?" Lon asked, joining his sister on the couch. He was irritated that Llen had sent them on such a ridiculous, time-wasting scavenger hunt, but Lon didn't voice his frustrations to his sister. "We'll need to figure out how to perform these two diagrams before we take our journey to the crystal cave, but I have no idea where to begin with something like this."

Mellai's eyes clouded over as she used her power to retrieve the rock Huirk had left sitting on the ground. "With experimentation, Big Brother. We'll work the science, and Huirk can test our skill."

Lon couldn't help but smile. "Big Brother, huh?"

"Hey," she answered, elbowing Lon in the ribs, "it's about time I come up with a nickname for you."

"No complaints," Lon said, placing his arm around his sister and calling upon True Sight, "but we need to hurry. Let's figure this out."

Chapter 17
Trudge

Tarek squinted, unable to shield his eyes from the shimmering light below. The rising sun had just crested Itorea's perimeter wall, bouncing off the half-mile wide Sylbien River. Trying to cross the arching bridge had been hard enough half-blinded, but the commander had an even more pressing concern. Nobody knew—not even Lon—that Tarek battled a mortifying fear of heights.

Although the bridge was a good fifty feet wide, the only barriers along its edges were small stone curbs. The Rayder bridge, Justice, had been torturous to traverse, but at least it had only been a hundred feet long, with solid wood barriers boxing them in. Now, at the highest point on Itorea's bridge and knowing that only four stone columns kept the entire thing aloft, Tarek silently thanked his horse for doing all the work. The Rayders had no idea, but their commander was frozen with fear.

The closer they drew to the west gate, however, the more distracted Tarek became by the wall surrounding the Fortress Island. He knew it was three hundred feet tall, but the number meant nothing to him since he had never stood on something that high. He was close enough to see King Drogan on his horse, a tiny speck at the base of the white stone wall. It was absurdly huge, and no man could convince Tarek to fight from up there. He would defend the gate with his feet firmly planted on solid ground.

If only Drogan would allow the Rayders to help defend the city.

Despite its size, Itorea's wall had one major weakness. Thick vinery grew out of the limited amount of soil on both sides of the gate, meeting above it to form a massive web that climbed all the way over the crenellations at the top. The vinery had been growing for centuries, so thick one couldn't see the wall behind it. Tarek shook his head with disgust over Appernysia's planning. Given enough time, Rayders could even climb the vines, but the calahein would scale it faster than Tarek could down a pound of mutton. The flanking towers on each side of the gate, even with their countless arrow slits, would be useless.

"You need to burn those down," Tarek called to Drogan, pointing at the vines.

Drogan reared his head to glance at the wall, then turned back to smile at the commander. "Perhaps you're right."

Perhaps I ought to punch you in the face, Tarek thought, knowing that the king had given little thought to his warning.

Both leaders and their mounted escorts were standing on a wooden bridge, the first defense of Itorea's city. The stone bridge had stopped abruptly, making it impossible to cross onto Itorea's shores without a fifty-foot extension. The drawbridge served that purpose. Stout chains ran from its front corners to holes through the perimeter wall, allowing the bridge to be retracted. When pulled tightly, it would also create a barrier over the gateway. *An effective defense against humans,* Tarek thought, *but kelsh would rip through the planks in no time. Hopefully they have something stronger to defend the entrance.*

"Are you ready?" Drogan called, pulling Tarek out of his thoughts.

He nodded.

"Very well," Drogan continued. He began turning his horse, but stopped to speak again. "Oh, I forgot to explain the rules."

Tarek sighed with annoyance. "No killing people. We got it."

Drogan replied with a dry laugh. "It's a little more complicated than that, I'm afraid. You see, I need to ensure the safety of my people, so I'll need you and your men to follow some standards I've set in place for you."

Tarek clenched his jaw. He had feared something like this would happen.

"No need to be angry. It's just a couple of simple things."

"Get on with it," Tarek growled.

"First, there will be no riding horses. This is for your protection as much as ours. I can't guarantee that everyone in my city will lovingly welcome you, and I'd hate for you to be shot. Let's not make it easier for them, hmm?"

Tarek nodded. That one made sense.

"Secondly, you will travel side-by-side in pairs. Of course, for those with horses like yourself, your horse will be your partner."

"That's ridiculous," Tarek answered. "That would stretch my men out for miles. What about our safety?"

"A valid concern," Drogan continued. "My soldiers will provide safe escort. They're already lined up inside, waiting for you. Your Rayders will be protected by a thick wall of my Appernysian soldiers on both sides of the road. Fair?"

Tarek gripped his reins with frustration. The escort wasn't for their protection, but for the civilians. "I give you my word, King Drogan. My men are only here to protect Appernysia from the calahein. To ensure our joint survival. There is no need for these precautions."

Drogan's formality disappeared, exchanged for impatience and distrust. "This culture you speak of, where a mere promise can be relied on unreservedly, doesn't exist. Experience has taught me that men can't be trusted. The greater the promise, the greater the guile. Millions of lives hang in the balance and I will not be taken for a fool again. So, you can either enter Itorea by my standards, or you can turn yourselves around and march back to Taeja."

Tarek's heart cried out in defiance, demanding that he lash out at the king, but Tarek's mind held control of the situation. Unlike many of his commander predecessors, he would not be labeled as a passionate fool. "Dismount!" he called, sliding out of his horse's saddle. "Form columns of two!" While his order trickled through the Rayder ranks, Tarek stood tall to face Appernysia's king. "I will prove you wrong, Drogan. If you have not experienced the reliability of valiant men, then you have surrounded yourself with the wrong people. There is honor left in this world, and you will experience it firsthand from the Rayders. Now, what is your next request?"

Drogan stared at Tarek, obviously startled by their decisive compliance. Maybe the king had hoped for the Rayders to refuse, to flee to their own deaths, but Tarek would not be swayed. While struggling with his own decisions the night before, Tarek remembered one distinct fact. Beholders always seemed to do what was best for their nation, and both Lon and Mellai had agreed that everyone—*everyone*—retreating to Itorea was the wisest choice. Tarek would see it through, on faith in Beholders if nothing else.

"Don't touch your weapons or move out of line," Drogan finally said, turning his horse to ride away, "and supply wagons single file at the rear."

Tarek didn't need to pass that order along. His men had enough common sense to know better.

The king's escort stayed a reasonable distance ahead of Tarek while they passed through the gateway. Once underneath the wall, Tarek saw that two portcullises hung from the ceiling, one at the front edge, and the other halfway inside. Two other gaps ran across the gateway, too, and Tarek had to carefully lead his horse over the large grooves cut into the stone floor. From what he could see, it looked like two enormous stone doors could be moved to block the gate, but without seeing it from the access rooms hidden in the curtain wall, he couldn't be sure. *They'd be heavy doors, though,*

Tarek thought as he looked at the ceiling arching fifty feet overhead. *Easily a million pounds.*

Just as Drogan had described, the road inside Itorea was lined with soldiers on both sides. And it looked like the entire city had turned out for the parade. Tarek's eyes lifted upward, amazed by the ghraef statues holding the raised aqueduct system above the city, until a rotten tomato hit him in the face. It was the first of many, along with a roar of insults and death threats at the Rayders.

"How far to the keep?" Tarek shouted over the noise, dodging a few more vegetables aimed at his face.

"Fifty miles," one of the nearby Appernysian guards shouted back. His chainmail was also spotted in splattered vegetables that had missed their mark. "A five-day journey from here."

Tarek groaned and tilted his face toward the ground, wishing the Appernysians had enough common sense to preserve their food for a siege. *This is going to be a very long five days.*

✳   ✳   ✳   ✳   ✳

"Can't we do something?" Kaylen asked, staring down at the city from above Itorea's west gate.

"What do you propose?" Kutad answered.

Kaylen shook her head. "I don't know, but did King Drogan really have to announce this to the entire city? The Rayders don't deserve this."

Kutad grabbed Kaylen's arm and turned her toward him. "Would you have them hailed as champions, Kaylen? Heroes, perhaps? Think of how many people have died at the hands of the Rayders, even in Pree. What about Myron and his family?"

"That's his youngest son!" Kaylen screamed, jabbing a finger at the man leading the column of Rayders.

"Not anymore," Kutad answered, signaling for his crossbowmen to lower their weapons. Fifty soldiers set their crossbows on the stone wall and stood at attention. Kutad nodded. Much to his surprise, it appeared that the Rayders would endure the berating without retaliation. Indeed, the protective lines of Appernysian soldiers might end up defending the Rayders from the civilians instead of the civilians from the Rayders.

"How can you say that?" Kaylen said, yanking her arm free. "You rode with Lon and the Rayders. You've seen they aren't as barbaric as everyone seems to think they are."

"But they are just as deadly," Kutad said. "If it weren't for Mellai, they would have slaughtered us. I guarantee it."

"Why would you say that?"

Kutad interlocked his hands behind his back. He had not told Kaylen, nor did he intend to, that Lon's squad had attacked Mellai at Réxura. Only with True Sight had she been able to deflect the arrows. Emotions had been strained, sure, but that was no excuse for the Rayders' actions. They did not try to negotiate, but resorted immediately to violence at every contention.

With an angry scream, Kaylen pounded on Kutad's breastplate with her fists. "Do something, Kutad! You're King Drogan's sergeant. You have the authority to stop this."

"Take her back to the keep," Kutad called as he walked to the other side of the wall. From there, he had a perfect view of the approaching Rayders. They had obeyed Tarek's order and were stretched in pairs for many miles past the bridge, almost reaching Sylbie's west gate.

"What happened to you?" Kaylen shouted as two crossbowmen dragged her toward the nearest tower staircase. "You used to care about injustice. Remember Linney!"

Kutad ignored her, leaning forward between the jagged crenels and pulling the note from his pocket. He stared at it for a moment, thinking of the emotion he had invested in such a pointless love. Lon's return had ruined any chance he had at winning Kaylen's heart. Kutad knew that now.

He blew out a burst of air, tore the note in half, and tossed it over the side. Kaylen was lost to him, but not Appernysia. He would still defend his kingdom, against the Rayders and the calahein at the same time, if necessary.

Returning to his men, Kutad noticed a dark spot barely visible on the northern horizon. A large group was traveling along the west banks of the Nellis River, about fifty miles north of his position.

"Lieutenant Wade," Kutad mused. "I have to be honest, my friend. I didn't think you could convince them to leave Taeja." He chuckled. "Too bad for you."

＊　＊　＊　＊　＊

By the end of that day, the entire Rayder army was inside Itorea, their flank a safe four miles inside the perimeter wall. Outside the wall, however, Wade Arneson and the rest of the Rayder civilians had moved closer, bringing them only five days north of Sylbie. But General Astadem would make Wade's group wait for Appernysia's soldiers to return before he allowed the Rayders into the city.

Ninety percent of Kamron's army was tied up in escorting the Rayders, including Kutad and his fifty crossbowmen assigned to protect King Drogan. That left ten thousand soldiers for Kamron to manage. He divided them into two groups. Five thousand would police the city from atop the aqueducts and among the civilians. The other half would prepare the battlements for a calahein attack.

During his many years as Appernysia's general, Kamron's greatest fear had been that he might have to manage a full-scale defense of the city. It was a daunting task. Hundreds of miles of walled shoreline surrounded its perimeter, fifty of which ran along its western shore. These fifty miles were where Kamron decided to make his stand.

Traditionally, every general of Appernysia's army was required to study a collection of documents describing the calahein. Kamron had only sifted through the papers fifteen years earlier, but a few key details still stood out in his mind.

One – The calahein had a deadly fear of water. That meant the Gaurelic Waste and Asaras Sea provided safer boundaries.

Two – He already knew the calahein contained two races, the kelsh and seith. The seith could fly, which meant his men would need to watch the skies as equally as the ground. Also, Kutad's report from Réxura revealed that a third race, venom-spitting terror hounds, had joined forces with them.

Three – The calahein were expert tunnelers, which meant they had sharp and powerful claws. Fortunately, Itorea's perimeter wall had been built in such a way that it was perfectly smooth and completely indestructible. This meant the calahein wouldn't be able to climb the perimeter wall by their own power. In the skepticism of his youth, Kamron had tested the wall's solidity many times, striking the top and insides of the wall in various places with whatever tool was closest. He couldn't even chip the stone, not even with a two-handed steel hammer.

Four – The calahein were faster than a horse, tougher than a bear, and fiercer than a wolf. If one ever bypassed the perimeter wall, it would kill many before it could be destroyed.

Five – Never had the calahein penetrated deep enough into Appernysian territory that a battle took place at Itorea. In other words, the Beholders really had no idea how effective their defenses would be when they built the city. Their design had been based completely on guesswork.

Kamron rubbed his forehead again, standing over a table covered in maps and records. *This won't be easy,* he thought again. He was in the guardhouse of Itorea's west gate, alone while his men kept watch outside.

He glanced over the defense of the west gate. Once they dropped the two portcullises, the calahein would never get through. And the two Furwen doors seemed silly to even consider using. *But I guess they wouldn't hurt,* Kamron thought, *if Mellai can actually move them.*

A few measurements and calculations later, the general counted two hundred and sixty-five drum towers along the western wall. Each circular tower held sixteen ballistae—one between every crenel—and each ballista required a minimum of three men to operate.

"That's almost thirteen thousand men for the aerial defense alone," Kamron said aloud. He could cut that number in half and man only the ballistae aiming outside of the wall, but that was impractical. The seith would attack from all directions and they needed to be prepared for a circular defense of ground and air.

"Let's see . . ." he mumbled, studying a cross-section diagram of the inner battlements of each tower. "Four hundred arrow slits per tower . . . that's over a hundred thousand men. Way too much . . . hmm . . . ah ha! This might work!"

A soft knock sounded on the guardhouse door.

"What do you want?" Kamron called.

"Everything alright in there, General?" a muffled voice called.

Kamron slapped the table in frustration. He had lost count. "Leave me alone!" he shouted back at the door. "Now where was I? Oh yes . . . if I cut that number in half, stationing fifty-two thousand crossbowmen inside the towers, then subtract the thirteen thousand ballistae operators, it leaves . . ." He scratched some numbers onto a blank sheet of parchment. ". . . thirty-five thousand men stationed on top of the west wall. Over fifty miles . . . that's one man for every seven feet of wall."

Kamron sat back in his chair and threw his hands up. "Success!" His calculations were perfect, and would make for an impressive display to scare away the calahein.

He stood and opened the door, called in a few of his lieutenants, then closed it again before carefully explaining his solution.

"What about inside the city, General?" one of them asked. "Don't the seith fly?"

"We have ballistae to deal . . . with . . ." Kamron started to argue, but then he realized what the lieutenant meant. He flipped through the maps until he found the agricultural layout of Itorea. "The west half of Itorea's blade will be holding Appernysia's entire population, all packed into less than six hundred square miles of land. If a seith lands in the middle of them, the death toll would be catastrophic, especially with all of our soldiers stationed at the wall."

"Place crossbowmen on the raised aqueducts," the first suggested, tracing vertical lines running through the city.

"Good plan," Kamron replied. "I'll pull another twenty-five thousand crossbowmen from the battlements for your idea, but the aqueducts are spaced five miles apart. Too many would still die."

"Move everyone into the Cavalier Crook," another recommended, pointing to the southwest quadrant of the Fortress City. "The nobles won't like it, but their castle walls will provide added protection."

Kamron shook his head. "Against humans, maybe, but not when fighting the flying seith. Besides, packed that tight, our people would kill each other before the calahein even got a chance."

A younger lieutenant raised his hand.

"Yes?" Kamron said impatiently.

"Could we use the Rayders?"

Awkward silence fell over the room, every man looking at their general. Kamron shifted his sword belt, then pointed at the door. "Wait outside."

The young lieutenant immediately complied and shut the door.

"Any other suggestions," Kamron asked, "preferably not completely void of all common sense?"

"Draft more men into your army."

"Arm the civilians."

Both suggestions came at the same time, and Kamron liked them both. He nodded his head slowly. Together, they would make the perfect solution. He didn't have enough weapons in his armory to distribute them to the civilians, but he could send a proclamation among them. He could convince the civilians to act as soldiers. Make their own weapons from whatever they could find. Defend each other as if they were part of the same family. Become an active part of Itorea's defense.

"Very good," Kamron said, picking up the quill once more. "While I write a proclamation, why don't the rest of you take inventory in the armory. Distribute the bolts and ballistae spears among our battlements, but save the rest of the weapons as a gift from King Drogan. Every citizen will be a soldier by the end of this week."

"Yes, General," the men called with a salute, then began filing out the door.

"Oh, and send in the young lieutenant," Kamron added.

A few minutes later, only Kamron and the summoned lieutenant stood in the room.

"Yes, General?" the young man spoke timidly, his head bowed low and his fist over his heart.

"What's your name, Lieutenant?"

"Char." He cleared his throat. "Char Gemott. I didn't mean to—"

"Take two hundred men with you," Kamron interrupted, "and scout the west edge of the Perbeisea Forest. If the calahein intend to attack, I want to know about it."

Chapter 18

Perseverance

December had finally come, besieging Appernysia with blanketing snow and biting winds. Aron resisted the urge to hug his wool cloak. Shalán, on the other hand, was wrapped like a cocoon. She didn't need quick access to a sword, nor was she holding a glaive.

This is the most beautiful glaive I've ever seen, Aron thought, admiring yet again its perfect design of pure Beholder steel.

Halfway between Humsco and Toj—a fishing town—the first heavy snowstorm had draped over them. Wading through another foot of snow had been exhausting, slicing their progress in half to ten miles per day instead of twenty. An extra day had been wasted making up the distance. With only a couple hours of sunlight left, the combined residents of both villages had camped along the West River just north of Toj, while Aron and Shalán led the two delegate couples into the fishing town.

Trev and Anice were doing well enough, all things considered, but Nadjor and Laecha looked as exhausted as their villagers. They could barely lift their feet high enough to trudge through the deep snow. Aron moved slowly, not wanting to push them any harder than necessary.

During this part of their journey, Aron had learned from Snoom that a fallen member of their guard was from Humsco, an Appernysian by the name of Jareth. But neither Aron or Snoom thought that Humsco's villagers could handle such a report. At least not yet. The villagers were suffering enough already. News of Jareth's death could wait.

Ever the loving type, Shalán had commented many times on Pree's villagers and their selfless service to Humsco's suffering people. Aron acknowledged her observation, but wasn't about to praise them for it. Even after combining with Humsco, Pree's men still jabbed at him with insults. The Beholders' guard, on the other hand, had been absolutely loyal to the Marcs. This had surprised Aron, considering his defection from the Rayders, but he trusted in their faithfulness. When Channer offered to punish the disrespectors, Aron had considered it briefly before smiling and politely declining. The men of Pree were prideful and no amount of physical abuse would change their perspectives.

The Beholders' guard spent most of their time protecting everyone from outside threats, running patrols up and down their sides and flank. Little squabbles erupted now and then, mostly from people getting in each other's way, but never had the guard involved themselves. They just sat quietly on their horses and watched until both parties either worked it out themselves, or glanced up to check if anyone was watching and quickly returned to their own business when they locked eyes with the horsemen.

The greatest motivator of all had been the underlying calahein threat. It kept people working hard beyond the point of exhaustion, knowing that the farther they traveled, the safer they would be.

But Itorea was still three hundred miles away. Only the strongest would make it there alive.

$$* \quad * \quad * \quad * \quad *$$

The town of Toj was much larger than Pree and Humsco combined, with its own network of roads and communities of at least twenty thousand civilians. During warmer months, when the rivers weren't frozen, brave fishermen would travel down the wide Saap River on barges and navigate through its delta maze to the east point of the Kerod Cluster. A large port had been built there to hold their seaworthy vessels. These fishermen would disassemble their barges for other uses, swapping them instead for the fishing ships. They would spend months catching big game in the Asaras Sea and trading with Draege via a path through the mountains.

When Aron and his family had fled Roseiri, Toj had been the first town he considered joining. He liked its economy and change of scenery. In a town like Toj, he would have been able to stretch his restless legs. But a real danger was present in Toj, too. They traded with Humsco and Draege, and the caravan circled through it every year. His family would interact with people from all over the kingdom, people who had heard the rumors about his children in Roseiri. When Aron came to this realization, he had known that Pree and its independent economy was the only practical option left.

As they entered the town, Aron made no attempt to hide his weapons, and he instructed everyone else do the same. The people in Toj were used to seeing armed travelers. Hiding their weapons would be what drew suspicion. Sure, Aron wielded a glaive, but four Rayders would follow after him. If Toj couldn't handle his weapon, seeing Rayders would bring disaster.

Once they reached a packed road of snow, Aron brought Nadjor and Laecha forward to lead their group. Just as Trev had been their political contact with Humsco, Aron knew that Nadjor would provide the same in Toj, and on a much more personal level because of their people's regular interactions in trade.

Toj was strangely still, muffled by thick layers of snow. Nobody was in sight, but columns of smoke rose from engineered rows of brick chimneys. Just as in Pree, they had obviously heard nothing of the calahein. They were ignorant and unafraid. But scarcely populated, too. Half the buildings looked abandoned.

Nadjor led them through town to a quaint house at its south end, on the northern shore of the Saap River. "Kátaea is an elderly woman," Nadjor said as they approached the house, "so make sure to speak loudly, but make no mistake—her mind is as sharp as Aron's glaive. She will not tolerate disrespect, especially about her age. She's been the delegate of this town for fifty years."

"And what of her husband?" Aron asked.

"She never married," Nadjor replied, eyeing Aron judgmentally. "Some say that having a woman delegate is unnatural, breaking traditional conformity. I disagree with such shortsighted statements, as does this community. I've never met a person more respected by their people."

*　　*　　*　　*　　*

Their discussion was quick—and loud. Kátaea resisted the reports at first, but when they pulled her north on her sled to view the entirety of Pree and Humsco's populations on Toj's doorstep, a crowd of over five hundred souls, she began to see reason. Learning of Beholders and ghraefs defending their kingdom again brought a wide, toothless smile to her face. A town meeting was called and, illuminated by torches, Kátaea explained their precarious situation to her people.

"I wouldn't survive the journey," she called through toothless gums, "but I ask you to leave our village. Travel with them to Itorea and reinforce King Drogan's defenses."

For what must have been the first time in Kátaea's life, her villagers disobeyed. They refused to leave her behind, arguing that most of their men had already been drafted into the army. Despite Aron's urgings that every individual man played a vital role in battle, they wouldn't listen.

"Once spring melt is here," one of the villagers argued, "we will float down the Saap, then up to Itorea by sea. If the city still stands, we will gladly join the fight then, bringing all the fish we can catch along the way."

"But Serglo—" Kátaea started.

"Save your strength," Serglo cut in respectfully. "You will survive another winter, Kátaea Ann, and we are staying to make sure that happens. But they are welcome to join us, right, Kátaea?"

"Of course," the aged delegate confirmed.

"We have plenty of food and warm beds to spare," Serglo continued. "Your people are already spent. You won't survive the journey."

Trev placed his hand on the delegate's shoulder. "He's right, Nadjor. Stay here with your villagers. We'll see you in the spring. I'll explain your situation to King Drogan myself. He'll understand."

Tears filled Nadjor's eyes. His lips pulled tight, unable to speak. He only nodded his head and wrapped his arms around Trev.

"Thank you for your hospitality," Anice said in place of her husband. "We had already come to the conclusion that we would die along the way, but we had no choice. We are doomed either way." Her voice caught, and she paused to regain her composure. She took Kátaea's hand and kissed it. "Thank you. At least we will enjoy a brief respite before fate reaches us."

Kátaea hugged her. "You two will live with me."

"Wait here," Aron said as he took Shalán by her free hand and pulled her back toward their own camp. "We will let everyone know what you've decided."

Shalán whispered as they returned to their camp, holding a torch forward to light their path. "If the calahein attacks Toj . . ."

Aron squeezed her hand gently. "I know. All we can do is keep pressing forward. Maybe the people in Draege will see things differently."

Chapter 19

Banished

Tarek sat up on his bedroll, sore and stiff. The Rayders had not been allowed to leave the cobblestone road for three days, not even to answer nature's call. They had been forced to squat at the road's edge, in full view of everyone. The Appernysian footmen had been served an equal injustice, forced to remove all Rayder waste, be it human or horse. The resulting smell was already beginning to bother Tarek, and he was at the front of the line. He couldn't imagine the mess miles back.

He ate a quick meal of salted pork, offering a small bite to his starving horse. With the supply wagons five miles back, none of their horses were being fed anything more than dirty snow off the road. It infuriated Tarek to see their animals treated so unjustly, but he was quickly learning the powerlessness of his situation while traversing the city. Once they reached Itorea's hook, though, he was counting on better conditions.

On a more positive note, the civilians had finally given up on watching the Rayder parade. From what Tarek had seen, and from reports being passed up and down their ranks, not one Rayder had retaliated with violence. Many were shouting back, but the crowd's noise overpowered anything they said. Tarek had been surprised at the report. This passive display was uncharacteristic of anything he would have expected under Rayben Goldhawk's rule, and perhaps even when Omar was acting commander. The Rayders were changing. When Lon returned, he'd definitely argue they were becoming Taejan.

"And maybe he's right," Tarek said to his horse, his white mane stained with red tomato juice, "but the Taejans were respected by Appernysia." He patted the horse's neck. "We have a long way to go before that happens."

Once again, Tarek absently reached for the saddle horn and stuck his foot in the stirrup.

"My Commander," Lio called, a reminder about King Drogan's no horse-riding policy.

Tarek cursed and pulled his foot loose of the stirrup. He knew he should thank the lieutenant, but his heart wouldn't have been in it.

Their camp was in front of another three hundred foot wall running longitudinally through the middle of Itorea. Although Appernysian soldiers weren't supposed to speak with the Rayders, Tarek had begun conversing with the guards around him after the crowds had disappeared.

"So does this gate lead into the keep?" Tarek asked, stretching his back. The Appernysians had been rotating night shifts, but all of them were beginning to rouse for that day's march.

"We're only halfway to the keep," one soldier answered, a man Tarek had started to befriend. "This wall separates the east and west halves of Itorea's blade. We're about to enter the farmland and livestock preserve. Three hundred and forty-two thousand acres of land, all fed by the same type of freshwater aqueducts that supply the west half."

"Seriously, Leland," Tarek jested. "You need to get more sleep. It's unhealthy to stay up all night memorizing pointless facts."

Leland laughed. "My family manages the collection and distribution of the crops. It's my responsibility to memorize pointless facts."

Tarek sobered. "I'd bet every soldier here would rather be doing that than pointlessly marching to the wrong side of this city."

He touched his fingers to his brand. "May the Jaeds watch over your family."

"Thank you, Commander Tarek." Leland saluted in return, a fist over his heart.

Tarek nodded and faced the fifty-foot opening ahead, waiting for their signal from Drogan. The king and his escort had camped on the other side of the wall. Its access was rigged with the same four-gate system as the perimeter wall's entrance, a defense prepared against a calahein invasion.

"This massive wall is ridiculous," he said. "If you get pushed back this far, there won't be anyone left alive to defend your crops."

The soldiers surrounding Tarek, both Appernysian and Rayder, acknowledged the commander's observation with wary silence.

* * * * *

When the Rayders entered the agricultural preserve of Itorea, half of the Appernysian soldiers stayed behind, leaving a three-deep line on each side instead of six. Leland was among those who continued.

"They are returning to defend the west wall," Leland commented. "I will earn my leave once you safely reach the hook. With the potential of more people entering the city, King Drogan personally asked for my help managing the storehouses through the winter." He pointed to the king's escort riding two hundred yards ahead.

"Managing," Lio asked, "or protecting?"

Leland shrugged. "Probably some of both. People are bound to get desperate, at least until winter ends. This calahein business has seen to that."

"Indeed it has," Tarek observed. "I get it. Everything we're doing seems like overkill, all based off of one dying tradesman's words and the report of a small group of scouts. I'd be skeptical myself, had I not seen Lon's eyes when he reported on his skirmish with kelsh last summer."

"Your Beholder fought the calahein?"

"He did." Tarek grew quiet, recounting the rest of Lon's report. He hadn't really fought the calahein, so much as desperately tried to protect himself and his squad. The ghraefs, if that's what they really were, had done the actual killing and driven the calahein away.

"Was it that terrible?" Leland asked in response to Tarek's silence.

Tarek nodded. "A good man died that day. Riyen Stotritten, a member of Lon's squad and one of the best archers I've ever seen." Tarek turned to address the Appernysian more directly, hoping he would heed his counsel. "Don't underestimate the calahein, Leland. They are vicious—without mercy or reason. They won't stop until everyone is dead."

* * * * *

Two days later, the Rayders crossed another wooden drawbridge— over the top of a moat one hundred feet wide—and through another four-gate passage into Itorea's keep.

All of the city's excess water had been dumping into a stone-lined channel that flowed through the city's center. The cobblestone road ran along the northern edge of this channel, and the Rayders had followed it all the way to the keep.

After living for so long in the swampy Exile, the Rayders had become experts at water flow management, so it was with high compliments that Tarek acknowledged the ingenuity behind Itorea's creation. They had traveled fifty miles over an uneven plateau with swells and valleys, yet the deep water maintained a constant surge east toward the keep. At times the channel flowed across aqueducts of its own, while other times wedges had been cut through the land to open a path.

The cobblestone road, on the other hand, usually followed the natural curves of the land. More than once Tarek had led his horse down into a valley, staring up at the bridged waterway and cursing, knowing he'd have to hike up the other side again.

This constant rush of water eventually dumped into the moat lining the west wall of the keep. The wall surrounding the keep rose another fifty feet at this point, providing extra protection to the city's center. Yet even at three hundred and fifty feet high, the west wall of the keep couldn't hide the five-hundred foot watchtowers positioned behind its north and south corners. These colossal watchtowers had been placed sporadically along the perimeter wall, too, providing extra viewing distance beyond Itorea's borders.

Tarek sighed. Again, the defenses were impressive, but against the calahein? He just didn't know how effective they'd be. If only he and his men had been allowed to protect the west wall. They'd make sure the defenses would hold.

Drogan's castle was built five miles inland, halfway between the east and west walls of the keep, yet the king didn't stop there. He continued riding east with his escort, leading the Rayders toward the hook, as promised.

When the Rayders passed in front of the castle, hundreds of ragged men appeared under armed guard. It was with great delight that Tarek saw the King's Cross brand on their right temples. These were his brothers that had been captured during their infiltration diversion under Rayben Goldhawk's rule. Tarek had assumed the Rayder prisoners were executed once Taeja had been taken. An armored Appernysian soldier shouted an order, and the prisoners joined the rest of the Rayders.

But Tarek's joy was cautionary. He had never heard of a situation where a prisoner was released without some sort of payment or expectation. King Drogan would undoubtedly use this act of kindness as an attempt to manipulate the Rayders in the future.

A meager audience of Appernysian humanitarians also awaited them—in front of a small army guarding the castle's entrance. The few appearing on the front steps held food, blankets, and medicine in their arms. They rushed out past the Appernysian escorts to gift the Rayders with much needed supplies. Kaylen Shaw was among them.

"Any word from Lon or Mellai?" she asked.

"Not yet," Tarek replied, taking a loaf of bread. "I haven't seen you since Sylbie. Where have you been?"

Kaylen frowned and looked down the line of Rayder soldiers.

Tarek dropped the bread onto the snow for his horse, then took the supplies from Kaylen and handed them to Lio. "Distribute these, Lieutenant." He then turned to Kaylen and took one of her hands between both of his own. "What troubles you, Kaylen? This seems bigger than Lon."

"Much bigger," she admitted. "My whole life, I've hated the Rayders, and I hated Lon last July when I heard he was fighting for you. So much time and energy wasted on a misinformed position. Now that I meet you and your men, I understand why Lon loves you. You are good people, better in many ways that our own soldiers." She glanced back at the nearby Appernysian men and gave them an apologetic shrug.

Tarek couldn't help but laugh when Leland refused her apology, instead agreeing with her wholeheartedly.

"What a tangled mess we've caught ourselves up in," Tarek observed, a broad smile on his bearded face. "I welcome your candor, Kaylen, and I see why Lon loves you, too. Don't give up on him yet. He's been fighting for a cause much bigger than anyone in Pree. Little did any of us know—including Lon—that your Beholder was preparing us for this moment. He sacrificed his relationship with you and his family to save us all."

Kaylen pulled her hand free to give Tarek a hug. Lio took a step forward, his hand on his sword, but Tarek waved him away and returned Kaylen's embrace. From the way she held him, Tarek knew she had been fighting with her feelings for quite some time. Unable to find the words, she was apologizing the only way she knew how—service and affection.

"Your father made the same sacrifice," Kaylen said, wiping away the tears spotting her cheeks. "Did Lon tell you about that, how Myron saved Lon's family?"

"Indeed he did."

Kaylen stepped back and dipped her head, her arms hugging her waist. "Thank you, Commander Tarek. May the Jaeds watch over you."

Tarek nodded in return. "And may they see you and Lon together again." He took hold of his horse's lead rope and followed after Drogan.

"Wait!" Kaylen called, forcing her way through the soldiers to his position. "I have news for you! While I was on the perimeter wall, I saw Lieutenant Wade escorting your civilians from Taeja. They must have reached Sylbie by now. It sounds like King Drogan will have them wait there until these men have finished escorting you, then they'll return and do the same with the rest of your people."

Tarek nodded again and resumed following the king's escort. *I sure hope so,* he thought.

The Rayders followed Drogan across the keep, through another gateway, and finally into the hook. By that time, the sun had set and left them in stifling darkness, with thick clouds blocking all light from the firmament.

With only torches to illuminate their way, Tarek continued to follow the path after the king's escort. They traveled quicker than normal, and Tarek found himself disoriented when he caught sight of another massive wall ahead. *Another wall?*

When Drogan and his escort passed through another gateway, Tarek began to grow suspicious. "What is this?" he asked his escorts.

The Appernysians faced forward, marching rigidly with their hands tight on their weapons. Tarek stopped, halting the progress of his men. Even in torchlight, he could see sweat running down some of the soldiers' faces. They were terrified.

"Leland," Tarek continued, "where are we?" He could see the young soldier's torn expression, until Leland finally drew his sword and faced the Rayder commander.

"I'm sorry," he said, tossing his sword into the snow. "I had no idea until now, but I won't enforce this. King Drogan is leading you out of the north gate of Itorea into the Gaurelic Waste."

The men surrounding Leland balked at his insubordination, but eventually followed his example and disarmed themselves.

"It's your choice, Commander Tarek," Leland continued. "The Gaurelic Waste isn't as boggy during the winter, but you'll still be sleeping on ice."

"You are an honorable man," Tarek replied, pulling his glaive from his horse's saddle. Grinding steel echoed down the Rayder line as his men drew their weapons. Many Appernysians recoiled. A few even dropped to their hands and knees, frantically digging through the snow for their swords.

Ignoring the mayhem, Tarek flipped his glaive in his hand and extended the butt-end of the staff to Leland. "Please accept this gift as a token of my appreciation."

Leland took the glaive, then picked up his sword and placed it back in his scabbard.

Tarek pointed at the cluster of plate-armored knights under the gate. "I need to speak with your king about this course of action."

The anxiety in Leland's face returned. "He's not here. I saw him enter the donjon when we crossed through the keep. Only his escort stayed to lead the way."

Tarek thought deeply over the choice before him. To stay meant to annihilate Drogan's escort and sow leaderless chaos across Itorea, while crossing the Nellis River into the Waste would only impact his own people. Although Drogan had relied on the deceit hidden behind partial truths, the king had led them through Itorea on a six day march. Even in the Waste, the Rayders were farther from the threat than anyone else. His people were as safe as they ever would be.

For the sake of humanity, the choice was obvious, though Tarek's pride tugged at his will.

"We will depart peacefully until your king summons us, then not even the calahein will be able to withstand our fury. Now go get my people from Sylbie, and bring them safely to us."

Chapter 20

Blockade

Aron clenched his fists to stifle his desperation, but really wanted to punch a hole through the perimeter wall of Draege and drag all of its people to Itorea. "I've spent my whole life arguing that the Rayders were misguided and stubborn, but now I see Appernysians are just as prideful. You will sentence this city to destruction if you hide in your caves."

"Then so be it," a man replied. He stood tall, his thick arms folded across his broad chest. "We haven't heard from anyone in Jaul for a month, which means the trade route is no longer safe. Our path to Itorea is blocked. Would you have me lead my entire city across open plains?"

"Yes!" Aron shouted. "Don't you see, Thuan? Not only has your king ordered you to Itorea, but your own survival demands it. I'm not denying that your defenses are formidable, but not nearly enough to resist the calahein. You're responsible for over forty thousand people here. Imagine the strength your numbers could add to Itorea."

"More strain than strength," Thuan countered. "Itorea is not as roomy as everyone believes. We would be packed in like the pebbles at the bottom of Drae Lake, unable to move or breathe. We are a city of riches and no stranger to attacks. I know how to adequately defend my people."

"Your experience doesn't matter," Aron shouted again. "They'll sweep over your defenses and kill everyone, including your women and children."

Thuan shook his head. "I don't think so. Now turn around, Master Aron, and lead your own people to Itorea. I will do what's best for mine."

With that final statement, the man disappeared through the gate into his city. It locked shut behind him, and crossbowmen immediately appeared atop the forty-foot stone wall. They aimed at Aron, encouraging him to obey their leader's order.

"He'll lead you to your deaths!" Aron shouted at the men, then turned and stomped down the stone causeway, away from Draege's perimeter wall.

*　　*　　*　　*　　*

"I don't blame them," Shalán responded after hearing Aron's report. She knelt next to Nybol, examining his frostbitten feet. "They're just doing what they think is best."

Aron stabbed his glaive into the snow. "Our children trusted me to bring everyone to Itorea, Shalán. Three settlements later, we are but a company of ten families. Hardly a noteworthy contribution to King Drogan's army."

"Plus one," Reese Arbogast added. Despite many pleas from Nadjor and Laecha, he had chosen to continue with the Marcs. His reasoning was understandable—to share the full story of Theiss's sacrifice with Mellai when she returned.

Aron nodded at the young man. "Even with you, I have still failed. I'll be the one held responsible for tens of thousands of deaths."

"The Beholders said to save as many people as we can," Nybol observed. "You've done your best, Master Aron. Now let it go."

Aron balked at Nybol's response, unsure of how to respond. It had been the first not-unkind thing any of the villagers had said to him since they left Pree.

"Don't be frettin' over things you can't control," Scut added. "We might be angry with your lies—furious, even, especially about my Kaylen—but we're not fools. We've seen you and Shalán's sacrifices to keep us alive, and who knows the risks your Beholders are taking. Don't be misunderstandin' intolerance as distrust."

Trev clapped a hand on Aron's shoulder. "You deserved punishment for your deceit, and I think your full sentence has finally been served. Now find that confidence of yours, Master Aron, and see us safely to Itorea. We will follow you unequivocally."

*　*　*　*　*

Three weeks of travel had taken their toll on Pree's villagers. Elora and Hadon also had frostbitten feet, and Ramsey's arm was in a sling after wrenching his elbow trying to fix his wagon. Everyone's faces were sunburned, with dead skin flaking from their chapped lips. Yet, Aron knew these villagers would fight all the way into Itorea. They had not survived generations on their own in Pree by luck alone, but through hard work and unquenchable willpower. And now they trusted Aron with their lives. It was because of this that he called a brief council with the Beholders' guard.

"Thuan said he hasn't heard from Jaul for a month," Aron relayed to the seven men. "What do you think? Has the trade route been overrun?"

"His timing matches our own experiences," Channer answered. "If what Thuan says is true, then Réxura was destroyed at the same time Jaul became silent. Perhaps the calahein have moved beyond the Vidarien Mountains to infest the Briyél Forest."

"It would be a strategically wise move," Snoom added, "effectively cutting off the Western Valley from reinforcing King Drogan's forces."

"Then we're running out of time," Aron said. He scanned the northern horizon. Even from his elevated position in the Kerod Cluster, he couldn't see the forest. But it was there, sixty miles north and twice as wide, wrapping Casconni Lake in a boycott of death.

"How do we get past?" Shalán asked quietly. Her eyes were worried, but determined.

That was the question that plagued Aron's mind. "Let's weigh our options. What if we circle west in the perimeter of the forest and use it to bypass Réxura?"

"We'd have to find a crossing over the Pearl River," Snoom answered.

"And travel dangerously close to Réxura again," Channer added.

Aron nodded. "So option one isn't feasible. What about swinging east, to the shores of the Asaras Sea?" He pointed at the Pearl River, a thick layer of solid ice covering its surface. "This will be easy enough to cross, but we'd still have to find a crossing over the Casconni River. On the other hand, we'd be on the opposite side of the Briyél Forest, as far away from Réxura as possible."

"Better," Duncan commented, "but not ideal. I used to play in that region as a child. On the south side of the Casconni River, there's a gap between the forest and the sea, probably twenty miles wide. If we move further east, that would leave us exposed on the open plains, easy for the calahein to spot and destroy without Beholders to protect us. That might be worse.

"But if we cut through the southern forest, we couldn't cross the lake without boats or barges. Even if we could, we'd move deep inside the Briyél Forest on the northern shore. The calahein might dwell there."

"*Might* in both cases," Aron repeated, "but only the river crossing is a possibility. I suppose that's an improvement, though. Any other ideas?"

Shalán cleared her throat. "Kátaea spoke of—wait, no, it was Serglo—he said they could travel down the Saap River, then journey north by sea. They must have a dock down there, on the other side of these mountains. We could take one boat and bypass the forest altogether."

"Good idea," Aron said, "but does anyone here know how to sail a boat?"

No one responded.

"Before we start asking villagers," Aron continued, "let's think about this. We'd have to travel around the Kerod Cluster to an unknown destination. That journey alone could take a week, plus the time loading a boat and figuring out how to man it. There goes another couple of days. Then once out at sea—"

"We'd probably sink the boat," Shalán cut in. "It won't work. Maybe if Toj's villagers had joined us, but it's not practical on our own."

"I wish it were," Aron replied, rubbing his sore thighs. "A boat ride sounds really nice right now." He looked up at the guard. "Any other ideas, besides giving up and returning to Toj?"

"Another ghraef ride would be fantastic," Shalán said, smiling as she shouldered her husband. "Even if Bromax and Huirk had to carry us one by one, it would be the fastest and safest solution."

"Indeed it would," Aron agreed, "but Lon and Mellai have an entire kingdom to protect. We need to assume we're on our own."

"Option two, then?" Snoom asked.

Aron nodded. "We'll try our luck with the Casconni River crossing."

Shalán took Aron's hand. "And may the Jaeds protect us."

Chapter 21

Infested

"**B**ut you didn't enter the forest yourself?" Kamron asked, drumming his fingers impatiently on the guardhouse table.

"I collected and analyzed their reports," Char said, his dry tongue fat in his mouth. "My men traveled seventy miles into the Perbeisea Forest and found no sign of—"

Kamron slapped his hand on the table. "You already said that. Stop your mumbling and answer my question. Did *you* enter the forest or not?"

"No, General."

"Then congratulations," Kamron spat. "You've earned an even higher responsibility."

Char's face flushed pale. "General?"

"Since your findings show no sign of calahein movement," Kamron said, standing to pace the floor, "I feel reassured that we can help Beholder Mellai gather the outlying villages into Itorea. Jaul is the closest town that hasn't been destroyed for sure, so that is where you and twenty of your finest soldiers will journey first."

"Yes, General, but—"

"But what?" Kamron interrupted, stepping toe-to-toe with the young lieutenant.

Visible trembling was Char's only response.

Kamron grabbed Char under his jaw. "Let me make it extra clear for you, just in case you didn't understand. Bring back everyone from Jaul, or don't bother coming back at all. And remember," he paused to take a deep breath, "a lieutenant's responsibility is to lead his men, not use them as a shield."

* * * * *

Char returned to the Perbeisea Forest and gathered the first twenty men that he encountered. "We've been sent on an errand for our king," he told them, doing his best to sound confident, despite the terror he felt inside. He knew this was a suicide mission, but he had no choice. "Our group will travel to Jaul and bring everyone safely home."

An hour later, and well-stocked for the one hundred and eighty-mile journey, they were cutting south through the Perbeisea Forest. "To bypass Réxura as far away as possible," Char told his men.

While his explanation was true, Char also felt insecure when surrounded by the six hundred-foot Furwen trees. Any number of beasts, calahein or not, could live in those canopies. He wanted to hurry through the forest as quickly as possible until they reached the open fields west of Wegnas. At least there he could see the enemy coming.

They searched the shores of the Prime River for a spot where it had been completely frozen, but the river was too wide and swift for much ice to form. Eventually, though, they did find a crossing. A Furwen tree had finally succumbed to its size and fallen over the river. Its wide trunk—over sixty feet in diameter—acted as a bridge, making the crossing easy for the men and their horses before its canopy of branches even began. Their horses' iron-shod hooves clacked on the rock-like trunk as if they were traveling on Itorea's cobblestone road.

Even with the shortcut, Char had to endure the forest for two full days before he could breathe the fresh air of the open plains.

Another three days' ride brought them to the northern edge of the Briyél Forest. Despite Char's dislike for dense woods, he decided that the forest would provide essential cover for their journey around the northwest shores of Casconni Lake. Réxura would be closer now than at any other point in their journey, a mere fifty miles northwest of the lake.

A day into their travels through the Briyél Forest, Char was feeling rather confident in his ability to navigate while off the beaten path. His anxieties started to dissipate, as did the worries of his twenty men. They talked casually as they rode, often singing and laughing at each other's jokes. They were only a day or two away from Jaul and all seemed well.

Then Char realized they hadn't seen or heard any signs of wildlife for an entire day, ever since they entered Briyél.

Courage fled, replaced instead by mortal fear. He immediately ordered his men to retreat. They backtracked frantically over their trail through the snow. Everyone held a spanned crossbow, ready to shoot the first critter that moved. Char could only pray it wouldn't be calahein.

Less than an hour after Char called for a retreat, the forest began collapsing around them—quite literally. It started with a mature pine—ninety feet tall and needles as thick as rice pudding—dropping on top of the three leading men and their horses. Char's men cried out, buried under the spruce's canopy. The young lieutenant barely heard them while a net of other trees crashed to the ground, until only he and two other soldiers sat uninjured on their horses.

The fallen trees had created a tight circle around them, leaving only one exit about six feet wide. In the middle of that exit stood a solitary kelsh, the ground troop of the calahein. The three survivors raised their crossbows and shot the hideous beast in its broad chest. The armor-piercing bolts sank deep into its red fur, but the kelsh stood tall, growling menacingly while it reached up and removed the bolts with its three-fingered claws. Then the beast glared at them with its crazed eyes, snorting through its flat snout while its tiny ears twitched on the sides of its head. It made no move to attack, but seemed content to block their escape.

Char's breath stuttered out of his terrified lungs in bursts, creating little pockets of moisture in the frigid air. He dropped his crossbow and drew his sword, readying himself to die for King Drogan. This one kelsh had not pushed over all the trees by itself. Other calahein lurked about. Char knew this, as did his two surviving men who followed their lieutenant's example, drawing their own swords.

"Charge!" Char shouted, kicking the sides of his horse. He rushed forward, intent on trampling the kelsh, but never had the chance. With abnormally long arms, the kelsh grabbed a foreleg of Char's horse, whipped the poor animal through the air, and impaled it on the branches of a fallen pine tree. Char toppled off the horse and landed on his back in the snow, just a few feet behind the kelsh.

While he listened to the tortured screams of his dying men, Char looked up at the branches overhead, wondering how long it had taken the trees to grow so tall. Hundreds of years of effort, at least, just to be thrown down by kelsh. The young lieutenant sighed. He had no idea how many calahein had come to Appernysia, but he was certain of one thing. They were intent on destroying his entire kingdom, just as they had felled the trees, and there was little the puny humans could do to stop them.

Only a miracle would secure Appernysia's victory.

The lieutenant felt a large paw reach underneath and take hold of his leather armor, lifting him into the air. He was now hovering directly in front of the kelsh, face to face with its blood-splattered snout and teeth. With a final cry of courage, Char stabbed and slashed the kelsh's chest repeatedly with his sword, until the beast's double row of fangs wrapped around his head and freed him from this world.

Chapter 22

Indestructible

Many stones, varying in size and shape, circled Huirk. One by one, he smashed them with his bone-tipped tail, then huffed and returned once again to his nest.

"Another total failure," Mellai growled.

Lon placed a reassuring hand on her shoulder. His sister's skill with True Sight was phenomenal, but her growth had been natural—almost effortless. Lon, on the other hand, had suffered through every aspect of his power, accepting his failures along with his successes. Consequently, while he evaluated their experimentation, Mellai only despaired. What must have been weeks of disappointment was wearing her patience perilously thin.

"This has to be doable," Lon said, "so let's review and try something else."

"Nothing works. How's that for accurate?" Mellai breathed out her frustration. "Remind me of the point of all this? Why is this necessary, when our whole kingdom is in danger? They're fleeing to Itorea and we're hiding in a cave, playing with rocks."

Lon eyed Huirk, hoping her words didn't anger the ghraef. "Llen must want us in Itorea more than we want to be there ourselves, yet he ordered us to stay. He has to know something that we don't, so I'll trust him above my own anxieties."

Mellai grumbled, but Lon ignored her as he munched on the cooked leg of a rabbit Huirk had caught for them to eat. "Take a look at this new one." He picked up a black fist-sized rock that Bromax had brought into the cave as part of a collection the Beholders requested.

"Obsidian?" Mellai asked, but Lon knew otherwise.

Lon shook his head. "It's too dull, and much heavier." He tossed half of the rock to Mellai. "Heavier than even granite, don't you think?"

She caught it with her essence and pulled it into her hand. "Probably. What's your point?"

"We've been testing the wrong kinds of rocks, Mel. Huirk has shattered the hardest rocks, like diamond or obsidian, but this one only split in half. Why?"

Mellai raised her eyebrows, glaring at her brother with obvious annoyance.

"This rock is heavier," Lon continued, "even though it's the same volume as all the other rocks. Kind of thicker, if that makes sense. Density is the key, not hardness."

Mellai's head tilted, her expression transforming to curiosity. "So we make them thicker, and they'll become stronger?"

"I think so, but how—"

Mellai yanked the rock from Lon's hand with her power. "Grab more of this out of the pile," she called while she knitted the two halves into one solid piece again. Lon smiled with satisfaction and retrieved six more similar rocks. Mellai took them and placed them on the ground next to her own.

"I hope this works," Mellai said, then began pulling the mass from one rock and weaving it into the other, taking care not to manipulate the host's size. Once finished, she proceeded to weave the remaining rocks into the host. At least that's what it looked like to Lon, and his apprehension replaced his sister's frustration as the process became increasingly difficult for her, until there was so little space in the host's mass that in her attempts, Mellai began to supply the rock with energy instead of matter. It began glowing brighter, but Mellai immediately withdrew the excess energy and released it into the air.

Lon stepped forward to lift the resulting black rock from the ground with his bare hand. Just as he suspected, it was far too heavy to hoist, even though it was no larger than an infant's head. This was becoming a regular pattern for them. He supplied the logic and she supplied the skill. It would be nice for once to accomplish a difficult task with True Sight before his sister.

"How about some help, Huirk?" Lon called, pointing to the dense stone.

The ghraef lazily sauntered over and batted the rock with his paw. Rather than tumbling across the cave, it only flopped onto another side. Huirk's eyes widened, then he gripped it with his paw and with a little bit of growling, raised it above his own head. He smiled at the two Beholders, his tongue lolling out the side of his mouth.

"Yes, you're very strong," Mellai teased. "Now drop it."

The ghraef obeyed. The stone hit the cave floor with a resounding thud, barely bouncing. Without waiting for further instruction, Huirk twisted and swept his bone-tipped tail into the air. Lon and Mellai dove out of the way, barely dodging the ghraef's bludgeon weapon as he bashed the rock.

An ear-shattering crack reverberated off the walls, followed by howls of pain. This was no act. Huirk had fallen onto his side, scratching his foreleg claws across the cave floor while grimacing, but the rest of his body remained rigid.

Lon gaped at the ghraef's tail. The bone sphere had cracked wide open. While Mellai tended to Huirk's injury, Lon turned his attention to the rock. It was partially sunken into the slate rock floor, but it hadn't chipped, nor was any surface scuffed. It was still perfectly intact.

"You did it, Mel," Lon whispered, stepping forward to stroke the undamaged boulder.

"That's great," Mellai answered half-heartedly, more focused on repairing Huirk's injury. "Now you figure it out. And hurry up. We're running out of time."

*　*　*　*　*

Mellai reassured her brother, carefully watching as he knitted a broken rock back together. "Stay focused," she called. "Don't try to force it. Let them blend together, just like you said."

She felt her impatience growing, but Mellai reminded herself that Lon hadn't been tutored daily by a Jaed. Although he had mastered a few techniques, his overall skill was still rudimentary. And it wasn't his fault. Given time, he would become just as skilled. He just needed practice.

"Good enough," Lon said, withdrawing his essence and sitting down, legs crossed.

Mellai pulled the rock to herself and examined it. Tiny fissures still ran through portions of the weave, but just like Lon proclaimed, it was good enough for now. "Alright," she said, "time for the true test. Let's make this one indestructible, too. Want to use that heavy black rock again?"

Lon shook his head. "We're out. How about limestone instead? If we do it correctly, it shouldn't matter what the stone is, right?"

"I have no idea, but I'm willing to try." She pulled a few fist-sized rocks from their pile and laid them side by side. "I'll start, then you take over when I say. Got it?"

"Of course," he replied with a weak smile.

"I don't want anyone else getting hurt," Mellai continued, "so I'll protect us with an energy shield. You'll have to work through it."

"We tried that before. You kept cutting off my access."

"Partly my fault," she agreed, "but there's a trick to it on your end, too. I'll choose to let you in, and you have to allow yourself to flow through. I don't know how else to explain it. That's how I penetrate my own barriers."

Lon raised an eyebrow. "Just flow through?"

"Mm-hmm. Let's try that first." She created a small barrier between herself and her twin, but eased her mind, permitting his essence to bypass it. Lon extended his own essence to it and struck the barrier.

"*Flow* through it," she said again calmly.

"Just flow through it," Lon teased as he reattempted. "Like wind through the trees. Like a waterfall into a pond. Like Tarek's good looks into my twin sister's heart."

"Grow up, Lon."

Lon laughed. "You know that you like him. When I connect to your emotions, I can feel—" With a burst of light, Lon's essence poured through Mellai's energy shield, only to be cut off again just as quickly.

"Whoa!" Lon called. "Did you see that?"

"I *felt* that," Mellai answered. When Lon attempted to link their emotions while they both used True Sight, Mellai had felt a distinct awareness, like a tingle in her brain. It was disconcerting, much more than when she spoke with the trees. Her twin brother wasn't just in her mind. He was a part of it.

"Forget the shield for a second," Mellai said. "Just focus on me and try that again. Feel for my emotions as if you weren't using True Sight, but don't let go of your power."

Mellai needed no cue to know when he reached out to her. There was no visible connection through their vision of True Sight, but she immediately felt that tingle in her brain again. This time, she answered, reaching out for her brother in return. *This is so weird,* she thought.

It was Lon who recoiled this time, jerking back and dismissing True Sight. "How'd you do that?"

"The same as you," she answered. "My brain kind of itches now. You?"

"No, no," Lon answered, leaning forward and summoning his power again. "I heard you, Mel. 'This is so weird.' Right?"

"That's impossible," Mellai replied at first, but then she remembered. Llen had spoken to her mind on many occasions. It was obviously possible, and they had just figured out how.

"Want to try again?" Mellai asked.

Lon nodded. "Can ghraefs fly?"

"Alright, but let me go first this time. When you feel my presence, reach for my emotions.

This is crazy! Lon shouted in her mind once they had connected.

I know, right? Now we know how to talk without Huirk or Bromax hearing us.

Oh, secret stuff. Like we're spies?

Don't be daft, Mellai thought, rolling her eyes. *For real, though, this could be helpful. I could sense your emotions from Pree all the way to the Exile. It was difficult, but I could do it.*

Lon's eyes grew big. *We can communicate across Appernysia, no matter where we are!*

Mellai nodded. *We'll just have to both be using True Sight.*

Very helpful, Lon agreed. *We'll just have to figure out a time of day when we both summon our power. Like a daily update.*

Sounds good, once we're in a place where we can actually keep track of time again.

Seriously.

Mellai used her power to create another energy shield. *Let's try this again.*

Lon extended his essence and with no resistance at all, slipped through Mellai's wall. She raised one rock into the air and wrapped it and its resting companions with a dome shield. *Now combine the rocks.*

He concentrated on weaving each subsequent rock into the limestone Mellai held aloft. It was more difficult for him at first.

He supplied energy instead of matter, which Mellai would have to absorb into her shield, but he eventually succeeded and slowly blended the rocks into one.

Mellai noticed that even though the limestone's mass grew, her ability to keep it in the air didn't ebb. This was the first time she had considered the limitlessness of her power, and she shared her thoughts with Lon.

Then why don't we just drop a mountain on the calahein's heads? Lon replied, just as intrigued. *I mean it, Mel. A literal mountain.*

"Because the calahein nest is below the soil," Llen spoke aloud, his glorious essence floating high in the cavern and penetrating every corner of the room. "I protect this world's energies, Beholders, and I forbid such a rash act with limited results."

"How do you do that?" Lon said, releasing his emotional connection to his sister. "Have you been here the whole time eavesdropping, and just now chose to appear to us?"

Llen's form slowly lowered to hover just above the ground. "I live in a different realm, Lon Marcs, where all essence flows after withdrawing from your mortal world. As a Jaed, I am one of few permitted to move between realms. Yes, I have been listening to your conversation, and for good reason. Your words are irrational."

"We understand," Mellai said, attempting to temper the confrontation. "We became too excited over what we could do. So counsel us. How can we be sure not to abuse our power?"

Llen's glowing eyes maintained their intensity. "True Sight is not a tool of convenience. It is a resource, only to be used in times of need. Every time you act with True Sight, you are manipulating some portion of this world. Do not change it unnecessarily."

"Then how do we fight the calahein?" Lon asked. "They hide in shadows and ambush us when we least expect it. For all of their kind we've killed, two entire civilizations have been destroyed and three of our own guard. We are losing this war." By the time he finished speaking, Lon's cheeks were hot, his speech strained, and his eyes brimming with tears.

"I understand," Llen said, his eyes softening. "The calahein destroy everything they touch, affecting both our realms. But do not despair, Lon Marcs. You are more adequately equipped to battle them than you think. After just over a month together, you have discovered one of the Beholders' greatest secrets, a talent that few ever developed. Lon and Mellai Marcs, you have been using synergy."

Mellai glanced at Huirk, wondering if the ghraefs already knew about synergy, but Huirk had fallen asleep. *Probably from the pain,* Mellai remarked after connecting with Lon's mind to maintain quiet for her recovering ghraef. She then directed her attention to the Jaed. *Synergy?*

"Yes," Llen continued. "It is a difficult concept to explain, but I will try. Lon, think back to your life in Pree. Remember building the corral for Dawes, how you and your father were capable of completing it in one day. Compare that to your efforts building the house for Kaylen Shaw."

Lon visibly flinched at the Jaed's mention of what could only be his worst memory, but Mellai gratefully noted that he maintained his connection with her.

The house was much harder to complete, Lon answered, *but I also had to haul every tree a mile after I felled it.*

"True, but you miss my point. While laboring in companionship, you must admit that every task becomes significantly easier."

Lon nodded. *Yes.*

Llen's voice slowed, deepening in intensity. "Some believe this a byproduct of social interaction, but they do not fully understand what is truly at work."

One man alone can lift a solitary boulder, Mellai thought, quoting her father, *but with another he can carry four.*

"Correct," Llen answered, "but your statement is more than just a statement on functional relationships. There are very real metaphysical interactions taking place. When energies work together, mathematics no longer apply."

One plus one is literally greater than two, Lon thought, his hand tugging at the stubble on his unshaven face.

The Jaed's eyes flared bright. "Exactly."

My head hurts, Mellai thought. She had never been much of a fan of philosophy, and these two were speaking in riddles.

"Allow me to demonstrate." Llen relocated the two unbreakable boulders they had just created. The black stone he set in front of Mellai, and the limestone by Lon. He then removed matter from both stones, storing their excesses as one swirling mass above his glowing hand.

"The stones should be manageable," he finally said. "Lift them with your hands."

Only with considerable effort was Mellai capable of raising the black rock from the cave floor. She held it aloft for just a few seconds, then dropped it again. A second later, Lon dropped the limestone, his chest heaving from his exertion.

"Observe," Llen said, using his free hand to move the two rocks together and knit them as one. "Did I add any extra matter to these boulders, Mellai?"

She shook her head.

"Then the two of you should be able to lift them together. Try."

The twins each took hold of the rock's sides.

Ready? Lon thought. *Lift!*

Not only were they able to lift the morphed rock, but they did it with relative ease. Mellai furrowed her brow and stared at her brother. He smiled in return.

"Now to prove my point," Llen commented, then slowly began adding matter back into the combined rocks. Mellai could feel the rock becoming heavier and she matched its weight with her own exertions.

Don't you dare drop it, Lon, she thought, fearing for the safety of her toes.

No problem, Lon answered, veins bulging from his neck.

"Together, you can carry the entire weight of both boulders," Llen said, then lifted the mass from Lon and Mellai, relieving them of their burden.

Mellai's breathing was labored as she glanced between the Jaed, Lon, and the boulder. *That shouldn't be possible.*

But it is, Lon replied. *One plus one equals more than two. Get it now?*

Slowly, it registered in her mind. I guess so. *Together, Lon and I can do things we could never do on our own.*

Times two, Lon added, smiling.

"A crude, but accurate enough description," Llen replied. "Now consider these same factors of synergy while using True Sight. Your combined power is no longer 'times two,' as Lon explained, but exponentially higher. Functioning as one, there is nothing you cannot accomplish. Think about this, Beholders, and the value therein."

We will, Mellai answered. *Thank you for this knowledge, Llen, and the hope it brings.* She turned to her brother. *Maybe we'll be able to defeat the calahein after all.*

Chapter 23

Unaided

For what must have been hours after Llen departed, Lon and Mellai practiced their new skill on the remaining assortment of rocks. They refused to leave anything to chance when the time came for their ghraefs' ceremony. The bonding had to be perfect if the tail crystals were to be used as weapons. Soon there were only a few boulders left on the ground, all absolutely indestructible—outside of Beholder manipulation, of course. Some they had created alone, others synergistically, and they had even perfected blending different styles of rocks into one, as they would have to do with the crystals and the ghraefs' tails.

Mellai teased Huirk, asking him to test their work again, but the ghraef found her comment far from funny. He yawned and licked his chops before turning around and dozing.

"I feel bad for him," Lon said as he used his essence to move the boulders to one side of the cave. "I'd be bored out of my mind, laying there with absolutely nothing to do."

"He hunts for us," Mellai responded, "which reminds me. I'm starving."

"Go ahead and eat. There's still part of a deer by him. I'll keep working."

Mellai thanked her brother as she crossed the cave. She used True Sight to remove a portion of the deer's flank, then wrapped it with fire fueled by another part of Huirk's nest. Once the meat was cooked through, Mellai sat down and leaned against the ghraef, nuzzling into one of his soft feather wings. Her physical exhaustion was obvious.

Lon nodded to himself when Mellai's glow diminished, signaling that she had released her power. *So she won't be able to read my mind,* Lon thought to himself. Although he and his sister were getting along well together, he had grown tired of Mellai's firsts. Everything seemed to come from his sister, leaving him to copy what she discovered on her own. It was about time he contributed. One of Llen's floor diagrams still remained unmastered, and Lon took it upon himself to figure it out.

Lon crossed the room and sat on the divan, deep in thought. Mellai said she had seen real sun crystals while she was in Itorea, and had described their glow as pure white. The only pure white glow Lon had ever seen came from Itorea, a light so bright that it was even visible beyond the horizon of Taeja, at least one hundred and forty miles away. The brightness had been so intense that the Rayders knew that another Beholder was in Appernysia—so confidently that they had marched to war.

"I've been meaning to ask you something," Lon said, lying back on the couch, "about something I saw two weeks before our battle in the Taejan Plains."

"What's that?" she answered, her voice sleepy.

"There was a huge burst of light in Itorea that illuminated the entire Taejan Plains, right before we went to battle. I assume that was you?"

"You saw that?" Mellai replied. "Well, that explains a lot. I've been wondering how you knew we were coming. Your ambush was clever."

"Was it you?" he asked again, not wanting to talk about the fighting.

"No. It was Llen, during my ceremony when he marked me with the Beholder's eye." Lon saw her dull hand touch the skin around her left eye. "Llen had been transforming the Lynth petals into living sculptures for each part of my tattoo. He called them the marks of the ghraef, the King's Cross, and of True Sight. The burst of light had been for True Sight."

"Did it hurt?" Lon asked, thinking of his own branding with the King's Cross.

Mellai shook her head. "Not at all. Llen was using True Sight to do everything, and sort of blended the petals into my skin. I only felt a tingle."

Lon carefully planned his next questions, trying not to draw attention to the fact that he was researching. "That must have been fascinating for everyone, watching a Jaed."

"No one can see him but us. Not even ghraefs. Right, Huirk?" She elbowed his wing, and the ghraef grunted.

From his sessions with Omar, Lon had learned a few things about the Lynth flower. He knew it was blue, poisonous, and that it only grew in the keep of Itorea. "So everyone just saw the flower dancing around you? Did anyone scream?"

"More gasps than anything, except when the ghraef phantom roared. A few children squealed at that one. My eyes were clouded as I watched Llen, though. They thought I was the one performing the show."

"The sculpture roared?"

"It did." Mellai laughed. "Startled me, too. Llen made that roar *really* loud."

"And the King's Cross? Did he do anything special with that?"

Mellai shifted and nuzzled further into Huirk's brown feathers. "He spun it sideways into my face. Made me flinch."

Now for the real question, Lon thought. "What about the light?"

"That one was strange." She took another bite of the cooked meat, pausing in her dialogue as she munched. "Llen lifted three petals and spun them around each other. A small white light appeared in their center. The faster the petals spun, the brighter it grew, until they burst into a ring of light that flew out over the city."

"Like an energy blast," Lon said. Her answer had confirmed everything he deduced so far. "Did it destroy the flower?"

"That's what was strange. After the light disappeared, all that was left was a large ball of blue dust. He used that to mark me." Mellai turned and summoned her power to look at Lon. "Why do you ask?"

Lon shrugged. "Just wondering. I read a few things about the ceremony in these journals and was curious what yours was like."

"Maybe you'll have your own someday," his twin said, "now that we're allies and all."

Lon chuckled. "And I'll brand you with the King's Cross."

Mellai snorted. "In your dreams, Big Brother." After a stifled yawn, she released her power again and rolled onto her side. "I think it's bedtime for me."

As his sister drifted into the dream world, Lon pondered everything he had discovered. If he had learned anything while living with the Rayders, it was that ceremonies were often inflated with formal speech and flowery actions.

The trick was recognizing the difference between Llen's performance and the actual skill. The ring of light running over the city seemed unnecessary, as did the spinning petals. But the sphere of light—that was essential, and it sounded like Llen had used the petals as a host so everyone could see it.

So that's step one for the sun crystals, Lon thought. *I need to use a physical host.*

Lon nodded to himself. When he created energy blasts, it had been by pulling raw energy from surrounding objects. Never had he used an actual item—visible without True Sight—to hold the energy.

The problem with an energy blast, though, was that it was unstable. It wanted to pull all loose energy into itself, to interact with its surroundings. *Not to mention the exploding part,* Lon thought, but then an immediate solution entered his mind. The sun crystals Mellai had seen—they must have been indestructible. Any normal rock or gem would combust under the influence of an energy blast, but not if it were impervious to damage.

Perfect, Lon thought. It will protect everything outside the crystal, while at the same time keeping the blast contained.

But another complication entered Lon's mind, one that he had learned to fear more than anything since first tutoring under Omar. Too much energy equals massive explosion.

The more energy Lon used for a blast, the brighter and more powerful it became. That had never worried him. Yet, packing the energy into an actual physical object was completely different. If he wanted the sun crystal to glow brightly, he would have to fill it with as much energy as safely possible.

An energy shield barrier wouldn't help, either. If the object exploded because of too much energy, that energy would transfer to the shield and create the same effect, perhaps even on a larger scale.

Bottom line—this would be very dangerous, far more than anything Lon had ever attempted.

Lon checked his sister, making sure she was asleep, then stood and walked to the table at the far end of the room. He guzzled the remaining water in his goblet and the accompanying flagon, then shouldered a full water skin opposite his sheathed sword. After silently bidding farewell to Mellai and Huirk, Lon slipped into the passage leading farther into the mountain.

It was time to find the crystal cave, and quickly.

*   *   *   *   *

At first, Lon's excursion was painfully boring. The long stone passage was dull, void of life, and ran on forever. Miles later, though—Lon had hurried through most of it—the passage began to change. Little chasms began speckling the floor, with openings no larger than a pillow, but sizable enough to swallow Lon whole and gulp him into their endless depths.

Along with the danger of falling to his death, Lon also had to protect himself from losing his way. When he encountered the passage's first offshoot, Lon stuck with the wider path and continued forward. A few steps later, though, he thought it wise to return and mark his path. He retraced his steps and praised the Jaeds for his intuition. Had it not been for the larger size of the passage that led him from the Beholders cave, he would have been lost. His view of the natural corridor from the opposite direction looked completely different.

Lon breathed a sigh of relief and sought for a way to mark his path, when he realized that one of his predecessors had already taken the liberty. A curved arrow had been carved into the ceiling connecting the two passages, its head pointing where Lon should return.

That simplifies things, Lon thought, hoping that the same markers were present at all intersections. Not only would they help him find his way back, but they would also confirm he was traveling in the correct direction. Most important of all, this would speed up his travel.

The farther Lon descended, the narrower the passage became, until he could barely walk upright. *No wonder ghraefs don't come down here,* he thought as he turned sideways and sucked in his belly to slip through a particularly thin path.

Somewhere off in the distance, Lon heard running water. It had started faintly, no more than a suspicious whisper, but steadily grew in volume as he descended. At one of the intersections, the noise and atmospheric pressure of the underground river plugged his ears and made his mouth water. His water skin was empty and in desperate need of a refill.

Lon eyed the ceiling and cursed. The reversed arrow came from the quieter path. Adding more to his dismay, the word 'NO' also had been carved at the opening into his preference.

"No, what?" Lon asked.

It was the first time Lon had spoken aloud since leaving the Beholders cave, and it shocked him how his voice echoed off the walls. Maybe that was the explanation for the ceiling's warning, that Lon's senses were deceiving him. Perhaps the water wasn't nearly as close as it seemed.

Still, Lon's thirst got the better of him and he chose the forbidden path. He rationalized his decision after reflecting on his many trips across Appernysia. He had experienced dehydration before and wasn't interested in enduring it again. He needed to refill his water skin.

After a quick check of his surroundings, Lon continued toward the water's source. He could barely hear his feet on the stone floor, and swirling energy poured past him, flicking his short locks of hair. He placed his hand on the wall to steady himself and marveled at the coolness of the stone.

Soon the swirling air became saturated with moisture, cooling Lon's face. And his journey became easier, too, as the passage steepened in decline. He knew the return journey would be more difficult, but he didn't worry. He would be gorged on an ice-cold natural spring, with a full water skin of the same. One hundred percent worth it.

Lon pulled his hand back, having touched something fuzzy on the wall, but True Sight revealed that he had only discovered moss. It would grow anywhere in a humid climate, even in a solid stone cave. Completely harmless.

His next step, however, shattered all of Lon's self-reassurances. He had stepped on a slimier deposit of moss and felt his foot slip. The rest of his body followed. He slid down the passage, clawing for a handhold on the slippery rocks, until he shot out of the corridor into a massive cavern. Lon was hundreds of feet in the air, tumbling alongside a raging waterfall toward a solid bed of smooth rocks.

With only seconds for action, Lon thought quickly through solutions, ultimately deciding on a slide. He hardened the top layer of falling water into ice and curved it toward the ground, then manipulated the smooth rocks where the ice touched to extend the curve upward. He lifted the reverse slide higher than himself, not knowing how far his momentum would carry him.

Once the slide was complete, Lon focused on righting himself in the air. The slide would only work if he eased onto it, so he fought the air currents to get his feet aimed down, where he could still watch ahead and make adjustments, if necessary.

He hit the ice hard, smacking the back of his head, then whipped down the ramp toward the ground. Fortunately, Lon had angled the ramp enough that gravity held him against the ice. If he had overestimated, he'd be dead already; underestimated, and he would have bounced off.

As his body battled the physical consequences of such violent changes in motion, Lon concentrated on keeping his feet centered on the ramp. If he aimed them true, the rest of his body would follow. He grunted in pain, his head pounding as the curving ice changed into stone and lifted him into the air again.

Lon could feel his movement slowing, so in one final act of desperation, he gauged ahead and caved in a portion of the ramp he was sliding up in order to catch himself. His body shot into the opening, crushed against the stone ceiling, then crumpled to the ground.

Chapter 24

Stalked

Channer ducked low behind a fallen log, trying to steady his trembling hands. "This will be no different than at the Quint River," he had told his men, but it had been a lie, and they undoubtedly saw through it. Even so, it still gave him courage that his squad had followed his order without reservation. Beholder Lon had asked them to visit every settlement while traveling to Itorea, so despite the complaints and reservations expressed by many of Pree's villagers, Jaul was as much a priority as anywhere else—and it was Channer's duty to search for any survivors, no matter the danger.

Channer requested the service of his three Rayders, but had hesitated when Aron also volunteered. It was not that Channer did not trust Aron—he had trained Beholder Lon to become a master swordsman, after all—but Channer did not want to risk Aron's injury or death for a scouting mission into the Briyél Forest. Pree's villagers needed his leadership, but Aron could not be swayed.

While the Rayders readied themselves, Aron had spoken to the Appernysian half of the Beholders' guard. He left Snoom in charge of Ric and Duncan. They were waiting in the south edge of the forest with Shalán and the rest.

In actuality, this scouting mission was the exact opposite of what had happened at the Quint River. Channer and his men were walking into the trap this time, which the calahein in turn might spring. But with a small group of only five men, Channer hoped they would go unnoticed until they had confirmed the condition of Jaul.

According to Aron, the shipping town was twenty-five miles north of their position, buried deep in the forest on the western shores of the largest lake in Appernysia. Both the Vidarien Mountains and the Kerod Cluster fed the lake, where the deep water pooled for eighty miles before finally draining into the Asaras Sea.

Twenty-five miles, Channer thought again, peering over the snow-covered log into the dense forest. It was not nearly as foreboding as the Forest of Blight, but knowing that the calahein might be hidden inside was intimidating enough to frighten even Commander Tarek.

The other four Rayders—Channer made a conscious decision to think of Aron as one of them—huddled next to Channer. Elja and Nik were wielding their composite bows, and Aron gripped his glaive of pure steel. Dovan and Channer had decided to rely solely upon their swords.

"We are not looking for a fight, especially one that we know we will lose. Remain unseen. That is your only order."

"Yes, Lieutenant," they replied with a salute.

Aron hesitated, but only for a moment before he, too, touched the scar on his right temple. "Lead the way, Lieutenant."

They stole swiftly and silently through the woods, dashing from tree to mound as they searched the ground and branches for signs of the calahein. Despite the mortal threat looming over them, Channer could not help but think of Beholder Lon's night stalker campaign in the Rayder Exile. The test of stealth had been forcibly difficult, nearly impossible, but Channer had been one of the few to survive on the attacking team. He had even captured the diamond himself once.

It was this experience that fed Channer with confidence to press forward, as it must have to the rest of his squad. They had all shown equal skill in stealth, which is why they had been selected to join

Lon's infiltration squad in the first place. Even so, Channer and his men had started early, just before sunrise, to maximize their daylight hours. The Taejan Plains had taught them that the calahein were even more deadly in darkness. And despite Aron's age, he kept up adequately and without complaint.

Whether by luck or allowance, they made it ten miles before the inevitable happened.

The Rayders had reached the southwestern tip of Casconni Lake, where it touched the South Pearl River. Ice wrapped the borders of the lake, but the residents of Jaul had obviously planned for such a thing. Far into the lake, well past the layers of ice, were anchored sizable fishing boats. Smaller row boats and rafts had been tied on the shoreline, meant as transportation to the larger fishing boats, but most of them were swallowed up in ice. They had not been used since the lake first began to freeze months earlier.

This was the first warning to Channer. He immediately called a halt and whispered his concerns to his men.

"Should we retreat, Lieutenant?" Dovan asked.

"If there is any chance that survivors are in the town," Channer replied, pointing to the shoreline structures fifteen miles farther north, "we cannot abandon them."

"But is there any chance?" The question was from Aron, and Channer could not tell if he was sincerely asking or challenging his decision.

"What do you think, father of Lon?"

Aron shrugged. "That's not my decision to make. I'm just anxious to move. It's not safe here."

As if on cue, noise began to fill the forest from all directions. Hissing, howling, snarling, but with no visible creatures to accompany the unnerving threats.

"Follow me!" Channer shouted, sprinting across the ice toward the nearest raft. It appeared to be free, and he intended to use it as an escape to à fishing boat. At least from the boat the Rayders would have a better chance of survival. His men could shoot the calahein as the beasts tried to swim aboard.

He heard Nik and Elja's bowstrings twang repeatedly as they ran, but Channer kept his focus on the raft. When he finally reached it, he grabbed hold of the stout rope and pulled with all of his might, but the lashed logs didn't budge.

Seconds later, Aron and Dovan arrived, but it was Aron who began shouting orders. "Pull from one side. We need to break it free from the ice."

While Channer and Dovan tugged, Aron used his glaive as a lever, sliding it under and lifting the logs.

"Now slam into it," Aron shouted, so Channer and Dovan dropped their ropes and charged full-speed into the corner of the raft. Ice crackled, but the raft remained unmoved.

"Again," Aron said, moving his glaive to a new spot while Channer and Dovan repeated the same two steps. This time, the raft broke free and slid several feet across the ice, leaving Channer and Dovan sprawling on their faces.

As he pushed himself to his feet, Channer drew his arming sword, expecting the calahein to overwhelm them at any second. To his surprise, they had stopped at the edge of the frozen water. A dozen terror hounds and three kelsh stalked back and forth, their fur an array of deep fall-colored leaves, but none ventured forth.

"They are afraid of the water," Channer shouted as he sheathed his sword. "Save your arrows and help us with this raft."

With five men assisting, the raft easily slid across the ice. But the danger had not passed, nor had Channer forgotten the calahein weapon that had killed Riyen.

"Watch the skies," he shouted, and not a moment too soon. Large boulders began raining around them, both recoiling off the ice and crushing through it.

Channer let go of the rope and reached for his own bow, but Nik told him to wait as he turned himself.

"We need to stop this bombardment or none of us will survive," Channer argued.

"And I will, Lieutenant," Nik replied. He took careful aim and loosed one arrow. It struck true, piercing one of the kelsh in its eye and dropping it dead. Nik had already pulled another arrow from his quiver and drawn his bow, but the remaining calahein disappeared from view. However, they continued to reign terror down on the Rayders from their covered positions.

Nik stowed his arrow and resumed pushing the raft, but Channer remained frozen in place. In the midst of the launching stones, something far more horrifying rose from the behind the trees. It looked like a kelsh, with dark orange fur encasing its large body, but it was leaner and carried by enormous black membrane wings. The calahein had finally unveiled their greatest threat, and the seith dove straight toward them.

"Volley!" Channer shouted, grabbing his bow and taking aim. "Ready . . . release!"

Four arrows whizzed through the air, tearing through the wings. One arrow—most likely from Nik—aimed directly at the seith's face, but the beast used its arm as a shield. The arrow sunk deep into its forearm, which the seith lowered as if it were no more than a scratch.

Channer drew his sword, knowing they didn't have time for another volley. He ran at an angle, brandishing his sword and shouting, luring the monster away from the rest of his men. The seith complied and redirected its diving path at the young Rayder lieutenant.

Taking position for a kill stroke, Channer gripped the sword with the blade aiming down from his hand. He would only have one chance at this.

But that chance never came.

Just before the seith landed, Aron's flying steel glaive pierced its neck. The beast immediately keeled over, and Channer was barely able to dive out of the way before it crashed through the thinning ice and disappeared with the glaive forever.

Channer knew his escape had been miraculous, but there was no time for celebrating. Along with ear-shattering howls of mourning, the kelsh continued to hurl boulders at them. Stones crashed all around, and the five men had just lunged onto the raft before the ice finally broke away, leaving them floating on the frigid water. They had no oars, but continued to drift farther away from the bank as the boulders splashed in front of them.

"I am sorry about your glaive," Channer said, saluting Aron, "but I will be forever in your debt for saving my life. Your throwing arm is as precise as Nik's bow."

"You would have done the same for me," Aron answered, turning away from the shore. "I'll have Mellai make me another one when I see my children again."

They drifted a little farther, but once the boulders stopped falling, their progress slowed. Channer heaved a sigh of relief, glad to have escaped the danger. The rippling water lapped against their raft, its repetitive sound soothing him even further. It had been their first calahein conflict that did not bring the death of one of their men.

Elja was the first to speak. "Without oars, how will we reach one of the boats, Lieutenant?"

"More importantly," Aron added, "how am I going to let my wife know that I'm still alive?"

"Do not worry," Channer counseled. "We will reach a boat eventually, and Snoom knows to lead the villagers around the forest if we do not return. They will believe we are dead, but their grief will be temporary. We will join them soon."

No one responded, but that did not surprise Channer. After all, what could they say more? He doubted that even a seith had the courage to fly over open water. With the sun setting and darkness approaching, they were as safe as they could ever hope to be.

Chapter 25

Retrospect

Huirk pushed Mellai underneath himself with his wing as he stood snarling, ready to take on whatever danger threatened them. Bromax also entered the cave moments later, teeth flashing.

Mellai had been similarly jolted from her sleep only one time before, when Wade had slashed her brother down his side. That had been back when Mellai was living with her grandparents, and she had woken up screaming at the top of her lungs. Allegna had comforted her then, but this time, Huirk had been there to protect his Beholder.

It took Mellai only a brief pause to realize what had happened. Lon was nowhere to be seen, and Bromax had come from above. That left only one other option. Lon had gone in search of the crystal cave, and he was hurt. Badly. Mellai explained this in one quick sentence as she sprinted across the cave barefoot, leaving Huirk and Bromax whimpering at the mouth of the second passage. They wouldn't enter, and she didn't have time to find out why.

It didn't take long for Mellai to navigate her route through the narrowing caverns, and she easily bypassed all the dangers. She stopped to catch her breath and examine the ceiling. After finding another carved arrow, she sprinted down the next passage.

"Lon!" she screamed again, both aloud and in her mind in an attempt to wake her twin. His emotions were present, but unresponsive, which meant he was unconscious. Mellai had become far too familiar with that sensation during Lon's trials in Pree.

Ouch, Lon finally answered in her mind.

You idiot! she shouted back, still sprinting. *Where are you?*

Down the passage marked "No." Whoever put that there was dead serious.

Are you in danger?

Not anymore.

Can you walk?

Impossible. A bone is sticking out of my thigh, and my right foot is turned the wrong direction.

Stay where you are. I'll find you.

Whatever you say, Lon answered, then his mind slipped away again.

Mellai doubled her speed, rounding every corner in a full sprint and slipping under protrusions in a gentle slide across her leather slacks. She cursed the darkness and its absorption of time, wishing she knew how long her brother had been hurt. His fractured leg could be bleeding severely. It was only a matter of time before . . .

No, Mellai thought, refusing to think that way. *I'll find him, heal him, and break his leg again to remind him of his foolishness.*

When Mellai turned one corner, a burst of air blew her brown curly hair across her face, followed by the tantalizing sound of rushing water. A quick check verified the word "No" on the ceiling, and Mellai carefully stepped into the passage.

Immediately, she knew what had gone wrong. The cool, wet stone soothed her bare feet, but also warned her of the danger of slipping. Lon had not been attacked by a beast. His injuries really were the byproduct of his own foolishness.

Mellai used her power to remove the moisture and reform the stone floor into broad steps, carefully descending until she reached the passage's opening. The resulting view was altogether spectacular and terrifying. A broad waterfall poured from an opening in the cavern above her, splashing on the rocks below before collecting into a powerful river that weaved through a sea of glimmering stones. Lon had discovered the crystal cave.

But where is he? Mellai thought, searching the cavern floor hundreds of feet below. The peculiar stalagmites first caught her attention. At a quick glance, they looked like a natural formation from the falling water, but the way they curved together, transitioning at their base between clear crystal and stone, was too perfect. Too crafted.

Then Mellai realized the clear stone wasn't stone at all, but ice. *He formed a slide,* she thought, wide-eyed as she followed the ramp up toward the ceiling. Had he disappeared up through a crack in the ceiling, into some hidden cavern? *If he did this on purpose, I'll break his arms, too.*

That's not very nice, Lon said in her mind.

I can't find you, Mellai replied.

Lon's mind winced in excruciating pain.

Stop trying to move, Mellai shouted, but her brother's pain continued. She frantically searched the cavern roof for openings.

Down here, Lon finally thought, *halfway up the stone ramp.*

Mellai relocated her gaze and saw half of Lon's glowing form hanging out the front of a break in the ramp, a small gap she hadn't noticed before.

Be careful, Mellai warned, *or you'll fall off again.* She extended her essence across the cavern and added a protrusion to the ramp to support her brother. *I'm coming.*

Mellai redirected her attention to the waterfall and the ice Lon had created in front of it. She first melted the ice and let it flood the rocks below, then began pulling a steady stream from the waterfall to form an ice staircase to her brother.

Bad idea, Lon thought. *You'll slip right off.*

Do you have a better suggestion? Mellai answered, melting the new ice. She had to admit it was an intelligent observation on his part. What fool would ever trust themselves on a staircase of ice?

Use stone instead, Lon answered, obviously annoyed.

Mellai shook her head. *You have no idea where you are, do you? This is the crystal cave. I'm not going to destroy it with a bunch of unnecessary stone manipulation. The water was safe. It can be melted.*

Just grab me and pull me up.

It was a good idea, but she didn't dare without knowing the extent of his injuries. *I could hurt you worse if I move you.*

Lon's thoughts were full of exasperation. *Then move what I'm LAYING on.*

Alright, hold still.

Just hurry. I think I'm going to pass out again.

Indeed he was. Mellai could feel his mind dimming. She raised a safety barrier around her brother, then retracted his section of rock to her location and weaved it together. By then, Lon was unconscious, so Mellai decided to get right to work.

Mellai gasped when she discovered that the back of her brother's skull was also cracked. The skin was split open, supplying the main blood flow out of his body. She quickly examined Lon's brain. It was lightly bruised, but nothing looked debilitating. It didn't take long for her to fuse the bone back together and heal the skin.

She next healed the most obvious injury, his left thighbone protruding out the underside of his leg. She pushed the bone back into place, mended it, then began healing the muscle and tissue that had been damaged. Lon came to, crying out and thrashing, so Mellai created more ice from the waterfall and used it to secure his entire body in place. It wouldn't help much if Lon went into shock, but her brother was tough. It would help with a more pressing matter. Blood was pooling under Lon and she wanted to slow its flow.

Once that task was complete, Mellai scanned Lon's body for further injuries. His right foot was a twisted mess of fractured bones and severed tendons, but not life threatening, so she moved on. A shattered tailbone. Dislocated shoulder. Bruising all over his body, along with a few shallow lacerations, which she closed.

"That feels much better," Lon spoke aloud, his cheeks squishing together as he tried to smile through the encasement of ice surrounding his mouth.

Mellai laughed. "You look ridiculous."

"It's nice to see you smile."

Mellai nodded. "Even better to hear your voice. You had me worried." She frowned. "I still have more bone work to do, Lon. It's going to hurt. A lot."

"Well, put a stick or something in my mouth and get on with it."

"Just keep your teeth clenched. Don't bite your tongue." Mellai thought of the repairs she did on Kaylen's legs. "Your foot first." She'd start with the most painful repair this time, then move down the hurt ladder. Maybe that would work better at preventing shock.

With Lon awake to consciously respond, Mellai was able to work more quickly. Besides a clenched jaw and a slew of curses shooting between his teeth, her brother remained relatively motionless while Mellai repaired his foot. It was tedious work, with many little bones that had to be relocated and repaired. A few times, Mellai had to study his other foot before she knew exactly how to heal him.

By the time Mellai finished, Lon was pale and disoriented. "I'm t-t-t-too c-cold," was the only intelligible thing he said, so Mellai removed the ice and tossed it over the edge. Lon was still shivering uncontrollably, even after Mellai dried his clothes and hair.

"You need a fire," Mellai said, searching the cave for a source of fuel, but all she could find was water and stone.

"Wrap m-me in s-s-stone," Lon suggested, "and m-make it hot. L-like an oven."

Mellai followed his advice, doming stone over him and manipulating some of the rock's energy to create friction. Heat slowly filled the space surrounding him. It took some time, but eventually Lon was able to relax enough that he could lie still.

"Quick thinking," he said to Mellai, his head poking out one side of the dome.

"On your part," Mellai replied. "I'm sorry, Lon, but I still need to repair your tailbone and shoulder. They'll be much quicker, but . . ."

Lon tried to smile. "It's alright, Mel. I developed a pretty high pain tolerance with the Rayders. I'll be fine. Just give me a few more minutes to warm up." He breathed slowly, soaking the heat into his skin. "Why'd you use all that ice, anyway?"

"You were bleeding a lot. I had to do something to slow it down."

"Ice does that?"

Mellai nodded. "But it has its side effects."

"Indeed it does."

Mellai raised her knees and hugged them. "Why are you down here, Lon?" She wanted to say a lot more, but she withheld the lecture. Lon already knew he was daft. Reminding him of that fact wouldn't make any difference.

"I needed a clear stone, Mel." He paused, closing his eyes and breathing deeply. "I think I figured out how to make a sun crystal, but the only way to know for sure is with something like a diamond; a rock that light can shine through."

"But why on your own? I could've helped, and this wouldn't have happened if I had been with you."

Lon reopened his eyes and looked at his sister. "That's exactly why I came by myself. It's no secret that you're better with True Sight than me, but I wanted to do something on my own. To figure it out by myself. To know I can still contribute."

Mellai's first instinct was to argue, but the more she considered her twin's point of view, the more she identified with him. Only a year earlier, she had been battling with similar feelings while Lon received all the attention. Ironically, those feelings had pushed her into her own dangerous quandary with Braedr.

"I understand, Lon. I really do. But the last time I ran away because I felt invisible, a predator took advantage of my solitude. The only reason I escaped is because of you. You loved me enough to watch out for me. *You* kept me safe, and that was just against

Braedr. Now we're dealing with an entirely new kind of enemy, one that literally feeds on the abandoned. We have to stick together." She paused, surprised by the hurt building up in her chest. "What if you had died? Aside from the pain you would have dropped on everyone who loves you, think about the rest of Appernysia. We're outnumbered already, Lon. I can't do this by myself. Not even the ghraefs' help is enough."

"But I didn't think I was in any danger, Mel."

"Neither did I."

Much to Mellai's surprise, Lon didn't shut her out or even turn away. He stared back at her, visibly digesting her counsel.

"You're right," he finally said. "I'll be more careful. No more solo missions."

Mellai gaped at him, wondering when he had discovered this part of himself.

Lon chuckled. "Easy, Little Sis. I may seem stubborn, but if the Rayders have taught me anything, it's humility. I know when I'm wrong."

"Most of us do," Mellai replied, "but admitting it requires an entirely different level of maturity. You've grown up, Lon."

"So have you," Lon said, accompanied with a sincere smile. "Now fix me up so I can show you what I figured out. How many repairs are left?"

"Only two. Your shoulder should be a simple fix—it's just dislocated—but your tailbone is shattered."

Lon groaned. "I hate tailbones. They always hurt way more than they should."

"Just like elbows," Mellai agreed. "You ready?"

After clenching his jaw again, Lon gave a quick nod.

Mellai removed the stone doming over his body and worked as quickly as possible, piecing Lon's tailbone together and knitting the bone. Again, much to Mellai's amazement, her brother dominated his pain and held reasonably still, simplifying and speeding up the process for her. A few minutes later, his tailbone was cured and his shoulder was moved into place.

"What about your bruises?" Mellai asked. "I can heal them, too, if you want."

"No thanks," Lon answered, finally capable of sitting up. "I could use a few days of manageable pain to remind me of my stupidity." He tested his various joints and muscles, then shook his head. "You're amazing, you know? I would have been crippled for life."

"You'd be dead," she answered seriously, then sat down next to her brother. "Now how about you repair your damage to the rest of the cave?"

Lon immediately used his power to push the stone slide down into the floor and smooth the surface. "It's weird, isn't it? Who knows how deep we are in this mountain, but we've gone . . . I don't know, maybe three weeks without the need of light. A fire now and then, just to cook the meat Huirk brings us, but otherwise, nothing."

The same thought had crossed Mellai's mind more than once. "The ghraefs, too. I can't help but wonder what makes them capable of seeing in pure darkness. Think it's some form of True Sight?"

"I doubt it," Lon replied. "Probably just an enhanced sense, like dogs. I think it's time we head down." He paused and glanced over the precarious ledge that he stood upon, then pointed up the passage. "That way."

"I've been thinking," Mellai said as she followed her brother, ready to intervene if he slipped again. "I don't think we need to create a sun crystal before the bonding ceremony. We each just have to choose a crystal and bring them back for Bromax and Huirk."

"But how will you know their color?"

Mellai opened her mouth to answer, but stopped short. Lon was right. True Sight changed their view of the world, revealing all energy while at the same time dulling color. Mostly just a haze of varying shades of gray.

"If we want to pick the perfect crystal," Lon continued, "we need to see it as it truly is. A diamond sun crystal would do exactly that. It's a clear stone with pure light. We could use a fire, but it would distort the genuine color of the crystals."

"But who's to say there are any diamonds in here? Who knows how many Beholders have been choosing crystals out of this cave. We might only have the ugly scraps left."

They had just entered the crossroads where "No" was written on the stone ceiling. Lon turned to his sister before continuing down the other passage into the cave of crystals. "You don't really think that, do you, that you have to find the most rare and beautiful crystal?"

Mellai shrugged. It seemed logical, but with Lon questioning her, she began to doubt herself.

"Choose what you want for Huirk," Lon continued, "but I'm going to choose one that matches Bromax. One that fits his personality and his body. I've already decided on which color, too, if I can find it in an appropriate shape. Remember when we saw Bromax and Huirk kill those four kelsh in Roseiri?" Lon suddenly paused.

Mellai guessed he was thinking of their grandparents because the same thought had entered her own mind, along with Theiss. "It seems so long ago, doesn't it?" Mellai asked, sullenly. "Almost a dream, like it never happened. I wish it hadn't."

"It was no dream. This cave is just messing with our connection to reality. You're the one who saw them through that tree's memories, remember? Eaten alive in their own house while it burned to the ground?"

"Stop it," Mellai demanded. "I don't want to remember."

Lon placed a gentle hand on her shoulder. "That's just it. You have to remember, Mel, and deal with the problem. Trust me. I've been there. Don't stifle painful memories, or they'll break free on their own terms and drown you in a sea of unmanageable despair. Even worse, until they force their way out, you'll become cold and heartless like the Rayders I used to know. I've seen too many people die, some of whom were my closest friends, but I've finally come to terms with my life. I did everything in my power to protect them—physically and mentally—and I'll continue to fight for the principles they believed in. There's nothing more I can do."

Tears filled Mellai's eyes. "It hurts so much Lon. I don't know how much more of this I can handle." Her throat and lungs burned, and her chest throbbed. Every breath was torture, like inhaling tiny needles and spitting them out again. Over and over and over. The agony multiplied until it became too agonizing. Lon was right. Her restraint wasn't worth the effort.

Mellai thumped her brother's chest with a clenched fist and exploded into hysteria. "Is this our calling as Beholders, to kill or be killed? Will we ever experience anything but death and suffering?"

Lon pulled her into a tight hug. "I'll bet every soldier has asked that exact same question, especially those specifically tasked with protecting their people. I don't like this any more than you, but I get through every day because of the vision in my mind. I never let it go, Mel, no matter the pain I'm enduring."

"What vision?" Mellai asked, not altogether interested in what he had to say.

Lon stepped back from his sister, took her hand, and led her down the correct passage. "Omar was a brilliant man. I was intimidated by his wealth of knowledge, but eventually I dared to argue with him over observational points. You know, claims based off of interpretation. Things that weren't solid facts. Make sense?"

"Philosophical discussions," Mellai said, wiping the tears from her eyes with her free hand.

"Exactly. Even when we were experimenting with my abilities, Omar and I always took opposite stances. One argued the logic, and the other sought all the flaws. But there was one subject that always brought us together. No matter how much we questioned or speculated, we could never disprove it. It was infallible."

"What, Lon?" Mellai replied, annoyed with his propaganda. "Just tell me."

"*Foresight only comes from hindsight.* Go ahead. Try to disprove it."

"I would, Big Brother, if I had any clue what you're talking about."

Lon teased her hand with a quick squeeze. "You know exactly what I mean, Mel. You can never develop indisputable knowledge of the future without a full reflection of the past."

Mellai pulled her hand free and quickened her pace, anxious to escape Lon's nauseating wit. "What does that have to do with the vision you keep talking about?"

Lon stopped walking, forcing his sister to turn around and listen. "Think about the First Age of Appernysia, Mellai."

"I have been, Lon, and probably too much. That's why I'm so scared. If hundreds of Beholders barely defeated the calahein, what hope do we have?"

"Besides the synergy Llen talked about?" Lon asked, smiling shrewdly. "That's not what concerns me, though. What bothers me, more than you can imagine, is that you're wrong. They all were, and we still are."

"*They* who? Wrong about what?"

Lon spoke quietly, but with uncomfortable intensity. "Mellai, the First Age Beholders thought they completely destroyed the calahein. Obliterated their entire population. Made them extinct. That's what *defeated* meant to our ancestors."

Mellai's annoyance fled as she realized where her brother was taking this conversation. This wasn't just a passing thought. Lon had been deeply pondering this very subject for a long time, undoubtedly since his skirmish with the kelsh on the Taejan Plains.

"They were wrong," Lon continued, "and we've been passing down their misconception for twelve hundred years. How can we expect to have foresight to prevent the same mistake from happening again unless we fully understand where the Beholders went wrong?"

"Hindsight," Mellai uttered.

Lon nodded. "Now you see my point."

"So let's figure it out," Mellai said. "What do you know about the final calahein battle? Did you learn anything new that Father hasn't shared with us?"

"Not really, and that's what frustrates me."

"Maybe the calahein had another settlement farther west," Mellai suggested.

"Simple enough, but it doesn't feel right. Llen said that Beholders only maintain their powers with pure hearts, right?"

"Correct."

Lon heaved a frustrated sigh. "They swore to all of Appernysia that the calahein had been completely destroyed. *Completely*. We both have our secrets and little lies, but a promise like that is too far-reaching to be ignored by the Jaeds. The Beholders couldn't have made that claim unless they absolutely believed it was true. They must have flown everywhere on this continent to verify their assertion. Checked every tunnel and passage. They had to." Lon twisted his hand over the pommel of his sword. "So where did the calahein come from now? Where were they hiding?"

"Think about what you're suggesting," Mellai countered. "You really think that the Beholders checked every cubic foot of livable space for miles under the surface? That's an impossible task. Even when you had buried all of the Rayders a few feet under the ground on the Taejan Plains, I couldn't see your essences. I had no idea we were marching over the top of you. The kelsh could have dug a hole under a boulder and closed it up, leaving no sign."

"For a little while, but—"

"And we have no idea how many calahein have returned. There are plenty of those venom-spitting terror hounds, but I don't think they were originally part of the calahein. In all of your reading of the Beholder journals, did you ever come across a description like them?"

"No, but—"

"So maybe the terror hounds have become pets to the few surviving kelsh, bound to serve their masters."

"Will you just let me talk?" Lon shouted. "I've thought through all of this already, but what you're suggesting is impossible. Regular calahein don't live a hundred years, let alone over a thousand. Only their queen can live that long and repopulate, but the First Age Beholders killed her before she could flee."

"So they have another queen."

Lon resumed walking. "That's the only plausible solution, but still without explanation. How could there be another queen and the Beholders not discover her? If we can't solve this riddle, Mel, then we're doomed. Even if by some miracle we win this war, another thousand years will bring another bloody conflict. I can't live with that."

Mellai agreed with her brother, but had an entirely different concern knocking around in her brain. It was she who stopped walking this time, overwhelmed by her thoughts. "Lon, if there was another queen, that means she has been birthing offspring for over a millennium. There could be an innumerable host of kelsh and seith hiding in the Vidarien Mountains, waiting for the perfect time to reveal their full strength. So why are they waiting?"

"Because they're afraid of us and the ghraefs."

"Maybe, but I think it's something bigger. Maybe the calahein understand us even better than we understand them. They could know the might of Itorea, and that our kingdom under threat would retreat behind those walls. We might just be making it easier for them, gathering all together for one final slaughter." Mellai tasted bile in the back of her throat and felt a strong need to throw up.

"Even so," Lon replied, "what choice do we have? Remember that vision I keep talking about? It's of a free Appernysian society united together with Taejans. If the Jaeds have the same vision, then—"

"That's a huge misunderstanding among the Rayders," Mellai interrupted. "Llen has told me many times that the Jaeds aren't concerned with the affairs of the world. They only care that its energies are kept intact. Don't expect help from the Jaeds, because we won't receive any. Jaeds don't protect us. Beholders do."

"And who trains Beholders—well, at least one of us?" Lon spoke with a hint of a smile playing at his lips. "They may not intervene directly, but they are assisting us every time Llen appears to you or me. They have to be concerned because if the calahein win, the world's energies would be decimated."

"What are you getting at?"

"Tell me one more time what Llen said in the mountains, during his first visit."

Mellai paused, searching her memory for the statements she had memorized. "*The balance of the world's energy has shifted. Appernysia needs you.* That's the first thing he said, but you're probably more interested in his speech when I left Roseiri. *War is coming. Appernysia is divided and unprepared. You must travel to Itorea and unite the king with his council, then lead his army in the approaching conflict. This is your purpose, Beholder. Without you, Appernysia will fall . . . Protect Appernysia. That is your primary focus. Your survival is dependent upon your ability to adapt and improvise. For you, change is essential. Even the mightiest oak must adapt with the seasons.*"

Lon's smile was so big that Mellai could almost feel it without looking. "Wow," he said. "I've never heard that one, but . . . it definitely strengthens my argument that Jaeds care about us. He sounded concerned to me."

"And?"

"Jaeds bestow True Sight to those worthy of it, and we are the only two Beholders in Appernysia. To me, that means Llen believes we can handle this on our own."

"Or maybe he's just trying to give us courage," Mellai scoffed, "all the while hoping that more Rayders will develop pure hearts."

"Or maybe he sees greater power in us than we even realize," Lon countered. "Oh, wait. He absolutely does. He already told us so."

Mellai rushed past Lon, leaving her brother behind. She was done talking, not because she disagreed with him, but because her brain felt like it was going to explode. Lon had always been a deep thinker, but she had never been interested in trying to figure out more than what was immediately pressing.

"Just promise me you'll think about it," Lon called as he followed her. "We need to be absolutely sure."

Sure of what? Mellai thought to herself as she nodded to appease her brother. *I don't know anything about the calahein, so how could I be sure where they came from, let alone how to destroy them? I don't have—*

A familiar tingle in her brain interrupted Mellai's thoughts. Lon was connecting to her emotions. She allowed it and immediately sensed curiosity from her twin.

What are you searching for? she shouted in her mind.

Hope, Lon answered, *and I found some. You'll be alright.*

Oh, thank you, Mellai thought, full of sarcasm. *Now I feel much better.*

She pulled free of Lon's emotions and thundered down the corridor.

Chapter 26

Sun Crystal

Lon had slowed down, giving his sister the solitude she sought, so it caught him by surprise when after a reasonable length of travel, he rounded a sharp turn in the descending stone passage and nearly tripped over her. Mellai was huddled over something on the ground. Her essence dimmed from dismissing her powers.

Before Lon could ask what she was doing, Mellai stood and turned around with a small crystal cupped in her hands. At its center was a bright sphere of energy unlike anything Lon had seen before. The energy was perfectly circular and constantly spinning while it floated independently of the diamond shell encasing it. Lon stared more closely, confirming that there were zero interactions between the separated energies of the sphere and the crystal, then shook his head in surprise. Everything he had experienced thus far proved that energy was constantly moving between objects. Even rocks and air regularly swapped part of their glow as heat passed between them. The crystal his sister held in her hand was a phenomenon.

"Queen Cyra's necklace looks exactly like this," Mellai said, glancing up at her brother. "But you have to look at it with your normal eyes to understand what I mean."

Lon immediately dismissed his power, bracing himself for the heavy darkness that would press in around him, but it never came.

It was being fought back by a dull glow coming from the diamond, just bright enough to light Mellai's hands and face.

"Exactly like Queen Cyra's," Mellai said again. "Even the intensity of the light is the same."

It was the first sun crystal Lon had seen, and it looked much different with the naked eye. There was no visible swirl of energy. Just a faint and steady glow, like a firefly, but whiter than the purity of scattered clouds on a clear summer day.

"Who would leave this here," Lon asked, "just lying around waiting to be found?"

"The last Beholder before us," Mellai answered. "He must have used this for the same purpose you wanted to create a sun crystal. Is it what you had in mind?" She handed the crystal to Lon.

Lon summoned his power again and examined the two separated energies. "Not exactly, but I didn't really know what to expect from the reaction. Makes sense, I suppose."

Mellai's glow brightened as she called upon True Sight. "What reaction? For the light?"

Lon nodded and held out the sun crystal so they both had an unobstructed view. "I had planned to pack as much energy as possible into a host object—without making it explode—then lock it inside an indestructible crystal. The host object would supply light that everyone can see, and the indestructible crystal would keep it stable." Lon looked at the sun crystal. "If this was created the same way, then I guess the two don't like interacting with each other."

"Or they can't," Mellai added. "Good idea, Lon."

"But I expected a brighter light than this."

"Oh, trust me, it can get brighter. You should see the sun crystal hanging in Itorea's great hall. It lights up the room as bright as the sun would."

Lon turned the sun crystal over in his hand. "So do you think we can add more energy to this? Make it brighter?"

"We?" Mellai answered. "Are you sure you want my help?"

Lon reached for his sister's emotions and felt her accept the connection. *Yes,* he said in his mind. *If synergy is the key to our survival, we better use every available chance to practice.*

If you say so, Mellai replied. *How can I help?*

You create a gap in the crystal and maintain its balance, then I'll slip through the gap to add more energy to the light.

Take your time, Mellai advised, *and don't try to add too much. We don't need Bromax and Huirk to see this shine.*

Lon nodded, thinking once again of the glow Llen had created out of three tiny Lynth petals. He was absolutely certain they could make it glow that bright, but Mellai was right. It was unnecessary and dangerous.

While his sister picked apart the sun crystal to create a small hole, Lon evaluated his surroundings and what energy he should use to supply the light. It was then that he realized a slight breeze was pouring from farther down the tunnel. The extra flow of air would be perfect, and he could use it without distorting the formation of the passage. He shared his idea with Mellai and she complimented him again on his ingenuity.

Careful, Lon teased. *You don't want people to start thinking you're a nice person.*

Get ready, Mellai answered with a smirk. *I'm almost through and neither of us know how much raw energy is in this light.*

Lon still held the crystal in his right hand, so he extended his left hand's essence to touch the hole his sister was creating. She was still capable of working through him while they maintained their emotional connection. *You ready?*

If you are.

Mellai had weakened the crystal's lining by unweaving the energy and withdrawing it, which she transformed into a smaller diamond with her left hand. Without losing control of the smaller diamond, she pushed into the lining with her right hand's essence and tore away a tiny physical chunk of the main crystal.

Lon pushed into the gap, taking immediate control of the light. It was condensed, but not significantly. Its energy was easily manageable and offered little danger to the Beholders.

Now that Lon was interacting with the light, he was finally able to identify the source object that held the extra energy. *Looks like whoever created this used a part of this diamond to store the light,* he thought as he slowly absorbed the passing wind into his body and pushed it through his right hand.

Ever so slowly, the swirling light energy contained within the diamond host began to spin faster and glow brighter.

Careful, Mellai thought again, probably not even meaning to speak to her brother's mind.

Seal the hole, Lon told his sister. The swirling light had grown significantly, but was still very stable. He wanted to see how bright it actually had become before he added any more energy.

Mellai replaced the chunk of diamond, but its density was still thin enough for Lon to reach through with his own essence. He waited until she had securely weaved the edges back together before he finally withdrew. The plug held, and Mellai weaved all of the extracted diamond into the crystal's lining.

"It's really packed in there tight," she growled aloud as she forced the final supply into the gaps.

"Want to place bets on how bright it is?" Lon asked.

Mellai considered the question before answering. "It will light this passage, but it'll still be relatively dull."

"Like a torch," Lon agreed. "Let's find out."

Lon dismissed his power and was immediately blinded by the intensity of the crystal's glow. He turned his head and shut his eyelids to guard his pained eyes and heard the crystal drop onto the stone floor.

"I think we were wrong," he said.

"No kidding," Mellai answered, having also released True Sight. "I can't see."

"Hang on." Lon squinted just enough to locate the sun crystal and cover it with his left hand. The skin lining the edges of his hand and fingers glowed red from the light hidden inside, and white beams of light shot out of holes he couldn't fully close.

"That's one of the strangest things I've ever seen," Mellai commented, having reopened her eyes.

"And that really means something coming from a Beholder," Lon agreed. "It's like I'm hiding the entire sun under my hand."

"Start lifting fingers," Mellai suggested. "We've been in this cave so long . . . maybe our eyes can adjust to it."

Her suggestion worked, although neither of them could look directly into the light without experiencing high levels of discomfort. The entire passage glowed as if they were standing at the exit with the sun pouring in.

While they were questioning what to do with the sun crystal, an idea entered Lon's mind. He hesitantly grabbed the stone off the ground, fearing it might be hot but finding it as cool as the stone floor. He gripped it tight in his right hand, then slowly uncoiled his index finger. A beam shot out of his fist, illuminating his sister.

"Watch it!" Mellai cried, shielding her eyes with her hands.

Lon apologized and turned his fist away, then experimented against the stone wall. The tighter he coiled his finger, the narrower the beam would become, and contrarily, too. It was just like holding a shuttered lantern in his hand, but much brighter and without the risk of spreading fire if he dropped it.

"Nifty trick," Mellai said, slugging Lon on the arm as her eyes clouded over. "Let's get moving."

"I like this thing," Lon said, deciding not to call upon True Sight. "I'm going to use it to light the path for awhile."

"Then get in front of me. I don't need you blinding me again." As Lon passed her, his sister spoke more solemnly. "Llen's journal said we need to make a sun crystal, or at least we think that's what it said. Does this one belong to us? Do we need to make another one?"

"We're in a hurry," Lon answered. "I'm sure Llen will let this one go without complaint. Who knows? Maybe he even broke his own rules and left this sun crystal for us. Either way, I'm not standing around to find out."

Chapter 27

Tension

Kaylen waved at the approaching Rayders. She danced on her tiptoes, prohibited from crossing onto the drawbridge, but anxious to talk with Tarek again.

The Rayder soldiers had been dwelling in the Gaurelic Waste for over a week, and this was the third batch of supplies King Drogan provided for them. Kaylen had made sure she helped with every shipment, then she and Tarek would spend hours talking outside the north gate while his men transported the supplies into the Rayder camp.

Through Tarek's stories, Kaylen had learned much about Lon and his experiences as a Rayder. All of the remaining hatred she had been storing in her heart had melted away, replaced by awe over Lon's continued sacrifices. From the way Tarek described him, Lon had not changed since he left Pree. He was still the same man, just more experienced and fighting for a greater cause than his own happiness. He still seemed like a man she could love.

But Lon was the furthest thing from her mind at this moment as she continued waving at the Rayder commander.

As usual, Tarek was leading his men and their horse-drawn wagons across the half-mile bridge. He raised a hand of greeting to Kaylen, but once he had crossed the bridge, he grew more sober. "What news do you have for me? Will Wade and the rest of my people be joining us soon?"

Kaylen's shoulders slumped. "I just found out that they're still in Sylbie."

"How could that be?" Tarek growled, red in the face. "Drogan promised to take care of them."

"He said you'd say that," Kaylen replied, sitting on one of the wooden crates, "and he said to tell you that he promised to treat them in *like*-manner, not *exact*-manner."

Tarek cursed. "Too much of a coward to tell me this himself?"

"You're a scary guy," Kaylen teased, placing her hand lightly on the commander's arm, "but he isn't being totally selfish. He can't afford to escort more people through Itorea, Tarek. His army needs to be on the walls, where the calahein threat is the greatest. But he's still taking care of your civilians. They receive regular supplies and they're protected inside the walls of Sylbie with plenty of comfortable lodging. I stayed at an inn there once. Probably the most comfortable bed I've ever slept in, although I didn't sleep much."

Tarek began pacing the drawbridge, deep in thought. "You heard what happened with Leland and all the Appernysian soldiers. They trust us now, so why can't everybody else?" He paused and looked at Kaylen. "My people can't stay in Sylbie. You know this. They're not safe there, nor would they be even if my men were with them. It's not built to defend against the calahein."

Kaylen's heart throbbed. She had delivered the message, but her heart wasn't in it. Everything Tarek said was true. There was no denying it. "But there's nothing we can do at this point, Tarek."

The commander resumed his pacing. "What if I talk to Drogan? If I could just get a few minutes with him, I might be able to change his mind. I wouldn't even use my fists. Just talking."

"You know that's not true. This is bigger than his own opinion. Who would escort your civilians through? Your army isn't big enough to surround seventy-five thousand civilians. Even if it were, that would only anger the Appernysians. Your people are just going to have to stay there or return to Taeja."

"Not good enough," Tarek said, his volume growing along with his temper. He raised a hand and jabbed a finger west. "That's our women and children out there, and they deserve defending as much as your own people. I've tried to be peaceful about this, Kaylen, but my patience is wearing thin."

"I'm doing everything I can."

"Then maybe it's time to move above you." He stepped to the edge of the drawbridge and addressed one of the Appernysian sentries stationed there. The soldier watched Tarek closely, but didn't respond aggressively. "I am Commander Tarek Ascennor, and it is my job to protect the Rayders. I demand audience with your king. Tell Drogan that if he doesn't climb down from his hiding spot and speak to me within three days, I will make him and the rest of your city suffer."

The sentry glanced over his shoulder at the gate into Itorea.

"Don't look at them," Tarek said, pulling back his attention. "I ordered *you* to deliver the message. No one else. Just you. And if Drogan refuses to answer my summons, then I suggest you start running the opposite direction because I'll hold you personally responsible."

"But Tarek—" Kaylen began, desperate to intervene.

"Don't bother," he interrupted, raising his hand at her. "I need to start thinking of my own people, and it's time I start acting like their commander, even if it costs me your friendship." He reshaped his palm into a finger and pointed it at the sentry. "Now I suggest you move along. You have a thirty-mile roundtrip to make in three days. Not much time to dawdle."

The sentry hesitated a moment longer, then turned around and sprinted into the gate.

"That's a good boy," Tarek muttered, then pulled the crate out from under Kaylen and marched back across the bridge. "Don't bother looking for me again, unless you're with your king."

Kaylen watched him leave, torn between sympathy for the Rayders and loyalty to Appernysia. She had no words of comfort or kindly perspective. If King Drogan didn't do something about this, blood would be shed on both sides. That was the only irrevocable truth.

She turned and sprinted after the sentry, desperate to make sure their king received Tarek's message.

*　*　*　*　*

"And what exactly does he intend to do?" King Drogan said. "Attack our city with his meager fourteen thousand? My crossbowmen would cut them down before they could even scratch at the walls."

Kaylen didn't answer, nor did the sentry next to her, with whom she had shared a horse for the duration of that day. Their king was just speaking rhetorically as he vented, and she knew that no soldiers manned the flanking towers at the north gate.

"You can't blame Tarek for feeling this way," Queen Cyra said. "His entire civilization is trapped out there like we're sacrificing them to the calahein."

Drogan dropped onto his throne at the head of the table. It screeched on the stone floor, echoing across the great hall. "Don't be ridiculous. Nobody is that heartless."

"Then prove it," Cyra continued.

"And how am I supposed to do that?" Drogan glanced around the table at those present.

Lord Teph was sitting next to Kaylen, opposite the sentry and visibly preoccupied—perhaps the other responsibilities he needed to take care of as the combined steward and chamberlain of Itorea. Advisor Haedon Reeth and Chancellor Anton Vetinie were also present, sitting across the table and ever willing to give council to their king and queen. General Astadem would also normally attend the King's Council, but he was busy with the west wall's defenses. Of course, the other Lords of Itorea had not been summoned. It would be years, even decades, before King Drogan trusted them in the keep again.

The only other person in the room was Kutad, and he stood a few feet behind King Drogan with his arms interlocked across his chest. His responsibility was only to protect the king, and Kaylen was grateful he wouldn't be speaking. Everything he had said lately only made her angry.

"Well?" Drogan said, "Let's hear some ideas."

"We could send some of our soldiers into Sylbie," Cyra suggested first.

"If the calahein attacked," Drogan countered, "they'd be slaughtered along with the Rayder civilians."

"Our scouts in the Perbeisea Forest would warn us of an attack," Cyra continued. "They would give adequate warning for your soldiers to evacuate into Itorea, along with the Rayder civilians."

Drogan shook his head. "We'd be no better off than if we just brought their civilians into Itorea now. I know our soldiers have developed a level of respect for the Rayders, but neither of us can make that argument for the rest of our people. Their hatred is at its peak right now, and it's my fault for spreading the propaganda."

"*Our* fault," Lord Teph inserted, "along with every leader of our past. We didn't know any better."

Kaylen watched Kutad visibly squirm behind the king. He obviously disagreed with where this conversation was headed. Kaylen couldn't help but smile at him, smugly of course.

"Which is why I won't bring the Rayders into the middle of our population to be mocked, ridiculed, and beaten. As patiently as the Rayders have endured it, everyone has a breaking point. Blood would be inevitably spilled and we'd have a civil war on our hands."

"Then only use a part of our soldiers to escort them through Itorea," Cyra argued, "just enough to remind our citizens to behave."

Drogan leaned forward on the table and interlocked his fingers together. "Haedon. Anton. You've both been uncharacteristically quiet."

"I admit I'm a little distracted, my king," Anton commented, "lost in memory of the last time I sat in this great hall." He nodded to Kaylen. "I've not had a chance to personally thank you for saving our lives. I wish I had been conscious to witness it."

Kaylen's throat burned. "No you don't, Lord Anton. Aely was still young and full of life, and they killed her right in front of me. She was my best friend. Nobody should have to see something like that."

Lord Teph placed a hand on Kaylen's shoulder. "If we don't resolve this Rayder problem, I'm afraid everyone will experience it, if not their own deaths first. We need to stay on topic. Lord Haedon, how about you?"

Haedon shook his head. "If the calahein attack while part of our army is escorting the Rayders across Itorea, our defenses would be severely crippled. A warning from your scouts would provide a day's notice at most, but the escorting soldiers could be up to five days away." He shook his head again and shifted in his chair to face his king. "You took enough risks when you sacrificed the first ten days to the Rayders, King Drogan. You can't afford to do it again."

"What about your armada?" the sentry next to Kaylen piped in, then immediately put his hand over his mouth and sat back in his chair. "I'm sorry, my liege. I didn't mean to speak."

"It's alright, Braj," Drogan replied. "It was a good suggestion, one I've already given great consideration, but it's impractical. My largest ships only carry one hundred people at a time, and they would have to travel forty miles upriver to reach Sylbie. For seventy-five thousand civilians and their supplies and livestock, it's just not practical. You've done exactly as you should, bringing this conflict to us. Now let us handle it from here."

Braj stood and bowed, his right fist over his heart. "By your command, King Drogan."

As Braj crossed the great hall, Drogan paused to drink the rest of the wine from his goblet. "Wait, Braj. I need you to escort Kaylen back to the Gaurelic Waste before you return to your post." Drogan turned his attention to Kaylen. "You will gather information for me."

Kaylen stood and curtseyed. "Information about what, my King?"

"You are close with Tarek. Speak with him and his lieutenants. Find out if there is a way we can appease him without this turning to bloodshed."

"But Commander Tarek threatened to attack if we don't bring his civilians to him. He told me not to return without you."

"We are at war, Lady Kaylen. Everything and everyone is at risk. Just do the best you can."

"As you wish."

Questions still racked her brain, but Kaylen knew pushing the matter was pointless. As she turned to leave, Queen Cyra caught her eye. The queen was fiddling with the glowing crystal hanging from her neck, her eyes full of concern.

"Follow me," Kutad said as he took hold of her arm and led them across the great hall.

Even though she was no longer welcome, Kaylen was wroth to leave. The fires circling the domed great hall were roaring with heat, a luxury nonexistent outside of royal presence. The torch-lined castle hallways would be as cold as the snow-covered ground outside, and they'd feel especially gloomy after sitting under the glowing crystal chandelier for so long.

Without a word, Kutad closed the door abruptly and latched it shut, locking them out of the room.

Kaylen stared absently at the door. Since becoming sergeant, Kutad had grown increasingly distant. The warmth he used to radiate when he led the trading caravan had completely disappeared, replaced instead by a cold and hardened soldier. He no longer expressed interest in Kaylen, leaving her with no other friends. Aely was dead. Mellai had left with Lon, with no foreseeable time of return. Queen Cyra had been kindly enough, but with irregular encounters. Above all, though, the severance of Kutad's love made Kaylen miss one person more than any other—her father, Scut. Sure he was quirky, but he was the only other person besides Kutad who had loved her unconditionally.

* * * * *

The stable doors opened and Braj entered with a bundle of supplies in his arms. He stared at Kaylen for a moment, then stepped forward with curiosity written across his face as he pulled straw from her hair.

Kaylen forced a smile. "I just needed a quick nap. I've been up for a few minutes. Thank you for your help."

Braj nodded. "It is my pleasure, Lady Kaylen." He restocked his horse's saddle bags, then mounted and extended a hand to Kaylen. "Are you certain you are fit for travel?" he said as he pulled her up onto the saddle behind him.

"I have no choice. I need to talk with Tarek and stop this madness."

Braj tapped the sides of his horse and steered out of the stable. "Let me know if you start to get sleepy. There are a few army shelters along the way. We can stop at any moment for you to rest." He paused for a few seconds before adding, "Do you really think you can convince the Rayders to maintain the peace?"

Kaylen rested her head against the soldier's back. "Again, I have no choice."

* * * * *

Once Braj traded positions with the sentry outside the north gate, Kaylen was easily able to slip across the half-mile bridge into the Gaurelic Waste. Although they had stopped at a small barracks for an hour so she could take a quick nap, they still arrived before sunrise. Braj had recommended the urgency, since darkness would ease her passage into the Rayder camp.

When Kaylen reached the opposite side of the bridge, she slowed as she stepped into a ring of light. One torch glowed at the entrance to the Gaurelic Waste. No Rayders were in sight, making her blind to any opposition. But she knew everyone could see her.

"Who approaches?" a man called from the darkness.

"Kaylen Shaw," she shouted back, as loudly as possible. The deep river silently passed behind her, but it still absorbed an alarming amount of sound.

A man appeared, moving quickly toward Kaylen. Her hand instinctively reached for the dagger hidden in her dress, but only temporarily. She knew this Rayder, and he was a good man.

"What are you doing here, Lady Kaylen?" He stepped closer to Kaylen and grabbed her arm urgently. "Commander Tarek ordered me to shoot all Appernysians on sight, so I ask again. Why are you here?"

"I have to speak with Tar . . . I mean, Commander Tarek. I have a message from King Drogan."

"Is he with you?"

Kaylen shook her head.

"Then your presence will anger Commander Tarek further. He only wishes to speak with Drogan."

"Well, I'm all he'll get," Kaylen countered. "Please let me see him. I'm trying to prevent unnecessary bloodshed."

"But Drogan does not share your same interest in the preservation of life. He sees fit to use my wife as a sacrifice to the calahein."

Kaylen laid her hand gently over the Rayder's. "I promise you that he isn't. That's what I'm trying to explain to Tarek. King Drogan is doing everything he can to resolve this peacefully."

He shook his head. "I cannot allow this, Lady Kaylen, or I will—"

"Let her pass," another voice called from the darkness. Kaylen recognized it as Lio Cope's, the head of Tarek's escort.

"Yes, Lieutenant," the sentry said, immediately stepping to the side and motioning Kaylen forward.

Thank you, she mouthed as she passed. He nodded, then disappeared beyond the torchlight again.

"This way," Lio called, leading Kaylen with his voice. "Tread carefully. The ground is covered with a solid layer of ice."

At the same moment, Kaylen's feet slipped out from under her and she landed on her rump with a solid thump.

"Ow," she grumbled as she pushed to her feet.

"Are you injured?" Lio called.

"I'm fine," Kaylen answered, sliding her feet along the ice to keep from falling. But the process wasn't fool-proof. Her foot struck a lump of ground jutting out of the ice, sending her tumbling forward. Fortunately, Lio was close enough that he caught her in his arms before she crashed onto the ice again.

"Welcome to the Gaurelic Waste," he muttered as he lifted the young lady to her feet again. "So kind of your king to share this premium estate with us."

"I'm sorry, Lio. I don't suppose it helps to know that I completely disagree with his decision?"

"No, it does not. Now what do you want with Commander Tarek? He has become far less approachable since your last visit."

"I know," Kaylen said, reaching for Lio's hand, "and I'm here to fix it. I just need to talk with him."

Lio recoiled before she could touch him. "Your feminine charms hold no sway here, Kaylen Shaw. I will inform Commander Tarek of your presence once he awakes, but do not expect an audience until Drogan arrives."

Kaylen shuddered, partly because of the cold, but mostly because she doubted King Drogan would come. Despite all of her rushing, she would be stuck in the waste for another two days. Not an encouraging thought. "What will I do in the meantime?"

"Find a cozy spot on the ice and make yourself at home." Lio gestured to the bridge with his chin. "Or you could always return to Itorea. I would hate to inconvenience you with our inhospitality."

"I'm not going anywhere," Kaylen said, drawing herself up and crossing her arms.

Lio smirked. "Have it your way," he said, then turned and walked away.

A few empty crates had been piled nearby. Kaylen used one as a seat and waited for the sun to rise. Navigating the Gaurelic Waste in the dark was proving dangerous for her, and she didn't know exactly where she was going, anyway.

A faint glow began to bud in the east, growing ever brighter as the time passed. Without any mountains to interfere, the sun crested the flat horizon a short time later. Its beams rained across the Rayder camp, offering light void of warmth.

The scene was detestable. Before her were fourteen thousand Rayder soldiers, slowly stirring. Canvas tents spotted the waste, but many people slept in the open with nothing more than a cloak and bedroll to fight the cold. They had been there only a week, but signs of their harsh environment were already beginning to show. Even after their conditional surrender, the Rayders had been so full of purpose while crossing the Taejan Plains. They had marched with honor, heads held high and eyes forward—even the injured men sitting in wagons had been full of pride.

None of that former enthusiasm existed anymore. The Rayders' spirits weren't defeated, but their eyes were full of exhaustion and hatred. King Drogan had pushed their patience too far. With every day that passed, chances of an alliance between the Appernysians and Rayders became less likely.

It wasn't until then, as Kaylen scanned their dismal conditions, that she noticed the bodies piled farther down the river. She turned her head away, too ashamed to count their numbered dead. Even the hardened Rayders were unable to defeat the Gaurelic Waste and its deplorable ability to kill.

Kaylen carefully stood and made her way toward the closest camp of soldiers. All traces of Kaylen's assignment to report on the Rayders disappeared from her thoughts.

Even if I can't talk with Tarek, she thought, *I can still help make a difference. I can still show him and the rest of the Rayders that I'm their friend.*

Chapter 28

The Garden

Having already descended most of the way down the corridor from the crossroads, the Beholders didn't have to travel far before they finally reached the mouth into the cave of crystals.

Mellai stepped forward. Her unclouded eyes were wide and her jaw slack with amazement at what the sun crystal's beam revealed. *And rightly so,* Lon thought, knowing he was responding exactly the same way to the view in front of them.

The Western Valley of Appernysia—the southwestern region containing smaller villages like Pree and Roseiri—was speckled in rolling hills. During growth months, these mounds were beautiful, covered in colorful foliage and mature trees of oak and birch. Lon had only experienced their beauty once, when he and his family had fled Roseiri. It had been during the end of Lon and Mellai's twelfth year, just before their October birthday.

Generally speaking, that year's celebrations had been pathetic. His family had been completely absorbed in building their new home in Pree while Aron worked tirelessly to earn the villagers' trust. But it hadn't mattered much to Lon, because he had already received his gift during their journey to Pree. For three days between Roseiri and Pree, Lon had absorbed the breathtaking hills of the Western Valley, brilliantly painted with an array of colors.

This was the scene that had now unveiled itself to Lon and Mellai, only it was dressed with an invaluable field of crystals. The cavern seemed even more massive while standing at its foundation. The waterfall was a hundred yards to their left, forming a river that weaved through the hills of gems that sprouted out of the stone in varying shapes and sizes. Some grew at ground level like shrubbery, while others protruded from the tips of proud stalagmites like branches on a tree.

Lon's sun crystal sparkled through a rainbow of colors in every shape and size imaginable. "Still worried we only have the scraps?" he teased.

Mellai turned her head to Lon and shouted, her voice muffled by the roaring waterfall as she numbly stepped forward into the garden. "Sun crystal."

Lon handed it to her, then Mellai raised her hand and the sun crystal floated into the air. She moved it over the center of the garden and placed it on the tip of a rounded stalagmite fifteen feet above the ground.

Lon didn't think the cavern could get any more breathtaking, but with the elevated light source, everything glowed even more brilliantly. He summoned his power and connected with Mellai's mind, but she spoke first, pointing at his feet. *Take your boots off. There's a lot of humidity in this cavern. I don't need you hurting yourself again.*

Do you think that's what made all the crystals? Lon thought, sitting down to slip off his footwear. *Is it the water?*

Mellai shrugged. *I have no idea, but it makes everything more dangerous. Just imagine if you had landed in here. You'd have—*

I get it, Little Sis, Lon interrupted. *No need to point out the obvious.*

A brief pause followed, Lon removing his boots while Mellai continued to search about. *I'm worried that anywhere I step, I'll be crushing a baby crystal that's just starting to grow. How are we going to do this?*

There, Lon answered, standing again to point past his sister. A ledge extended from the wall on the other side of the cavern, curving upward until it connected with a stout stalactite hanging from the cavern roof. It was a strange formation, creating an arching bridge of stone well above the crystals. *If we can get up there, we'd have a perfect view of everything. We could pluck our crystals without hurting anything else.*

Mellai eyed the path of the bridge and vigorously shook her head. *No way, Lon. That stalactite is hundreds of feet long, just hanging there. It might break if we stand on the platform.*

Don't be ridiculous, Lon thought. *Do you have any idea how much it weighs? I promise that an extra three hundred pounds won't make any difference.*

Mellai was still skeptical. *And how are you going to get up there?*

Like this, Lon answered, grabbing Mellai around her waist with his essence and lifting her into the air.

"Put me down!" Mellai screamed at the top of her lungs.

I can't now, Lon replied in his mind, *or you'll fall on the crystals.* He had already lifted her halfway up to the arch.

Mellai screamed again, too far away for Lon to hear.

What was that? Lon thought.

Put me back! Mellai screamed in her mind.

Lon gently set his sister safely on the highest point of the stone platform, directly next to the stalactite. *See, you're just fi—*

All conscious thought left Lon's mind as he felt himself being yanked forward. Faster than he could process, his sister had reached out her essence, grabbed him, and tossed him through the air. Unintelligible grunts escaped his lips as his lungs constricted in terror, then he felt himself stop midflight and whip back the other direction. Three more times he felt himself violently change direction, but could no longer process what was happening. The forces on his body had crippled his awareness and he blacked out.

✳   ✳   ✳   ✳   ✳

"Wake up!"

Lon flinched and rolled sideways off the stone bridge, but felt himself immediately stop and redirect back to where he had awoken.

"Can you hear me now?" Mellai screamed, dropping him onto the platform from a foot above. He landed on his side with a grunt. "I told you never to do that again! Never!"

"Calm down, Mel," Lon said, raising his hands as a gesture of peace. Even a fool could see that this was not the time for jokes.

"Don't you tell me to calm down. Don't you dare tell me that."

"I was just trying to—"

Mellai stepped forward and slapped Lon across his face, hard enough to stun his thoughts. "I know why you did it, Lon, but that doesn't make it right. I told you never to do that again!"

Lon licked his lip, which had split open on his teeth and drizzled blood into his mouth. He racked his brain, desperately seeking for an explanation. Lifting her into the air was the obvious problem, but when had he ever done that before? Then he remembered. He had raised Mellai onto Dawes after her horse had died. He remembered her complaining, but not anywhere nearly as explosive as what Lon witnessed now.

"I don't understand, Mel. Why are you so angry?" Mellai tried to slap Lon again, but he grabbed her wrist. "I'm trying to talk this out."

"Stop it!" Mellai screamed, yanking her hand free and immobilizing Lon with True Sight. Lon just stared back at his sister, not daring to call upon his own power. "No one will ever restrain me again, Lon. No one!"

Her final statement brought everything together in Lon's mind.

"I'm sorry," he said, sincerity pouring from his eyes. "It'll never happen again, I promise." His sister was talking about when Braedr had attacked her in Pree. The experience had transformed Braedr into Clawed and brought many Rayder deaths. But never had Lon considered how it had transformed his sister.

Mellai stood facing Lon, with just enough light from the sun crystal below to illuminate her flaring nostrils. She still seethed with anger, but Lon would patiently wait it out. She had every right to be angry.

Slowly, her heaving chest diminished, her strained muscles loosened, and her face softened. As a final signal of her calm, she released Lon and sat on the stone bridge with her knees tucked under her arms. Her clouded eyes had become clear again.

Lon carefully crossed the stone and sat down beside her, his legs dangling off the edge. "You alright?"

"I could've killed you."

"Easily," Lon agreed, "and I would have deserved it."

"That's just it," Mellai said, tears slipping into her eyes. "You didn't deserve any of it. I was completely out of control, Lon. It's me who should be apologizing."

"Thanks," Lon replied, nudging her lovingly with his shoulder. He leaned forward and peered at the crystal garden below. "This really is a good spot. Look at that view."

Without speaking, Mellai rolled onto her belly and leaned her head on her folded hands. Lon watched her as she searched the stones, glad to see she hadn't lost her desire to bond with Huirk, then he began his own treasure hunt.

"I started telling you back in the cave," Lon said as he searched, "that I'm choosing a crystal that matches Bromax's fighting style. He's large and powerful, and I think he'll really like something that he can keep using as a weighted flail."

"That's considerate," Mellai said. "Huirk, on the other hand, is nothing like Bromax. He's young, goofy, and spry. He'd probably like something more sleek so he won't lose his maneuverability." She pursed her lips. "You're lucky Bromax has black hair. What color matches light brown?"

"No clue. I thought that was your skill."

"More like Kaylen's. She'd choose both of ours in no time."

Lon smiled. It would be good to talk with Kaylen, to reconnect and see if they were still fit for marriage. He longed to hold her again, to feel the warmth of Kaylen's arms wrapped around him. It had always been so soothing and therapeutic. Even a little kiss would be nice.

"What are you grinning about?" Mellai said. "Wait, don't tell me. I've seen that look before. Something to do with . . . Kaylen? Oh, Lon. Even as an all-powerful Beholder, you still get the butterflies when you think of her, don't you?"

"You got me," he answered, grinning even wider. "When we get out of here, she'll be the first person I contact."

"Even before Tarek? He'll want a report of where you've been." As his sister spoke, a romantic smile crept onto her face, too.

"Whoa, what's that?" Lon jested. "Seems like the thought of Tarek is having the same effect on you."

Her smile immediately disappeared. "I could throw you off of here."

"Yes, we've established that."

They searched the stones for many hours, casually talking about the crystals and any other subject that came up. At one point, Mellai pulled a sphere of water from the river to drink. Lon couldn't help but lick his lips in delight. He had never tasted anything so cool and refreshing. It revitalized his energy and attitude.

Lon eventually twisted around on the platform to search the crystals on the other side of the garden. And there, right in front of him, was the cluster of crystals he had been searching for. A treasure trove of obsidian. *Black stone for my black ghraef,* Lon thought to himself. Now he just had to find the right shape and size. As with the majority of the gems in the crystal garden, most of them were elongated prisms with dangerously sharp pyramid tips. Not anywhere near what he had in mind.

"Do you think our crystals have to be shaped naturally?" he asked his sister.

"I've been wondering the same thing. Every shape I saw on Itorea's perimeter wall seemed to be genuine. What do you think?"

Lon scratched the thick brown beard that had been growing on his face. "I say we do whatever we want. Beholders may have chosen natural stones in the First Age, but there are plenty of differences about our time. Like you, for example. I say we create our own crystals, like we did over Jareth's grave."

"Can you do it by yourself?"

Lon shrugged. "I might need a little help."

Mellai glanced around as if someone were watching them. "I don't know, Lon. It might make Llen angry. Or maybe it will offend the ghraefs. Bromax seems especially traditional."

"Let's ask the Jaed." Lon cupped his hands around his mouth and shouted. "We're going to make our own crystals, Llen. If you want us to stop, now is the time to speak up."

No response.

"Good enough for me," Lon continued.

"But what about Bromax and Huirk?"

Lon extended his essence and began collecting piles of obsidian together. "We're going to make the crystals so unique and stunning that the ghraefs won't have any choice but to love them."

Once Lon had collected more than enough obsidian, he slid away from Mellai and moved the pile between them. The narrow mound was stacked so high that Lon couldn't see his sister, even after he stood, so he connected with her mind.

Mellai's thoughts immediately entered his head. *I'm guessing that you're ready?*

Absolutely.

To Lon's left, a bright sphere began forming as his sister collected the wind to form an energy shield. *What's the shape, and how big?* she asked.

Tell me if this makes sense. I want it to look like two shallow saucers cupped against each other, with their joined edge sharpened all the way around the seam. Basically, Bromax will be able to use it like his bone tip right now, bludgeoning anything he wants. But then he'll also be able to swipe it sideways like a glaive to slice the calahein in half.

Lon felt an emotional shudder from his sister. *Terrifying.*

That's the idea. Can you shape it while I supply the obsidian?

The glowing energy shield reshaped into a perfect vision of Lon's idea, only too small. *Bigger,* Lon thought. *Large enough so that I could curl up inside of it if it were hollow.*

Mellai enlarged it as instructed. *Like this?*

Perfect. Now hold it steady. Lon picked up a prism of obsidian with his essence and tried to move it through Mellai's energy shield, but it recoiled and dropped out of his grasp. He barely reacted in time to grab it before it shattered on the crystals below.

Try this, Mellai said, opening a hole in the top of her formation for Lon to deposit the obsidian. Lon followed her lead and soon the shining black stone was brimming at the top.

Now what's your plan? Mellai asked. *You can't shape the obsidian while it's solid.*

You'll melt it and let it naturally fill the shape. Just don't heat it too much. I don't want it changing into some other type of stone.

Mellai closed the opening. *I'm holding the energy shield. You get to melt it.*

Lon nodded, forgetting that his sister couldn't see him as he pierced the lining of Mellai's energy shield and began heating the black stone. It was difficult at first, but as each prism melted, the contained heat assisted with the rest. Eventually it was all liquefied, but a small gap still remained at the top of the shield.

Drop a few more in, Mellai suggested, *but carefully. No splashing.*

Lon worked as quickly as possible before the obsidian cooled, but he found it impossible to add the perfect amount of crystals to fill the shape. It was overfilled, oozing slightly up the shield's porthole.

Wait a second, Mellai said as she wrapped the energy shield closed and compressed it enough to reshape it as Lon desired. *Alright, now cool it.*

How?

I already showed you this once. Soothe the energy with your essence. It's not difficult.

Lon pierced her energy shield with his essence and began interacting with the melted obsidian. He casually swept through it as if he were swishing his hand through the water of a pond. *Like this?*

Good enough.

Quicker than usual, the obsidian solidified so that Mellai could remove the shield and place the large crystal back on Lon's side of the surplus pile. *It's magnificent, Lon. Truly. Bromax will be amazed.*

But it's not finished yet. I still need to harden it. Let me know when you're ready for my help with your crystal.

Lon directed his attention to the unique black crystal glistening from the sun crystal below. The top of the obsidian dome was just high enough that it would hit Lon under the chin, if he could stand close enough—but that was impossible because of the foot-deep obsidian blade wrapping around its middle. If Lon were shoved into it, he was certain his belly would be split wide open on its sharpened edge.

But just to make sure, Lon thought, stepping forward and running the sleeve of his tunic lightly along its edge. His eyes widened with delight when the pale cotton fabric sliced apart with hardly any effort. He stepped back and began weaving more obsidian matter into his ghraef's new tail crystal. *You're right, Mel. Bromax will love this.*

Chapter 29

King's Cross

It really is beautiful, Mellai thought to herself, having severed her power and emotion bond with her brother. She wasn't afraid of sharing such a thought with him, but she didn't want him to feel her jealousy. Lon had known from the beginning what crystal to choose for Bromax, but Mellai was clueless. She had been searching the gem garden for what seemed like forever, but nothing had caught her eye or prompted an idea.

She glanced at her brother. Lon's beard and dark brown curls obscured his face. He looked silly, but ruggedly handsome. His face was as lean as when he had left Pree, but not in an I'm-going-to-die sort of way.

His features were more chiseled than before, along with the rest of his body. Lon had been living a very different life with the Rayders. His physique had transformed from a dairy farmer to a seasoned soldier.

Lon's blue eyes were deeper, too—not in color, but in wisdom and experience. As she watched him, Mellai knew why the Rayders followed him. He bore a contagious confidence. Lon had truly become a man, someone Kaylen could gladly marry. Nearly flawless in appearance, were it not for that scar on his face.

Yet the King's Cross didn't represent what it used to. It was still carried by the Rayders, but if their population had evolved to standards even close to those upheld by Lon and his squad, they would be a people worthy of joining Appernysia.

No, Mellai thought, *not just of joining us, but of protecting us. Even leading us.*

As much as she wanted to, Mellai couldn't deny it.

But how could she ever convince her own leaders of this opinion? She hoped they had experienced similar changes of heart while retreating to Itorea with the Rayders, but it was a desperate hope. Their feud ran deep—twelve-hundred years deep—while Mellai had only been alive for a meager eighteen. Maybe Kaylen had learned a new perspective, and perhaps even Queen Cyra—she seemed kindly enough—but doubtfully Kamron or King Drogan. Mellai had seen the way they both talked to Tarek and Lon. No, her general and her king might not ever change.

Unless I do something to help them along, Mellai thought, her mind unveiling a fantastically petrifying idea. Something drastic, even borderline treasonous. But the potential for changing hearts was too tempting to ignore, and Mellai felt she owed it most to her brother. If any part of Lon still doubted her love for him, this one act would sweep all reservations away.

Having made up her mind, Mellai recommenced her search, but this time looking for blue crystals. It would be a complicated design, one that most definitely required her brother's help.

A cluster of azurite had formed at the far edge of the crystal garden, gleaming from the sun crystal's light. It pained Mellai to think of destroying such natural beauty, but her mind was set. She was transforming them into something even greater.

"Figured it out?" Lon asked, stepping next to her.

"Where's yours?" Mellai asked, searching around.

Lon pointed to the opening where they had entered the cavern. "I'm done, so I thought it might not be such a bad idea to move it off this platform. Piling two indestructible tail crystals on here might be pushing our luck."

"Not the worst idea you've ever had," Mellai agreed, "but I need you to step back so I can move this between us again."

She piled the first layer of azurite between herself and her twin, then a tingle in her brain signaled that Lon had summoned his power again and reconnected to her emotions.

What are we making? Lon asked.

You'll just have to wait and see. It's a little bit more complex than yours, so I'll create the molds again while you pile in the stone.

This color is heavenly, Lon thought, picking up one of the crystals to examine it more closely. *Reminds me of the deep blue sky right before sunset. I can't tell you how nice it'll be to see that again.*

Mellai laughed out loud. *Believe me, I understand completely.*

Realizing that the design would require far less fill than Lon's, Mellai stopped collecting the blue crystals while the top half of her brother's body was still visible.

I haven't sculpted something like this before, Mellai thought as she began gathering wind energy for the shield encasing. *No judging.*

I'd never, Lon replied, his thoughts oozing with sarcasm.

Just before she reshaped the energy shield, Mellai decided to create her design in pieces that she would knit together afterward. She began by forming an empty javelin shell, with a two-foot shaft as thick as her leg, and a six-inch conical tip slightly larger in radius where it touched the shaft. She aimed the tip down so Lon could load the azurite into its open shaft.

There, she thought to her brother. *Let's make six of these first.*

Six?

Yes, and they have to be exactly the same.

Oh, that'll be easy. More sarcasm.

Just fill it as close to the top as possible and I'll match their lengths later.

Mellai focused all of her effort into maintaining the shape while Lon filled, melted, and cooled six identical javelins. It took time, but they turned out exactly as Mellai had imagined. She lined them up side by side on the stone arch to trim and shape them equally.

Now for the reveal, she thought, taking a deep breath.

After moving two of the javelins out of the way, she rearranged the remaining four so that their shafts were touching each other in the center of the design, with their four sharpened tips pointing outward like a map's compass. Exactly like the King's Cross, but blue—as it should be—and still missing a few parts.

Mellai felt her brother's reaction long before he communicated any words. At first, he was apprehensive, surely worried about the politics behind such a statement by Appernysia's Beholder. But slowly, the apprehension gave way to heartfelt gratitude.

I don't know what to say.

You don't have to say anything, Mellai responded as she knitted the edges of the four shafts together and wrapped their hollowed center with a tiny circular energy shield. *Fill that gap, please.*

Lon complied, melting a small amount of azurite to fuse the four javelins together at the center. Then Mellai knitted their seams to strengthen their bond.

It looks good, Lon commented as Mellai lifted it into the air with her essence.

We're far from done, Mellai answered as she twisted the King's Cross forty-five degrees and formed an arcing shaft between two of the javelins, close to their tips. Lon filled the form and hardened it, then Mellai rotated three more times as they repeated the same action.

Now it looks like the King's Cross, Mellai thought once they finished. A hollow circle ran completely around the four javelins.

So what are these other two for? Lon asked, pointing at the unused javelins.

Mellai smiled and lifted the structure into the air while keeping it parallel with the ground. *We're going to add more personality.*

Under careful instruction from Mellai, Lon helped her to knit the extra javelins at the center, pointing directly up and down, as if she were creating an oversized version of a child's spinning top. After that, they created two more intersecting, hollow circles through the two new javelins. The final effect gave the full design a spherical shape, with six javelin tips poking out in all directions.

That was harder than I thought it would be, Mellai thought, still weaving more azurite into the design to make it impervious to damage. She took her time to fill every available space in the crystal, knowing that her design was far more brittle than Lon's.

This is perfect for Huirk, Lon observed. *It's still crisp and angular, but more artistic than Bromax's tail crystal.*

But do you think it will interfere with his ability to maneuver in the air?

Lon paused and examined the design. *I don't think so, but it might cause problems when he's fighting. A calahein's arm or leg might get caught in those empty spaces, or a kelsh or seith might even grab hold of it on purpose to try and pull down Huirk.*

Mellai slumped to the ground, completely discouraged. In her attempt to heal Appernysian and Rayder relationships, she would kill her own ghraef. *I wish we had thought of that before we started.*

Wait, though, Lon continued, searching around the cavern. *What if you fill in the center with clear diamond, up to the outer edge of the hollow circles? Everyone will still be able to see the King's Cross design, but the crystal will be solid like Huirk's current bone tip.*

Mellai grabbed her brother with her essence and pulled him around their creation until she could hug him with her real arms. "Thank you, Lon," she said aloud. "Not just for this, but for everything you've done—everything you've sacrificed—this past year. You're stronger than I ever could hope to be."

"Don't be so sure about that," Lon answered as he returned the hug. "You came back from the dead, remember?"

Mellai chuckled. "I forgot I told you about that."

Lon stepped back. "Now let's fill this thing in and harden it so we can hurry back up to the Beholders cave. We've taken too long already."

Chapter 30

Impasse

Shalán glanced over her shoulder again, searching for her husband. Even while sitting on Dawes's back, she saw no sign of Aron or the other four Rayders.

After waiting two days, Snoom had finally decided that they'd leave the road and travel northeast along the forest's edge. He had obviously given the order with a heavy heart and Shalán didn't begrudge him for it, but she hadn't given up hope that her husband was alive.

She turned her attention northeast, in the direction they were moving. It had taken them four days after crossing a frozen section of the South Pearl River to traverse most of the tree-filled terrain. No attacks had reached them yet, but Shalán stayed alert. They were near to the east edge of the forest, which would present an entirely new set of problems.

Aron had left an arming sword hanging on Dawes's saddle. "Just in case," he had told Shalán, but the likelihood that she would need it was growing every day. In addition, Shalán felt a stirring in her blood, an overpowering desire to draw the sword and rush into the Briyél Forest for rescue or retribution. It was an unnerving temptation, almost as if she were a Rayder herself.

"Any sign of him?" Reese asked, walking beside her in the deep snow.

Shalán forced a smile. "Not yet, but I'm sure he's fine." Despite her many efforts, Reese had refused to ride Dawes, arguing it was her right and privilege as Lon's mother.

"I was a fool to hold back my apologies," Scut said from the other side of Dawes, "and now I might never have a chance to tell him so myself." He wiped a tear from his eye. "Aron is a good man, as is your son. You raised 'em right, Shalán. If time ever sees my Kaylen together with Lon again, I'll still be a proud father-in-law and do my best to show it. Not just because he's a Beholder."

"Thank you, Scut." Even while sitting on Dawes, she was easily able to lean over and reassuringly squeeze the tall man's shoulder. "And I'd be the happiest mother-in-law in Appernysia."

"If there's still an Appernysia to be happy in," Ric commented. He was following behind Shalán on his own horse.

"You can keep those thoughts to yourself," Snoom called from the front of their line.

"Yes, Lieutenant," Ric answered, followed by low grumbles and curses.

As soon as they reached the forest's east edge, Shalán realized what Duncan had meant. They were at least five miles away from the northern shore of the lake, and even more miles west from a feasible spot where they might cross the Casconni River.

Snoom counselled with Ric and Duncan, then they decided it would be best to move as far east as possible. Whether one mile or twenty miles from the forest, they would be easy to spot—better to create as much distance as possible.

*   *   *   *   *

A burst of freezing wind tore through the trees, cutting through Shalán's layered clothing. She leaned forward against Dawes, sharing his warmth. The wind had steadily increased as they traveled east, a result Snoom attributed to the nearing coastline. Another day had passed without any sign of Aron or the four Rayders.

Shalán had never seen the Asaras Sea, until they crested a swell in the terrain and had an unobstructed view. Even from two miles away the view was breathtaking. Snow covered the beach and thick layers of ice along the shoreline, but beyond that, the sea swelled and waves rolled over themselves before crashing back into the deep blue water. Another gale of wind hit Shalán in the face, leaving a taste of salt in her mouth and a determination to return during summer months. It was beautiful. Absolutely breathtaking.

"There's our crossing," Reese said sarcastically, pointing farther north and drawing everyone's attention.

Shalán's hope immediately dimmed. She had thought its size would reduce as they traveled east, but Shalán knew they were trapped. The river was still too deep and wide to endure in their weakened condition, and the current too swift for ice to form.

A quick glance around proved that everyone else had come to the same realization. Their eyes were darkened and shoulders slumped.

"Let's keep moving forward," Snoom called, tapping his horse's sides with his heels. "There has to be a manageable crossing somewhere."

Shalán doubted Snoom's positivity, but another danger concerned her even more. The southern half of the Briyél Forest had ended twenty miles west of their position, but on the opposite side of the shore, it extended all the way to the coastline. Just as Ric had warned, if the calahein infested those woods, Pree's villagers would be walking right into a trap.

She tapped Dawes's sides with her heels and moved up next to Snoom. "Can I talk to you for a moment, Lieutenant?"

"Of course," Snoom answered, dipping his head at her.

"I'm sure you've considered the danger waiting for us on the other side of the river. What is your plan?"

Snoom glanced over his shoulder, then turned to Shalán and spoke for her ears only. "My plan is to keep your villagers moving,

Shalán. We can't stay here, the leaders of Draege would never let us in, and Toj is too far away. All that remains is forward."

"But what about the calahein?" Shalán pressed. "They might kill us before we even set foot on the opposite shore."

"If we give up, we die, too." He breathed a deep sigh, his warm breath creating a cloud of mist in front of his face. "In all honestly, I've been hoping since Draege that your children would show up. We could really use their help right now."

Shalán didn't respond, too caught up in her emotions. A full month had passed without signs from Lon or Mellai, and Shalán's apprehension grew with every passing day. She doubted any foe could defeat their combined strength, especially with allied ghraefs fighting with them, but Shalán had never encountered the calahein. Their enemies might be able to . . . *No.* She kept pushing the thought aside. Her parents were dead and her husband missing. She couldn't allow her mind to tread down this path, too.

Shalán absently fingered the ghraef pendant hanging around her neck, thinking of her twin children. *Where are you?*

Chapter 31

Bonding

"Just be careful," Lon warned, sitting on his ghraef's back.

Bromax huffed and grabbed the obsidian creation by his teeth, keeping his tongue and lips reared to avoid the sharp edge wrapping around the black tail crystal.

"Didn't really think that one through, did we?" Mellai said. She had already braided her legs securely with Huirk's hair, while he slobbered incessantly down the King's Cross tail crystal in his own mouth. "Bromax is going to cut himself again."

Lon shook his head and turned away, glad to be partnered with Bromax. While Huirk had loped around excitedly when he saw Mellai's creation, Bromax had methodically circled Lon's and evaluated it for imperfections. He must have recognized it as obsidian, which is naturally very brittle, because he hurled it against the cave wall. The resulting thud had been so loud that Lon could feel the vibrations in his chest, and the ghraef had sliced open his paw in the process. But the tail crystal held true, and Bromax had bowed before Lon to show his appreciation.

"May I?" Lon had answered, touching the top of Bromax's bleeding paw, and the ghraef had flipped it over in compliance. It had been the first time Lon ever healed a wound, but it came easily after the weaving and blending he had done in the cave of crystals. But it had also brought a flood of regret and frustration, which Lon still fought to push aside. With this healing skill, he could have saved many lives—most importantly, Omar's.

With the tail crystal still in his mouth, Bromax pawed the rolled-up rug of crystal designs and motioned to the floor. Lon understood and used his power to lay it out over Llen's journal carved into the stone. "We'll have to come back another time to stitch your designs into the rug," he said, patting Bromax on the thick mat of black hair covering his back, "but I'm afraid we may have taken too long already."

"We're concerned about our parents," Mellai added, glaring at her brother from her spot on Huirk, "but not too concerned to ignore our bonding ceremony. Are we ready, Huirk? Do we finally get to meet the rest of the ghraefs?"

Huirk directed the question to Bromax, who roared in approval before sprinting up the passage leading out of the cave. Lon had to duck low to avoid the stone ceiling, and he took the opportunity to quickly braid Bromax's hair around his own legs. The speed with which Bromax moved was amazing. Lon could feel the ghraef's back muscles stretch with every stride, then snap back together as he powered forward. With thick padded paws, he navigated every turn without slipping, sometimes even using the wall at sharp corners.

Lon glanced back and saw Huirk following easily behind Bromax, his slobber splattering on the floors and walls as he ran. Lon doubted the smaller ghraef was as fast as Bromax, but his size seemed to make it easier to maneuver in that enclosed space.

Just then, Lon felt his body wrench backward as Bromax burst ahead, leaving Huirk far behind. When Lon was finally able to turn around, he saw that Bromax had entered a straight passage, miles long with an opening at the far end. Lon immediately released True Sight to confirm what he hoped, reveling at the natural vision. Bright sunlight poured into the corridor. They were finally leaving the mountain.

Lon threw his fists into the air and shouted in triumph. His euphoria was founded on his escape from the pressing darkness and inability to tell time, but so much more added to his joy. His skill with True Sight had grown tremendously. His knowledge of Appernysia's previous Beholders was sound. His bond with Bromax had grown, and after finalizing it with a deadly tail crystal, they would finally return to Appernysia. He had anticipated this day for weeks and couldn't contain himself, so he shouted again.

Mellai's own screams of delight echoed up the passage, bringing tears to Lon's eyes as they continued to put on speed. He and his twin sister were now fully equipped to protect their kingdom from destruction.

Bromax burst out of the opening with his black-feathered wings tucked against his body, diving forward along the face of a sheer cliff. The rushing air made it difficult for Lon to breathe, along with his own apprehension, but he stayed focused as his eyes adjusted to the bright sunlight. He kept telling himself that Bromax wouldn't do anything to put their lives in danger.

Farther they dove, thousands of feet toward a canopy of snow-covered tree tops, until Bromax finally spread his wings and lifted high into the air. They circled around, floating on the wind, while Huirk took Mellai on a stomach-churning adventure of twirls and loops. But Lon's sister seemed just as thrilled as the ghraef. In fact, she even leaped from Huirk's back and dove through the air, testing the currents with her extended arms and legs before tucking into a tumbling roll and flaring out again. Huirk had responded with his own loop and dive, slipping underneath Mellai for her to weave her legs into his hair before they leveled out.

As Bromax began flapping his wings to climb higher into the sky, Lon took the opportunity to speak with his sister. He summoned True Sight and connected to her emotions, turning around and pointing at his eyes for her to do the same.

You are crazy, you know that? Lon said in his mind.

Oh, Lon, doesn't it feel good to be out? I can't stop smiling!

I totally understand, but we need to start thinking tactically, Mel. What's our plan once the ceremony is over?

We'll have a full-blown planning party. Now try to relax, even if just for a minute.

As Bromax continued to climb, Lon laid on Bromax's neck and let his arms fall to the sides. "Mellai's right. It is nice to be out of that mountain. How long were we in there, do you think?"

Bromax answered by tipping sideways and rolling once in the air.

"Once?" Lon said, trying to decipher his meaning. "Maybe one cycle? . . . obviously not one day or week, and there's no way we were there a full year. One month?"

Bromax nodded.

"Wow," Lon continued, baffled by the lapse of time. "It's strange how reliant we've become on the sun. Warmth, light, growth, direction, time—all byproducts of that big yellow thing in the sky. Remind me never to take it for granted again."

Bromax only huffed, then turned and began circling a large meadow planted in the intersecting valley of five separate peaks. Unlike the rest of the mountains and despite its size, this valley was completely absent of snow, explained by wisps of steam venting through spotted fissures in the soil. The grass was flat and yellow, though, still obedient to the season's control. And a strange pile of spherical stones had been heaped on one side of the clearing.

Lon thought he spied movement around the borders of the meadow, so he called upon his power to verify. Indeed, the entire pasture was circled with dense clusters of living essences.

He dismissed True Sight and sat tall, hoping to honor Bromax's decision to bond with him, yet the lower they circled, the more excited and nervous Lon became. This was a momentous occasion, and the other ghraefs had come to pay witness in a sacred meadow.

It wasn't until they landed that Lon realized the pile of rocks was actually bone tips, all bitten from the ghraefs by their own mouths.

The mound was huge, even larger than Bromax, from an age when Beholders and ghraefs served together regularly.

Huirk landed next to Bromax, placing his tail crystal next to Bromax's while Mellai smiled reassuringly at Lon. But he felt no such peace. As the ghraefs had begun filing into the meadow, he realized that he had no idea what to do. Sure, he would bond the crystal to Bromax's tail, but what about the formalities? Should he remain sitting on the ghraef's back, or should he stand off to one side?

Deciding on the latter, he began to unbraid Bromax's hair, but the ghraef stopped him with a quick shake of his head and a snarl. It didn't take long for Lon to realize why, and he relayed the warning to Mellai. The approaching ghraefs were stalking, bodies close to the ground, wings tucked back, and unblinking eyes locked on Bromax. They varied in size and hair color, but Lon paid little attention to such trivial details. He was more interested in their numbers, and how to defend himself. From what he could see, at least thirty ghraefs had entered the clearing, fully grown and frightening, with more ghraefs pouring out of the woods behind them. All of them looked ready to attack.

Huirk leaped in front of Bromax, his tail coiled up like a scorpion and teeth flashing. Mellai had obviously summoned her power, because her voice filled the clearing.

"Stop!"

The ghraefs momentarily paused their approach, giving Lon time to call upon True Sight and connect to his sister. *What are you doing? Get out of the way.*

Shut up, Lon, she demanded. *These are renegade ghraefs, and they've been waiting here since we entered the mountains so they could stop this ceremony. They'll kill us if they have to.*

Lon stammered. *How do you know all this?*

I begged, so Huirk let me read his thoughts for a second. Everyone here opposes Bromax and the rest of the ghraef council. They don't want their kind to be reunited with Beholders.

The ghraefs began stalking forward again, edging around Huirk and Mellai.

Lon's sister was searching about when seven enormous ghraefs dropped between the opposing lines, facing the renegades with their own tails raised defensively.

As Lon wondered if this was the ghraef council, the ghraef in the center—nearly twice as large as Bromax and wrapped with dark brown hair streaked with gray—turned and spoke gutturally at them. Huirk immediately leaped back to face Bromax's tail, then together they bit off each other's bone tips.

The two ghraefs snarled in pain as they tossed their bone tips onto the pile, but not nearly as loud as the roars of opposition from the renegades. They poured forward to attack, but the seven larger ghraefs held the protective line.

Hurry, Mellai shouted at Lon, already fusing the King's Cross to Huirk's armored tail at one of the six javelin tips.

Lon followed her example, using his essence to place the ridge of the obsidian crystal against his ghraef's tail. "This is going to hurt," Lon called, then he split the tail with the sharpened edge. Bromax shuddered, but remained still while Lon blended each half of his tail into the crystal's sides.

"How does that loo—" Lon began to ask, when two ghraefs dropped on top of them—about Huirk's size. Lon looked to his sister for help, but she and Huirk were already occupied with their own opponents.

One of the ghraefs snapped at the Beholder's head, and Lon barely managed to lean out of the way before extending his essence to grab the ghraef by his throat. It thrashed and flailed under Lon's grip, until Bromax whipped sideways and decapitated the ghraef with his new obsidian tail crystal. The other ghraef tried to leap away, but Bromax sunk his teeth into his cowardly opponent's tail and pulled him back, whipping him sideways through the air. One of the ghraef's wings broke under his own weight when he crashed to the ground, but he remained motionless, signaling his defeat to Bromax.

The leading gray-haired ghraef, now splattered with blood from the civil battle, roared something else at Lon's ghraef. Bromax took a step in his leader's direction, his eyes screaming that he wanted to help, but he coiled onto his hind legs and leaped into the air. Huirk was right behind him, and they flew side-by-side in the opposite direction. A few of the renegade ghraefs tried to follow, but Lon and Mellai fought them off by breaking wings or throwing them to the ground.

"*Why are we running away?*" Mellai shouted aloud and in her mind, seething with anger. "*We need to help the council.*"

I agree, especially if that's the ghraef council, but the gray one told Bromax to flee. Lon searched the carnage below. A pile of dead renegades were strewn around the seven ghraef council members, and the rest seemed to have lost their initiative. A few were still fighting, but most had fled back into the forest.

"Why would they do that?" Lon asked Bromax, but he already knew the answer. Just as Appernysia had experienced a civil fallout at the end of the First Age, so must have the ghraefs. It made sense, since the ghraefs were as intelligent as humans, but it still broke Lon's heart to see so many of their kind needlessly dead.

"I'm sorry," Lon said to his ghraef. "Are you hurt?"

Bromax shook his head, still flapping his wings to gain altitude, so Lon checked with Mellai.

Huirk hit himself with the tail crystal, Mellai answered, *but it barely broke the skin. He'll be fine. What about Bromax?*

Not a scratch, Lon answered, then directed his attention to the ghraef. "Bromax, we need to stop in Pree first, but not too long. Let's make this quick."

Chapter 32

Strategy

An hour's flight northeast brought the Beholders out of the mountains and to Pree. Lon shook his head in amazement. All this time, the ghraefs had been living this close to their village.

After circling Pree twice to search for danger, Bromax and Huirk landed in the front yard of the Marcs' old property. The frame house was still standing, except the front door was swinging open and the windows were shattered. A quick evaluation inside proved Lon's suspicions to be true. Their home had been looted of provisions.

"Looks like Master Delancy has been preparing himself for a long winter," he said, kicking at loose floorboards that had been ripped up in search of hidden treasures.

"We should pay him a visit and return the favor," Mellai answered. "Maybe if we dump a cask of mead on his head he'll think twice next time."

"Hopefully there won't be a next time. I can't blame him, though. He has a daughter to look after."

Mellai scoffed. "Sonela is of age, and plenty capable of taking care of herself."

"Maybe not," Lon countered. "Delancy has been protecting her since she was born. She might not know how to do anything."

"Except cry."

Lon returned to the doorway, his hand resting on his falchion's pommel. "Let's go. Bromax and Huirk should be part of our planning."

"That's a no-brainer," Mellai growled as she shouldered her brother out of the way. He let her go without dispute. He was upset, too, but there was no punishment they could give Delancy that the brewer hadn't already brought upon himself. By the end of winter, he'd realize his choice to stay behind was foolish, and he and Sonela would suffer plenty for it.

Outside the Marcs' house, the two ghraefs were lying on the ground, their bodies forming a connected circle with their shining tail crystals in front of each other's snouts. Their inside wings were also carpeted across the snow for their Beholders to rest on. Lon smiled at the planning nest and sprawled out on Bromax's black feathers while Mellai sat against Huirk's side.

"On with it, Master Lon," she said, her voice oozing with sarcastic formality. "We need to make this as fast and efficient as possible."

"What happened back there in Ursoguia, Bromax?" Lon asked, ignoring his sister. "Why did those ghraefs try to attack you? And who were those other seven who came to our rescue?"

"They were huge," Mellai added. "I thought you were big, Bromax, but they put your size to shame."

Bromax growled and flipped the tip of his wing, tossing Mellai a foot into the air before she sprawled flat on her back.

Lon burst into laughter. "You do that any time you want, Bromax. I think you're the only one who can get away with it." He paused as Mellai sat back against Huirk, but on her own ghraef's wing instead. "I don't suppose you have a way to talk to us, do you Bromax? It's not fair that you can understand our language, but we have no clue what you're saying."

Bromax only shrugged his shoulders.

"Then let's play 'yes or no.' We'll guess, and you tell us if we're right."

The ghraef huffed again.

"I'll go first," Mellai said. "Those seven larger ghraefs looked old and important. I'm guessing they're your leaders?"

Bromax nodded.

"So obviously they supported our presence," Lon added, "which means the other ghraefs must have been dissenters. Kind of like Rayders used to be, right?"

Another nod.

Lon continued. "And those renegade ghraefs have been fighting you since the First Age?"

Huirk answered this time. His tongue hung playfully out the side of his snout as he nodded.

"So just like Appernysia versus Rayders," Mellai continued, "there's no real good explanation as to why you're still fighting. Maybe bonding with Beholders will help to heal it?"

Bromax's burst of breath fluttered his lips as he rolled his eyes.

"Or maybe not," Lon observed. "They seemed pretty radical, didn't they, Mel? That's probably why Bromax spent all his time guarding the mouth into the Beholders cave."

Mellai stood. "All that time I thought Huirk was protecting the Beholders archive from us, but he was really being protected by Bromax." She crossed the space between the two ghraefs to place her hand gently on Bromax's nose. "Thank you. You're very brave."

Bromax pushed his head forward and nudged her with his nose.

"Along those same lines, I've been thinking about that skirmish with the ghraefs," Lon said. "We were cut off from each other, Mel, surprised and completely preoccupied by our own fights. We did nothing together."

"No synergy," Mellai replied.

"Exactly. Llen told us that synergy was our secret weapon, so to speak."

Bromax and Huirk shifted their weight to draw the Beholders' attention, and both ghraefs' eyebrows were showing notable interest. Bromax even cut in, speaking to the younger ghraef in their guttural language. Lon tried to decipher some portion of it, but the mix of bear and dog intonations still sounded completely foreign.

"You two know all about synergy," Mellai commented.

Both nodded vigorously—even the usually mellow Bromax.

"I think back frequently to the way you fought together in Roseiri," Lon added. "It was almost like a dance, how you worked around each other in unspoken synchronization. Kind of like a wolf pack, you know?"

"So that's how we're supposed to work together?" Mellai said skeptically. "Like a wolf pack?"

Bromax answered with a very slow, methodical nod of his head, and Lon completely agreed.

"Before we took back Taeja," Lon said, "Tarek and I trained the Rayder soldiers for many months. We worked hard, fighting and failing together. Every single day and with every weapon. By the time we crossed the Zaga Ravine, every man understood exactly what was expected of him and what everyone around him was capable of doing. We knew each other inside and out. No situation surprised us, not only because we had planned for everything, but because we had the skill to respond." He paused to calm himself, realizing that he was getting wrapped up in the excitement of his own experiences. "The Rayders have plenty of flaws, Mel, but in battle, we are deadly because we are completely unified. Synergy. Just like the wolf pack."

Mellai replied with her own slow nod. "And the Rayders had leaders who fought alongside them, ready to die with their men. I saw you and Tarek. You two looked just like Bromax and Huirk."

Silence fell over their council. Lon knew that all four of them were masters of their own skills, more than capable of defending themselves on their own, but what they lacked was training together. They didn't have six months to set aside, but even one day could make a huge difference. Mellai would be the most difficult with her lack of military training, but she'd learn quickly with the proper guidance. And she didn't need to know how to wield anything besides True Sight. She could create an energy barrier faster than any Rayder could raise his shield, and no weapon was more deadly than her essence.

Lon opened his mouth to suggest a plan of action, but Mellai cut him off. "One day to train," she said, "until sundown. That's all I'll give you, and only on one condition."

"Name it," Lon replied, knowing they were sacrificing time they didn't have—but it was absolutely necessary for their survival.

Mellai crossed the ghraefs' wings one more time to stand in front of her brother, where she dropped to one knee and brought her right fist over her heart. "You must lead us, Master Beholder Lon Marcs." She looked up and smirked at him, drawing a chuckle from Lon. Even in genuine formality, his twin sister was incapable of staying totally serious.

Bromax and Huirk added their own approval, dipping their heads toward Lon.

"We need a leader," Mellai said, standing up again and extending her hand to her brother, "and there's no one more qualified than you. Someone who will have the final say. I promise to do what you ask—unless you abuse your power, then I'll stomp you into the ground."

Lon took her hand and stood in front of her, saluting her with two fingers to his King's Cross brand. "I'm honored, Beholder Lady Mellai Marcs."

She pushed him back onto his rump. "I'm no lady, and don't you forget it. You can save that title for Kaylen."

"She's a lady now?"

"A lady-in-waiting. Close enough, and it suits her. She'll never be a warrior."

Lon thought back to his experiences with his betrothed; her kind-hearted nature and ability to diffuse any conflict. Mellai was right. Their kingdom needed people like her, too, just as much as soldiers.

Mellai summoned True Sight and angled her arms down from her shoulders, palms facing toward Lon. "So what will it be, Beholder? What's my first training exercise?"

"To finish this planning meeting," Lon said, pointing to her spot at Huirk's side.

"I hate training already," she grumbled as she skulked back and sat down.

"We can work on our skills in a minute, but we still have one more topic to cover. What route will we use to return to Itorea, and what will we do once we get there?"

"Our path is a no-brainer," Mellai answered. "We're going to follow the trade route around southern Appernysia until we find our parents. Then we escort them the rest of the way to Itorea." She paused. "That is, if you agree."

"Simple enough," Lon answered, "unless we encounter settlements that have refused to join Pree's villagers. Do we spend time trying to get them to follow, or allow them to make their own choice?" Mellai was about to respond, but Lon cut in. "Think for a second before you speak, Mel. Every man we bring to Itorea is another block in our defensive wall. Leaving them out here unprotected might not only sentence them to death, but the rest of us as well. Especially if it's a bigger city like Draege. We need every reinforcement possible."

"You've been gone so long that you've forgotten how Appernysia operates," Mellai said. "King Drogan already drafted most of the able-bodied men from the big cities. That's why his army has a hundred thousand soldiers. With a few exceptions, only old men, women, and children are left."

"All the more reason to bring them to Itorea, right?"

Mellai stopped to contemplate his perspective. "You're playing Omar with me right now, aren't you? Arguing the counterpoint, even if you disagree with it?"

"Yes, but who says I disagree with it?"

Mellai groaned. "Stop it. Just tell me what you think."

Lon couldn't help but smirk, remembering when he had been on the opposite side of similar conversations. It felt good, almost as if he were bringing Omar back to life for the moment. It was an effective method, too. "I think there's no simple answer. We'll have to address each situation uniquely."

Bromax clicked his teeth together, then stood up, rolling Lon off of his wing before stretching his legs and fluttering his wings. When he finally stopped, he faced Lon with his tail coiled up over his back in fighting stance.

"Time to train," Mellai said, jumping to her own feet. "You ready, Huirk?"

The smaller ghraef tucked his wings and rolled sideways, opposite Mellai, onto all four legs.

Lon was the last to get up. After replacing the arrows that had spilled out of his quiver, he twisted his belt into place and shifted his tunic under his bow. "Let's begin."

Chapter 33

Groundwork

"That would've knocked you off Huirk's back," Lon said, pointing into the air where Bromax's tail grazed the full length of Huirk's spine. "How would you have reacted?"

The two ghraefs had been aerial sparring on the cleared terrain south of Pree for an hour. Since humans were far less familiar with the ghraefs than inversely, Lon decided it was the best place to begin. He and Mellai watched them closely. Once they understood the many ways aerial fighting occurred, they would know how to become one with their ghraefs.

"Assuming I saw it coming," Mellai answered, "I would have thrown his tail over my head. Or maybe I would have just grabbed his tail and flung him around for awhile."

"Only serious answers," Lon requested. "What if he had knocked you off?"

Mellai hesitated. "If Huirk couldn't get to me in time, I'd grab the seith, pull it underneath me, and control its wings until we landed. Then I'd break its neck."

"I tried to restrain Bromax," Lon said, "but he was too powerful and broke loose. What if the seith can do the same?"

"I'd break its neck first, then use its dead carcass to glide down."

Lon shook his head. "That's possible, but forget about the seith. Think larger. What other options do you have?"

Mellai glared at him. "Why don't you tell me?"

"You're the True Sight expert, and I'm trying to push you past your limits. Now answer my question."

Mellai blew out her breath and bit her bottom lip, but recoiled, pained by the open sores she had created in Réxura. "Your slide idea in the cave wasn't the worst option, if you hadn't thrown yourself back up into the air."

"No room for a gentle slope," Lon added, constraining her options even further. "You have to stop right where you land."

"Would you stop it?" Mellai growled, but then her eyes suddenly brightened. "I would create an air pond."

"A what?"

"I'd condense the air below to catch me, just like water, only I'd make the top section less dense so I'd gradually slow down."

"Like a cyclone?"

"Sort of, but without moving wind."

"Have you tested this before?"

Mellai shook her head, so Lon retrieved True Sight and called for the ghraefs to return before speaking to her again. "Now's as good a time as any. Give it a try."

Mellai stared at him. "You're serious?"

"Don't worry. I'll catch you if you mess up."

His sister thought about it for a moment, then folded her arms. "If you try something first."

"As long as it doesn't kill me."

Mellai used her power to slice open the palm of Lon's right hand. "Heal yourself."

Lon grimaced and cursed, shaking his head. But he had agreed, so he focused on his hand and tried blending the flesh back together. The pain was overwhelming, far different than when he had carved into his forearm. It was easy to cut his skin with a knife, but to knit every individual fiber back together required an entirely different focus. He gave it his best effort, but was ultimately incapable of maintaining a controllable connection to True Sight.

"Don't feel bad," Mellai said, finishing what Lon had started. A few seconds later, his skin was back together with no signs of a scar. "Llen did the same thing to me. He said only two Beholders had ever been able to heal themselves, and Llen was one of them."

"You made it three, didn't you?"

Mellai nodded. "How'd you guess?"

"You're just like Mother and Grandmother. A natural born healer. It's in your blood, I guess."

"Not really," Mellai countered. "Allegna wasn't our blood grandmother, remember?"

Lon grew silent. "You know, I—"

"Wonder if you've met our great grandparents?" Mellai inserted.

Lon shook his head. "No. They'd have to be dead by now."

"You've probably been fighting alongside distant relatives, though."

"Perhaps, but will you let me finish what I was trying to say?" Mellai remained quiet, so Lon continued. "I know the man responsible for their deaths. His name was Lars Marsen. I selected him as part of the original twelve men in my squad."

Mellai's face transformed into a furious scowl. "Did you find this out before or after you chose him?"

"After, although it wouldn't have mattered. When he told me the story, I had no idea he was talking about my own grandparents, and he was more than apologetic about it. That choice alone had tormented him for his entire life, a secret he nearly took to the grave. He finally confided in me right before he died, with an arrow sticking out of his stomach." He paused. "I could have healed him, Mel, but I didn't know how."

His sister didn't respond, and Lon preferred it that way this time. If she didn't speak, she didn't risk saying something that would upset him.

Before the silence became too awkward, Huirk and Bromax alighted in front of them. Mellai hopped onto her ghraef's back and told him to fly.

Mellai had Huirk glide in a circle a few hundred feet above ground while she manipulated the air below. Once she thought the air pool was ready, she leaped off the ghraef's back and twisted her body to aim feet down.

Lon watched carefully. He didn't need to intervene, but it was close. When his sister hit the air pool, she sliced through the thin upper portion and barely had time to realize her mistake and further condense the air below. She stopped just a few feet from the ground, then released the air altogether and dropped the rest of the way to land on her feet.

"Are you alright?" Lon called, but his sister ignored him as she hopped back onto Huirk and he took flight again.

She practiced a few more times, each a little higher than the previous, until she had mastered this new skill. By then, everyone's stomachs were aching for want of food. While Bromax and Huirk flew into the mountains in search of larger game, the Beholders broke through the ice and pulled fish from the river. Lon ate his fish raw, but Mellai cooked hers over a small fireball she held above one hand.

Lon watched his sister work, marveling over her effortless skill with True Sight as she gutted, cooked, cooled, and skinned the fish, producing a tasty looking cuisine he had only seen the equivalent of at Rayder banquets. Even with the brutality Lon had endured from the Rayders under Commander Rayben Goldhawk's rule, it had been a simpler time. A part of him still missed it.

"What's next, Big Brother?" Mellai asked, after she consumed the entire fish and began cooking another.

"It's our turn. You'll first defend against me, then we'll practice battling Bromax and Huirk with different arrangements. Us versus them. All of us versus one ghraef. Bromax and Huirk versus one of us. All combinations and scenarios possible."

"What about you defending against me?"

Lon grinned. "I'm set. There's nothing you can teach me about regular weapons, and I won't be fighting against another Beholder."

Mellai picked up a stone and hurled it at his head, barely missing him. "I'm not talking about normal weapons, dummy. As skilled as you think you are, you can't fight the kelsh in close combat. We'll have to leave that to everyone else while we stay a safe distance away."

Lon sighed, contemplating the logic of her statement. He was used to getting into the fight, even leading his men into battle. But that would be impractical against the calahein. They were too large and powerful. He would live a lot longer and save significantly more lives fighting from afar.

"You're right, Mel." He stood and pulled his bow from his back. "You ready?"

"Are you?" Mellai said, hopping to her feet and facing him.

"We're working solely on your defense, so no fighting back."

Mellai groaned. "That's convenient for you."

"But necessary. The calahein attacked my squad at night, and they stayed far enough away that even with a roaring fire, I was still the only one who could see them."

"Because of True Sight?"

"Indeed. They had us completely surrounded, and began hurling head-sized boulders at us from over a hundred yards away. That's why Riyen died, struck by a boulder while I was facing the other direction. They knew my weakness, Mel, and that weakness will be the focus of this session. I'm going to bombard you with snowballs from all directions, and you must stop them all. If you miss one, even if it's not aimed directly at you, a soldier just died."

Mellai's arms dropped to her sides and she released her power. "Are you sure you're alright with this, Lon? I know that Riyen was a—"

Lon hit her in the back with a large snowball, knocking her face-first into the snow. "The calahein ambush when we least expect it, Mel, and you just let everyone die."

"Try that again," his sister responded after pushing herself back to her feet and summoning True Sight.

"You know I will," Lon replied with a wink as he began creating piles of head-sized snowballs scattered around his sister, "but remember that you can't attack me. This is a defensive exercise."

"I can see everything you're doing, Lon. There's no way you can surprise me, not even if I wanted to let you."

A slight chuckle escaped Lon's lips when he realized his ignorant mistake. "Right. Well, I guess we can still talk about it. How would you respond?"

"I'd grab the incoming boulders mid-air and fling them back," Mellai answered, "or I'd start piling them as cover for my soldiers, but low enough that I could still see the calahein."

Lon nodded absently, realizing his own mistake during the ambush he had referenced. Instead of directly manipulating the boulders, he had tried counterattacking through other means. "It's my fault Riyen died."

"You were completely surprised by the calahein," Mellai added. "Don't be so hard on yourself."

"When Father started training me in weaponry," Lon continued, staring at his sister, "he first told me two things. I needed to be able to use all weapons on the battlefield, and each weapon had its specific advantages and disadvantages against others. I should have realized his advice applied to True Sight, too. I never even thought to use the boulders, Mel. I just defaulted to the skills I thought were the most powerful. Fire worked great during the Battle for Taeja, so why wouldn't it work against the calahein? I was so stupid."

"And now you know better. Remember what else Father told you? *This was something you've never experienced before. Just focus on calming your mind.*"

Lon couldn't help but smile. "I can't believe you still remember that."

"It was good advice. It helps, you know, when I feel myself starting to get worked up over something. I just take a few minutes to put it in perspective. Now teach me something else."

"I don't think I can, not without both of us using True Sight."

"Try."

Lon shook his head and stared down at the snow, then an idea popped into his head. Without using his power, he knelt and made two fist-sized snowballs, then stood with only one in his hand. "See if you can block this."

He hurled the snowball high into the air, arching toward his twin sister. When he saw Mellai lean back to watch it, Lon grabbed the other snowball and threw it straight at her. Mellai flicked her hand and knocked it aside, all the while waiting for the other snowball to fall next to her.

"You still remember that trick?" Lon said, dejected that she had blocked it.

"Yes, but I understand what you mean. Something about being constantly aware of my full surroundings, especially in battle. Am I right?"

"Yes, and I hope you'll take that seriously. One critical mistake is all it takes, Mellai. Just one."

Mellai nodded. "Anything else for me?"

"Not really, unless you want to learn how to use real weapons."

"No thanks."

Lon sat in the snow. "I figured you wouldn't, and you saw everything else I'd share during our battle on the plains—Rayders versus Appernysians, I mean. It's difficult, isn't it, watching all those people die? Especially when they're people you care about."

"I haven't really experienced that yet," Mellai replied as she walked over and sat next to her brother, "at least not firsthand. I don't count anyone from Roseiri. I wasn't actually there to watch them die."

"What about Jareth?"

Mellai shrugged. "I appreciated his protection and everything, but I don't really know any of my guard except Snoom."

Lon stared west, searching the sky for their ghraefs. "So who do you care about?"

She didn't answer immediately, and when she finally did, her response surprised him. "Why does it matter to you?"

"Because I love you, Mel," he said, turning his head to look at her, "and I don't want you to endure any more suffering than necessary. If it's in my power to keep the people you love alive, I'll do it, even if it brings my own death."

Mellai shouldered him. "That would defeat the purpose, Big Brother, because you're at the top of the list. You just barely edged out Mother and Father. And, of course, Kaylen is right below the three of you."

Lon was undeterred. "Who else?"

"I mentioned Snoom already. Everyone in Pree, too. Even the annoying ones—I've known them long enough to develop a sort of loving hatred, if that makes sense."

"Of course. Anyone in Itorea?"

Mellai sighed. "Kutad. Our king and queen. And maybe Kamron."

"Kamron, the general?" Lon asked, trying to hide his distaste as he resumed watching the skies for Bromax and Huirk. "I don't know if I'll be able to help you there."

Now Mellai was looking at Lon. "Why do you hate him so much?"

"You explained it yourself, when you said a proper leader should do just that—lead. Kamron is a perfect representation of cowardice. When Appernysia tried to drive us from Taeja the first time, Kamron hid behind his soldiers. He even launched three oil casks on top of his own men, trying to kill me in the process. I deflected the casks, but I couldn't save everyone. Hundreds of his own men were burned to death, all because of Kamron."

"I never knew that," Mellai said quietly.

"Of course you didn't, just like you never heard that he tucked his tail between his legs and galloped away, leaving all of his men behind. I could have killed so many of them, Mel, but I didn't. I'm sure no one talks about how I let your army retreat—*forced* them to retreat—even though they had attacked with full intentions to kill us all."

Tears had begun filling Mellai's eyes. "But why, Lon? Why did you let them live, when you had every excuse not to?"

Lon placed his arm around his sister and pulled her tight against his side. "Because the Rayders weren't in Taeja for blood. We just wanted to return home. I admit it wasn't always like that, but most desires for revenge died with two Rayder leaders—Commander Rayben Goldhawk and Captain Vance Talbot." He spit out the two names with venom.

"They died in battle?"

"Rayben was assassinated by Appernysian refugees he had enslaved. Vance and his cavalry murdered all of the slaves, though. He didn't die until later. Omar cut off his head, took control of the cavalry, and saved my life." Lon paused, contemplating whether he should bring more heartache to his sister, but decided she had the right to know the truth. "I don't suppose you heard about that part, either?"

"What part?"

"Kamron forced five thousand Appernysian peasants onto the battlefield, with nothing more than crude weapons and wooden shields. They were used as fodder to test the throwing distance of our trebuchets. Do you know what happened then?"

"Go on."

"The most terrible part—the worst of Kamron's secrets. We threw one stone into their midst to scare them, and they fled back to their own lines for protection. Your general refused to allow it. He shot a volley of crossbow bolts at them. Hundreds died and the rest fled back to the battlefield, not welcome on either side. That's when I intervened. I rode out to rescue the Appernysians and bring them into our protection. I was exposed and vulnerable, and Kamron sent his horsemen to kill me. I only survived because Omar brought our own cavalry to my aid."

"And these Appernysians you saved . . . are they slaves now?"

Lon turned onto his knees and grabbed his sister's shoulders. Her eyes were swollen red and tears poured down her cheeks. "Of course not, Mel. We brought them back to Taeja. Most of their families even joined them, having been ostracized because their husbands, fathers, and brothers had been proclaimed traitors to the crown." He lifted Mellai's chin so she would look at him. "I won't lie to you. Not everyone in Taeja was excited to receive the Appernysians, but they were generally accepted, especially by those who mattered. Tarek spent most of his free time training them in weaponry, and I even branded them as Rayders before we marched off to battle. We left them in charge of the city's protection."

Mellai fell forward, her forehead against Lon's shoulder. "I don't know how to respond."

"Let me tell you one more thing," he continued. "If I were King Drogan, Kamron would be the last person I'd put in charge. If Kamron wants to curl up in a hole somewhere and die, that's his choice, but he can't be trusted with the lives of anyone else."

"But he's not a traitor, Lon. He's very skilled in fighting, and one of the only people King Drogan can trust enough to keep in his company."

"Maybe, but that doesn't change the fact that he's completely gutless, regardless of who chooses to recognize it. If he didn't have the mettle to stand and fight against us, then how long do you think he'll last against the calahein?"

Mellai leaned back, looking as though she were going to answer, but her eyes shifted to the sky behind Lon. "They're done hunting."

*   *   *   *   *

When Bromax and Huirk landed by the Beholders, Lon had them take turns attacking his sister instead. Bromax folded his wings and stood on his hind legs, acting like a kelsh, and Huirk attacked from the sky like a seith.

The battles were fierce, and neither Beholder nor ghraefs held back. Just like Lon, they understood the threat that awaited them in Itorea and pushed themselves hard to be as prepared as possible.

"Huirk looks tired," Mellai jested as she threw her ghraef to the ground and dragged him across the plain. She picked up a fallen tree and dropped it on him for emphasis, distracting her just enough that Bromax drew within reach and batted her to the ground with the padded section of his paw.

"You'd be dead, Mellai. A calahein wouldn't have swatted you. If you were lucky, it would have bitten your head off, or stabbed through your back with its knee or elbow spikes. If you were unlucky, it would have maimed you just enough to incapacitate you while it ate you alive."

Mellai stood and brushed off the snow. "I get it, Lon, but don't ever bring that up. I'm serious."

Lon apologized, knowing his sister was thinking of their grandparents again. "You were distracted by Huirk. There's no time for victory celebrations or displays of dominance. Remember, as soon as you're done fighting one enemy—"

"Three more will take its place," Mellai interrupted. "Am I done?"

Lon nodded, then had to dive out of the way when Huirk swept out of the sky at him. He spent the next hour sparring with Bromax and Huirk, too preoccupied defending himself to criticize how unlike calahein the ghraefs were behaving. He only used True Sight, following the same advice his sister had proffered. They both needed to fight from a distance.

Battling an airborne ghraef was easy, just as it had been in Ursoguia. He simply had to grab Huirk and toss him aside—of course if the ghraef had been a seith, Lon would have destroyed him in the process.

Bromax was more difficult, mostly because Lon was unable to overpower him with his essence. Instead, he had to erect walls of dirt as barriers and use projectiles made of snow and rock to attack him.

By the time they finished training, the sun had disappeared behind the western wall of mountains, painting the sky in orange. Mellai caught a hare for dinner, then retired against Huirk's side to eat it.

"I'll be right back," Lon said, taking his portion of the rabbit in his hand.

"Where are you going?" Mellai asked, voicing the same question already in Bromax's eyes.

"I'm going to give Delancy one more chance to come with us." He paused and turned to his ghraef. "That is, if Bromax is willing to carry him and his daughter until we reach my parents."

The black-haired ghraef nodded, then motioned for Lon to climb onto his back.

A quick flight brought them to the northwest corner of the village square, next to a large windmill. Lon battled the emotions swelling up inside of himself as he slid off Bromax's back. This had been where he became engaged to Kaylen. The Ascennor Estate was directly south, where Tarek's parents and siblings had been buried. And farther north was Mellai's hill, where she had spent most of her time during their five years in Pree.

Lon crossed the road and tried the front door of the village tavern. It was bolted shut.

"I know you're in there, Delancy," Lon called, taking a step back. "Either open this door for me or I'll break it down. Your choice."

A metallic scrape sounded through the door as the steel latch was moved, then Delancy's head poked through the cracked door. "What do you want?"

"Mellai and I are leaving tomorrow. I'm giving you one last chance." He paused and pointed at Bromax. "My ghraef will be more than happy to carry you and your daughter. Come with us."

Delancy stared at the ghraef, and his eyes bulged when he saw the black crystal attached to the tip of his tail, but his stubbornness won through. "I've been listening to your ruckus all day. Do me a favor and fly yourselves out of here tomorrow so I can have a little peace. Sonela and I have more than enough provisions to see us through the winter."

Delancy slammed the door, leaving Lon with no choice but to honor the man's wishes.

Chapter 34

Foreboding

Mellai caught sight of Bromax as night fully draped over the village. The ghraef eventually landed near her in the clearing south of Pree.

After Lon briefly explained what had happened, Mellai nodded and summoned True Sight, pointing at her head so that Lon would do the same. She didn't trust herself to speak the words weighing on her mind.

We've run out of time, Lon. Can you feel it, tugging at your soul?

I told Bromax the same thing today, Lon thought.

I'm worried that we're too late, Mellai continued. *I only feel this way when something bad is about to happen.*

Or already has, Lon added. *I should leave right now. I won't sleep tonight, anyway.*

Then go, Mellai answered. *Seriously, Lon. If you leave now, you'll reach the Asaras Sea by morning.*

But what about you?

Huirk needs to sleep. He's not as conditioned to this kind of life as you are. I'll wake him up in a few hours and follow after you. Mellai took Lon's hand. *But you have to promise me you'll stay with Bromax. I won't be there to protect you.*

Lon squeezed her hand, obviously realizing that Huirk was just the scapegoat of her own exhaustion, but he let the matter go. *I promise, and I'll follow the trade route so you can find me. Or you can just ask.*

Not if you aren't using True Sight, Mellai answered, *so let's make it a standing rule. Whenever we're not together, we stay connected to True Sight as much as possible.*

And always at dawn and dusk, Lon added, *when the sun is touching either horizon.* He stood and walked to Bromax, who had been watching the Beholders carefully. "Mellai and I fear something bad has happened."

Bromax nodded and clicked his teeth.

"Then you agree we should leave now?"

The ghraef stood and shook the snow off his underbelly.

As Lon ran up Bromax's angled wing and braided his legs into the ghraef's black hair, Mellai brought her fist over her heart. "Be careful, Master Lon."

"You too, Beholder," Lon answered, then Bromax leaped into the air and flew east. *Now get some sleep,* Lon added in his mind.

Mellai only rolled her eyes.

*　　＊　　＊　　＊　　＊　　＊*

Rather than the typical week of travel through unpacked snow, Lon arrived at Humsco a short two hours later. Bromax's black hair made them basically invisible against the night sky, but they still approached cautiously. Lon hoped his father and guard had led the villagers safely across the southern loop of the trade route, but he still had to be careful. The calahein could have overrun any settlement, as well as the route between.

As Bromax circled a safe distance above the village, Lon used his Beholder vision to search for signs of life. Only a dim glow of elemental energy existed. Either everyone had been killed or they had joined the residents of Pree on their journey east.

"They made it out safely," Lon said, evaluating the perimeter wall of logs and thin planks. "The calahein would have torn that barrier apart. I say we move on."

Bromax clicked his teeth and turned southeast. Another forty-five minutes of flight brought them to a completely different scene at the fishing town, Toj. People still lived there, and no defensive perimeter had been established.

Why are they so scattered? Lon thought, peering through windows at the glowing essences of living bodies. For every occupied home, at least three had been vacated.

Mellai's voice filled Lon's mind, making him flinch sideways. *Who's scattered?*

I didn't realize we were still connected, Mel. Why aren't you sleeping?

Don't be daft, she answered. *Now who are you talking about? Did you find our parents?*

Not yet, Lon replied, *unless they decided to stay with everyone else in Toj.*

You're there already? I thought you'd just be reaching Humsco by now.

Lon couldn't help but smile. *Bromax can fly pretty fast when he's in a hurry.*

Silence followed for a short time before Mellai responded. *Do you see our parents?*

I don't know. Everyone's inside for the night. We might have to land.

Just be careful. And don't you dare stop using True Sight. I'm worried enough with you out there by yourself.

I'm not alone. Bromax is with me. As soon as the thought entered his mind, Lon realized what a fool he had been. The ghraef's vision had to be exponentially better than his own, even in the dark.

"Do you see anyone from Pree?" Lon asked.

Bromax didn't immediately answer. He flew a careful pattern above Toj, angling up and down, veering sharply, and doubling back repeatedly.

"Well?" Lon asked when the ghraef resumed a casual loop above the town.

Bromax shook his head.

"Neither do I, but we should still talk to the delegate. Any chance you know where he lives?"

The ghraef dropped into a steep dive and alighted with uncanny stealth behind a quaint house along the Saap River. As Lon climbed down from his back, Bromax snorted with amusement.

Lon froze and looked at him. "What are you laughing about?"

Bromax turned his snout and looked up at the stars, refusing to answer.

"Have it your way," Lon grumbled as he walked around the house to the front door. After rearranging his clothes and weapons, he knocked softly.

A middle-aged woman answered a short time later with a torch in her hand. She gasped and recoiled into the house. "Help!"

Before Lon could respond, a man jumped between Lon and the woman. He held a rusted sword in his hand and aimed it at Lon. "What business do you have here, Rayder?"

Lon breathed out a sigh of frustration, realizing the source of Bromax's amusement. The ghraef knew how this village would react to Lon's brand on his right temple. "Good evening, Delegate. I'm looking for Aron and Shalán Marcs. Did they pass through here?"

The man cautiously took the torch and held it aloft. "Your eyes . . . you're a Beholder, aren't you?"

Lon nodded. "And I'm looking for my parents. Have you seen them?"

The woman stepped around her husband and peered closely at his face. "He looks just like them, doesn't he, Nadjor?"

Nadjor? Lon thought, trying to remember how he knew that name.

Humsco's delegate, Mellai answered in his mind. *What's he doing in Toj?*

"Have you taken up management here?" Lon asked, echoing his sister's question. "I saw that your village was abandoned."

"No, Master Lon," he answered, "My people were too ill to continue and Toj's delegate was kind enough to give us housing. Only your village moved on."

"But what about all the empty houses here? Did some of Toj's residents go with them?"

A creak sounded on the wood-planked floor farther inside the house. It startled Lon and he instinctively reached for his sword, but he realized the action was completely unnecessary when an elderly woman shuffled into view.

"You are not welcome here, Rayder," the elderly woman said.

"He's a Beholder, Kátaea," the middle-aged woman replied.

"All the more reason you should leave," Kátaea continued, glaring at Lon. "Nearly every man in my town had to answer the king's conscription last summer, and it's completely your fault. How many of them did you kill, Rayder? Did you get your fill of Appernysian blood, or are you here to finish the slaughter?"

Lon was speechless, unsure of how to respond. Kátaea's words were true. The threat of a Rayder Beholder had forced King Drogan to draft as many men as possible. It was his fault.

What's on your mind? Mellai's voice asked in his head.

Toj's delegate only sees me as a Rayder.

Does she know you're a Beholder?

Yes.

Are Mother and Father there?

No.

Then leave.

Lon wanted to argue with his sister, but her logic was sound. There was little he could do. He stepped back from the porch and dipped his head. "I'm truly sorry for the suffering of your town. If it's any consolation, I saved far more Appernysians than I killed, and all survivors are now safely behind Itorea's walls. I go to join their defense, and I advise you to follow after me. I swear to you, the Rayders are no longer your enemies."

"The Rayders will *always* be my enemies," Kátaea shouted. She spit at Lon, then wrenched the sword from Nadjor's hand and raised it above her head as she stomped out the front door.

Again Lon was dumbstruck, unsure of how to respond to this elderly attack, but Bromax intervened. The massive ghraef dropped from the sky, pounding his obsidian tail crystal on the ground. He stood tall and proud, his bone-armored tail wrapped protectively around his Beholder.

Kátaea stumbled backward, falling onto her rump in the snow. She didn't move as she stared wide-eyed at the beacon of Appernysia's past.

"It's true, Laecha," Nadjor uttered, taking his wife's hand. "It's actually true. The ghraefs have returned."

Lon climbed his ghraef's curved tail and sat between Bromax's shoulder blades. "I'm sorry," he said again to Kátaea as he braided his legs into Bromax's hair, then the ghraef leaped into the air.

This is going to be harder than I thought, Lon communicated to his sister. *Everyone still only sees me as a Rayder. Maybe you should have come instead.*

Oh, that would work brilliantly, Mellai answered sarcastically. *If they're afraid of you, imagine how they'd respond to Huirk's tail crystal. 'Run for your lives! It's a Rayder ghraef!'*

Indeed, Lon thought, chuckling as the frigid air bit at his cheekbones. *We're on our way to Draege now. It should take us at least an hour, so you really should try to get some rest. You won't be any use to me if you're falling asleep all day.*

Perhaps you're right, Mellai thought, but Lon could feel the weariness in her mind. She might actually listen this time.

✳ ✳ ✳ ✳ ✳

The journey to Draege was unlike anything Lon had experienced before, and he was especially grateful for True Sight's power to allow him vision that night. He had always known that the Kerod Cluster was a small group of mountains in southeast Appernysia, but no one had ever told him of the endless groves of aspens. The quantity of stout trees was as dense as the mosquitoes in the Gaurelic Waste, forming a rousing web from the mountains' bases to their very tips.

Lon also knew of the wealth hidden under those trees, and it was the responsibility of Draege's citizens to mine the vast assortment of precious stones. The shipments would be transported up the North and South Pearl Rivers, joined in the middle by a huge lake and the shore town of Jaul.

Lon shuddered. While training with the Rayders, he had been warned repeatedly to stay away from Jaul's citizens above all others. They were experts in weaponry—comparable even to Rayders—because it was their sole task to escort the invaluable shipments to and from Draege. So treasured was their elite duty that they had never served in Appernysia's army, despite the strength they would have provided. Only a few squads of Rayders had ever attempted to attack a Jaul-escorted shipment, and the results had been disastrous every time.

As Lon crested an especially broad mountain peak, Draege came into full view, glowing brightly from countless torches. The large city was wrapped on all sides by sheer cliffs hundreds of feet tall, with the exception of a stone wall that ran a hundred yards along its north border, just touching the shores of Drae Lake.

Although the city's civilians were just beginning to rouse in the dim morning hours, a thick mass of soldiers stood atop the curtain wall, all armed with crossbows. A large catapult was also centered on each of the four drum towers. Lon unconsciously fingered the pommel of his falchion. These people were prepared for battle, and a Rayder could easily spark them into a rampage of death.

Bromax had obviously made the same observations, for he stayed close to the mountains and avoided moonlight wherever possible.

"Look over there," Lon said, pointing to his right. A large portcullis blocked the entrance into the underground mines, its iron web barring all who desired access. A host of armed men stood ready with spanned crossbows at that location, too.

"We can't fly into this city," Lon commented. "You're the most powerful creature I know, Bromax, but even your thick hide couldn't stop all those bolts."

Bromax huffed and stretched his front paws forward, mimicking a Beholder using True Sight.

Lon shook his head. "An energy shield would be pointless because we can't let them see me up close, either. If they notice my brand, they'll stop listening to me before I even have a chance to speak. How can we get their attention without putting our lives in danger?"

Without further consultation from the Beholder, Bromax dove straight at the citadel positioned against the back cliff wall of the city.

"What are you doing?" Lon called, ducking low to avoid the blinding wind, but Bromax didn't respond. He flared out his wings just before crashing into the citadel, landed softly on one of its tall spires, then spread his feathered wings and roared louder than Lon had ever heard before.

A soft glow from a roaring fire atop the citadel illuminated their position, but Lon didn't wait to see if they thought Bromax was a seith. He projected his voice across the city.

"Citizens of Draege, you are in grave danger! The calahein attack from the west, and your only chance of survival is to join me in Itorea. You must leave at once, before it's too late!"

"You and I will talk about this later," Lon added quietly to Bromax.

An eerie silence followed. All crossbows were trained on their position, and nobody moved, until finally a cluster of men appeared on the roof of the citadel below.

"Who are you, to order my people about?" a man called. He was dressed in polished plate armor, but Lon doubted he had ever experienced a true battle.

Lon created a fireball above his left hand, illuminating the unbranded side of his face. "I am Lon Marcs, son of Aron Marcs and protector of Appernysia."

The man spat on the ground. "And my name is Thuan. I've been baron of Draege for thirty years. Twice now I've been lectured over what is best for my city, but I won't have it. Not even from a Beholder. Not even if he rides a ghraef."

Despite his air of confidence, Thuan jumped behind his men when Bromax turned to face him.

"Twice, you say?" Lon answered, hoping it had been his father who last spoke to him. "Who was this other messenger?"

"A filthy traveler, with an ugly scar running past his right eye. He couldn't convince me to leave, nor can you. Now fly away, Beholder, and greet your doom wherever you best see fit. We will meet ours here, and we will defeat it."

Lon surveyed the soldiers manning the battlements, finding them as loyal to their baron as the Rayders to their commander. No amount of pleading or threats would displace them, not without causing irreparable harm.

"So be it," Lon shouted, then extinguished his fireball as Bromax skimmed above the city and continued north. Fortunately, no one had been foolish enough to shoot at them.

Chapter 35

Signal

*M*ellai! Lon shouted in his mind even though it would make little difference. *Wake up!*

What is it? she answered groggily, finally connecting to their emotional bond.

The sun's rising. Time to get up.

Obvious annoyance radiated from his sister. *Next time you scream at me for something so stupid, I'll—*

Something's wrong, Lon cut in. *There's a huge column of black smoke rising from the middle of the forest.*

The weariness in Mellai immediately disappeared. *Which forest?*

Briyél. I'm at the south end. Forget the trade route and fly straight here. If you hurry, it should only take you a few hours.

We're coming, Mellai answered. *Stay out of that forest, Lon.*

There are tracks along the south edge of the forest that lead east toward the sea. I'm following them.

I'm serious, Mellai pressed. *Don't you dare enter that forest without me. I can't make that promise. Just hurry.*

Mellai cursed. *I knew you'd say that. We're in the air now. Please wait for me.*

Lon didn't answer. Knowing that his sister was awake and traveling his direction, he focused his attention on the tracks just inside the forest. A small group of human travelers had made them, along with a cluster of livestock prints along the edge of the open terrain. It fit Pree's size.

"Quickly, Bromax. I'll watch the forest."

If the calahein are in the forest, Lon thought, searching for glowing life behind the trees, *this is probably the first time they've seen a Beholder riding a ghraef. That'll scare them for sure.*

But only for so long, Mellai replied. *Keep your distance. If they see any opportunity to attack, they'll take it.*

And if they do, Lon thought, his anger rising with every glance at the black smoke, *we'll destroy them mercilessly. We'll remind them how pointless it is to fight us.*

Not unless you have to, Mellai insisted again. *This isn't the real fight.*

Lon saw a bright glow of energy suddenly appear deep inside the tree line of the forest. He grabbed it with his essence and yanked it onto the plains, but it was only a deer, flailing to get free. Lon relaxed as he dropped it into the snow and watched it sprint back into the trees.

"If a deer willingly runs back into the Briyél," he said to Bromax, "then the forest must be safe. Maybe the citizens of Jaul are just burning garbage or something."

Bromax shook his head and flapped his wings hard to gain altitude. From that high, Lon could see a huge lake. "That's the big lake . . . uh . . . Casconni. It's Casconni Lake. And look. The fire's coming from an island."

The ghraef clicked his teeth and lowered closer to the ground at the edge of the forest.

What are you thinking about? Mellai asked. *You feel confused.*

I am, Lon answered, realizing his sister could hear his thoughts, but not his speech. *The fire's coming from an island on the lake. Why would they do that? It points out their exact position.*

I know I'll regret saying this, but it's probably a signal fire.

Or a trap, Lon countered. *But I just saw a deer run into the forest. Maybe the calahein aren't here after all.*

Or maybe a ghraef scares it more than anything. Deer are Bromax's main source of food.

All anxiety returned to Lon. *I hadn't thought of that.*

And that's why you need to wait for me, Mellai added. *You're not perfect. You can't think of everything by yourself.*

You've made your point. I'll be wary.

Finally, Mellai thought. *Sometimes you're more stubborn than a donkey.*

Lon continued to contemplate the black smoke. "Why would they do that, Bromax—light a fire on an island, I mean? Why not at Jaul? And did you see where it was burning? Right on top of one of the small mountain peaks, just like a signal fire from Three Peaks. Almost like my own Rayder brothers were trying to warn me."

Bromax clicked his teeth again.

"Wait," Lon asked, leaning closer to his ghraef, "there *are* people there?"

The ghraef nodded and tapped next to his right eye with a sharp claw.

Lon's insides twisted when he realized what Bromax was saying. "Rayders?"

Another nod.

"My squad?"

More clicking teeth.

"Then we need to rescue them," Lon shouted, pulling Bromax's long black hair to the left like reins on a horse. "Let's go!"

Bromax rolled his shoulder blades to free Lon's grip, followed by a slow shake of his head.

"Why not?" Lon shouted again. "It's my duty to protect them."

The ghraef lifted his paw and pointed directly ahead.

Even from that distance, Lon could see the massive expanse of water on the eastern horizon. "Yes, it's the sea," he jabbed his left hand north, "but that's my squad."

Bromax growled and licked his chops, then spoke. "Paarreeaa."

"Pree?"

The ghraef huffed.

"But if Pree's villagers are over there, then why is my squad trapped on the lake?"

Bromax pointed ahead again, this time with more emphasis.

"Fine," Lon grumbled, gripping his sword hilt as he glared at the black smoke. "I'll let them explain it to me."

*   *   *   *   *

"You've been doing this for almost two hours," Lon complained as the ghraef dove down the steep side of another hill. "We'd be there by now if you'd just fly higher."

Bromax pointed left at the tree line of the Briyél Forest on the opposite side of the river, and Lon searched it again. Still no signs of life. He knew it was Bromax's intention to remain unseen, but the effort was costing precious time.

The sun had finally risen, making it difficult for Lon to see with his regular vision. Two blinding lights beamed directly in their faces—one from the sun, and the other from its reflection on the Asaras Sea. They were close enough now that Lon could see the rolling waves and smell the pungent air. Even with the worry that plagued him, the experience still offered Lon a reprieve of peace.

Bromax continued following the natural contours of the land, until he crested a particularly large hill and Pree's villagers finally came into view.

I found them! Lon thought to his sister. *They're on the borders of the sea.*

Stay with them, Mellai answered. *I can see the Pearl River ahead. I'm almost there.*

Lon consented, anxious to speak with his father.

But it wasn't a joyous reunion.

A cry rang out from the camp and everyone rushed into organized ranks—spearmen kneeling in front, swords in the middle, and archers standing in the back. Everyone was armed for battle. Even the young children held daggers.

Four horsemen sat behind them all. Even from two miles away, Lon could tell his mother sat on Dawes. The other three had to be Mellai's guard.

Lon expected them to lower their defenses once they recognized Bromax, but when he flew within a mile, the archers drew their bowstrings back to their ears and aimed high into the air.

"Wait!" Lon called, projecting his voice forward to the villagers, but it was too late. Eleven arrows shot into the air, a wasted volley from too far away. Lon reached out his essence and grabbed the arrows one by one, but two still escaped his reach and disappeared into the snow.

With the threat neutralized, Bromax was able to fly directly into their camp. Shalán met Lon on the ground, having already dismounted Dawes, and wrapped him in a tight hug.

"I'm sorry," Snoom said, bowing before him. "This blinding snow has distorted our vision. We couldn't tell if you were friend or foe."

"Here," Lon said, returning the nine arrows in his hand. "You'll need these."

Snoom dipped his head again. "Thank you, Beholder."

"Your father is missing," Shalán said, a hint of hysteria in her voice, "and black smoke fills the sky. I fear the worst."

"You didn't tell me that Father was with them," Lon said, glaring at Bromax, then he turned back to Shalán. "They're alive, Mother. Bromax saw them on our flight here. And the black smoke is from their signal fire on an island centered on the lake."

"Taie Island," Duncan commented. "It's at least five miles away from the nearest beach."

"How did they get there?" Snoom asked. "Does the lake freeze over?"

"Only along the shoreline," Duncan answered. "They must have taken a boat or a raft."

"Then why not continue sailing here?" Snoom asked again.

This question wasn't as easy to answer. They stood staring at each other for quite some time before someone came up with the answer.

"That smoke isn't a just a signal fire," Ric said flatly. "It's a distress beacon. They can't leave, probably because they're burning their boats to get our attention."

"It's not from their ships," Lon said. "It burns on one of the mountains. It's obvious they need help. Maybe they're shipwrecked."

Ric blew out his breath and shook his head.

Neither Lon nor Snoom had a chance to intervene, because Shalán ripped her sword from its scabbard at Dawes's side and placed it against Ric's neck.

"That's my husband you're mocking," she spat, but she wasn't trembling. Her sword hand was steady and her eyes narrow, waiting for Ric to respond. "If you do that again, I will slit your throat."

Ric glanced between the other members of their guard, but the only response he received was from Snoom, who folded his arms across his chest and stared back at him. "Last I checked, Ric, it was the Rayders who volunteered to scout the forest, not you. Do you really want to get into some sort of a competition over courage and skill? Because you'll lose. We all would."

Lon stepped forward and pulled his mother's sword away from Ric. The soldier breathed deep and swallowed.

"Mellai will be here in an hour. We'll let her deal with him."

Shalán looked past her son and raised her eyebrows at Ric. "Never again. Do you hear me?"

Ric nodded and walked away.

"What's gotten into you?" Lon said, placing the sword in the scabbard at Dawes's side.

Shalán leaned against the horse with tears in her eyes. "I don't know, Lon. Insults that didn't used to matter will get under my skin and fester. And I'm constantly battling an overpowering desire to fight—physically fight for the people I love. I have no idea where this is all coming from."

Lon glanced around at the surrounding villagers. The children were climbing on Bromax again, and he kept his obsidian tail crystal high in the air, out of their reach. Most others had returned to their tents and bedrolls, but Scut Shaw and the Pulchrias stood watching them, along with Snoom and Duncan.

"Let's take a walk," Lon said, offering his arm to his mother. She took it, and they wandered closer to the sea. The salted wind blew hard from the east, bitter cold and refreshing all at once. Lon glanced over his shoulder to make sure no one had followed them before he spoke. "I have news for you. At another time, it may have destroyed you, but now it should only serve to give you perspective."

Shalán took her son's hand between hers. "What is it, Lon?"

"You are a Rayder."

Shalán stared back at him, her eyes distant and contemplative. It was some time before she formed a response. "How did you discover this?"

"Simply put, Mellai saw it happen through a tree's memory. Your real parents hid you in a tree hollow before they were taken away for execution. Their relationship was forbidden, so when they discovered she was pregnant, they fled into the Vidarien Mountains to birth you. Grandfather found you hours later and brought you home."

Shalán sat on the snow-covered beach and stared out at the sea. "What were their names?"

"Sévart and Geila," Lon answered, sitting next to her.

Her next question surprised him. "Have you met any of your relatives?"

"I don't know . . . maybe? I first heard your parents' story from a member of my squad, but he died shortly after and I haven't thought much of it since. I didn't even know he was talking about my real grandparents until Mellai told me on our way to Pree."

"I didn't expect *this* to be the reason," Shalán said quietly, "but I always wondered about the way people used to look at me growing up. How they'd whisper when I walked by. I always felt like I didn't fit in, and that became poignantly clear when I married your father. I guess it explains why I was attracted to him in the first place, but it's still a lot to take in."

Lon placed his arm around her. "And it might also explain how you're feeling now. This tendency to fight, the need to defend—it's in your blood. Our blood. Now that our lives are under threat, this bred desire is forcing its way out."

Shalán leaned against her son. "So what am I supposed to do? You saw what I did back there. I almost killed him."

"No you didn't. You just warned him. That might not make any sense, but it's the Rayder way. You made sure he knew you were serious, but I doubt you would have actually killed him. Even if he had insulted Father again."

"Maybe not, but I felt like challenging him. That would have been foolish."

Lon laughed. "Yes, it would have. We need to train you before you try anything like that. Especially against Ric. He's strong and dangerous."

Shalán kissed her son on the cheek. "Thank you for trusting me with this secret."

"It wasn't easy. I was worried you might be angry with Grandmother and Grandfather for never telling you."

"No," she said, shaking her head, "it only makes me love them more. They raised me as their own daughter. They trusted me, housed my husband, loved my children. Even gave their lives to save Mellai's betrothed." Her voice caught, and she wiped away a tear. "If only Theiss had survived. Mellai deserves happiness—she's spent so much of her life full of anger. But I suppose that might be explained by our blood, too."

"Perhaps." Lon retrieved his arm and stood. "I need to talk to Snoom. Will you be alright?"

"Go ahead. I'll be fine."

Chapter 36

Rescue

When Lon returned to the main body of the camp, Scut was the first to stop him. "I need a minute of your time."

"Anything, Master Scut. What can I do?"

"Ah," he replied softly, "I bet most of your conversations are about things someone else is needin', but you'll never be hearin' that from me. I only want to tell you I'm sorry. I've been judgin' you too harshly, all the while forgettin' the honorable man you've always been to me and my Kaylen. Why, I'd even offer you back your apprenticeship, but I'm sure you have more important things on your mind besides milkin' my cows."

"But that's no reflection on your responsibility," Lon answered. "Our villagers need you just as much as they need me."

Scut laughed and slapped Lon hard on the back. "That's an embellished truth if ever I heard one, but I appreciate the thought. My Kaylen will be lucky to have you." With those words, he marched away, smiling.

Next were the Pulchrias. They weren't nearly as forthright as Scut, but they stood looking at Lon expectantly, and he was certain he already knew the reason.

"Good morning, Master Hans," Lon said, dipping his head. "And how are you, Lady Ine?" he added with a kind wink.

"Oh, Master Lon," she replied, taking him by his left hand, "I wish we had the energy or disposition to joke around, but that opportunity has abandoned us. What I wouldn't give for the old days in Pree, sitting around your table and munching on your mother's mouthwatering cuisine."

"The road has been hard," Hans added, ever a man of few words.

"Indeed it has," Lon agreed. "What can I do for you both?"

Ine let go of his hand and moved behind her husband, nudging him forward.

"Our son," Hans finally said. "He became a Rayder?"

"He did," Lon said. He poured his entire focus into remaining kind and neutral, despite the death and hardship Braedr caused among the Rayders. After all, the path he chose wasn't his parents' fault.

"And he died in battle?" Hans pressed.

"Yes."

"Why?"

They could have asked how, but they wanted to know *about* Braedr—what he had done as a Rayder and why he was killed.

Lon struggled to come up with a response. Should he reply honestly, disgracing Braedr's memory eternally, or smooth over his acts and preserve what remaining love his parents still held for him?

Hans resolved Lon's conflict for him. "Do not lie to me. I know my son, and I want the truth."

"As you wish, Master Hans." Lon organized his thoughts. "Braedr joined the Rayders last March. I found him on the edge of death, but he recovered and quickly gained a devoted following of Rayders. He fought valiantly with me during the Battle for Taeja, but when I began using my power to stop the fighting, he developed an intolerable hatred for me."

"Why?"

"I'm not exactly sure, but I think it had something to do with jealousy. Braedr always believed I stole Kaylen from him, and he probably felt the same way when the Rayders bowed to me—like I had stolen his reputation, too." Lon paused. "The rest of his story will only bring you sorrow. Are you sure you want to know?"

Ine hugged her blacksmith husband's thick arm. Hans nodded slightly.

Lon heaved a lengthy sigh. "He and his following began killing Rayders every chance they could get, usually men in positions of leadership. Some of my dearest friends fell to his blade, including my mentor. Braedr was determined to become the new Rayder commander, but he eventually failed and his plot was exposed. I imprisoned him myself and left him under the guard of fifty men, but he somehow escaped. His last act was an attempt to end my life. Mellai stopped him, and . . . the new Rayder commander ended Braedr's life because of his crimes. As far as I know, his body still lies on the Taejan Plains."

Ine was blubbering at that point, but Hans remained stone-faced. The only sign of his inner turmoil was the tightened muscles in his neck. "So he is dead?"

"I'm sorry," Lon said, daring to place a hand on Hans's shoulder.

Hans nodded slightly again, then returned to his camp with his wife. Lon watched them for a few minutes, but neither appeared angry with him. They just sat there, quietly processing what Lon had told them.

"Sorry for eavesdropping," Snoom said, stepping up from behind Lon, "but I just wanted to make sure you were safe." He paused to look at Hans and Ine. "I remember the man you spoke of. Beholder Mellai trapped him in dirt, correct?"

"Yes."

"I didn't know he was their son. Do we need to worry about them?"

Lon shook his head. "Braedr has been like that his whole life. If anything, the greatest emotion they might be feeling is guilt for their relief that he's finally dead." Lon turned to face Snoom. "I was glad to hear you defend my squad and my father. I was worried your groups had a difference of opinion."

"No conflicts at all," Snoom replied. "You chose wisely when you placed Lieutenant Channer in charge. He led us well."

"And my father?"

"Aron insisted that he go with them into the forest. Channer tried to discourage him, but your father wouldn't be refused. We waited two days for them, but they never returned."

"I understand. My father's more stubborn than Mellai, if you can believe it. What about here? Why are you camped on the shores of this river?"

"The journey took its toll on us, Beholder. We're too weak to cross."

Lon searched the opposite bank of the Casconni River, a quarter mile away and dangerously close to the forest. "That may have been for the best, Snoom. An ambush probably waits for you in those trees."

Snoom dipped his head. "We share the same concern."

"Have you been attacked already?"

"No, but our anxiety grows with each day we're stuck here. I can't see them, but I'm certain the calahein are closing in around us. I've been running defensive drills with the villagers in case of an attack."

Lon clapped him on the shoulder. "It was an impressive display. You should be proud."

"But it would have done little good. We can't see anything clearly."

The whites of the young lieutenant's eyes were plagued with red, as sunburned as his nose and cheeks. His lips were dry and cracked, too, much as Lon's must have been when he traveled to the Exile a year earlier.

"Mellai will be here any minute. Let's wait for her before we make a plan."

As Snoom signaled his obedience, Lon connected to his sister's mind. *How long until you get here?*

I'm right above you, Mellai answered.

Lon leaned back his head and searched the sky. Huirk was just a tiny speck, and Mellai an even tinier spot next to the ghraef.

Are you falling again? Lon asked his sister.

Why wouldn't I? Mellai answered. *It's the fastest way down, and the most thrilling thing I've ever done.*

It's also reckless.

Maybe for you.

Lon shook his head and pointed upward. "Here comes my sister now."

Pree's villagers joined Lon in searching the sky. Only a few of them—those with the keenest eyesight—stated that they were able to see her at first, but soon the whole village was voicing their concern over her independent flight.

"Why on earth would she do that?" Shalán asked, gasping. "You tell her I said to get back on that ghraef at once!"

Mother's heart is failing her, Lon passed along to his twin sister. *Time to end the fun.*

Mellai didn't answer, but Lon felt her irritation as she angled back to Huirk and took her position on his back.

"Did you really tell her?" Shalán said, staring at her son. "I wasn't sure you actually could."

Lon smiled slyly and tapped his head with his finger. "It's a convenient update to our emotional connection, now that we're both using True Sight."

Shalán's eyes widened. "You can—?"

"Shh," Lon whispered, touching his finger to his lips. "Family secret."

"I'm so glad you can," she whispered back as she subtly glanced around. "I've been worried while you two were away. At least now I'll know that you can keep track of each other."

Lon's eyes softened. "I never really considered how all of this has been affecting you. You're stronger than either of us."

"Hardly," she answered, returning her attention to the sky above. "Oh, what's she doing now?"

Huirk was spiraling downward with intermittent zigzagging. Mellai sat tall with her arms spread wide.

"They're more spirited than me and Bromax," Lon answered dryly, "especially when they're flying. And I think Huirk's showing off for his audience."

"Those maneuvers could make—oh, Mellai!—could make a big difference at Itorea."

"Indeed."

As soon as Huirk landed, Bromax swatted at the other ghraef's snout and let fly a stream of guttural reprimands. Huirk was barely able to dodge the blow, then cowered with his tail flat against the ground. Mellai ducked, her clouded eyes bulging at Lon.

Lie still, he counseled his sister. *Bromax is just lecturing.*

That's all? she thought sarcastically. *Next time, he should let me dismount first.*

You were just as much a part of it as Huirk. Now keep quiet and listen closely.

Mellai rolled her eyes, but remained still until the rebuke had ended. After she slid off of Huirk's back, the ghraef skulked away, dragging his King's Cross tail crystal through the snow.

"There." Lon patted Mellai on top of her head. "That wasn't so bad, was it?"

Even though he watched his sister with True Sight, she moved so quickly that he didn't have time to think of how to defend himself, let alone actually respond. Mellai swept his legs with her essence and dropped a pile of snow on his face. Lon gasped at the cold, but smiled nonetheless.

"Be kind," Shalán said, stepping between her twin children and facing Mellai. "Now let me look at you. Did Bromax hurt you?"

"No, Mother," she replied impatiently, then she caught sight of Reese. Her eyebrows softened and tears flooded her eyes at the sight of her betrothed's younger brother.

"You're alive," she said, reaching out to him, but Reese recoiled.

"You left us," he said, his own eyes damp with anger. "You ran away and left us all to die, Mellai. Everyone's gone and it's your fault. You could have stopped it!"

Reese stomped away, leaving everyone awkwardly staring at each other.

"He's right," Mellai finally said. "I could have saved them."

"At what expense?" Lon countered. "Our battle and everything since never would have happened. We'd still be enemies, and I'd be back in Taeja with the Rayders, waiting cluelessly on death's doorstep."

"Give Reese time," Shalán added. "He'll forgive you."

While Mellai stood staring after the boy, Shalán turned and pointed a finger at Bromax. "And don't think I've forgotten about you. I don't care who you are or where you come from. You treat my daughter and Huirk with more respect from now on. Do you hear me?" She placed her fists on her hips and glared at him.

Lon stopped breathing, terrified of how Bromax might react. It shocked him even more when the ghraef nodded his head and laid his snout in the snow submissively.

"Hmm," Shalán grunted, blowing air out of her nose, then turned back to her children. "Now what are you going to do to rescue your father?"

* * * * *

Lon leaned low against Bromax's neck, the ghraef skimming over the partially-frozen water on his way up the Casconni River. It was the safest place to fly. Before Lon and Bromax had departed, Huirk—with his over-animated body language—had communicated the calahein's fear of water. The people on Taie Island were taking full advantage of that fact.

As they flew, Lon had been searching for life in the surrounding forest, but not one glowing essence had appeared yet.

How much farther? Mellai asked.

I'm about halfway to the lake.

Despite her protests, Lon had ordered Mellai to stay behind and protect the villagers while he and Bromax flew to Taie Island. The ghraef would carry all four of the Rayder squad to safety—assuming they were all still alive—then return for Lon and his father.

Once they all returned, Lon and Mellai would work together to escort Pree's villagers across the river and through the east tip of the Briyél Forest.

Lon hadn't expected the journey to be safe, so it didn't surprise him when two large boulders and a sharpened sapling shot out of the forest. Bromax lifted slightly to dodge the attack and the projectiles fell harmlessly below them. An intensifying series of bombardments followed, increasing in quantity and speed, but all were easily dodged.

"Remember to stay low," Lon said, right before he noticed that a crude dam had been constructed a short distance ahead of them. It was lined with kelsh and terror hounds. "Fly, Bromax! Get into the air!"

Bromax ignored Lon's order and barreled headlong into the center of his enemies, raging with bloodlust. Poisonous phlegm flew past them. One caught the tip of Bromax's left wing, bringing a roar from the ghraef, but Bromax didn't divert his course.

Lon suddenly had an idea. He extended his essence and tore huge sections of logs from the dam. Only the calahein near the shores were able to escape, leaping clear just as the dam fully collapsed. At least fifty kelsh and twice as many terror hounds dropped into the freezing river. Their panicked screams and whimpers filled the forest, ringing in Lon's ears, but he ignored them as he lifted a log and began swatting at the surface of the water. Skulls crunched and bodies crumpled under his rain of death blows.

Bromax jerked into the air, causing Lon to lose hold of the log. The Beholder looked up just in time to see a group of calahein rise from the north bank. Their membranous wings beat furiously to gain altitude, and Bromax met them stroke for stroke.

"Four seith!" Lon shouted aloud and in his mind.

Run! Mellai shouted back. *That's too many!*

Now it was Lon who ignored the warning. He remembered sitting at the table in Omar's study, listening intently while the scholar described the greatest enemy Appernysia had ever seen. "*The seith were the only creatures in Appernysia that were dangerous to ghraefs. Do not misunderstand me. A ghraef would still win in a fair fight with a seith, but the seith did not fight fair.*"

Lon lost all sense of reason and calculation. Death had ceaselessly plagued him, stealing the lives of those closest to him for over a year. Bromax had become one of his dearest friends and Lon refused to lose him, too. He shouted at the top of his lungs and let loose with True Sight. Passion had taken full control, driving him to ruthlessness. He ripped wings and limbs from the two closest seith, then used them to impale the third. Three dead carcasses fell from the sky, and Lon gathered himself to attack the fourth. But Bromax snarled and shook his head.

Lon understood perfectly. The ghraef wanted one for himself.

Lon laid low on Bromax's neck. "Tear him apart!"

Even without its companions, the seith didn't back down. It turned directly at Bromax and reached out with its three-fingered paws to attack a beast at least three times its size.

Lon expected a jarring confrontation, two behemoths crashing together in the air. He clenched his jaw, readying himself to be clawed and slashed.

Never had he considered that Bromax might pull an aerial stunt like Huirk.

Just before Bromax reached the seith, he tucked his black-feathered wings against his sides and spun forward. Lon became completely disoriented, gripping the ghraef's black hair with all his might, until Bromax leveled out and turned casually west again.

When Lon glanced back, he saw the fourth seith tumbling toward the forest canopy. It's head was split wide open through its neck. A few flecks of blood stubbornly clung to Bromax's tail crystal, too. Lon's eyes grew wide. The ghraef had timed his spin perfectly, catching the seith directly on top of its skull with the sharpened edge of obsidian.

Lon guffawed. "That was amazing, Bromax!"

The ghraef clicked his teeth, undoubtedly pleased with himself, while Lon took a few minutes to heal the wounded wing. He used his essence to peel away the phlegm and toss it aside, then weaved the dissolved bone and flesh back together. A few feathers were still missing, but the rest of Bromax's wing was whole.

There were no more confrontations on their way to the island.

✳   ✳   ✳   ✳   ✳

He did what? Mellai asked in her mind.

You heard me right, Lon answered. *It was incredible.*

Even so, you have to be more careful. What if there had been more?

Then we would have killed them, too. We taught the calahein an important lesson today, Mel. We reminded them how dangerous we are.

Desperation flooded Mellai's consciousness. *That's what I'm worried about. Your need to emphasize your skill trounced your common sense. Why pick up a log and swat at the kelsh like a little boy hunting dragonflies when you could have drown the beasts in one massive wave of water?*

Their mental conversation ended there, leaving Lon alone with Bromax, but he couldn't shake his sister's concern. He had been overzealous with the log, and the calahein may have just been testing the combined strength of a Beholder and ghraef. If so, what would the next attack look like?

He relayed Mellai's message and his own concerns to Bromax. The flying ghraef slowly nodded, digesting their thoughts.

"We have to hurry," Lon urged.

Taie Island was only a few miles away. The black smoke had diminished to a subtle trickle and a large crowd of tiny shadows were congregating along the east shore. They must have seen the approaching ghraef and were rushing to meet him.

"Who are all those other people?" Lon said aloud, but he needed no answer. Masses of fishing boats were scattered around the island. These were survivors from Jaul.

Everyone was carrying an assortment of weapons and they were garbed in various layers of leather armor, making it impossible for Lon to distinguish his father or squad in the masses. He even searched for his father's shining glaive, but couldn't spot it. Only when they finally landed on the beach did his kin finally appear, Aron standing uninjured at the front.

"I'm glad you came, Son," he said, stepping forward to wrap Lon in his arms.

"What happened?" Lon asked, returning the embrace. "How did you end up on this island with all these people?"

"We walked right into a calahein ambush," Channer said, placing his hand on Bromax's snout. The ghraef passively allowed it. "Nik shot a seith from the sky, and we avoided the rest of the kelsh by raft. It appears they fear water."

"That's what Huirk told us, Lieutenant."

Dovan moved next to Channer, staring curiously into Bromax's eyes. "You can speak our language?"

Bromax huffed, amusement filling his eyes.

"He understands us," Lon said, "but he has a language of his own."

"Then how do you communicate?" Dovan continued.

"With difficulty. They act things out, and we ask a lot of yes-or-no questions." Lon scratched behind Bromax's ear. "It was frustrating at first, but we've learned to deal with it, haven't we boy?"

Bromax knocked Lon flat and growled at him.

"I'm sorry," Lon said, hands raised in surrender. "I was just trying to make a point." He stood to address everyone, broadcasting his voice over the sizable crowd. "Bromax is a ghraef, a creature of more intelligence than any of us. He's not a pet, and he'll maim anyone who treats him as such. Keep your distance and you'll have nothing to fear."

While whispers filled the air, Channer stepped back from the ghraef. Lon flicked his hand dismissively at him. "You're fine, Lieutenant. Tell me, how did you earn the trust of these people?"

"Shared fear," Channer replied. "Too many of their people have already died, and we have a common enemy. Our placement in the Beholders' guard helped, too, although they were beginning to doubt our story. You arrived just in time, Beholder."

Lon scanned the crowd. Nik was standing close to Aron, his bow slung over his back and his quiver empty. Lon nodded at him and continued surveying. "How many men are here?"

"Maybe two thousand," Aron answered, "plus women and children. Many of their soldiers in Jaul died safeguarding the town's escape."

One of the Appernysians stepped forward. He was lean, but moved as one familiar with battle. A deep scar parted his hairline near the crown of his head. "I'm glad to see you, Beholder," he said, taking Lon's hand. "My name is Darius. Our governor died in the evacuation, leaving me in charge."

"All survivors from Jaul are on this island?"

Darius nodded as he stepped back and ran his right hand through his hair, his left hand gripping the pommel of his sheathed cutlass.

"And how long have you been stranded here?"

"About three weeks. We've been catching fish for food, but even they have stopped biting. Our resources are depleted."

"Then we have no time to waste," Lon said. "Gather your leaders and meet me here in five minutes."

"That's not enough time," Darius said. "Many of them are still on the south tip of the island."

Lon climbed onto Bromax's back. "I'll see to them."

Chapter 37

To the Sea

Mellai cursed, angry at her brother for taking such extraordinary risks. *Any attacks yet?*

Surprisingly, no, he answered. *Every arrow I made for my squad still sits in their quivers. It's been an unnaturally quiet journey. You should see the first boat any minute now.*

Huirk was carrying her, flying above Pree's villagers for a better view, but close enough to the ground that Mellai could still intervene in their defense. She peered into the setting sun. Just as Lon said, the first of their fleet appeared on the horizon, a few miles away and sailing toward the Asaras Sea.

There you are, Mellai thought, relieved that the wait had finally ended. She had been forced to stay there the entire day, while Lon helped Jaul's citizens load into fishing boats and sail east. Mellai had been especially worried once they reached the river, but they had met no resistance. *You said there are a hundred boats after this one?*

Almost, Lon replied, *but I'll worry about them. You just get the villagers ready. These boats sit deep in the water, so you'll have to extend a long dock from the shoreline to reach them.*

I don't like this, Mellai grumbled for the umpteenth time, then told Huirk to land.

"They're finally here," Mellai told the villagers, and they responded with a cheer. They had taken down camp during the first part of that day, then waited just as anxiously as Mellai for the fishing boats to arrive.

"And they'll be carryin' us all the way to Itorea?" Scut asked, too skeptical to believe such an extravagant promise.

"That's the plan," Mellai answered. "Fetch your cart, Master Scut, and follow me."

She crossed through the villagers, pausing for a moment to caress the soft cheeks of Meriwald's young baby. He cooed and smiled back at the Beholder, having grown accustomed to the cold. Tirk stood close to his mother and baby brother, his hand interlocked with Nybol's daughter, Hannah.

"Tirk will make a great husband," Mellai said, squeezing Hannah's arm. "Stay close to him and he'll take good care of you."

"I will," Hannah answered, leaning closer to Tirk and gripping his forearm with her free hand.

At the river's edge, Mellai raised a wide stone pathway for the village carts to travel safely along. She extended the dock fifty yards toward the center of the river, where the water was deep enough for the approaching boats, then she intersected it with another raised path that ran with the current.

"Let's go over this one more time," Mellai said, turning to face the village. The three members of her guard were next to her, sitting on their horses. Shalán was also standing nearby, her nervous hand gripping Dawes's lead rope. Reese was standing on the opposite side of Dawes, refusing to make eye contact with Mellai, but the Beholder smiled reassuringly at him anyway before continuing. "The boats are moving faster than I had expected, so boarding will be a little tricky. Even so, if everyone does what I've asked, it should work."

Nine-year-old Tragan raised his hand, his face half-concealed behind Nybol.

"What is it?" Mellai asked kindly.

"Can't you just move the whole dock onto the boat instead of lifting us in one at a time?" He hugged his father's leg. "I . . . I just don't want to lose anyone else."

Mellai assented, understanding the grief he must still be feeling over the death of his mother, Hykel. "That's an excellent idea, Tragan. Will you do me a favor, though? Will you sit on the dock so I can make extra sure you don't slip off?"

Tragan nodded his head vigorously. "As long as I get to sit next to Father."

Mellai smiled and addressed the whole village again. "I'm using Tragan's idea, and the first boat is only a couple of miles away. Quickly file onto the dock and ready yourselves for transport. You're all boarding at the same time."

Shalán moved forward, but Mellai caught her hand and spoke softly. "Stay with me and my guard. It's not that I don't trust myself. I just want to make absolutely sure you are safe."

"Very well," Shalán replied, pulling Dawes and Reese aside to allow others past.

Wellesly's and Ramsey's two families led the way, followed by Nybol's. Elora followed her four sons onto the dock next, then Landon and Haden forced their wives and masses of children forward. The three smallest families took up the rear: Scut, the Pulchrias, and Coel, with his wife and two daughters.

"Are you certain this will work?" Trev asked as he and Anice entered the dock last. "Can you really lift us all at once?"

"Yes," Mellai answered. "What's the worst that could happen?"

"I fall into the river."

"Then I'd scoop you back out again. Don't worry, Trev. You're finally safe."

"We'll never be safe," he muttered, continuing down the dock. "Not as long as the calahein are alive."

One thing at a time, Mellai mentally grumbled.

Everything alright? Lon asked.

We're all on the dock. I hope your idea works, Lon.

It'll work, as long as you don't screw it up.

Right . . .

While she waited for the first boat to reach the nearest bend in the river, Mellai added a back wall of stone to the dock, with a low stone bench in front of it. She requested that everyone sit down to ease her task, then breathed deep and let the air waft out her nose. This wouldn't be especially difficult. It's just that people's lives were on the line. That's all.

"I was wondering," Mellai said to distract herself, glancing at Reese. "Would any of you like to fly with me for awhile? I'll need to drop you off on the boat eventually, but I thought maybe—"

"I would love to," Shalán said as she handed over the reins, "if Snoom will watch over Dawes." She was obviously catching on to Mellai's true intent—to heal the Beholder's relationship with Reese. "How about you, Reese? Would you like to join me?"

Reese gazed at Huirk for a short time, then slowly nodded.

"Let's climb up on him now, then," Shalán said, placing her arm around Reese and leading him next to the ghraef. "Now use his paw as a step. There you go . . ."

Mellai stopped listening. The boat had just rounded the corner and was approaching quickly, faster than she had anticipated. Fortunately, Channer's squad and Aron were there to receive the villagers.

"Hold on," Mellai called, extending her essence. A few villagers screamed when she hoisted the full length of the dock into the air and moved it upstream, hovering over the boat's deck.

"Hop down," Aron called, waving his hands forward. Little children jumped first, straight into the Rayders' arms, then the older villagers began to follow. All was going well, until the dock cracked in half from the displaced weight.

Tirk and Hannah toppled over one side, and Mellai was able to split her essence to catch them and fling them onto the boat. But she panicked as the dock broke into more pieces. She couldn't manage them all, nor could she drop the dock on the deck—it would sink the boat and crush the people standing there.

"Come on!" Aron shouted, reaching up to pull on Elora's dangling leg. The middle-aged widow toppled forward onto him, and he pulled her out of the way just as a large section of stone dropped down where they had been standing and cracked the wooden deck.

The boat had moved downstream, directly in front of Mellai. She could see that everyone had evacuated the dock except Meriwald. Her husband was standing in front of her, shouting for her to jump.

"I can't!" she screamed, clutching her baby against her chest. "I'll drop him!"

"I'll catch you both!" Ramsey shouted back, but his wife was frozen with fear.

"Wait!" Mellai called, tossing aside the remainder of the dock until just the portion holding Meriwald remained. She gently brought it down beside the boat until Ramsey could reach under his wife's armpits and lift her safely down.

"Is anyone hurt?" Mellai asked as she cleared the debris from the river.

"We're fine," Aron called back, waving her off. "Go help Lon."

"Not yet," Mellai answered. She next wrapped Dawes in an air pocket, effectively immobilizing him as she pulled the reins from Snoom's hands and moved the horse onto the boat. Dawes whinnied and rolled his eyes, unable to protest in any other way. When she was certain that Elja had a firm grip on the lead rope, Mellai released Dawes. Elja was able to quickly soothe the horse and tether him to the main mast.

"That was a disaster," Mellai spat, turning away.

"But still a success," Snoom replied, still standing next to her. "Everyone is safe. That's all that matters."

"That was just the people," Mellai said as she shook her head. "Move the rest of the supplies forward. We're not done yet."

As the ships continued to pass, Mellai dropped the rest of their supplies and livestock onto the boats. She moved her guard last, placing the three men and their horses on the fourth ship back. "I'll meet you in the keep," she called as the boat sailed away, and her three protectors bowed in response, their fists over their hearts.

"Glad you stayed with me?" Mellai grumbled as she climbed onto Huirk. Reese sat behind her, with Shalán in the rear.

"Of course," Shalán answered, "but only because it means that I get to spend a few more minutes with you."

"Don't be dramatic, Mother," Mellai commented as she braided all three pairs of their legs into Huirk's brown hair.

"What are you doing?" Reese said, panic in his voice.

"It's to keep you on his back," she replied softly. "Huirk can fly pretty fast. I don't want you tumbling off his back."

"But he won't do anything like what he did earlier, right?"

"Not unless you ask him to," Mellai added with a wink, then connected to her brother. *We're coming, Lon.*

*   *   *   *   *

The twins patrolled above the boats—Mellai in the front and Lon covering the back half—until everyone had escaped onto the Asaras Sea. By then, the sun had set and the ships were nearly invisible against the dark sea, even with torches glowing on every deck. The captains of each boat watched the shoreline carefully, making sure to keep it constantly in sight from the bright moon shining overhead, but not close enough that the rolling waves could push them inland.

Once out at sea, Lon and Mellai moved side by side, hovering over the front of the long fleet. Huirk didn't seem to mind the extra weight, but his exhaustion became more obvious. He barely flapped his wings, angling them instead to ride on the breeze from the east.

It was an accident, Mellai said to her brother a little too defensively.

But why didn't you just move groups of people to the ship instead of trying to do it all at once? Lon replied.

The whole idea was idiotic. I should have just stopped the boat in front of the harbor and let people climb aboard themselves.

It's alright. I'm just glad everyone is safe.

A short span of silence followed before Mellai felt like communicating with her brother again. *We'll need to rest once I drop off Mother and Reese,* she thought, turning at look at Lon.

Lon nodded. *I'm still amazed that he survived the trip to Humsco. If I didn't know better, I'd say the Jaeds were watching over him.*

But you do know better, Mellai retorted. *It's just us. We're all that stands between survival and utter destruction. That's a reassuring thought, isn't it?*

At least there are a lot fewer calahein to worry about, Lon replied, obviously trying to reassure himself as much as his sister, *including four dead seith.*

Mellai nodded absently. She hoped it would give them an advantage, too, but her heart told her the opposite. The worst fighting was yet to come.

When the lead boat came into sight, Huirk angled downward until he was floating right above the deck. The Beholders had forgotten to warn them of their approach, so many of the villagers screamed when Huirk appeared in the torchlight.

Aron caught Reese in his arms and carried the young man to the far side of the deck, laying him next to Dawes. Reese curled up against the horse's side and immediately closed his eyes.

"Are you sure you have to leave?" Shalán said, hugging her daughter from behind.

Mellai nodded. "We've been away for far too long. You'll be safe. Just aim straight for the south end of Itorea's keep. There's a dock there for the royal armada. I'll warn King Drogan that you're coming and he'll let you into the city."

"And I hope to see you there, too," Shalán added with a kiss on Mellai's cheek. "Be safe."

"You, too," Mellai answered, lowering her mother to the deck.

"Take care of my family," Lon called down to his squad. The four men kissed their fingers and touched their brands in response.

"For Appernysia," Channer said, standing proud.

"For Appernysia," Lon replied, returning the salute.

Lon motioned for Mellai to follow, then led her and Huirk to the shoreline, where they landed on the beach. The ghraefs dropped onto their bellies while their Beholders filtered the salt out of the ocean water and placed the liquid in stone troughs for them to drink. They drained the troughs multiple times, then casually lapped at their snouts as they nestled into the sand for the night.

Although her brother seemed content to sprawl out next to the ghraefs, Mellai took more caution. She melted the sand, forming it into a thick dome of glass over their entire company with an opening just large enough for Bromax facing the sea.

"Now we have protection and can still see danger approaching at the same time," Mellai said, finally lying next to her brother.

"Brilliant, as usual," Lon said. "That's why I keep you around, Little Sis."

"I like the new Rayder motto, too. 'For Appernysia' is a lot more inclusive than that 'For Taeja' garbage." Mellai allowed her voice to waft away as she stared at the stars overhead, the rolling surf beckoning her to sleep. She felt her eyes begin to close.

"Tomorrow's an important day," Lon interrupted.

"How so?" she answered, half awake.

"Think about it, Mel. Everything we've done the past year—*everything*—has led up to this moment. It's like our destiny is waiting for us in Itorea, and I don't know if I'm ready to meet it yet. It's not that I'm afraid or resistant—I just don't know if I've been adequately prepared, you know?"

"You'll be fine," Mellai answered, turning sideways to face him. "Look at what you did today."

"But it scared me, Mel. I felt my emotions take control of me again, just like in Pree, only I had full control of True Sight."

"Maybe that's not such a bad thing. Your heart is still pure. Let it guide you."

Lon sighed and brought his hands behind his head.

"What's really on your mind, Big Brother?"

Her brother's face winced, as if he were in physical pain. "I feel an overwhelming sense of foreboding, Mellai. Kind of like what we experienced in Pree—you know, what drove us to fly here so quickly?—but exponentially larger."

Mellai propped up on an elbow. "Like we're in danger?"

"Not really, but it still keeps me awake at night. I'm confident that we'll eventually win this war against the calahein. I really am. But I can't shake this feeling that something eternally significant is still about to happen. I know that sounds ridiculous, but there you have it."

"I've heard stranger things, especially considering everything that we're facing right now."

"Maybe, but the strangest thing of all is that it fills me with sadness. Why would I be sad that we're going to win?"

"It's late, Lon, and you didn't sleep last night. Everything feels heavier when you're tired. Get some rest and we'll talk more about it in the morning."

Lon nodded and closed his eyes, so Mellai rolled onto her back again. "I love you, Lon. Try not to worry. We'll get through this."

"I love you, too, Mel."

As Mellai felt herself slip into the dream world, a clear voice began singing *The Song of the Dead*, yet so overpowering was her exhaustion that Mellai couldn't identify the source. She allowed herself to join in, casually humming along until sleep finally took her.

Chapter 38

Slander

*L*on stood knee deep in the Asaras Sea, facing east and welcoming the rising sun's warmth as it soaked into his skin. He closed his eyes and thought of Kaylen—what their future would hold. Taeja would be their home, and they'd have children. Maybe even a son who Lon would train as a Beholder. He was so caught up in his thoughts that Lon barely noticed as the sea water began to rise. It touched his hips, then climbed slowly up his chest. It wasn't until it reached his shoulders that Lon sensed the danger. He opened his eyes and called upon True Sight, pushing the tidewater back into the sea. But a massive wave resulted. It rose hundreds of feet into the air, blocking out the sun as it barreled toward the Beholder. No . . . the sun had already crossed the sky and settled in the west. Lon looked back just in time to see its last sliver of light drop below the horizon, then water crashed over him. He tried to cry for help, but couldn't find his voice. As Lon felt himself drowning, a kelsh appeared, swimming up to him from the depths of the sea. Before Lon could react, it reared back and swatted him across the face.*

Lon's eyes shot open as he sat up, reaching for his sword. Mellai was prostrate in front of him, retreating backward across the sand.

"Are you alright?" Lon asked.

"Are you?" she countered.

He held out his arms and examined himself. He was dripping wet, and the left side of his face still stung. "What happened?"

"You wouldn't wake up," Mellai said, slowly rising to her feet, "not even when I dumped water on your head. I had to slap you."

He absently rubbed his cheek. "I was dreaming."

"Next time, don't attack me when I try to wake you," she spat, climbing onto Huirk. "Come on. The sun rose an hour ago."

Lon was exhausted, but he forced himself to stand. He stretched his tired body, staring contemplatively at the sunrise, then reached down to straighten his belt. It was then that he noticed his hands were trembling, still fighting the effects of his dream.

"Did I do anything dangerous?" he said, thinking of the last time he had experienced such an intense dream. He had thrown handfuls of wind around the camp, startling his Rayder squad.

"Nothing worth talking about," Mellai answered, then her voice softened. "Tell me about your dream."

"I'd rather not," Lon said as he mounted Bromax. The ghraef looked as weary as Lon felt. "I'm just fatigued. I'll be fine."

"Eat this," Mellai said, using her power to place a cooked fish in her brother's hand. "You said it yourself. Today's a big day, and you'll need your strength."

Both ghraefs leaped into the air and turned north toward Itorea. Where the Casconni River touched the sea, twenty more miles of coastline extended east before finally turning north. It was for this reason that Bromax led them inland, in the straightest path possible toward the Fortress Island. An hour or so into their flight across the barren plains, domed buildings of all shapes and sizes began to appear, their white stone half buried in the snow.

The catacombs of Wegnas, Mellai replied to Lon's mental inquiry. *This is where all citizens of Itorea are placed after they die. It's seems illogical to house their dead so far from the city, but I guess it maximizes Itorea's usable space. At least that's what Kaylen told me. Aely is buried here.*

Sorrow flooded Mellai's thoughts, speckled with memories of intense pain. Lon left her alone as he focused instead on the northern horizon. The Perbeisea Forest had begun to appear, which meant the outer walls of Itorea would be close behind. Another hour of flight would see them safely at the south gate of the Fortress City.

*　　*　　*　　*　　*

"You're needed on the wall, General Astadem," a soldier said, saluting at the entrance into the guardhouse.

"Very well," Kamron answered. He sat up on his cot and rubbed the sleep from his eyes. Although he expected the main attack at the west gate, the general had been traveling down Itorea's perimeter wall to the south gate once per week. The trip was exhausting, and he spent more time fighting the deteriorating morale of his soldiers than on any other task.

After donning his leather traveling armor, Kamron stepped out of the guardroom and followed the soldier up the rounding staircase until they were standing on top of the gate's flanking tower. The wind already blew with great force at three hundred feet up, but it came with even more power this close to the Asaras Sea. The cold air burned in Kamron's lungs, but he ignored it as he looked up at the nearby watchtower, rising another two hundred feet higher behind the curtain wall.

A soldier stood on the watchtower between the staggered crenels. He held two bright red flags, one raised high in the air, and the other pointing directly south.

Kamron took a metal cylinder from the lieutenant, then extended the spyglass and peered through it. Two enormous beasts were flying directly at them. "Are we certain they are seith?"

"Not entirely. They could be ghraefs, flying in the open like that."

"Or they could be a diversion," Kamron said, turning to peer into the line of Furwen Trees that towered to the west. "Any signs of movement from the forest?"

"None, General."

Kamron licked his dry lips. He had not heard from any of his scouts for over two weeks, not since he sent Lieutenant Char to search the Briyél Forest. *They might be fine*, he thought. He had not given explicit orders to report lack of movement, after all. *But they also might be dead.*

"We will take no chances," Kamron said, handing the spyglass back. "When those beasts get close enough, shoot them down. In the meantime, keep your eyes glued on the forest."

"Yes, General," the lieutenant replied, then relayed the message to the other soldiers. While the ballistae teams cranked winches and retrieved spears, a flagman stood on a high platform and repeated a pattern of movements with yellow banners, signaling all other nearby drum towers. A runner also disappeared down the staircase to notify the crossbowmen hidden behind arrow slits in the flanking tower. Within thirty seconds, all ballistae teams were armed and ready.

"Not bad," Kamron said, strutting around the perimeter to evaluate. "Spotters, keep your hands off the release rope until you are ready to shoot. I don't need you wasting our spears."

He stopped to stare at one of the teams. "What exactly are you two doing?"

"He says he can do it himself," one soldier replied, his arms full of extra spears. He stood next to a bulky man who, alone, held the stout beam extending off the back of their ballista.

Kamron gripped his sheathed sword, struggling to contain himself. "I don't care what he says, soldier. Get back into position!" While the soldier returned the spears to a large barrel centered on the tower, Kamron shouted at his men. "Two men on every aiming arm, and one spotter to shoot the spear. Do what I say! All of our lives depend on it!"

He stepped closer to the bulky man. "You may think you're strong, but after an hour of raising the ballista by yourself, your arms will be useless. I always have need of more scouts in the forest. Am I clear?"

The soldier nodded. "Yes, General Astadem. I don't know what I was thinking."

"Bah," Kamron growled, then turned his attention back to the approaching beasts. "They're nearly in range. Aim!"

The teams worked together, the two men in the back angling the ballista under the instruction of the spotter. When the ballista was perfectly angled, the two men held the aiming arm against the stone floor to keep it in place. Each spotter sounded off as their team finished the job.

"Spotters ready!"

"Ready!" they shouted in unison, taking hold of the release rope.

"Hold," Kamron said quietly, waiting until the two beasts were close enough to accurately hit. "Release!"

The ballistae were secured between each crenel of the round flanking tower, making it impossible to shoot a massive volley at the enemy. Instead, only the closest-aimed ballista loosed their spear, hoping to drive the beasts sideways into the path of the others.

Their plan failed, even when the flanking tower opposite the gate released their own spears at the intruders.

Rather than darting sideways, the two beasts stayed their course, rising just slightly to avoid the steel spears.

"Reload!" Kamron shouted, frantically kicking over the barrel of spears at the ballista team.

While the team cranked the winch back, a mass of crossbow bolts shot out from the sides of both towers, finally accomplishing Kamron's intent. The two beasts veered apart from each other, allowing the other ballistae teams to release, and bolts continued to pour out from the battlements.

"We've got them now!" Kamron shouted, elated to see his soldiers in action.

"Stop shooting at us!" an angry voice sounded in the air. Kamron stammered, recognizing it as Mellai's, but unable to identify the source. He pushed aside one of the spotters and peered over the battlements at the bridge below, but saw no one.

"Where are you?" Kamron shouted back as he stared at the beasts, beginning to wonder if Mellai had somehow transformed herself.

"On the ghraefs, you idiot!"

Now Kamron understood. The two ghraefs had leveled out directly in front of the towers, their heads low to expose the Beholders sitting on their backs.

"Hold!" Kamron ordered, but unnecessarily. Everyone had heard Mellai's voice, and stopped shooting as soon as she mentioned the ghraefs.

With a quick examination, Kamron could see that Lon rode on the long-haired black ghraef. It landed on the tower opposite the gate, but Kamron's attention was drawn to Mellai's brown ghraef, which had just alighted with its two hind legs on separate crenels. As it sat up straight, Mellai slid down one of its curved wings onto the center of the flanking tower.

"I'm sorry, General Astadem," Mellai said, dipping her head. "I didn't mean to call you—"

"Mellai Marcs," Kamron boomed, cutting her off and grabbing the Beholder by her shoulders. "I've never been happier to see someone in my entire life. And you brought a ghraef with you, no less. I thought they were extinct." He stepped aside and evaluated the large creature. Its claws were long and sharp, and its snout large enough to swallow a man whole. Truly an intimidating specimen. Kamron stepped closer to examine the feathered wings. "Was it difficult to train?"

"*He* understands every word you're saying, General, so I'd keep your distance. Ghraefs are more wise than they are powerful, and you're insulting Huirk with your ignorance."

Kamron stepped back and looked up at the ghraef. Huirk was glaring at him, a tiny portion of his lip raised to reveal a row of dangerous teeth. "A pleasure to meet you, Hurick," he said, bowing low.

"Huirk," Mellai corrected. "Just one syllable—well, at least I think it is. I struggle to understand his language, let alone speak it."

"Huirk," Kamron repeated, still staring at the ghraef. "Will you accept my apologies, master of the skies?"

The ghraef blew a sharp breath out of mouth, fluttering his lips as he rolled his eyes and looked away.

"Have I offended him?" Kamron asked, taking another step back.

"Hardly," Mellai answered, smiling at the general. "He just finds your formality entertaining."

Huirk glanced back at them, a hint of amusement dancing in his eye.

"What a marvelous creature," Kamron continued. "Where did you find him?"

"Huirk found me, and saved my life. If you find his presence alone intimidating, just wait until you see him in battle. He and Bromax will make invaluable allies."

"Bromax?" he replied, pointing at the other tower. "That's the black ghraef?"

Mellai nodded. "He's in charge and twice the size of Huirk. A lot more serious, too. You'll have to watch what you say more carefully around him."

Kamron put his arm around Mellai and pulled her close. "But a Rayder rides him," he said in a whisper.

Mellai pushed back, her eyes narrow and clouded with True Sight. "That Rayder is my twin brother, Kamron, and your only hope of survival. I don't care if you're a general. Don't demean Lon again."

Huirk opened his jaw and clicked his teeth together hard, the glare back on his face as he raised his tail and dropped it forward onto the tower. Kamron's eyes widened at the sight. The entire tail was covered in bone armor, much like thick scale mail, but with brown hair poking out between the scales. An enormous diamond was connected to its tip—but its beauty diminished when Kamron recognized the blue King's Cross in its center.

"Was he born with that?" Kamron asked, pointing to the diamond.

"No," Mellai spat, folding her arms across her chest. "I put it there, and by my own choice."

"I mean no offense," Kamron replied, changing the subject. "I'm concerned about the relationship between our nations. If your brother—as a Rayder—is riding the alpha ghraef, that might cause a power struggle."

"Then let's clear the air right now and speak with the Rayder commander. Where is Tarek?"

Kamron stammered, unsure of how to reply. It was clear that Mellai had developed an inappropriate love for the Rayders during her travels, so she wouldn't understand King Drogan's decision.

"Where is he?" Mellai asked again, more intensely. "You brought the Rayders to Itorea, right?"

"We did."

"Then where did you house them?"

Kamron raised his hands innocently, not wanting to anger the Beholder further. "In the Gaurelic Waste."

Chapter 39

Synergy

Huirk was flying next to Bromax, with Mellai tapping her head and looking at her brother, but Lon refused to connect. He had heard enough. Drogan had forced the entire Rayder army into the Gaurelic Waste, then abandoned the remaining Rayder civilians in Sylbie. Those were the facts, and no explanation would change them.

But Lon could fix Drogan's mistake. *Would* fix it.

Sylbie was twenty-five miles upriver from the south gate. Once Lon had climbed onto Bromax's back and shared the news with him, the ghraef had taken off at once in the city's direction. Bromax flew high, above the view of the arrow slits spotting every round drum tower, but still outside the perimeter wall. If Rayders were prohibited from entering the city, he and Bromax would live by the same standard.

Lon watched the towers carefully, making sure the flagman below kept waving their green flags ahead of his position. Not only did he not want to be attacked again, but the skirmish had been a tremendous waste of resources. Again, he had been foolish to think the Appernysians would recognize the ghraef. Lon committed never to enter friendly territory unannounced again.

"Please," Mellai said, projecting her voice to Lon, "just talk to me. Where are you going?"

"To fix Drogan's mistake," Lon shouted back.

"Good. I'll help you."

"What about your precious king?"

"He can wait."

The ghraefs traveled quickly and shouts of excitement followed them below, all the while Lon battling within himself. The rational side of his mind knew that the Appernysians had only been obeying orders when they escorted his Rayder brothers out of Itorea. But the emotional side . . . it wanted to knock them from the wall and drown them one by one in the river.

Lon summoned True Sight and interacted with the wind for a moment, testing to make sure he still had his power. He breathed a sigh of relief that his pure heart was still intact, thinking of another bit of advice from his father. Thoughts don't define a person's character. It's what they do with those thoughts that reveals the true intentions of their heart.

But the closer the Beholders drew to the west gate—the shore opposite from where the Rayder civilians had been abandoned—the quieter the Appernysian soldiers became. Every single one of them had to be worried about Lon's return. How would he react when he found his people stashed in an abandoned city?

The Rayders, on the other hand, barely noticed when Bromax and Huirk swooped down and landed at the east edge of Sylbie. Most of them were inside buildings, running fires to stay warm or eating lunch, and the few thousand soldiers Lon spotted were positioned miles away on the west end of the city, protecting their borders from the calahein threat.

Gratefully, Wade Arneson had been among those few stationed near the bridge into Itorea. The young lieutenant had the wisdom to recognize the ghraefs and waved off the archers long before Lon had to make any proclamation.

"Well met, Beholders," Wade said, touching his brand. The Rayder's long blond ponytail—usually well-kempt—was loose and disheveled, matching the weary expression on his face. Lon didn't have to ask to know that he had experienced many trials.

Lon placed a hand on Wade's shoulder. "I'm sorry it took us so long, Lieutenant. Is this everyone from Taeja?"

Wade hesitated before answering. "Everyone who would come, Beholder."

The answer didn't surprise Lon. Of course there would be those who refused to leave Taeja. "How long have you been in Sylbie?"

"Nearly three weeks."

"Do you have enough supplies?"

Wade sighed. "Ample, and that is what bothers me, Beholder. Weekly shipments have been brought to us from Itorea, and the housing is more than accommodating. I have nothing to complain about, yet my thoughts obsess over rejoining with Commander Tarek. I am strained. Perhaps I am not a fit leader for these people."

"You have everything to complain about," Lon replied. "Rayders aren't bait to be dangled from King Drogan's hook. This isn't where our people belong, Lieutenant, and Mellai and I have finally come to repair the injustice."

"We are honored by your tail crystal," Wade said, bowing at Huirk before turning to Mellai. "And thank you for its creation, Beholder." The surrounding Rayders followed their lieutenant's example and saluted them, too.

Mellai's jaw dropped. "How do you know about the tail crystals?"

"All Rayders are raised with this knowledge. Ghraefs and Beholders are part of our history. I still remember some of the tail crystal designs I drew as a child. May I?" he said, indicating to Huirk's tail.

Huirk huffed and nodded his head, so Wade stepped forward and ran his hands along the clear diamond and six blue javelin heads. "King Drogan will not be happy about this."

"I don't care," Mellai answered. "That's his problem, not mine. Anyone who spends time with the Rayders will know they are a people worth defending. My brother is our greatest example of that."

"No more than Tarek," Lon said.

"Perfect examples from our most prominent leaders," Wade inserted, glancing around. "Allow me to introduce these men who follow me."

"Some of the Appernysians I rescued and branded," Lon interrupted, taking the closest soldier by his shoulder. "I'm glad to see you standing at Wade's side, although I never learned your name."

"Quinten Witkowski," the man replied.

"A strong name. I see you still have my glaive. Has it served you well?"

"It has, Beholder. Thank you."

"And your son?"

"Alive and healthy, thanks to you."

Lon nodded and turned back to Wade. "We're leaving this city. Get everyone outside, then Mellai and I will escort you to join the rest of our brothers in the Waste."

✳   ✳   ✳   ✳   ✳

I wish there were something more we could do, Lon thought as they circled above Sylbie. *You can't imagine how much they've suffered since leaving Flagheim. None of them deserve this.*

I have an idea, Mellai replied, *but it will require that we remove part of this outer wall.*

I fail to see the problem.

Amusement filled his sister's mind. *Glad you agree.*

So what's your idea?

Remember our conversation on the way to Réxura? About different methods of travel?

Lon nodded.

I've been thinking about our parents, coasting on ships along the surface of the water and letting the wind do most of the work. Then it struck me. We can do the same for the Rayders using your sled idea. If we tear down the stone wall surrounding Sylbie and blend it into one massive sled, we could transport them all at the same time. And probably just as fast as our ghraefs can fly, if the terrain is flat enough.

The Gaurelic Waste is the flattest, most desolate place in Appernysia, Lon replied, growing excited over his sister's idea. *If there's anywhere that your idea could work, it would be there.*

The river will be tricky. Its widest part is right where we need to cross, at the fork of the two rivers.

We will deal with that when we get there. Just imagine, Mel—rather than taking a few days of travel, we reach Tarek in a couple of hours. Come on!

Lon shared the idea with Bromax, then the ghraef carried him outside the north end of the city to the top of a small plateau. Huirk followed and the two Beholders worked together to extract the wall's stone blocks and blend them together into one massive slate. They made the sled thick, knowing the weight and force they'd have to put on it to get it moving, then angled the front end up to keep it from digging into the snow.

A mass of Rayders had already climbed the steep hill, breathing heavily as they watched the Beholders work. Lon invited them onto the stone sled as they completed each section. The twins continued to labor like this for hours, well into the afternoon, before the sled was large and sturdy enough to hold everyone, their supplies, and their livestock.

How large do you think that is? Lon asked his sister, staring out from Bromax's back. The sled extended for miles across the plateau.

Maybe this wasn't such a good idea, Mellai answered. *We don't even know if we'll be able to move it.*

Lon smiled, his excitement overpowering his own concern. *There's only one way to find out. You fly up there and let everyone know we're ready to try. Make sure you tell them to sit down to keep from slipping.*

This is crazy, Mellai thought as Huirk leaped into the air. The masses of Rayders began sitting down once she relayed Lon's message. *Now what?*

Come back down here and help me. Land over there, he said, pointing at the opposite side of the angled front. *We should pull from the sides, just in case this is easier than we think it'll be.*

And don't yank on the top edge, Mellai added. *You'll just break the front off.*

Lon extended his essence, wrapping around and through the underside of the stone until he had a firm hold. *You ready?*

I guess.

Pull!

Both Beholders yanked with all of their might, throwing the sled forward fifty feet and sending many of the Rayders toppling backward. Terrified screams filled the air, intermixed with squeals of delight from the children.

Lon spoke aloud to Bromax as he projected his thoughts to Mellai. "We need to check the damage."

The ghraefs took flight and carried the Beholders across the sled, searching for broken stone and injured Rayders. Besides scattered bumps and bruises, along with nervous livestock, everyone was whole. The sled still held together.

I'm going to add a wall on the back of the sled, Lon thought. *A lot of people fell off the back.*

Mellai agreed, but also suggested they add cross-barriers along the full length of the sled. *Nobody was hurt because they could all move together. If a wall had been there, those people in the very back would have been crushed.*

Indeed, Lon thought, trying not to visualize the reality of her logic.

After another thirty minutes of prep time, Lon and Mellai were sitting on their ghraefs at the front of the sled again. Everyone was facing forward, their backs propped against the barriers. The cattle and horses had been walled off in their own individual stalls, while the smaller livestock were corralled into groups.

Try it by yourself this time, leader Beholder bossness, Mellai suggested. *Two of us might be overkill.*

Lon agreed, then slowly began exerting himself, pulling harder and harder with his essence until he could feel his face filling with blood. But the sled never budged.

I think I found the limit to my strength, he thought, breathing hard.

I didn't really think you could do it, Mellai responded. *I was just checking something.*

Lon breathed out with annoyance. *What's that?*

I wanted to see if synergy was at play here. It was too easy for us to pull the sled together. It didn't make sense in my mind, so I had to be sure.

Lon couldn't help but chuckle. Mellai had never really had to experiment with True Sight, not while training with Llen, so it was fun to see her investigate. *Well, if you're done sciencing, Little Sis, I'd like to get started.*

Don't start making up words, Mellai grumbled, taking hold of the sled with her essence. *Remember, slower this time.*

Pull, Lon said softly in his mind, almost at a whisper.

The sled creaked forward, almost unnoticeably, until both Beholders began adding more effort. They accelerated gently, but eventually built enough speed that Bromax and Huirk had to sprint to keep up with the sled.

Want to go faster? Lon asked.

Why not? Mellai answered, excitement radiating in her response.

"Fly, Bromax!" Lon called, and the ghraef spread its wings and lifted into the air, followed immediately by Huirk. "Speed up, but stay low to the ground."

The two ghraefs beat their wings, increasing in velocity while the Beholders kept a firm hold on the sled. Lon could feel the weight of the sled tugging at his essence as they sped up, but it was easily manageable.

"Is it pulling on you?" Lon asked Bromax. The ghraef shook his head. "Really? You don't feel any resistance?"

Bromax clicked his teeth, emphasizing his previous response.

That's strange, Lon thought to his sister. *Bromax says he can't feel any difference from when he normally flies. Even though they're pulling us, I think the entire strain is on us alone.*

It makes sense, Mellai answered, *in its own strange way. When we carried their tail crystals out of the cave, did you feel any extra weight on your feet?*

I guess not . . . but wait. This means that even if we we're standing on a rotting bridge, we could still lift any amount of weight without breaking the planks.

Unless you fall through because you're already too fat.

Ha ha, Lon answered sarcastically. *I've been living on a strict diet of malnutrition for over a year. No fat on these bones. But you, on the other hand . . .*

Don't even think about it, Mellai snapped.

* * * * *

Although they didn't move as quickly as Lon had hoped—he hadn't considered preparation and acceleration time—they still reached the tip of Itorea's blade within an hour. Lon was just beginning to consider how they would slow down when he saw the magnitude of the joined rivers. Nearly a mile separated them from the opposite shore of the Nellis.

So how are we going to cross? Mellai asked.

We're moving pretty fast, Lon replied. *Maybe I can keep the sled moving while you fly ahead and freeze the river.*

That won't work, Lon. Even if I could completely stop the river from flowing—which I can't—the front end of the sled will eventually drop down the embankment and crash into the surface. It won't be able to withstand that amount of force. It's not made out of indestructible stone.

Lon searched the horizon, contemplating solutions. A crossing wouldn't be nearly so difficult farther north. He and his squad had been able to do it on horseback during a flood, but that had been at the tip of the Vidarien Mountains.

How far away is the mountain range from here? Mellai asked in response to her brother's thought process.

At least another hundred and twenty miles. Maybe even a hundred and thirty.

Then let's keep moving north. You're talking worst case scenario, but we'll find a crossing long before we travel that far. Even so, that would only add another four hours to our journey. We could still reach Tarek before complete nightfall.

Good plan, Little Sis, Lon thought, waiting a moment to communicate his next observation. *So you're excited to see Tarek, too, huh?*

Mellai rolled her eyes. *Shut it.*

Chapter 40

Whole

"You alright?" Tarek said, lifting Kaylen back to her feet. "No," Kaylen replied, her feet still shifting around on the ice, "but who is in this place?"

Tarek smiled weakly as he continued following the Rayder scout through their camp. "It could be worse. Lon shared some pretty nasty experiences about the Gaurelic Waste during summer months. Nothing but death fills these swamps, except for swarms of mosquitoes that cling to your body so thick that it looks like you've been bathing in mud."

"That sounds terrible."

"Yes, it does. He lost one of his men and a horse to its madness. No matter what happens with the calahein, we'll have to evacuate before spring."

"Hopefully into Itorea," Kaylen added, her face downfallen.

Tarek pulled his lips tight. "If what you tell me is true, then the possibility of that is as farfetched as building a summer home in Meridina."

Kaylen's brow furrowed as she stared at the Rayder commander.

"You know . . . Meridina, the old headquarters of the calahein. A frozen tundra." Kaylen's expression didn't change, and Tarek breathed out with a sigh. "I was making a joke. It's never summer in Meridina."

"Oh . . ." Kaylen responded, still staring at her feet. "I'm sorry for being distracted. I just wish . . . I don't know . . . I guess I wish for a lot of things, but none of them seem to be coming true."

"Chin up," Tarek replied, lifting her face with his leather-gloved hand. "If there's one thing I learned growing up with the Rayders, it's that misery can't last forever."

"I know, but . . . can I just vent some honesty at you right now?"

Tarek laughed. "Sounds fun!"

"I wish I were back in Pree with Lon. I want Mellai there, too. I wish that I wasn't caught between the politics of you and King Drogan. I don't know how much more of this I can take."

"You're not giving up on me, are you? Lon would never forgive me when he gets back." He paused and chuckled. "And all my hopes of courting his sister would drown themselves in the sea."

"*If* they come back," Kaylen grumbled.

Tarek didn't respond. He had been grateful for Kaylen's insistence, that she had demanded an audience with him even after he told her not to come back without Drogan. Her intentions had been genuine, which became immediately clear when she told Tarek that Drogan had ordered her to return empty-handed. They had quickly reconciled and worked together ever since. But Kaylen was falling victim to the same enemy that plagued his entire camp. Despair. And regardless of how he tried, Tarek was incapable of curing any of them. He needed Lon back, inspiring hope in his men before it was too late.

"Right there, my Commander," the Rayder scout said, pointing northwest. "It appeared a few minutes ago, and it is moving fast in our direction."

Tarek peered at the horizon, into the failing light of the setting sun. A cloud of snow was billowing into the air, swirling around itself as it approached their camp. It looked exactly like the dust trail following a cavalry charge, except horses couldn't move that fast across the ice. Nothing could, unless they had sharp claws for traction.

"We're under attack!" Tarek shouted, drawing his sword. "The calahein have bypassed Itorea and come straight for us! Battle positions!" He grabbed the scout by his neck and pulled him close. "You get Kaylen out of here. I don't care who threatens you. You make sure she gets into Itorea and that they close their gates behind her." He hurled the scout at Kaylen. "Go!"

Rayder soldiers were rushing everywhere, slipping across the ice while they clamored for their weapons and armor. A few fell with sickening crunches as their arms and hips shattered on the frozen bog.

"There's no time!" Tarek called. The snow cloud was nearly upon them. "Ready your bows!"

Every Rayder froze in their location, and those with bows nocked an arrow.

"Take aim!"

Thousands of soldiers pulled the drawstrings back to their ears.

"Hold!" a voice commanded, flying upon the air. A few disoriented Rayders released their arrows, fooled by the unexpected command, but the majority held.

"You rotting sack of kelsh fodder!" Tarek shouted, relief washing over him as he recognized Lon's voice. "Where have you been?"

"Hang on," Lon's voice responded. The swirling snow was leveling, and it had angled away from the Rayder camp as it slowed in speed. Even from a mile away, Tarek could see an angled stone platform rising out of the mass, and flying above it all were two huge beasts, brown and black against the setting sun.

"Don't tell me you went and got yourselves ghraef cronies!" Tarek called, reeling at the sight.

"We did."

"And what is this thing you're toting along with you?"

"It's a surprise."

Tarek blew out his breath. "I hate surprises."

"You'll like this one. I promise."

Another five minutes passed before the structure came to rest, directly beside the Rayder camp. Tarek stared slack-jawed at what it held. Lon had been right. This was a surprise worth waiting for.

Rayder civilians poured from the giant sled, searching for familiar faces in the disarray of Rayder soldiers. Tarek was initially worried that they might trample each other, but when the first group slipped and fell on the ice, everyone else naturally slowed down. The ice didn't dampen their spirits, though. Soldiers wept openly at the sight of their families, finally rescued from the doorstep of death.

When Wade stepped off the sled, Tarek couldn't contain himself. He wrapped his thick arm around him. "You did well, Lieutenant," he said, squeezing the breath out of Wade.

"*They* did well," Wade said, diverting the compliment to the Beholders still flying on their ghraefs overhead.

Tarek laughed heartily. "What a journey we've been though, you and I. A year ago, I was warning Lon of your intention to kill him during his weapons trial, all the while expecting I'd have to beat you senseless for doing it. Now the three of us are here, working together to protect our whole nation's survival. Where's the rest of the squad? They deserve a feisty pat on the back, too."

Wade's brow furrowed. "Lon's squad? I thought they were here with you."

"I haven't seen them since you all left for Réxura."

"Nor have I, since I left them to report to you."

"Lon wouldn't just leave his men behind," Tarek said quietly, fearing the worst. He needed an explanation, but he suppressed his desire to shout at the sky. Every man in Lon's squad was an expert fighter, but even more, a respected member of their civilization. Their deaths would seriously impact the Rayders' morale on all fronts.

"Continue as you were, Lieutenant," Tarek said, turning around to return to his camp. "Make sure everyone has a place to stay and food in their belly."

"Yes, my Commander," Wade replied.

A woman's voice filled Tarek's mind as he walked. *Only Thad has passed, along with one member of my own guard. The rest are alive and well, sailing toward Itorea with the survivors of Jaul and Pree.*

It wasn't until the end of the message that Tarek recognized the voice as Mellai's. His initial reaction was rage, thinking she had just casually announced Thad's death to the Rayder masses. But as Tarek searched everyone's faces, not one gave a visual reaction to the news of Thad's death.

"Did you hear that?" he asked a soldier, grabbing him by the arm.

"Hear what, my Commander?"

"The girl Beholder," he continued, pointing at the ghraefs flying overhead. "Did she just speak to us?"

"I apologize," the soldier said, shaking his head. "I will listen more closely."

Tarek gave a sidelong glance at the ghraefs for a moment. "Never mind. On your way."

The soldier saluted. "Thank you, my Commander."

Are you in my mind? Tarek thought, directing his full attention upward.

Of course, Mellai's voice answered. *How else could I do this?*

I'd be careful how much you play around in here, Tarek continued, tapping the side of his skull with a finger. *You might not be able to handle what you find, being an innocent girl from Pree.*

I'm not that worried. If your thoughts offend me, I'll just let Huirk play with you for awhile.

Huirk? Tarek asked, having never heard that name before.

The brown ghraef flying over you. My companion.

Tarek snorted with amusement. *You're being courted by a ghraef? Why? Jealous?*

A little. He's got himself a thicker beard than me.

But not nearly as pretty, Mellai countered, and Tarek's beard transformed into an assortment of tight ringlets again.

I like this new look, Tarek thought, patting his manicured facial hair and winking at the sky, *but only because it came from you. Come down here and let me express my gratitude.*

In your dreams.

The black-haired ghraef broke out of his loop and dove straight at Tarek's position.

"Protect our commander," one of the soldiers shouted, and men began clustering around Tarek.

"As you were," Tarek ordered. "They're our allies, remember? Beholder Lon is sitting on that ghraef."

The soldiers reluctantly separated, clearing just enough room for the black ghraef. Despite the beast's size, barely a sound came from the solid ice when it landed.

"It's good to see you, Brother," Lon said after dismounting. He wrapped his arms around Tarek in a tight hug.

"Indeed, it is," Tarek said, returning the hug. "Did you have time to give Thad a funeral?"

Lon stepped back and nodded.

"Good. Now would you mind introducing me to your new best friend?"

"This is Bromax. I met him in Roseiri, but he began watching over me long before that."

"A pleasure," Tarek said, dipping his head at the shaggy ghraef. Bromax clicked his teeth in response.

"Any news," Lon asked, "besides Drogan's stubbornness?"

"That about sums it up." Tarek's face fell as he pulled the ringlets out of his beard. "Where have you been? I've needed you."

"With Mellai and the ghraefs."

Tarek's mouth parted with unsatisfied annoyance. "That's it?"

"That's all I can tell you about it. But don't worry. It was time well spent, and might be the ultimate factor in our survival."

Tarek rubbed his forehead, breathing out with frustration. "Commander Rayben never would have accepted that answer."

"Then it's a good thing you're not him. Come on. Let's return to your camp. We have a lot to catch up on."

"That's what I've been trying to do," Tarek grumbled, leading the way. "Your eyes still creep me out."

Lon laughed. "Good."

* * * * *

"A whole month?" Tarek complained, his gaze shifting between Lon and Mellai.

Lon grimaced. "I know. Spare me the lecture." There was so much he wanted to share about Ursoguia, the ghraefs, the Beholders cave—everything—but he knew it was forbidden knowledge. Not even Omar had known the location of the ghraefs' home, let alone the training a Beholder goes through there.

"Well, at least Jaul's civilians are coming," Tarek continued. "They'll make great allies."

"But not enough," Lon growled. "How can Drogan be so stubborn about the Rayders? Doesn't he understand?"

"Obviously not," Tarek replied, "but there's little good complaining can do about it. Last time I did, Kaylen was banished."

"Banished?" Lon stammered.

"Alright, she wasn't banished, but Drogan commanded her to come live with us and solve my problems. I don't see much of a difference."

"When did this happen?"

"A week ago. Kaylen ran straight here and told me all about it. She's been living with us ever since."

Lon searched around the camp, his clouded eyes able to see well beyond the ring of firelight. He noticed Mellai was doing the same.

"She's not here," Tarek continued. "I sent her away when your stone sled appeared. I thought you were the calahein."

"Where?" Mellai asked, climbing onto Huirk.

"To Itorea. I sent a runner with her to tell Drogan to drop Itorea's gates and forget about us."

After Huirk leaped into the air and flew away with Mellai, Tarek leaned closer to Lon. "She's a wild one, isn't she?"

"Mellai? I guess you can look at it that way. She's always done whatever she wants, and now that she has True Sight, not even I can stop her."

"Should we fear her?"

Lon shook his head, unable to tell Tarek about the pure heart requirement of a Beholder. "Never."

"Then where did she just go?"

Lon relayed the question to his sister through their connection.

To get Kaylen, Mellai replied.

Why don't you just use your new trick and tell him yourself? Lon said.

Because I can't see him.

Lon silently nodded. He and Mellai were the only two who could communicate in their unique way. When Mellai had spoken to Tarek's mind, on the other hand, she had used her essence to plant her words on his brain. It had been her first attempt at something like that, and even though it had worked, Lon still rebuked his sister for testing it on his best friend.

"Well?" Tarek asked.

"She's bringing Kaylen back," Lon replied, noticing that a broad grin grew on the commander's face. "What are you smiling about?"

A gentle hand rested on Lon's shoulder, one he had not felt since leaving Pree. "I'm right here."

Lon turned and saw Kaylen standing behind him, smiling sweetly with tears in her eyes. It reminded Lon of the day he had killed Gil Baum, only Kaylen's expression was now full of sadness instead of terror.

He turned to face her. "Kaylen . . . I don't know what to say."

"Then say nothing," Kaylen replied, stepping forward and kissing him softly on the lips. Afterward, she leaned her head against Lon's chest and wrapped her arms around his waist. "Oh, I'm so glad."

"About what?" Lon said, laying his cheek on top of her blonde hair as he held her. Her body felt warm and familiar against his, almost as though he had never left Pree.

"You still feel right." She paused, looking up at him. "*We* still feel right."

"Then I'm glad, too," Lon answered, leaning down to kiss her again.

Kaylen turned her head away. "That doesn't mean I've forgiven you." Her expression was genuinely heartbroken. "You left me, Lon, without any explanation. Not even a goodbye."

Lon stepped away, but Kaylen took hold of his hands, keeping him from escape. Lon could only stare at the snow-covered ice and wonder how long before the fire melted through to extinguish itself in the swamp. "It's easy to look back and see how foolish I was," Lon finally said, "but in that moment, I thought it would make everything easier. I had to leave, Kaylen, because I loved you. I couldn't hurt you again."

"But you did. The heartache I felt that day hurt far worse than any physical pain I've ever experienced. My heart was broken. If it hadn't been for your sister . . . I was in a dark place, desperate and capable of anything. Do you get that?"

Lon nodded. "I do, and I see my mistake for not trying to contact you after I left, too. But you have to understand something. I won't apologize for joining the Rayders. I missed you terribly, but the Rayders needed me. I couldn't abandon them."

Kaylen's face fell. "Do you see the irony in that statement?"

"Of course I do, and I did then, too. I even had dreams about losing you while I was in the middle of helping the Rayders fight for Taeja. But as much as I love you, Kaylen, you're still only one person. I couldn't put my love for you above the needs of so many people, not when I was the only person who could help them."

"Do you still feel that way?" Kaylen said, dropping Lon's hands and hugging herself. "I need to be my husband's top priority. I deserve that much."

"Yes, you do," Lon answered, unsure of how to respond.

"Bah!" Tarek shouted, moving around the fire to stand between them. "Look at the two of you, determined to destroy a perfect relationship. Don't you understand what you have here? How rare this kind of love is? Listen to yourselves. Even when you're fighting, you're not really fighting. You can't afford to toss this aside."

"But I don't see how we can make this work, either," Lon replied, searching the depths of his betrothed's green eyes. "Not when I'm a Beholder."

Tarek slapped Lon's face, drawing his attention away from Kaylen. "The difference between now and a year ago, Brother, is that you can take her with you. You ran away from her because you were a threat to her safety." Tarek stretched out his arms. "Look around. The threat is gone."

Lon absently let his eyes wander around the camp. A thick ring of watchful people had encircled them, a mixture of ages and experiences, but all with one thing in common. Every single person was a Rayder.

"You are born Appernysians," Tarek continued, "but you've never been more at home than you are right now. These people trust you, enough that they'll even die for you. And what about Bromax? He's more than capable of carrying you both in your travels. And when danger strikes, he'll keep Kaylen safe, even when you're away. He already proved that once in the mountains." Tarek leaned close to the ghraef. "That was you, wasn't it?"

Bromax clicked his teeth.

Lon felt his throat tighten, burning with emotion. Tarek had spoken wisely, but could it actually be true? Had the Jaeds finally opened a window, allowing him to experience a little bit of selfish happiness?

The Rayder commander took hold of Lon's hardened leather vest and pulled him close—so close that their noses were nearly touching. "Do you hear what I'm saying, Lon? You never have to leave Kaylen again."

Lon smiled. "Your breath stinks."

"Good," Tarek replied, slapping Lon again. "Now let's celebrate— for you both and for the reunification of our people!"

*   *   *   *   *

Huirk flew low enough for Mellai to scan the Gaurelic Waste. Her worries grew as they drew closer to Itorea's north gate—not that Kaylen had entered the Fortress City, but about the chaos her entry would have caused. If the soldiers manning the perimeter wall believed they were under attack, they would shoot at Huirk without hesitation. Mellai didn't really feel like that was an experience she wanted to have again.

When they flew close enough to see that the gate itself was still open—even though the drawbridge was retracted—relief rushed over Mellai. That meant Kaylen had not entered the city. But where was she?

They flew around the north end of the camp for a few minutes, but Mellai realized their efforts were becoming more and more pointless as the civilians continued filtering through. She'd never be able to distinguish Kaylen from the other Rayder women without carefully searching every one of their temples for a brand.

Just as Mellai was about to search minds, a cheer rang out from the center of their population. It came from Tarek's camp, followed by obvious celebrations. Rayders all over the camp lit torches, sang, and danced.

Mellai couldn't help but smile as she watched them. In a world where death and suffering became ever more threatening, people needed a good excuse to enjoy themselves.

But not us, she thought begrudgingly, reaching for her brother's mind. *I can't find Kaylen.*

She's here with me.

Were you two the reason behind that cheer? she teased, then told Huirk to return to camp.

Maybe a little, but mostly because Tarek just made an amazing speech.

Mellai chuckled. *He didn't strike me as an eloquent speaker.*

He's not. Now hurry back.

Huirk landed next to Bromax, but Mellai remained on the ghraef's back for a few minutes to enjoy the celebration. It reminded her of her time with Kutad and the tradesmen. Unfortunately, the Rayders had no musical instruments with them, having left them behind either in Flagheim or Taeja. But that didn't slow them down. They sang proudly and kept time with anything they could get their hands on, be it cracking sticks together or the clang of swords against shields.

Lon and Kaylen were in the center of the crowd, near the fire. They danced and danced, hardly leaving each other's sides. A light had returned to both of their eyes that Mellai hadn't seen in a long time, not since Lon's coming of age celebration. They were happy and in love again.

"How about that?" Tarek called, standing next to Huirk and pointing at the young couple. "If it didn't go against my better reasoning, I'd say we marry them tonight."

Mellai unbraided Huirk's hair from around her legs. "What better reasoning?"

"Appernysia is a mess," he continued, offering his hand to help Mellai climb down. "Why would anyone want to marry, let alone bring children into a world like this? For all we know, the calahein could attack tomorrow and destroy us all. Marrying would be like leaping off a high cliff. You'd have the time of your life for ten seconds, then splat."

"All the more reason to do it," Mellai said, ignoring Tarek's hand and hopping down herself. "At least you'd have those ten seconds."

"Wait. Are you serious? You want to marry me?"

Mellai rolled her eyes, secretly enjoying the playful banter. "Will you ever give up?"

"On you?" he replied, reaching for her hand. "Never."

She pulled her hand away. "Be serious for a moment, Tarek. You saw their reunion. Is marriage a practical option?"

Tarek shrugged. "Why not? Kaylen's a beautiful woman and she loves him. There's worse things that could happen to Lon."

"Then let's do it."

"What . . . right here?"

"Yes, and you'll perform the ceremony."

"What about your parents, and everyone else from Pree? Think they'd be happy this happened without them?"

Mellai heaved a sigh and leaned back against Huirk. "Alright, but as soon as they get here."

"Wherever *here* is," Tarek continued. "Lon's squad will come to the Gaurelic Waste, but what about everyone else? Where will they live?"

Chapter 41

Outcasts

"She's right there," Aron said, one arm around his wife and the other hand pointing to the top of Itorea's perimeter wall. "Can't you see Huirk?"

"Not clearly," Shalán replied, squinting. "Just a large blur."

"Wait a few minutes for your eyes to adjust."

The crew on Aron's boat had been sailing north for two days, with the long line of Jaul's other ships trailing behind. The weather had been fair, with a strong breeze pushing them faster than anyone had anticipated. Itorea's wall was now just a few miles away, and Pree's villagers climbed out to see. Most of them had spent the entire time below deck—including Lon's squad—resting their bodies and welcoming a chance to finally escape the sun.

Only Aron and Reese had stayed consistently above deck, helping where they could as they learned to manage a sea vessel from Appernysia's finest sailors. Reese especially enjoyed the crow's nest atop the main mast, and how the wind-filled sails pushed him out over the sea.

"It feels like I'm flying on Huirk again," he had told Aron.

Reese was the first to spot Itorea's perimeter wall, jumping up and down as he shouted the news before rejoining his shipmates on the deck. "Are those warships?" he asked, staring at a group of larger ships anchored off the coast. Large ballistae were clearly visible on the decks of every ship.

"Indeed they are," Darius said, drawing his cutlass to use as a pointer. "This is just a small portion of King Drogan's full armada. Most of his ships are stationed farther inland, near Itorea's south bridge.

"Then why do they keep these here?"

"Sometimes the king likes to go sailing," the sailor replied, sheathing his sword again.

Aron nodded at Darius, grateful for the man's tact. They had veered far away from the coastline of Appernysia, aiming for the middle of the Fortress Island. The ships anchored there were undoubtedly part of King Drogan's emergency plan, in case he needed to make a hasty escape. That kind of information would have struck too closely to Reese, who had fled for his own life just a few weeks earlier.

The warships were large, so they had to be anchored a safe distance from the coastline. Jaul's fishing boats, however, were perfectly sized to sail right up to Itorea's doorstep. Darius had his men dock at a smooth stone platform jutting out from the wall, then he stepped out and marched up to the iron portcullis. Aron followed behind him, glancing back to make sure the Rayders hid their brands, but none of Lon's squad were visible.

"We are from Jaul and Pree," Darius said to the sentries standing on the other side of the iron grate. "We seek refuge."

"King Drogan has been expecting you," the man replied. "Beholder Mellai warned us of your arrival."

"*Warned* you?" Darius asked. "Are we considered a threat?"

"Not all of you. Just a handful."

Aron stepped forward. "My daughter respects the Rayders traveling with us, as do the rest of us. She gave you no warning."

The sentry shrugged. "I wasn't part of the conversation, but I have my orders. The rest of you are welcome to enter, but all Rayders are forbidden in Itorea."

"Even my son?" Aron said, grabbing one of the iron bars.

"I'm sorry," the sentry said, stepping back, "but I can't let you in until the four Rayders have identified themselves."

"I want to talk to my daughter." When the sentry didn't respond, Aron stepped back and shouted up the wall. "Come down here, Mellai."

Mellai's head appeared over the edge of the wall, then her voice sounded in Aron's mind. *I can't, or none of you will be able to enter. King Drogan doesn't want me interfering.*

"Then why are you here?" Aron raged, disliking Drogan more with every passing second.

To keep the peace. Please don't fight this, Father. There is enough contention already.

Aron stared back at her, fuming as he tried to think of a response, when Huirk leaped off the flanking tower and dove straight down. He landed next to Aron, raised a claw to touch the scar on the ex-Rayder's right temple, then motioned to his own brown-haired back.

Huirk, on the other hand, Mellai continued, *can do whatever he wants. Tell Lon's squad to climb on. He'll fly them straight to the Gaurelic Waste.*

"For such a fearsome creature," Aron said, bowing to the ghraef, "you are more generous than any of us humans. You have my utmost respect."

Aron called to the Rayders, then turned to the sentry on the other side of the portcullis. He stared at the young soldier with an intensity that would make even the most courageous shake. "And you . . . you can march the rest of us straight through your blasted city to join the Rayders."

The sentry's eyes grew wide. "But why?"

"If our brothers have no place in Itorea, neither do we."

*　*　*　*　*

Although Aron hadn't spoken with Darius or Trev regarding his proclamation, he was certain they would back his decision. After all, it was Rayders who had saved their lives.

And they did, wholeheartedly, along with everyone they spoke for. After Huirk had flown away with Lon's squad, the sentries opened Itorea's east gate while Jaul's sailors moved each fishing boat up to the royal dock. After all passengers and cargo were unloaded, each boat was abandoned on the sea.

"Then secure them yourselves," Darius had responded when Appernysia's soldiers began complaining that the boats might damage the king's warships. "We don't need them where we're going."

When a sizeable crowd began forming inside the keep, Aron led the first group up the road that crossed into the hook and ultimately stopped at Itorea's north gate. They traveled quickly along the cobblestone, but it was still a twenty-mile journey and they hadn't started until late afternoon. They would be required to camp for one night inside Itorea's walls.

By that time, Huirk had returned from the Waste and picked up Mellai. They landed at Aron's camp just as they had finished that evening's meal.

"I thought you weren't allowed to intervene," Aron said, casually stoking their fire with a charred branch.

"I'm not," Mellai countered. "I'm just here to talk."

"Listen, Mellai, if you're going to try to—"

"I agree with your decision," she interrupted, sitting down next to her mother. "King Drogan is acting especially stubborn about all of this."

Aron paused to look up at her, searching her face for sincerity. Mellai stared back at him, her expression soft and understanding.

"Have you tried talking to him?" Shalán asked.

Mellai nodded, then leaned her head against Shalán's shoulder. "I met with the King's Council for a few hours yesterday. They claim they're doing this to prevent bloodshed—that Itorea's civilians still loathe the Rayders—but their argument is weak. The civilians wouldn't even know if the Rayders moved into Itorea's hook, and Appernysia's soldiers have developed a mutual respect with the Rayders. There wouldn't be any bloodshed." She thumped her own thigh with a frustrated fist. "Nothing I said made a difference, though. It was like arguing with a herd of dead donkey."

"Then why won't King Drogan change his mind?" Shalán pressed.

"Because he's ruled by his own fear," Aron answered, breaking the branch and tossing it into the fire. "He spent his whole life scared of the Rayders, fighting to keep them outside our borders. When Lon helped the Rayders defeat our army, it must have decimated King Drogan's sense of security. Now he makes all of his decisions defensively. He'll hide behind these walls until either battle or old age take his life."

"I think you're right," Darius commented, sliding a smooth stone along the sharpened edge of his cutlass. "We can only hope it comes from the latter."

"But what about us?" Trev asked, gesturing to Pree's villagers scattered around them. "Will we spend the rest of our lives drowning in the Gaurelic Waste?"

"I don't know," Aron replied.

"It's not as bad there as you think," Mellai commented, shifting her weight against her mother. "Lon has already begun building stone shelters. If we're still there in the spring, after the ice melts, he and I can drain the swamp and make the land livable."

"If *we're* still there?" Shalán said, leaning forward to look at her daughter's face. "Do you plan on staying with us?"

Mellai chuckled. "Look at Huirk's tail crystal. I belong with the Rayders."

"Your duty is to King Drogan," Aron argued. "That blue tattoo on your face can mean only one thing. You swore an oath to him. Am I correct?"

"Yes, but it doesn't mean I can't help you, too," she said pointedly.

Aron absently rubbed the scar on his face. "Not this time, Mellai. Lon can look after the Rayders. Your place is here, protecting Itorea's borders. Don't let King Drogan's mistake cost unnecessary lives."

"He's right," Shalán said, wrapping her arm around her daughter.

"Alright," Mellai said hesitantly, but then she shot upright with a smile on her face. "But not until after tomorrow!"

"Why?" Aron said. "We can find Lon ourselves."

"I can't believe I forgot to tell you this," Mellai said, giggling as she searched the camp. "Where's Scut?"

"Tell us what?" Shalán asked, grabbing her daughter's hand. Aron could see by the excited look on his wife's face that she had already anticipated the answer.

"I have to go get things ready," Mellai continued, forgetting about Scut as she hugged her mother and climbed onto Huirk's back. "Kaylen and Lon are getting married tomorrow!"

Chapter 42

United

Although the adornments of Kaylen's marriage were plain in design, there was nothing simple about the ceremony. Twenty thousand Rayder soldiers—including the five thousand Appernysian Rayders her betrothed had rescued—stood in two bodies, fully garbed for war with glaives in hand and bows slung across their backs. Their polished breastplates glinted under the setting sun, as did the seamless granite walkway running between them.

At the far end of the walkway—over a mile away—stood Tarek Ascennor, a simple villager that had become commander of all living Rayders. He stood on a raised platform, his thick hands gloved with blue velvet and adjusting a silver coronet on his head. His plate armor had also been polished, and the blue King's cross on his breastplate shone nearly as brilliantly as the one embedded in Huirk's tail crystal.

Both ghraefs were part of Kaylen's assembly, Bromax leading the procession and Huirk walking directly behind her with Mellai on his back.

"Just in case," Mellai had said, demanding that she stay where she could protect her best friend.

Scut Shaw also stood next to Kaylen. Although his clothes were tattered, they contrasted his internal merriment. A wide smile beamed across his face as he looked at his only daughter. "You ready?"

Kaylen smoothed her chestnut-colored dress one more time and nodded, still fidgeting with the gold piping stitched into its wrists. The material hung more loosely on her slender form than it had during Lon's coming of age celebration, but it was still beautiful. Kaylen was grateful that her father had packed it along for this special occasion; it was more comfortable and sentimental than all of the fancy gowns Tarek had offered for the ceremony.

"Hie then, Bromax," Scut said respectfully, following after the black-haired ghraef with Kaylen's hand wrapped around the nook of her father's elbow.

Kaylen smiled at the few citizens of Jaul she could see at the back of the wedding audience before they disappeared behind the ranks of Rayder soldiers. The next fifteen minutes of their march stayed this way, rows upon rows of armored men, with the occasional child that slipped between the soldiers to peek at their Beholder's new wife. Kaylen waved at one young girl, bringing a giggle from her before she slipped back through the soldiers.

"You'll make a wonderful mother," Scut said, wiping yet another tear from his eyes.

"Thank you, Father," she replied, hugging Scut's arm.

A drop of cold water trickled down the back of her neck, but Kaylen ignored it. Mellai had crafted an ice tiara for the occasion and it was starting to melt against her warm head.

As they neared the front end of the narrow walkway, the people Kaylen cared for most began to appear. Ric, Snoom, and Duncan, along with the five members of Lon's squad. Reese Arbogast, who never ventured far from Shalán and Aron, stood proud with the rest of Pree's villagers.

And there he was—Lon Marcs—her great love, finally to become her husband. His brown curly hair had been neatly trimmed and his face shaven. He was the only Rayder not in armor, dressed instead in brown leather slacks and knee-high boots, his sword belted over a royal blue tunic of silk.

Scut stopped at the base of the platform and turned to his daughter. Kaylen expected a thoroughly planned speech, but Scut only smiled at her and kissed her hand before stepping out of the column and standing next to Lon's parents. Bromax and Huirk leaped into the air, landing behind Tarek and turning to face the crowd, then Mellai dismounted and stood behind the Rayder commander.

Kaylen felt uncomfortable standing there by herself, so she hurried onto the platform and eagerly grabbed Lon's hand. The observing audience burst into laughter.

"Obviously, these two need no encouragement," Tarek said, while Mellai projected his voice to the masses, "nor do they require an introduction. But even I can't ignore certain traditions, such as the sacred union of this invaluable couple. We welcome you, First Lieutenant Lon Marcs, along with your better half, Kaylen Shaw. May the Jaeds watch over your journey together. Now let us hear your oaths, that we may bear witness of your devotion to each other."

Kaylen turned to face Lon, taking his other hand as she stared into his deep, blue eyes. "I love you, Lon Marcs, more than anyone else in Appernysia. For as long as I've known you, I've watched you put the needs of others before your own, even when it brought your own suffering. You've done more than your part for this kingdom and deserve all the happiness this world can offer. Thank you for choosing to share that future with me and our children I hope to bear. I pledge my heart, body, and soul to you. If there is anything I can do to bring you the happiness you deserve, I will do it full-heartedly. I am yours."

Light clapping poured from the crowd, a sign from all present that they heard and approved Kaylen's oath. Lon kissed Kaylen's hands and cleared his throat, his emotions battling to overpower his composure.

"I had begun to doubt this day would come," Lon said, beginning his own oath. "From the moment I met you, Kaylen Shaw, I loved you. Your kindness is unmatched, as is your ability to see into people's hearts. You loved me and my family when it felt like no one else could. You believed in me, supported me, and helped me, even when my pride refused it. Above everything, you never gave up on me. If anyone in Appernysia is pure of heart, my love, it is you. I promise to spend the rest of my life protecting and preserving everything I love about you, even if it is at the cost of my own desires. You are my all, and I pledge my life to you."

As more light clapping followed, Kaylen watched Lon carefully. He spoke from the heart, but seemed beset by a deep-rooted sadness. "What is it?" she asked, gratefully noting that Mellai wasn't carrying this conversation to the masses.

"What if I can't protect you? What if I'm not strong enough?"

Kaylen squeezed his hands. "There's no trial we can't defeat, if we face it together. I love you, Lon."

Lon forced a smile back at her. "And I you."

"Your oaths are approved," Tarek proclaimed with Mellai's assistance, once the clapping had quieted down. "By my authority as Rayder commander, I declare you Lon and Kaylen Marcs, husband and wife. Now kiss each other already and make this official."

Kaylen stepped up to Lon and wrapped her arms around his waist, pulling him close as he cupped her face gently between his hands. When their lips met, it was no longer as a betrothed couple, but as married companions, never to be separated again.

Thunderous applause ensued, followed by wild celebrations. With a bleeding hunk of meat drenching his velvet glove—where it came from, Kaylen had no idea—Tarek ordered that their full supply of ale be distributed amongst the masses.

Everyone joined in except the newlywed couple. Instead, Lon picked up his wife and carried her onto Bromax's back. They flew to an isolated location that Mellai had prepared to the east, on the shores of the Asaras Sea. There they spent the first of many nights together, alone and in love.

✳   ✳   ✳   ✳   ✳

"Bromax approaches!" a Rayder watchman called, pointing north at a dark speck in the purple sky.

Everyone had been watching for the couple's return, but Wade Arneson was the only Rayder dreading it. He stood, staggering across the ice to their camp's eastern border, then continuing on.

He was at least a hundred yards from the nearest Rayder when Bromax descended and landed on the ice next to him. Kaylen was sitting in front of Lon, his arms around her waist and their hands affectionately interlocked. They were both dressed in layers of casual linens.

"I told you he'd be waiting here for me," Lon said, kissing his wife on the cheek. "Any noteworthy reports, Lieutenant?"

"No updates on the calahein threat," Wade said, then dropped to his knees on the ice. "I have a confession, though—a truth I have been keeping from you, Beholder."

Lon unbraided his legs and dismounted the black-haired ghraef. "What truth?" he asked, helping Wade to his feet.

Wade unsheathed his sword and offered it to Lon. "Bryst Grayson deceived me. I am no longer a worthy protector."

Even with his gaze downcast, Wade could see Lon tense. "Who died?"

"Flora Baum, in Taeja. At first, I feared her three children were abducted by fifty remaining members of Clawed's following, but they are clever. The children avoided capture."

"Who killed her?"

"Warley Chatterton. He now lies dead near Taeja's keep, but it matters little. Avenging Flora's death was not my oath to you. She should be standing here beside me."

"Why did you keep this from me?" Lon asked, taking Wade's sword and tossing it to the ice.

"I realized my mistake when we were banished to Sylbie," Wade continued, ignoring the question. "The Jaeds were punishing us because of me and my choice."

"Don't be ridiculous," Lon said, his tone softening slightly. "Now answer my question, Lieutenant. Why didn't you tell me about this earlier?"

"Because I believed you deserved this," he replied, pointing to Kaylen. "I have never seen you as content as you were the night we arrived in the Gaurelic Waste. I could not ruin it."

Lon looked at his wife for a moment, then began pacing the ice. "That wasn't your choice to make, Wade."

"I see that now. I am sorry, Beholder."

"Where are they?" Lon pressed.

"The children? Somewhere near our Commander's quarters, if they obeyed my request. Flora's body is there, too. I brought her with me as proof of my error."

Lon paused, staring down at the ice in deep contemplation, then picked up Wade's sword and handed it to him. "Lead me to your camp, Lieutenant. Flora deserves a proper funeral."

Wade sheathed his sword and saluted. "Yes, Beholder."

✳   ✳   ✳   ✳   ✳

"Who is Flora Baum?" Kaylen asked as they flew toward Tarek's stone house, constructed from the giant sled Lon and Mellai had created.

"Remember that Rayder I killed in Pree?"

"The one you knocked off the horse?"

"That's him. His name was Gil Baum. Flora is his widowed wife. I devoted myself to her care, along with her three children."

"I have to ask," Kaylen said hesitantly, "not that it would matter now that I've convinced you to finally marry me . . ."

"Convinced me?" Lon said, followed by a laugh. "She was interested, even kissed me once, but I never reciprocated. Aside from my devotion to you, I wasn't in the place for a relationship. Gil was my first kill, and I still feel guilt over what I did. I have to make sure they're cared for."

"But why attack Flora, of all people? That doesn't make sense."

"I should've asked Wade, but I'm sure I already know the answer. They thought I'd be the one to come back to Taeja and were using Flora as bait to kill me. When I didn't show, they killed her and tried to capture her children as hostages to ensure a safe escape."

"So have they escaped?"

"I suppose so, for now. Maybe once all this calahein dust settles, I'll take you to Flagheim and show you the sights. Seek a little retribution on Clawed's following while I'm there, too."

Kaylen leaned into her husband, sharing warmth. "This man, Clawed . . . He died?"

"Yes."

"Was he Braedr?"

"How'd you know?"

"Mellai started calling him that after you left Pree. You know, because of the scars on his face."

"I eventually figured that much out, but it's amusing to hear where the nickname came from. I guess Braedr finally embraced it."

Kaylen grew more quiet. "Braedr was an evil man, but it still makes me sad to hear that he died."

"You wouldn't say that if you knew everything he did. I'll spare you the details, but some of the closest people I knew were murdered because of him. Even now, death still comes from his influence."

Silence overtook their conversation. Lon observed the activity on the ground, but people rarely moved as they readied themselves for bed. There was nothing to do and nowhere to go on the Waste. The Rayders couldn't even hunt, relying instead on the regular crates of supplies from Itorea.

"We have a lot to catch up on, don't we?" Kaylen eventually said.

"Indeed," Lon replied, kissing the side of his wife's head, "but there's no hurry."

Kaylen nuzzled even closer to him. "No hurry at all."

Yet, in his heart, Lon knew they both spoke erroneously. Their marriage and the few days since had been wonderful, but fleeting. The calahein threat was still very real, the looming attack drawing closer with every hour that passed.

* * * * *

Lon explained the situation to Tarek, while Kaylen disappeared with a few Rayder women to be fitted with leather armor. Lon thought it unnecessary to dress her for battle, but Tarek had demanded it, reminding Lon that the calahein weren't the only potential threat to his or his new wife's safety.

"And how was your honeymoon?" Tarek asked as Lon dressed in his own light armor.

"None of your business," Lon replied flatly, eyeing the three children in the tent.

"I'm being serious, Lon. All is well in your relationship? No fights or anything?"

Lon motioned for Tarek to follow him outside, then closed the door behind them before walking further away. "It's been pure bliss. I had forgotten how much I missed her."

"I'm glad," Tarek said, sitting down on an empty crate. "Maybe I'll have a relationship like that someday."

"With my sister?"

Tarek grinned. "I wouldn't complain about that."

Lon sat next to him, tightening his own vambraces. "Neither would I. You two are a smart match, but you still need to court her. She'll hold you to it."

"I'm sure she will," Tarek said, slapping Lon on the back. He surveyed the various tents and makeshift shelters scattered across the ice. "I can't tell you how good it is to have you back."

Lon nodded absently, his gaze drifting north toward Flagheim. He knew that just beyond the horizon was the Appernysian watch-towers that he and his squad had seized nearly a year earlier. He found comfort in the fact that the mountain remained free of smoke or fire. "How long since anyone visited Three Peaks?"

"Not since Wade left to fetch our civilians Why?"

"Want me to pay them a quick visit? I could be back in a few hours."

Tarek shook his head. "That's too far. Thennek can handle his men, and he has a whole cabin and forest full of food to last through the winter." He hesitated. When he spoke again, his voice was much softer. "I'm sorry to hear about Flora."

Lon returned to his seat on the crate, wondering how long it would take for Wade to arrive. "So am I."

*   *   *   *   *

"How do you breathe in this thing?" Kaylen said, pulling at her leather vest.

"You'll get used to it," Lon replied. "It's better than the alternative."

"I wish there weren't the alternative," Kaylen said, slumping back against him.

Lon breathed in the crisp night air as he stared across the Gaurelic Waste with his enhanced vision. They had been flying on Bromax for hours, circling high above the camp and scouting for danger. Lon couldn't help but contemplate his journey to the Exile. Over a hundred miles north were the jagged peaks of the Dialorine Range. It had been there where he first witnessed death on a large scale. Bodies had littered the mountainside, all Appernysian men desperate to flee their kingdom. Many didn't survive, while those who made it into the Rayder Exile wished they had died on the way there. Now the reverse was true. Rayders sought sanctuary with the Appernysians and had been banished into their own internment camp. Lon had never been much of a believer in reciprocated fate, but this was becoming awfully suspicious.

"Lon?" Kaylen said, turning to look at him. "Are you alright?"

"I'm fine," he replied with a quick kiss. "I'm just sorting through a lot of memories of this place. I had planned never to return."

"We can still leave."

Bromax replied with an aggressive huff and shake of his head.

"He's right," Lon agreed. "I can't leave these people to die. I'm about the only chance of survival they have left."

The ghraef huffed again, rolling his shoulders to jostle the two passengers on his back.

Lon chuckled and patted the ghraef on his back. "You can help, too, I guess."

"But what are we going to do?" Kaylen said, holding Lon's arm around her waist.

Lon didn't answer, unsure of the answer himself. No one knew what to expect from the calahein, except that their attack would be well planned and ruthless.

Chapter 43

Flame in the West

Mellai sat upright, startled out of sleep to see an Appernysian soldier nudging her shoulder.

"I'm sorry to wake you," he said, "but you should see this."

After rubbing the drowsiness from her eyes, Mellai stood and followed the soldier to the outer crenellations of the watchtower. When she and Huirk had begun patrolling Itorea's west wall a few days earlier, the ghraef had taken over the top of the watchtower as his temporary nest. At five hundred feet—two hundred feet higher than the perimeter wall protecting it—the watchtower offered a secluded place where Beholder and ghraef could peacefully rest. And because of its position halfway between Itorea's west and south gates, the entire front of the Perbeisea Forest was perfectly visible across the half-mile-wide river. It was a perfect scouting location.

The soldier didn't need to explain what had caught his attention. Mellai stared wide-eyed into the forest. Even though the Furwen Trees grew taller than the watchtower, she could still see that a fire raged inside its borders. The horizon glowed bright orange against the night sky.

"What does it mean?" the soldier asked, licking his dry lips.

"It means we need to prepare for battle," Mellai replied, reassuringly squeezing the soldier's forearm. "Warn your unit and ready yourselves."

The soldier disappeared down the tower staircase and Mellai climbed onto Huirk's back. She pulled at the hair between his shoulder blades, the safest place to wake a sleeping ghraef. Huirk unconsciously snapped, then licked his snout and snorted. Mellai frowned, knowing his exhaustion from flying endless patrols for nearly a week.

"I'm so sorry," she said, "but it's time to go. The calahein are approaching."

All signs of weariness immediately departed as Huirk pushed onto his feet and spread his wings.

Mellai secured her legs. "We need to get higher than the trees and verify what's happening."

Huirk leaped off the edge of the watchtower, catching the wind under his wings as they floated across the city before beating them to gain altitude. A minute later, they were soaring high above with an aerial view of the forest. Not only was the firelight more clear, but Mellai could see the orange flames flickering in the middle of the forest.

"That couldn't be an accident," Mellai said, mostly to herself as she examined the night sky. It was completely void of clouds. "We need to talk to Kamron."

Huirk clicked his teeth, veered north, and landed above the west gate ten minutes later. Mellai ignored the many questions from the soldiers stationed there as she descended the flanking tower stairs with no torch, perfectly capable of seeing in the dark with True Sight.

At the top of the tower, the staircase zigzagged in the center, but a third of the way down—one hundred feet from the top—the stairwell connected to tunnels that ran inside the wall. The hidden passages connected the towers in a continuous network. At the north wall of Itorea, the passages provided access to raised aqueducts. Pumps ceaselessly pulled freshwater from the Nellis River and fed the aqueducts as they ran south over the city.

Mellai glanced down a passage, then turned and cut through one of the guardrooms—where terrified crossbowmen stared at the glow through arrow slits in the flanking tower. At the far end of the room, Mellai pounded on a locked door into the guardhouse.

"Wake up, General Astadem," Mellai shouted, but there was no answer. Her patience was thin. She shattered one of the stout door planks and lifted the crossbeam to let herself in, finding Kamron lying on his straw mattress in a deep sleep. She grabbed his shoulders with her essence and shook him, drawing a startled shout from the general.

"The Perbeisea Forest is on fire," Mellai said once Kamron was alert enough to comprehend.

"Impossible," Kamron replied as he belted his sword around his waist. "The bottom of the forest canopy is at least fifty feet in the air, and Furwen trunks are as hard as stone, impervious to flame. No ground fire could reach those branches."

"That's what I feared," Mellai replied. "The trees must have been set on fire."

"Calahein?"

Mellai nodded. "That's the only logical explanation."

Kamron dropped his sword and reached for his full body armor, first grabbing the chainmail. "Then we must prepare for battle. What time is it?"

"A few hours from sunrise," Mellai replied, recalling the position of the stars.

"That fire is meant as a distraction," Kamron continued, shaking his head. "They will attack an hour or two after sunrise, when men begin to feel the effects of their sleepless night."

Mellai wanted to tell people to sleep, but knew it would be a futile request. She, for one, wouldn't be able to. "Should I warn King Drogan?" she asked instead.

"Have you gone mad?" Kamron said, his face screwed up with impatient mockery. "In case you didn't notice, our future is on the line *here*, not at the keep. Send a runner."

Mellai left Kamron in his quarters and called a crossbowman over, whom she knew to be hardworking and reliable.

"Yes, Beholder," he replied, placing a fist over his heart. "What—"

"I need you to carry a message to King Drogan," Mellai interrupted. "He needs to hear it directly from your lips. No handing it off to pages or any other messengers. I'm trusting you with this task. Will you do it?"

"Of course."

Good. Here is the message. 'The Perbeisea Forest is on fire and the calahein will attack at dawn.' Now go, and ride hard. I expect Drogan to hear this report within two days."

The runner disappeared down the staircase on his way to the stable yard, then Mellai returned to her ghraef on the wall top. "Back to your nest, Huirk."

Once on top of the watchtower, Mellai vented her frustrations to the ghraef. "I hate to admit it, but Kamron is right. King Drogan can do very little from his castle and he'll be days behind once the runner reaches him. We're on our own."

Huirk shook his head and pointed north.

Realization dawned on the Beholder. She immediately attempted to contact her brother, but he wasn't using True Sight. When Mellai reached for his feelings, she felt only calm. "He's asleep!" she shouted at Huirk. "After all this preparation for war, he's going to sleep right through the fighting!" But that didn't stop her from trying to reach him again, and again.

"Until Lon responds," she finally said to Huirk, "it really will be just the two of us. Should we split up?"

Huirk shook his head even more aggressively, then clicked his teeth to emphasize his opinion.

"Alright," Mellai agreed. "And hopefully it never becomes that desperate."

But just a few minutes later, Mellai felt her brother summon True Sight. She linked minds with him and immediately felt his anxiety.

What's happening over there, Mel? The wrong horizon is glowing.

The Perbeisea Forest is on fire. Kamron believes it is the beginning of the calahein attack, and I think he's right. I need you here now. I can't defend twenty miles of wall all by myself.

I'll need to talk with Tarek about it.

No you don't. Come here now.

Mellai felt the irritation grow in her brother. *I thought you put me in charge. I thought you trusted me.*

Not when you're making idiotic decisions. This is humanity's survival we're talking about. Get some perspective. You don't need permission.

Without a response, Mellai felt their connection sever as Lon dismissed his power. "What's wrong with him?" Mellai shouted at Huirk.

The ghraef only huffed and laid his head on one of his paws.

Mellai inhaled and let the air slowly escape her lungs. "I'm sorry, Huirk. I shouldn't be shouting at you. I just get so angry sometimes. Am I being irrational?"

Huirk turned to look Mellai in her eyes, then tapped on top of his head with a claw.

"I know. I need to think before I speak."

The ghraef shook his head and twisted his body to face her more directly. He methodically pointed at her, then tapped on top of his head again.

Mellai felt her face turn red with embarrassment. "Oh . . . you want me to read your thoughts again?"

Huirk clicked his teeth.

Upon entering the ghraef's mind, Mellai's awareness was filled with an image of her brother. He was kneeling before Tarek with two fingers over his King's Cross brand. Then the image morphed into Mellai kneeling before King Drogan, her fist over her heart.

Lastly, a scene filled her mind of Lon and herself side by side, each professing their loyalty to a beam of light streaming from the sky.

That light must be Huirk's interpretation of a Jaed, Mellai thought, understanding the message behind the images. "You made your point, Huirk," she said aloud. "Lon has a duty to Tarek, just as I do to King Drogan. And ultimately we both serve the same cause as Beholders."

Huirk nodded, but continued to hold Mellai's gaze.

Mellai stammered. ". . . and I . . . uh . . . should trust Lon's judgment?"

Huirk clicked his teeth, then returned his head to his paw and stared west at the burning Furwen Trees.

Mellai plopped down on the ground beside the ghraef. "I hate when you're right," she grumbled, then blew out another breath of frustration. "He better hurry."

*   *   *   *   *

Lon walked quickly across the ice, dressed in his leather armor.

"There isn't time," Kaylen said. She was wrapped in a thick wool blanket and sitting on Bromax's back as the ghraef followed after her husband.

"I know," Lon replied, "but I can't just leave. I have to tell Tarek." By then, he had reached the commander's stone dwelling. Lon reached forward to pull back the crafted door, but it swung out seemingly of its own accord.

"Tell me what?" Tarek said, stepping out into the night with naught but his trousers to guard against the frigid cold. He folded his arms across his burly, hair-covered chest, but looked past his visitors at the glowing horizon. "Tell me *that*?" He jabbed his finger west.

Lon nodded. "Mellai demands that Bromax and I leave immediately, but I don't want to abandon the Rayders."

It took a few seconds for Tarek to return his gaze to the Beholder. "You think helping your sister is abandoning us? I thought you were smarter than that."

"But I—"

Tarek slapped Lon across the face, stunning him. "Wake up, Brother. Some needs trump all other obligations. Now get on Bromax and go help Mellai and Huirk." He glanced one more time at the horizon and his expression resolved in unconquerable determination. "You won't be alone, Lon. I will march our army into Itorea by tomorrow. We'll be right behind you."

"Are you sure?"

The commander wrapped Lon in a bear hug, then stepped back and pushed him toward Bromax. "Go. Just save some of the killing for us."

As Lon climbed onto Bromax's back, he couldn't help but fear that the opposite was more plausible. A lot could happen during the Rayder's march. Lon's goal was simply to hold off the calahein long enough for is brothers to be of any help.

"I have to leave you again," Lon said to his wife. "I fear this is a continuation of a lifetime of interruptions between us."

"And the life I chose for myself," Kaylen replied, wrapping Lon in the blanket and kissing him passionately. "I'm much more concerned about your safety. Promise me that you'll come back this time."

Lon returned the kiss, holding his wife close and treasuring the warmth of her body. "I love you Kaylen."

"And I you," she said, followed by a softer caress of their joined lips. She then took Lon's face between her hands and forced him to look at her. "Promise me."

"I can't, not when I'm uncertain of anyone's future, let alone my own." He took Kaylen's hand and kissed it. "All I can offer is my best effort to survive. Please accept it."

Kaylen looked at him, even seemed to stare through him, but finally assented. After one more kiss on Lon's cheek, she slid off of

Bromax and walked to the ghraef's head. "Nothing heroic, Bromax," she said, rubbing him on the snout. "You have done so much to keep me and Lon safe and together. Don't give up on us now."

Bromax nodded, then turned and leaped into the air. As he and Lon turned west, Tarek's booming voice reached Lon's ears. "For Appernysia!"

Chapter 44

Battle for Itorea

At some point during the early morning hours, the wind had changed directions, darkening Itorea with enough smoke to burn in Mellai's lungs. The fire had become clearly visible at the front of the forest canopy, then the flames had torn through the Perbeisea Forest, consuming the Furwen trees lining the edge of the Sylbien River. Their immense trunks were charred black. Massive expanses of branches crumbled from the burning heat that had spread through their boughs. The frozen ground had morphed into a sludgy quagmire, as had the ice lining the river. Even from a half-mile away, Mellai felt the heat when the flames had touched the opposite bank.

With the forest destroyed, Mellai now had a full view of Sylbie while standing above Itorea's west gate. The neighboring city had also been consumed by the fire—well, what was left of it. She and Lon had already removed most of its stonework weeks earlier to make the Rayder sled.

Mellai rolled her shoulders, trying to ease her restlessness.

"What about your scouts?" Mellai said, still sitting on Huirk.

"There are none left to save," Kamron replied. "That forest has been overrun by the calahein for weeks." He paused, glancing around. "Where's your brother?"

"I sent him to the south gate," Mellai replied.

The general didn't reply.

"If the calahein have been in the forest for weeks," Mellai asked, "then why attack now? Their odds would have been much higher before Huirk and I arrived."

"I've wondered the same thing," Kamron replied, "and only one answer seems logical. They want us all in one spot."

"That's a foreboding thought," Mellai said, feeling her own mouth become dry.

"Perhaps, but you and your ghraef defend us. Imagine how that makes them feel."

Mellai stifled a sigh, not wanting to appear under-confident. But Kamron's trust was misplaced. She couldn't effectively defend their entire line, even with Lon's help. She connected with her brother's mind and received a report similar to her own observations. Even at his location, only small pockets of smoldering ash remained from what used to be a towering forest.

And to the north, rising from somewhere beyond the horizon, Mellai could see a faint trace of black smoke.

"Three Peaks," Kamron commented, pointing in the same direction. "Idiotic Rayders. What use is their signal fire at this point? This entire forest just burned dow—" Kamron paused, placing his hands on neighboring crenels and peering east.

"General?" Mellai said.

"The first wave advances!" Kamron shouted to Mellai and the surrounding troops, pointing at the west edge of the arching bridge. A large pack of terror hounds appeared, saturated in mud that covered most of their autumn-colored fur. "Ready yourselves!"

Men ran around the top of the flanking tower, bumping repeatedly into Huirk as they tried to collect spears and operate the aiming arms of their ballistae.

"I need you off this tower," Kamron said, waving a hand at Mellai without looking at her. "You're taking up too much room."

Huirk growled low, scraping his claws across the stone as he skulked onto the curtain wall between the two flanking towers and directly above the west gate.

"Easy, Huirk. He's on our side."

The ghraef huffed and faced west, spreading his wings in preparation for flight.

"Wait," Mellai said. "You can't charge them. Their toxic phlegm will bring you down."

Huirk whined, tossing his head and clicking his teeth in frustration, but he held his position, as did the terror hounds. Just as Mellai was beginning to wonder how this battle would commence, Huirk reared back and roared—so loud that the surrounding men dropped to their knees in fear. The hounds also visibly flinched, then burst into a run.

Halfway across the bridge, a hailstorm of ballistae spears began pouring down from the towers. Some found their mark, skewering hounds and carrying them over the edge. Howls filled the air as the beasts toppled into the river a hundred feet below.

Black clouds of crossbow bolts joined the attack soon after, consuming the remaining hounds in a rain of death.

Mellai breathed out, having been unconsciously holding her breath. None of the hounds had made it across the drawbridge or through the gateway. Then reality struck as she reconsidered her thought. The drawbridge was still down, and the gates were open.

"To the gate!" she shouted. The ghraef dove off the edge, landing abruptly on top of the twitching carcasses of the terror hounds. While Huirk consumed a couple of the more lively ones, Mellai dismounted and dashed into the arching gateway. She grabbed the rear Furwen door with her essence and yanked sideways. It resisted at first, having remained motionless for so long. But Mellai fought until the two-foot-thick slab gave way and slid across the passage, blocking access all the way to its crest fifty feet above.

She next yanked on the protruding spikes of the rear portcullis, until whatever levers held it aloft finally snapped. The iron grate crashed to the ground with an earth-rumbling clang, its spiked tips buried deep into openings in the hardened stone floor, but it wasn't the sound that startled the Beholder.

Centered over the mesh of metal was a massive King's Cross, made of shining blue steel and covering nearly the entirety of the fifty-foot iron gate. Mellai stared in wonder, knowing it had been created during the First Age when Taejans protected Appernysia.

Shaking herself into the present, Mellai followed the same process for the other Furwen slab and the front portcullis—which also had a King's Cross on its face. The gateway was now effectively blocked with four layers of protection, so the Beholder climbed onto Huirk and told him to take flight.

"Retract the drawbridge!" she shouted to Kamron, then realized Lon had been shouting in her mind. She asked Huirk to fly high, far away from danger as she communicated with her brother.

Are you alright? Lon asked.

We were just attacked by terror hounds, but no one was injured. Oh, make sure to close the—

But Mellai felt Lon's consciousness disconnect before she could finish her though. He had become distracted by something more pressing.

✳   ✳   ✳   ✳   ✳

Fighting at the south gate had also begun. Lon closed the front portcullis. Not knowing the inner mechanisms, he had just pulled the iron grid with his essence and hoped it wouldn't break. The ground shook when it slammed closed. Lon and Bromax were shocked to see a giant King's Cross emblem covering it, which distracted them just enough that the calahein were able to cross the entirety of the bridge. Bromax was hit a couple of times on his flank with poisonous phlegm, but Lon had cured the injuries quickly before any permanent damage had been done.

Dead terror hounds piled in front of the gate and a few dangled from its grid of iron beams. All were spattered with crossbow bolts from the watchmen inside both flanking towers. Lon had been surprised—impressed, even—with their accuracy. Not one bolt had struck Bromax.

They almost slipped through, Lon finally told Mellai, relieved to hear that no one had been injured under her charge.

After quick instruction from his sister on the function of Itorea's gate systems, Lon told Bromax to land behind the gateway. The ghraef was flying south along the front of the wall, roaring challenges at the opposite shore. Bromax rolled upside down to his left, over the wall and the stunned soldiers standing on top of it. While upside down, Lon could see that his gate had not been as fortunate as Mellai's. A few soldiers were lying in the middle of the cobblestone road, having been struck by poisonous phlegm during the attack. Their bodies glowed dull, void of life. There were no other civilians in sight. Lon decided the soldiers' gruesome deaths must have scared them away.

"Don't touch their injuries," Lon ordered, pushing a soldier back with his essence. "Leave them there until the fighting stops."

When Bromax landed on the inside of the wall, Lon dismounted. The rear portcullis had also been dropped, but not of Lon's own doing. A soldier inside the gatehouse must have hit the release lever with a maul. Lon peered through the gate's iron beams and dragged the front Furwen slab into place, then retreated from the gateway and closed the rear slab, too.

The surviving soldiers stationed there thanked him profusely as they stepped out from cover.

A horn sounded on top of the wall, drawing the Beholder's attention. Flagmen were signaling toward the opposite shore. The calahein were preparing to attack again.

"Who's in charge here?" Lon asked, berating himself for not asking sooner.

"Sergeant Leshim," a soldier replied, pointing to the top of the south flanking tower. "He arrived two days ago, sent by King Drogan."

Well, at least he knows what he's doing, Lon thought as he climbed onto Bromax. "Obey his orders," Lon called, then Bromax lifted into the air and returned to stand on the curtain wall over the gate.

Who? Mellai replied.

Sergeant Leshim.

That's Kutad, Lon. He's there?

Apparently. He's in charge of the defense here. Lon turned his head left and searched the many faces on the flanking tower, but he was unable to recognize any as Kutad.

✳ ✳ ✳ ✳ ✳

"Dive low, Huirk. Right over the top of them."

As the ghraef swung around the front of the curtain, Mellai created an energy shield with her left hand, wrapping around the front and side of Huirk. Her intent was to protect them from the approaching hounds.

What Mellai had not considered is that the energy shield absorbed or deflected the wind that Huirk needed to fly. The ghraef's right wing became useless and his body twisted in the air. Both he and Mellai crashed into the wide Sylbien River before she realized her mistake.

Despite the freezing water, Mellai focused on the energies swirling around them. She manipulated the water's current to bring her and the ghraef to the surface, but by then, they were hundreds of feet downriver.

Mellai was stunned that the scene had become so desperate in such a short span of time. Nearly a hundred terror hounds had crossed the bridge and were now climbing up the vinery that grew around the gateway. Many had already reached the top of the wall, wreaking havoc, while more continued to pour across the bridge.

"How did they—" Mellai began to ask, wondering how they had passed the drawbridge, but the answer was clear. Aged chains had snapped, their rusted links still dangling off the front sides of the wooden bridge.

Huirk climbed onto Itorea's banks to shake off the water, and Mellai set the bottom edges of the vinery on fire. Soon after, Huirk was in the air and attacking the forces on the drawbridge. He grabbed one hound with his front paws—crushing it to death and tossing it aside—and swept a few more off the bridge with his tail.

With Mellai still on his back, Huirk nosed up into the air, flapping his wings hard and arching upside down to dive at the top of the wall. Mellai took the opportunity to destroy the hundred-foot drawbridge, before focusing her attention on the terror hounds that were desperately clamoring up the vinery, trying to escape the rising flames. Their fear distracted the creatures enough that the few standing soldiers could fight back, hewing body and limb wherever their swords and halberds could reach.

From their aerial view, Mellai watched as one hound broke through the line of soldiers and raced along the top of the wall, dodging blows and slashing legs as it passed more soldiers. It hit one man in the face with its poison phlegm, and Mellai had to make a conscious effort not to recoil as she thought of Jareth's similar death. The beast made it all the way to Kamron's flanking tower and disabled two ballistae before the general finally thrust his longsword down its throat.

"What good is a wall if we provide free access with vines?" Mellai growled, cursing as Huirk dove at the main fight directly above the gate. She reached out with her essence to snap as many necks as possible. Just before they landed, one hound leaped inside the city to the courtyard below. Many soldiers were stationed there, behind the closed gates, but there were also many curious civilians. Women and children scattered when they saw the approaching terror hound, while the soldiers lined up with raised halberds.

As the terror hound fell, wad after wad of poisonous phlegm flew from its open snout. Soldiers and civilians alike were struck.

Without any spoken communication, Mellai dismounted onto the top of the wall and Huirk continued into the city to ensure the death of the rogue terror hound. The helpless sounds of dying victims stabbed at her ears. The true calahein hadn't even attacked yet, but already people were dying inside the city.

Mellai joined the soldiers around her to destroy the remaining hounds that had crested the wall. She killed and mangled them all, except one, which she captured in an energy shield and pinned to the ground.

"Why?" she screamed, pushing into its mind with her essence. Once again, just as she had experienced in the Vidarien Mountains, Mellai met a firm barrier protecting the terror hound's thoughts. But she didn't give up that easily. She pressed and fought against the barrier, trying to find a weakness, while the hound thrashed and snapped at her efforts. Just as with the ghraefs, this beast seemed consciously aware that Mellai was touching its mind.

She tightened the energy shield around the hound, hoping that pain would distract it enough to penetrate its thoughts. It howled and yelped, and Mellai broke through. Although it was only for an instant, a fully rounded vision filled her consciousness.

Mellai had become the terror hound, desperately fighting against her invisible bonds.

Then she shot across the river into the mind of a kelsh. She was hiding behind a charred Furwen tree with an innumerable host of other calahein ground troops. She ordered the terror hound to kill itself, furious that it wouldn't comply.

Once again, Mellai left her host, deeper into the Perbeisea Forest until she reached a section untouched by flames. Up she climbed into the forest canopy, where she became a seith, standing in the middle of her fellow lieutenants, directing the kelsh in their actions. She grew suddenly concerned. A foreign mind had entered her consciousness, and she frantically searched to locate the source.

Mellai began to move farther west, out of the mind of the seith, but a blinding pain struck her forehead. Faster than a bolt of lightning, she reversed completely through the three hosts.

Mellai was herself once more, staring down at the struggling terror hound. Her mind was weak and her limbs trembled. She killed the terror hound before she lost full control of her body, then collapsed onto the polished stone, unable to move. The flames had clawed through the vinery high enough to become clearly visible along the outside wall. She stared at them, wondering if they were burning her skin.

What was that? she thought as soldiers picked her up and carried her along the top of the wall. Strangely, she still seemed to have control of her mind, although it wouldn't allow her to command her body.

Lon's voice entered her head, full of concern, but Mellai couldn't make out any words.

Then a bright light appeared in front of Mellai, hovering above the ground. "You just entered the joint consciousness of the calahein," Llen said. He floated alongside her, above the oblivious soldiers. "The actions of each member of the calahein are dictated by higher authorities. Your severance from their network has cost you the ability to control your own body. Do not worry. This will last only a short time, until your mind cleanses itself of the calahein residue."

Why didn't you warn me?

The bright lights pouring from the Jaed's head softened. "I had not considered you would ever succeed at penetrating their telepathic barrier. That is not something you should attempt by yourself again."

But the vision was incomplete. I was moving somewhere else, beyond the seith, before I was finally stopped.

Llen moved aside as Mellai's body was carried up a small staircase onto the flanking tower. "It was their queen who halted your progress," the Jaed said.

Kamron's face appeared. His mouth moved but no words reached Mellai's ears. She looked past the general, at the Jaed floating behind him. *There were so many of them, Llen. These terror hounds are just the beginning. What am I supposed to do?*

"Keep fighting," Llen said, then disappeared.

Chapter 45

Breached

Lon dropped against the wall, out of breath. The afternoon was wearing on slowly. The Beholder was alive, but each opponent he faced seemed more skilled than the previous. Coupling that with his own exhaustion made every fight more difficult to win.

"Not much experience with these?" Kutad asked, squatting in front of him to stab a thrashing terror hound in the eye.

Lon didn't answer. He had lost interest in arguing with the former leader of Appernysia's trading caravan. Between each bout of fighting, Kutad had spoken unreserved hatred for the Beholder, but without ever directly vocalizing the source. Lon could only guess it was that he was a Rayder.

Lon's latest opponent had surprised him, throwing itself against the Beholder. Lon had decapitated it with his falchion, but the body was moving fast. The bone spikes protruding from its spine had pierced Lon's leather armor and into his chest. The injuries were shallow, but the attack had shaken Lon's confidence.

You said yourself that we need to fight them from a distance! Mellai shouted in Lon's mind.

He didn't answer. He and Bromax had decided to separate once the hounds had breached the wall. While Lon defended the soldiers, Bromax had personally torn down the vinery, earning a score of injuries from the approaching terror hounds. Lon had just finished healing the ghraef when Bromax dove into the air again, straight at the drawbridge. It was there he was making his stand, keeping the hounds away until the Appernysians had cleared the wall.

Kutad picked up the dead carcass and tossed it over the wall. "Do you need a rest?"

Lon ignored his mocking tone and nodded.

"Then return to your nest, little bird. Let us handle the defenses."

"We're on . . . the same side," Lon said, gasping between phrases as he pushed himself onto his feet.

Kutad scoffed. "Fighting a common enemy doesn't make us allies, Lon. That will never change."

*   *   *   *   *

"They've been doing that all day," Mellai said, shaking her head as another pack of terror hounds emerged from the charred forest and sprinted across the half-mile bridge. Kamron had ordered the ballistae to save their spears, but another volley of crossbow bolts shot from the two flanking towers, bringing the pack down in front of the west gate. A large mound of dead beasts had begun to form there. The portcullis was also covered in dripping phlegm, but the poison seemed to have little effect on the pure Beholder steel.

"How fares the south gate?" Kamron called, immediately followed by a ripple of flagmen passing the question south along the tops of each drum tower.

Mellai frowned, knowing a response wouldn't come for another twenty minutes. Huirk could fly the distance just as quickly, but Kamron had grounded the ghraef, arguing that he and Mellai needed to preserve their strength. Full control of her body had returned an hour after piercing the calahein consciousness, but Kamron wouldn't hear her arguments.

And Lon was resting, recovering from the injuries in his chest. Despite her desire to heal him, Lon had demanded she stay at the west gate. Bromax would rouse him if there was an urgent need only a Beholder could resolve. He had severed his connection to True Sight before Mellai could argue the danger.

"Why do they keep attacking?" Mellai asked, returning her attention to the dead beasts on their doorstep.

Kamron rubbed his chin between his thumb and index finger. "My studies would argue they are trying to distract us; a decoy from the real attack."

"That's why you keep sending messages south?"

"But no other threat has surfaced," Kamron said, nodding in answer to her question. "I can't figure out what they're up to. What do you see?"

Mellai heaved a sigh and, once again, searched the terrain with True Sight. It was a far more effective method than regular eyesight, especially with the setting sun blinding their view, but nothing had changed since the attack began that morning. Only a few signs of life existed on the other side of the river, visible only for a moment before disappearing behind the blackened trunks again. Even the fish seemed to have fled the water, as if they knew the threat stalking at their borders.

"Nothing," she answered.

"I don't like this," Kamron said, his brow furrowed in deep concentration as he turned and peered down the inside of their wall. Mellai followed him, looking over hundreds of thousands of defenseless Appernysians. One terror hound had killed many, just during its drop from the wall. Mellai didn't want to imagine what a full pack could do, let alone a group of kelsh or seith.

"I've made up my mind," Kamron continued, waving a trumpeter over. "Sound the retreat. I want these people out of here."

"Into the agricultural lands?" the soldier replied, bringing a bugle to his lips.

Kamron shook his head. "Farther. Move them into Itorea's hook. They belong safely behind three more walls of defense."

The trumpeter began blasting Kamron's order to the masses, and a chorus of more bugles soon joined in.

"Do you want my help carrying the message?" Mellai asked. Many civilians had already fled east earlier that day with only what they could carry in their arms. The majority had eventually begun to follow, no doubt because of the rumors and panic that had been spreading since, but an uncomfortable amount of people still remained. They searched around in confusion. "It looks like some of them don't understand."

"It's not that," Kamron replied, tapping his foot on the stone. "They've lived their lives like me, trusting these walls explicitly. Even with my order, many will refuse to leave."

"And they might not all fit inside the hook."

Kamron nodded. "But what else can I do?"

The Beholder and general stood watching for a time, but Huirk had leaped from the wall. He specifically flew over people who were misbehaving, be it rude or dangerous, and corrected their behavior with threatening growls. The masses moved quickly. Soon, most settlements within a mile of the wall were cleared, and more followed.

"Imagine how this would have gone with the Rayders in Itorea," Kamron said triumphantly. "Their extra numbers alone would have crippled this evacuation with congestion."

"That doesn't justify King Drogan's decision," Mellai argued. "I still disagree with him."

"Yet you swore to serve him," Kamron continued. "Remember? I was there, standing right next to you when you were tattooed with the Beholder's Eye. Whose side are you on?"

"I fight for humanity," Mellai spat, then she projected her voice to Huirk and asked him to return.

"But a corrupted life isn't a life worth living. The Rayders deserve every punishment they receive."

Mellai turned and glared at him. "And who designated you as the authority on that subject? Remember what else happened on that platform? You were nearly executed for leaving your soldiers to the wolves."

Kamron stepped closer to Mellai, gripping his sheathed sword. "Quiet down."

"Why?" Mellai shouted back. "Are you afraid these men might realize you're a coward? Sorry, but it's too late. They were there, standing in your wake when you turned tail. Even King Drogan still holds you responsible for the lives you abandoned." During the passion of her rant, Mellai's eyes grew wide with new understanding. "Is that why you're evacuating all these people? Afraid the fighting might get too intense again? Do you need a place to run, Kamron?"

"That's General Astadem," he whispered, glancing at the nearby soldiers, "and this isn't helping. My men need courage in their hearts, not mutiny."

"If it's rebellion they feel," Mellai whispered back, "then it's your own fault. These men don't lack courage. You can point that finger back at yourself."

Mellai's blood raged through her body, pounding in her ears as she stared at Kamron. He returned her glare, his fist twisting around the pommel of his sword, but the stare-off didn't last long. A strange sound—like the scraping of claws against hard dirt—tugged at the senses of the Beholder.

"Calahein!" a soldier shouted. "Inside the wall!"

The Beholder looked down just as a hole opened in the ground, widening quickly until it was large enough for a kelsh to climb out. The brute clawed at the opening to widen it, with intermittent bashes from the long bone spike protruding from its elbow.

Mellai reacted quickly, extending her essence to the hole and breaking the kelsh's neck before cramming it back inside and packing it down with more dirt. But this wasn't the only place the wall had been bypassed. Dozens of other tunnels opened up and the streets filled with kelsh.

She also tried to contact Lon, but he was sleeping. Mellai cursed. *That's twice now his beauty rest has put us at risk.*

Huirk roared, glancing between Mellai and the kelsh below. She understood his conflict. The ghraef wanted to dive down immediately and thrash the enemy.

"Bring me with you!" she screamed at him.

Huirk uttered a quick whimper, but complied. He flew past the wall, close enough that Mellai could leap onto his back. She grabbed hold of his hair to keep from tumbling backward, then secured her legs and peered over the side. The kelsh sprinted toward the defenseless civilians, away from Appernysia's soldiers. The situation was grave.

"Fly ahead of them," Mellai said to Huirk instead. The ghraef dove low, tearing apart any kelsh he could reach and swatting them with his spiked tail crystal until they were ahead of the rushing line.

"Higher!"

Huirk nosed straight up into the air, while Mellai leaned back and evaluated. The streets were full of kelsh and even more continued to emerge from the open passages, but no other holes had appeared in the ground. They all seemed clustered behind the west gate.

"At least they are for now," Mellai spat, knowing that other tunnels were undoubtedly close to the surface. She needed a way to plug the holes, while at the same time killing the kelsh and protecting the civilians. Only one practical option came to mind. She knew it would destroy much of the city, but it was a sacrifice worth making for the preservation of lives.

Mellai breathed deeply in concentration, then pulled a thick wall of earth out of the ground. It was a hundred yards in width and twice as tall, large enough to block the entire path of the calahein. But she wasn't done yet—the kelsh could easily run around it. With a grunt of effort, Mellai packed the wall together to harden it, then tipped it over.

Howls of terror filled the city as the kelsh realized their doom, but their voices were immediately silenced with a thundering crash of packed soil and rock. The watching soldiers cheered in triumph.

"That won't hold them long," Mellai shouted to Huirk, who was still climbing into the air. "Head south, along the river's surface. I have an idea."

Huirk roared and angled backward, flying upside down for a brief moment before rolling over and diving toward the river. Mellai shook her head with self-disgust. This was the real attack Kamron had feared. The kelsh must have been working for weeks on the underground tunnels.

Rather than attack the tunnel entrances in a forest overrun with calahein, Mellai chose a more effective method. She formed a massive hoe of pure energy. As Huirk flew with the river's current toward the south gate, Mellai tilled a deep trench down its center. Wherever the energy tore through the riverbed, the river water would fill the crevices—including the calahein tunnels.

"Quicker," Mellai pleaded with Huirk. "There might be other openings farther south."

Chapter 46

Overrun

By the time Mellai and Huirk reached the south gate, the Perbeisea Forest surged with furious life. The kelsh no longer hid behind charred bows, but stood openly on the riverbank, hurling boulders and snarling their protest. Mellai had not only discovered their queen's plan, but the Beholder had found a way to immediately neutralize it. Who knew how many of them she had drowned in the tunnels below.

When Huirk neared the south gate, the full fury of the calahein ignited. Their colony poured over the bridge, the terror hounds spitting and the kelsh gripping large stones. Huirk flew up to the top of the wall to avoid the attack and perched facing the bridge.

"What happened?" Kutad asked, running up to them. "Why are they so agitated?"

Lon and Bromax also landed on the wall next to Huirk and Mellai, just as Kutad finished speaking.

"Thank the Jaeds," Mellai replied, glad to see their position hadn't been infiltrated. She jabbed a finger and Lon. "No more sleeping!"

Lon nodded, rubbing the exhaustion from his eyes. "I must have been more tired than I thought."

Mellai released her energy shield and focused on healing the puncture wounds in his chest—curing his flesh and the damaged armor. "The kelsh tunneled under the wall farther north," Mellai continued. "I barely managed to stop them, then we flooded any other potential passages on the way here. Keep your eyes open. They're more clever than we thought."

As if to emphasize her statement, a volley of phlegm splattered an energy shield Lon had just created. It startled Mellai at first. She didn't think the terror hounds could spit far enough to reach the top of their three hundred-foot wall, but an explanation immediately followed. The kelsh had dropped their boulders and were throwing the terror hounds instead. None had reached the top yet, but they were easily high enough to spit over the wall before falling to their own deaths.

Many soldiers were being struck, both above and inside the flanking towers. More screams of pain pierced Mellai's ears, causing her to visibly wince. Some terror hounds were still clinging to the narrow arrow slits, snarling as they spewed venom inside. But every attack met an equal response from Appernysian soldiers. They retaliated with their crossbows, piercing the hounds' skulls and knocking them from the wall.

The stone vibrated under the Beholders and ghraefs. The kelsh were not standing idly by, letting the terror hounds do all the work. They piled themselves against the wall, pounding and clawing at the impenetrable stone surface. Their attack seemed silly at first, until the clamoring mass of fur and claws began to grow. They soon reached halfway up the outer wall, scratching at the invincible gemstone sculptures of Mellai's predecessors. Their behavior was frenzied. They tore into each other's hides to climb higher, often tearing each other from the mound. The Prime River splashed with falling and drowning calahein, yet they continued to climb.

"Destroy the bridge!" Kutad ordered, ducking under a phlegm wad aimed at his face. "They're going to reach the top!"

Mellai joined minds with her brother and together reached out for one of the four stone pillars keeping the half-mile bridge aloft. With a focused amount of effort from such a great distance, they managed to crack the dense stone. The bridge sagged in the air for a moment, then its weight became too great. The pillar crumbled, as did the portion of the bridge it was supporting and the calahein standing on it. Stone and flesh crashed into the freezing river, leaving a gap five hundred feet long. The stone washed downriver, destroying most of the abandoned warships of King Drogan's armada.

"Again!" Kutad shouted, pointing at another pillar.

The Beholders repeated their actions, dropping another five hundred-foot section of bridge, then Huirk leaped down, gliding close to the wall while Mellai scooped away hundreds of calahein and drowned them in the river.

They're probably doing this at the west gate, Lon communicated to Mellai. She just caught a glimpse of him and Bromax as they flew north with tremendous speed.

Be safe, Mellai thought, thankful for the intervention. She was exhausted, her labored breath bursting from her lungs.

✳   ✳   ✳   ✳   ✳

Lon had predicted correctly, except the mass of kelsh had already reached the top of the wall at the west gate. The soldiers fought for their lives, but stood little chance in close combat with the kelsh. The top of one flanking tower had already been completely overrun. The ballistae circling around the perimeter were shattered, the operators were dead, and kelsh had moved on, killing more soldiers on their way along the wall.

The other flanking tower, however, was still functional. Spear after spear pounded into the mass of kelsh. But for every kelsh destroyed, three more took its place. The tower's supply of spears was nearly depleted.

"Fly straight at their base," Lon said, pouring as much energy into a sphere as possible. All manner of calahein projectiles flew past them, including terror hounds. Lon fought to keep the sphere stable while Bromax dodged and weaved.

Until they reached the bottom of the piled calahein.

Lon released the sphere, resulting in a massive blast of energy that he forced outward, away from himself and Bromax. The kelsh closest to them disintegrated, while most of the others combusted into a mass of fluids and fur. The outer portcullis was mangled from the blast, as was part of the bridge, but the other three gate barriers were still in place. And of course the wall itself remained perfectly intact, having been made of invincible stone.

Before the calahein recovered, Lon turned and created a shield behind them, and just in time. Another volley of phlegm flew from the top of the wall, striking the barrier and falling harmlessly into the river below.

But another vision caught Lon's attention. His energy blast had also removed the thick web of charred vinery that used to grow around the gate on its way to the top of the wall. Just as with the south gate, the vines had not been for decoration, but to hide what was underneath their mass.

Embedded in the wall above the gate was a blue King's Cross, centered between the crystal designs of Appernysia's first Beholders. It was unscathed by the fire or blast.

Lon cursed. All for the sake of pride—to hide what Appernysia's kings considered a tainted part of their history—good men had died that day.

Bromax rolled onto the wall to help fight off the remaining calahein, his teeth and claws bringing death to all that opposed him. His tail crystal, however, was used for a different purpose. The ghraef kept the obsidian dangling above his back, dropping it like a scorpion to block the poisonous spit attacks.

Lon dismounted and watched him for a moment, worried for his safety, before resuming his task. While Bromax protected his position, Lon destroyed the west bridge in the same way he and Mellai had at the south gate—albeit in smaller, more manageable pieces. Fearing the stone might wash downriver and create a dam,

Lon removed the stone fragments and tossed them at the calahein on the opposite shore.

"Where is General Astadem?" he asked a soldier, who sat curled up and trembling behind one of the wall's crenels.

"Dead," he answered, then clenched his jaw and pulled at his hair when another soldier screamed.

Lon knelt in front of him, placing a hand on his shoulder. "Look at me."

The man resisted at first, overcome with terror, until he realized that a Beholder knelt before him. Lon's presence gave the soldier just enough courage to return his gaze.

"Did you see Kamron die?" Lon asked.

The soldier nodded. "He led a group to defend us. A kelsh stabbed him through the stomach with its knee spike, then ripped him in half and tossed his body off the wall."

Lon shook his head. That was it, then. Appernysia's general was dead.

"What are we going to do, Beholder?"

"I'll take care of you," Lon answered, grabbing him by his arm. "Come on. Your brothers need our help."

The soldier stood, drawing his sheathed sword, but the fighting had stopped. All threats on top of the wall had been eliminated. No one celebrated, though; neither did they mourn. Everyone, including Bromax, stood motionless and staring west. The failing light glowed red, but it wasn't the foreboding sunset that held their attention.

A mass of seith had lifted from the forest, each carrying a kelsh or terror hound in its claws.

They were flying over the river.

Over the wall.

The skies filled with whizzing spears. Men poured out of the battlements to add their own crossbow bolts to the fray. But all efforts seemed to make little difference.

Itorea's vast defenses were breached, and more seith rose from the forest.

"Fly, Bromax!" Lon screamed, reaching out with his essence to kill as many seith as possible.

The ghraef matched the howls of the attacking calahein with his own deafening roar, then opened his wings and took flight, straight into the mass of seith.

Tears poured from Lon's eyes, but he fought the hopelessness that threatened to consume him. He froze a large section of the river's surface upriver, shattered it, and tossed the shards upward. It was a deadly stroke to match Bromax's efforts. Dozens of calahein fell from the sky, but it wouldn't be enough. Twenty miles separated him from Mellai, a front impossible to defend by themselves.

Lon drew his falchion and gripped it with white knuckles. *Fight, Mellai! We can't let them win!*

Chapter 47

Lightning

L on brought his falchion up as a last resort of defense, gripped in his left hand. With his right hand, he snapped spine after spine, but so great were the number of calahein and men in the passage that they were difficult for Lon to distinguish while using True Sight. Consequently, he had to fill himself with his power just long enough to attack, then release again to select a new target.

"Go, Beholder!" an Appernysian soldier shouted, stepping in front of Lon with his halberd aimed at the approaching force. "We'll hold the line here!" Twenty other soldiers joined the first and pushed toward the kelsh, but Lon sprinted in the opposite direction, the men's dying screams joining hundreds of others that echoed through the narrow passage.

The Beholder cursed, wishing he hadn't listened to Bromax. The ghraef had pushed him down a tower staircase and pointed east, then leaped into the air with ten seith chasing after him. Lon had entered Itorea's perimeter wall tunnels, fighting where he could to save the retreating soldiers, but the time for rescue had passed. Now he was just as likely to die as the Appernysians, trapped in a corridor of invincible stone that he didn't have time to manipulate with his power.

Minutes passed as Lon felt his body weaken, his pace slowing from a full sprint to a weary jog. His heart beat so intensely that he could feel his blood pounding in his ears, and his mouth was dry and sticky.

I can't keep running like this, Lon thought, using his power to peer down the dark passage. At least two hundred yards separated him from the next tower exit.

Then stop, Mellai replied. *Can't you take thirty seconds to catch your breath?* Her suggestion was immediately followed by a surge of energy as she used her power for some other task, but Lon barely noticed. He had long grown accustomed to the feel of his twin sister using True Sight, and he had his own survival to worry about at that moment.

Lon glanced back. A sizable gap now separated him from the calahein threat, but not nearly enough. Once the Appernysian line failed, nothing but an empty passage separated Lon from the threat. The kelsh would close that distance faster than Dawes could at a gallop.

No, Lon thought, returning his focus to the closed doorway ahead. He just had to make it to the tower, then he'd have more options.

As he ran, a regular pattern of arrow slits passed Lon on his right—lining the inside of Itorea's perimeter wall. Somewhere outside, the sound of screaming civilians rose from the city, so loud that it overpowered the shouting inside Lon's corridor. He was tempted to stop and peer out an arrow slit, maybe intervene in someone's behalf, but he shook his head and reminded himself that he had to keep running. He focused on the click-clack of his boots on the stone floor.

Mellai's shout filled his mind. *That's not your boots, Lon! The calahein are chasing you!*

She was right, and Lon should have known better. He barely had time to turn and release an energy blast, throwing himself and the kelsh in opposite directions. Lon slid backward down the hallway and slammed into the barricaded door, his sword landing beside him. Unlike the kelsh, who had quickly recovered and resumed their pursuit of the Beholder, Lon sat dazed and out of breath, unable to call for help. He slapped his palm repeatedly on the door, silently pleading for the guardsmen to let him in, but received no response. With a quick flick of his hand, he shattered the stout oak door and stood to run inside.

But Lon fell to the floor again before he could take his first step.

Confused, the Beholder tried again and failed, unable to support his weight.

As Lon drew himself up to attempt it for a third time, he caught sight of his left leg, hanging limply toward the floor.

I'm trapped! Lon shouted to his sister. *A hundred feet down with nowhere to flee.*

Fight! she screamed back. *Don't let them win!*

Lon recognized the counsel as his own, and it emboldened him. He fell to his backside and faced the approaching kelsh.

"If I die, you're coming with me!" he screamed at them.

He protected himself with a domed energy shield with his right hand's essence and grabbed as many kelsh as possible with his left. An assortment of boulders and debris broke against the energy barrier protecting Lon, hurled from the midst of the approaching force, but nearly all of the Beholder's concentration was fixated on the calahein in his grasp. Lon narrowed his essence and poured more energy into it, hoping to crush them into one mangled heap of furry death.

But Lon's efforts resulted in a completely unexpected effect.

A perfect combination of shape and concentrated energy created a surge of electricity in the Beholder. Forked lightning shot from Lon's hand, charbroiling the front beasts and exploding them into the surrounding walls. Their shattered limbs whipped through the air with great force, piercing those not cooked in the blast. None were left alive.

While staggering from the noise and shock, Lon released the energy shield and examined his leg. It had been broken more severely than he thought. A sharp bone protruded from his skin halfway between his left knee and ankle.

Shock began to set in as Lon realized the extent of his injury. His vision darkened and narrowed, barely allowing him to maintain enough coherence to turn and crawl up the stairs, one step at a time, until his reserve of energy depleted and his face fell to the smooth stone. The sound of nearby soldiers was the last thing Lon heard before passing out completely.

Chapter 48

Turmoil

When he opened his eyes again, Lon felt surrounded in darkness. Drowning in the smothering black of . . . ghraef hair.

He blinked his eyes and looked around. Indeed, he was. Bromax was flying high and fast, holding the Beholder against his chest with one paw to keep him warm. Lon's leg throbbed with pain, and a quick inspection revealed a belt secured around his left upper thigh.

"Did you do this?" Lon asked, touching the tourniquet.

Bromax shook his head, so Lon knew it must have been an Appernysian soldier.

Lon searched the ground below, wondering where Bromax was carrying him, and quickly found his answer. They were over the Gaurelic Waste—just north of Itorea's blade. The Rayder camp was barely visible to the east.

"Where are Huirk and Mellai?"

Bromax gestured to the right with his snout, indicating that they were somewhere inside the blade of Itorea.

"And my—" he tried to ask, but Bromax interrupted him by revealing the falchion gripped in his other paw.

Lon summoned True Sight and connected to his sister, wanting to let her know that he was alive. Mellai replied so urgently that her voice pounded in his head.

They're dying! she screamed.

Lon jerked his head south, searching for his twin. *Who is? Everyone! I can't save them!*

"Fly, Bromax, as recklessly as your wings can carry you! We have calahein to kill!"

The ghraef reared back his head, breathing deeply before roaring so loudly that it left Lon's ears throbbing. Bromax beat his wings hard, gaining altitude and speed with enough acceleration that Lon felt his stomach churn.

Where are you? Lon asked.

In the crops, near the water channel. But it has turned to pure blood! So many people are dead!

But you're not! Lon shouted back, then with practiced skill, he numbed his emotions. Mellai was panicked enough. She didn't need his own anxieties fueling her recklessness. He quickly gave Bromax directions to find the water channel, then resumed his communication with Mellai. *Is Huirk with you?*

He's up there, fighting the seith. I can't help him! There are too many down here.

Kelsh?

Mellai didn't respond immediately. Her brain surged with an expulsion of power, followed by anger and more panic. *I can't kill them fast enough, Lon. Our army has collapsed. Now the civilians are—*

No! Another burst of power ran through their emotional connection, followed by waves of torment.

Listen to me, Mellai. You won't agree with what I'm going to tell you, but you have to do it anyway. Promise me.

Just say it!

Focus on those you can save, then force yourself to ignore the rest.

I can't do that!

You have to, Mel. I'm injured and not much use to anyone right now. Bromax is keeping me out of the fight until you can heal me. You and Huirk are the only two who can protect them. If you die today, so will everyone else.

Mellai's emotions slipped further, dangling between desperation and capitulation. *I needed you, Lon.*

I'm coming. Just stay alive. I'll see you at the keep.

Although his twin sister withdrew from their conversation, Lon knew through her poignant shame that Mellai had complied. Lon remembered the first time he had experienced the guilt that now filled his sister. An Appernysian soldier at the Quint River. Lon had slashed his chest. Even now, that experience tugged at Lon's conscience. He knew that he'd never fully recover from what he had done.

Lon withdrew from his sister's emotions, but maintained his connection with True Sight as he shared everything with Bromax. He then turned his attention east, in the direction of the keep. "Come on, Tarek. Where are you?"

Chapter 49

For Appernysia!

Two days earlier, when thick smoke first began filling the sky, Tarek had called his lieutenants together for a war council. Their discussion had been quick, though—more of a "Here's how it is," conversation. Tarek didn't care who was interested in helping the Appernysians. Their fates were inseparable.

As did the Beholders, Tarek had suspected that the black smoke pouring into the air signified the start of the calahein invasion. There was little they could do from seventy miles away, but he had ordered full preparations at first light the next morning, "after everyone has a full night's rest."

Every Rayder soldier, totaling fourteen thousand, garbed themselves in full war attire. Chainmail, breastplates, shields, glaives, swords, and composite bows, with two full quivers at their sides. Horses were also a must, not for the battle itself, but to preserve each man's strength on their journey east.

Unlike any battle before, the Rayder women had also marched to war. Leaving the elderly to care for their children, the women followed closely behind their husbands, fathers, and sons. They would care for the wounded and, if necessary, join in the fighting if men began to fall.

The two thousand surviving men from Jaul also joined, led by Darius. They acquired weapons and armor wherever they could before combining with Lieutenant Wade's unit of five thousand newly branded Rayders on the south edge of the Gaurelic Waste.

Aron and Shalán had stayed with Kaylen and the Beholders' guard and been fitted only with hardened leather breastplates. There had not been any further armor to spare. Aron had found himself an ordinary glaive to supplement the sword hanging at his side. Shalán also had a sword, and her healing satchel still hung over her shoulder. Kaylen held nothing, refusing to ever carry a weapon again.

After one more night sleeping in the Waste, Tarek had led the combined army—over twenty-one thousand strong with another ten thousand women—to Itorea's north gate. The line of Appernysian soldiers guarding the gate's entrance had hesitated only for a moment before raising their halberds and stepping aside to admit the Rayders.

Refugees had already begun to fill the hook, whispering embellished stories of what was happening at the west wall. Their hatred toward the Rayders had also disappeared, replaced by overwhelming gratitude at the formidable force marching to war.

The farther the Rayders traveled, the more desperate Appernysia's civilians had appeared. Their accounts had also transformed from grandiose to simple statements of truth, numb comments regarding the horrors they had experienced firsthand.

"The venom is toxic."

"My husband is dead."

"I can't find my parents."

For ten miles, these accounts had increased in their morbidity, all the way to the keep's east gate. Yet, the worst stories of all had been the silent ones. Blank stares from those too traumatized to speak.

* * * * *

It was an hour before midday when the Rayders entered the keep. As Tarek led his army west, he glanced over his shoulder. Lon's squad rode close behind, five of the deadliest and most loyal Rayders in all of Appernysia. Tarek was glad to have them at his side again, along with the three surviving men in Mellai's guard who had proven themselves to be fierce allies.

The Beholders would never forgive Tarek for admitting the last two members of the guard. On his left trotted two war horses, Shalán and Kaylen sitting on Dawes and Aron riding the other. Tarek had already known Aron to be a weapons master, and Lon's stories of Shalán's medicinal skill were too tempting to ignore. When the couple had demanded inclusion, Tarek had to accept their service. And Kaylen . . . well, there was nothing he could have done to make her stay behind when every other Rayder woman marched to war.

Tarek had refused all other volunteers from Pree, and Reese was forbidden to join them. Even though the young man had begged for an opportunity to exact revenge for his family, Tarek could easily see that he lacked the skill to help with this battle.

Halfway across the keep, King Drogan's cavalry rode out to meet the Rayders.

"I'm glad you've come," Drogan said, taking Tarek's hand. "Forgive my pride."

"Save your apologies for later," Tarek replied, gripping the king's hand. "We have a kingdom to save. How many knights do you command?"

"Ten thousand."

Tarek bit his cheek, suppressing an overpowering temptation to punch Drogan in the face with his steel gauntlet. Despite the pressing need to protect Itorea, the king had kept thousands of soldiers for himself.

"Commander?" Drogan said.

Tarek blew out his breath to release his frustration. "How long is your west wall?"

"Of Itorea?"

Tarek shook his head and pointed at the ground. "This keep."

"It's ten by ten miles square," Drogan answered, growing impatient. "What do you propose?"

"Thirty-one thousand men," Tarek mumbled, looking west and calculating in his head. Any soldier who survived the onslaught in Itorea's blade would be completely spent. Everyone still capable of fighting was in his presence.

"My Commander," Wade called from behind, drawing Tarek's attention.

Tarek turned on his horse. "What is it, Lieutenant?"

"I have a suggestion, my Commander. When I was taking back Taeja, I came to a point when my superior numbers seemed to make little difference. I believed Braedr's cult had taken refuge in the keep. With only one entrance, they would have been able to hold that position indefinitely with their limited following. We could do the same—"

"—at the keep's west wall," Tarek cut in, already sorting the details of Wade's plan. He thanked the lieutenant and turned back to the king. "The calahein will be funneling toward this keep, into a more confined line of defense. We will be able to form two lines along the wall's full length. The Rayder women can take refuge inside the wall, where they'll have quick access to the soldiers." He paused, glancing around. "Where is Mellai?"

Drogan licked his dry, middle-aged lips and adjusted the crown on his head. "I'm not sure."

Tarek cursed and called to one of the refugees fleeing in the opposite direction. "Where is Mellai?"

"I don't know anyone named Mellai," the woman replied.

"Your Beholder?"

"Oh." The woman paused, catching her breath. "She and her ghraef are fighting at our rear."

"Trying to save everyone," Tarek mumbled, "just like her brother."

"And where is *your* Beholder, great commander?" Drogan asked sarcastically.

"Wherever Mellai is," Tarek countered, sitting tall in his saddle. "I would know more if you hadn't banished us. But no matter. We ride for the keep's west wall."

*　　*　　*　　*　　*

Huirk weaved back and forth, killing as many seith as possible while Mellai sat on his back, creating barriers to protect the civilians' retreat. Her muscles were sore, but not nearly as exhausted as her mind. She had been awake for nearly forty-eight hours. Even so, her skill was still infallible, but only where she was present. Every time she left an area, the calahein would overwhelm the defenses she had just created. The slaughter was merciless.

Anyone who had the courage to turn and fight, often in an effort to give their loved ones more time to escape, would add themselves to the tens of thousands dead. The water channel running alongside the cobblestone road was full of dead bodies, as were the elevated aqueducts that fed it. And the calahein had taken special interest in breaking and defacing the crafted stonework of the ghraef statues along the channel. Mellai knew it took a considerable amount of effort from Huirk to allow such atrocities as he fought to save the humans instead of the monuments of his ghraef predecessors.

Many soldiers had escaped into the tunnels inside Itorea's walls, fleeing east through the pump rooms, but that had only kept them safe for a short time. The seith began dropping kelsh and terror hounds onto the towers, where the beasts dove into the dark passages and resumed their hunt. While screams poured out of the wall's openings from men making courageous efforts to barricade, survivors had emerged onto the two hundred-foot aqueducts to stand knee-deep in the rushing water and shoot down the seith. Despite Mellai and Huirk's efforts to rescue them, most had died, either by the claws of the calahein or by throwing themselves over the side.

Kutad had been one of the aqueduct victims, near Itorea's south wall. Huirk had been nearby, trying to reach the sergeant, but incapable of fighting through an onslaught of seith. Mellai had been protecting refugees on the ground below. She had turned just in time to see the gravely injured sergeant drive his scimitar through his own heart before a pack of terror hounds poured over him. Mellai had torn down the entire aqueduct in retaliation, killing every beast on it, but she had been too late. Kutad was beyond saving.

And just as Mellai had foreseen while inside the calahein mind, they just kept coming. Wave after endless wave.

Mellai leaned forward, resting against the back of Huirk's neck. Her head pounded and her determination was precariously frail. Huirk read her body language and turned away from the fighting. Thrice she had healed wounds on the ghraef, two of which would have ended his life. She had not escaped unscathed herself, either. She could feel dried blood tugging the hair on the back of her head, where a boulder had struck her while her back was turned. She had been knocked unconscious in the middle of fighting, but Huirk had grabbed her from the ground and kept her safe until she came to a few minutes later.

As Mellai rested against Huirk, staring east over the retreating Appernysians, an unexpected sight caught her attention. The west wall of Itorea's keep was only a couple of miles away, where civilians sprinted across the drawbridge spanning a wide moat of blood. But the surprise had come from on top of the wall, which rose fifty feet higher than the rest of Itorea's perimeter wall.

Mellai sat up, feeling a small part of her courage renewed. Even from that far away, she easily recognized the mass of Rayder soldiers. The front line gripped glaives and diamond-shaped shields—etched with a blue King's Cross—while intermixed ranks of archers and crossbowmen unleashed death from behind the front line.

Tarek's here, Mellai shouted to her brother, *with the entire Rayder army!*

Lon didn't respond at first, but he couldn't hide his mixture of emotions. He felt honor, undoubtedly that the Rayders had joined the fight, but with a significant amount of fear for their safety. *Is Kaylen with them?*

Mellai's eyes widened at the thought. She peered at the line of soldiers, but she was too far away to distinguish anyone, especially behind the wall of shields. *I'll let you know. How far away are you?*

Five minutes. Bromax is flying straight to you.

Not here, Mellai said. *You're hurt, Lon, worse than you're telling me. I can feel it. Go to the keep until I can heal you.*

Not without you.

Mellai gripped Huirk's hair in her hands, furious, her momentary hope depleted. *What's the point? No matter what we do or how hard we fight, the calahein will just keep coming.*

I know it feels that way, but—

Just shut up and listen to me, Lon! I've seen our destruction!

A lengthy pause followed. *What do you mean?*

I broke in. Tears filled Mellai's eyes as she recalled the incapacitating experience. *The calahein are joined in one massive web of consciousness, all leading back to their queen. I saw them all, but I couldn't count their numbers. We're doomed.*

You read their mind?

That's what I just told you.

What's their intention?

Isn't it obvious? Mellai snapped. *They want our extinction.*

Lon's mind filled with anger. *It sounds like we have one thing in common with the calahein. I'll wait until you heal me, Mel, but then we will combine our strength. Only one race will rise victorious from this battle. We'll show the calahein who should be most feared in Appernysia.*

Chapter 50

The Flood

"There," Drogan said from on top of the keep's west wall, pointing at a black spot in the bright pink firmament. It was Bromax and Lon. They had been following the Gaurelic Waste toward Itorea's keep, outside the interest of the calahein.

Sunset was upon them, as was an increasingly aggressive host of calahein attackers. But the gates into the keep had been closed, the drawbridge retracted, and the valiant column of soldiers above held their line. No calahein had broken through yet.

Immediately after the king spoke, a group of five seith turned north, flying directly at the approaching ghraef and Beholder.

"Watch what you say," Tarek said, his face overly focused even for a Rayder. "They're listening."

Mellai stood and projected her essence into the sky, where a solitary seith had been circling above their position. She broke the beast in half. "Not anymore."

"That's my girl," Tarek said as he planted a kiss on top of Mellai's head. "You're the only reason Drogan got me up here on this wall," he whispered, having confided in her about his fear of heights.

Mellai was surprisingly flattered by Tarek's kindness, but her attention was focused on her brother. *Five seith are flying at you,* she told Lon.

Lon didn't reply, nor did Bromax change his course. As the seith closed their distance, Mellai became worried.

Do you hear me? Five seith are—

A bolt of lightning shot from the Beholder, flashing as it forked to strike all five seith at the same time. Three exploded, while the remaining two burst into flames and tumbled from the sky.

While everyone stared in wonder, Wade spoke calmly to the small group surrounding him. "As brilliantly as I had expected."

"He's been working on that, Lieutenant?" Tarek asked.

"Not to my knowledge, my Commander," Wade replied, "but I knew this day would come. Ever since Beholder Lon obsessed over the electrified sky during our infiltration mission to Three Peaks, our squad has often discussed when he would learn that power for himself."

Tarek burst into laughter, slapping Wade on the back.

Congratulations, Mellai communicated to her brother as she climbed onto Huirk and woke the ghraef. *Aside from causing quite a ruckus down here, you've finally learned a new trick before me.*

I won't let it go to my head, Lon replied. *How was your nap?*

Short, she answered, *but helpful.*

A few minutes later, Bromax landed next to Huirk.

"That's a new way to ride," Mellai said as Bromax laid her brother on the ground.

"I had a little accident," Lon replied.

Kaylen rushed to her husband's side as Mellai examined Lon's leg. Both bones in his shin were broken, and one stuck through the skin. "Trying to make this a regular habit?" she asked as she moved Lon's body to the ground.

Lon smiled through the pain. "Why? Does it inconvenience you?"

"You might need to hold him down," Mellai said to Wade and Tarek. "This will hurt." She then turned to Kaylen. "You sure you can watch this?"

Kaylen's lips tightened stubbornly as she nodded.

After the Rayders had secured Lon's body, with Kaylen holding his head in her lap, Mellai grabbed the lower half of his leg with her essence and pulled it. Her brother shouted in pain when the protruding bone slid inside the skin, but Mellai didn't stop. She realigned the bones, knitted them together, then healed the surrounding flesh and muscles. Ten minutes later, Lon was whole, though his face was paler than usual.

"You can't keep breaking yourself," Mellai grumbled.

"It wasn't my fault," he replied, standing to test his leg. Finding it satisfactory, he climbed onto Bromax's back and pointed at the sky. "Come on, Mel. We need to be up there."

"And what about us?" Tarek growled. "We walked all the way up here to talk to you."

"Now's not the time," Lon answered, "not when there are calahein to destroy." Bromax roared and jumped into the air with Lon.

"Sit behind me," Mellai said after a quick apology to Wade and the two leaders. "Huirk will carry you off the wall."

"And me?" Kaylen said.

Mellai nodded. "I especially want you and Shalán off this wall. For Lon's sake."

✳   ✳   ✳   ✳   ✳

Lon balked at the ferocity of the calahein forces. The entire west half of Itorea was infested. Everywhere the Beholder looked, the enemy was wreaking havoc. Many civilians were still trapped outside the keep, scattered across farmlands as they fled for their lives, but more and more died with every minute that passed. They were helpless on their own.

A thick cloud of seith also littered the sky, swooping down to occasionally assist in the killing, but more interested in grabbing kelsh and terror hounds to drop on top of the keep's wall. The Rayders were fighting valiantly, making full use of their training, but they wouldn't last forever. And their arrows only reached so far into the air. A few seith had already tried to pass high overhead on their way to the unprotected civilians farther east. Luckily, Mellai and Huirk had been there to stop them.

Lon cursed. The calahein fought on two separate fronts that he couldn't defend on his own. Just as he had experienced further west.

I'll focus on rescue, Lon thought to his sister. *You stay at the wall and prevent them from entering the keep.*

Be careful, Mellai replied, and stay away from the ground. *They'll swarm over you and Bromax quicker than you think.*

Lon understood his twin sister's advice, but it was advice he couldn't follow. Down there was where he had to be.

"Protect the people!" he shouted at Bromax.

While the ghraef dived at the calahein, Lon plucked the trapped Appernysians with his left hand's essence and placed them inside a protective energy sphere held in his right. They jostled around each other with the erratic flight of Bromax, but there was little Lon could do about that. It was better than the alternative.

Once the energy sphere was filled with ten or so Appernysians, Bromax would fly back to the keep and Lon would place them in front of the castle. Over and over they made this journey—with intermittent aerial battles with the seith—until hundreds had been rescued and there were no visible Appernysians left to save.

How are you doing? Lon asked his sister as Bromax swept one last time over the hundreds of square miles spanning Itorea's full blade. He tried not to look too closely at the mangled bodies below, searching instead for the glowing essences of humans as he continued to fight off the seith.

Well enough, Mellai answered. Her mind was exhausted, but her confidence wasn't nearly as shaken as it had been earlier that day. *Any more luck finding civilians?*

Nothing yet.

Maybe you should come back, then.

Lon shook his head, even though his sister couldn't see him. *There could be thousands of people still hiding out here. I can't give up on them.*

But the farther west Lon and Bromax traveled, the less confident the Beholder became. Kelsh were pouring out of the walls onto the raised aqueducts, looking down at innumerable hosts of terror hounds that dashed in and out of the buildings below. Occasional screams reached Lon's ears, but he could never identify the exact source. The calahein were performing the same task as Lon, but with an opposite objective and an incalculable increase in numbers. There was little left he could do.

He completely lost his resolve when Bromax reached the central wall splitting the east and west halves of Itorea's blade. They arrived just in time to see a host of kelsh pull back the final Furwen gate with an incredible display of strength.

Lon gaped as an endless stream of enemies poured into the farmland, as thick in number as the mosquitoes that had attacked him in the Gaurelic Waste. No longer did the ground troops rely on the seith to carry them into the city. Somehow, they had bypassed the Sylbien River and now raced into Itorea with unobstructed access. The front of this force would reach the keep by morning, with endless reinforcements behind them.

And the Beholders and ghraefs barely dominated the skies.

✳   ✳   ✳   ✳   ✳

Three seith dove at Huirk while two more flanked him, but the ghraef was unaware as he clawed and snapped at the other four that attacked from underneath.

"Drop!" Mellai shouted.

She had unbraided her legs and jumped from his back, rotating to face upward as she fell toward the ground. With the full group of attacking seith in her view, she pulled them together with her essence and crushed their bodies into a mangled heap of flesh and bones. Random knee and bone spikes stuck out of their mass like the spherical tip of a crude morning star. Mellai hurled it at another flock of seith farther west, then flipped onto her belly and waited for Huirk to swoop under her. But the ghraef never came.

With a quick glance over her shoulder, Mellai realized that one of the seith had crippled Huirk. A large section of his wing had been torn open, making it impossible for him to fly. He tried to slow his decent with his other wing, but the effort only flipped him sideways. His only choice was to tuck his wings and dive, too fast for a Beholder to heal him in time.

Only Mellai could save them now.

Thousands of people filled the keep below, forcing Mellai to catch herself and Huirk in an elevated air pond. She adjusted her position with her arms and legs until she was right next to the ghraef, then used her essence to pull Huirk underneath herself so she could save them as one body. With no time to spare, she barely managed to compress the air and stop their fall. But it wasn't perfectly executed, and Mellai had to heal more of Huirk's body than just his wing when they finally hit the ground.

Everything alright? Lon asked.

We survived, Mellai answered, climbing onto Huirk's back. *What about you two?*

You're right. There's nothing more we can do out here.

And? Mellai said, feeling that he was hiding something.

We're in trouble, Mel. Itorea is flooded with calahein, and more seith than ever are headed your way. We won't be able to hold them off forever.

Mellai looked below just in time to see another kelsh drop onto the wall of shielded soldiers. The beast's arms were outstretched, ready to kill, and the Rayders took advantage of its posture. While two men gripped their diamond-shaped shields protectively over-head, two more Rayders swung upwards, striking the kelsh in its shoulders with their shields' sharpened edges. The kelsh's arms fell harmlessly to the sides, but the berserker was still lethal. It dropped onto the men and kneed the two middle soldiers in their bellies with its knee spikes before a glaive finally removed its head.

After quickly dispatching the flying seith that had transported the kelsh, Mellai shook her head. Eventually, the calahein's superior numbers would win through. Lon was right. The beasts would pour over Itorea like an inescapable flood.

A flood, Mellai repeated in her mind. Her eyes brightened. *How far away are you?*

Five minutes. Why?

Hurry! I need your help!

* * * * *

Are you sure no human survivors are left? Mellai asked. She and Huirk had taken position on top of the watchtower at the southwest corner of the keep. From there, they would have a full view of the intersecting walls.

As sure as I can be, Lon replied.

He was sitting on top of Bromax while the ghraef used the fierce western wind to hover in front of the Rayder line. Lon looked over the ghraef's right shoulder at the north end of the keep's wall, where the bloody moat poured out of the north perimeter wall and into the Nellis River. Lon filled the iron-grated outlet with hardened stone that he had removed from a dismantled silo inside the keep. Corn seed now covered the keep's ground, but no one below paid it much attention. They were watching as the moat's water level rose at a quick rate. It would soon flood its banks and move out onto the farmlands.

Lon redirected his attention to the skies above the Fortress Island, dividing and extending his essence to all seith within his reach. *You ready?* he asked his sister.

Yes. Her voice was full of apprehension.

We need to do this at the same time to maximize our effectiveness. Just say when.

Lon pulled energy into himself and used it to concentrate his tendrils connected to the flying seith. *Now!*

A massive wall of water entered Lon's peripheral vision, hundreds of feet wide and pouring over the south wall into Itorea's blade. Mellai was supplying the tidal wave with an endless flow of water from the Asaras Sea. Her task was to flood the city as quickly as possible. The wave crashed down into the farmlands, washing over the kelsh and terror hounds as it made its way to the blade's north wall.

Now you, Mellai shouted in her mind.

In blinding flashes of light, webs of lightning shot out of Lon as he moved between two constant tasks—bombarding the water with electricity and frying all airborne seith. Over and over he struck until hundreds of beasts were dead and the rest were fleeing west. But Lon and Bromax weren't finished. Bromax flapped his massive wings, pursuing the seith as the flood continued to rise.

It's working! Lon shouted to his sister. *The calahein are in a full retreat!*

So I can stop?

Not yet, Mel. This will take time.

Mellai's core radiated with distaste at the city's destruction, but it was a necessary evil to cleanse Itorea of the calahein filth.

For an hour, Lon and Bromax chased down the calahein, until they finally reached the city's west curtain wall. Lon slid the Furwen doors back into place at the west and south gates, and Bromax jumped into the air just before the flood waters reached them.

There they waited, perched atop one of the moonlit watchtowers for hours and watching for more calahein to appear. The seith rallied forth on occasion, but Lon knocked them from the sky before they could cross the half-mile-wide river. In truth, not much happened until the floodwaters overtook the aqueducts, then masses of calahein began pouring out onto the walls. But there was nowhere for them to escape. They raced back and forth chaotically on top of the walls, often fighting with each other until the flood waters finally reached three hundred feet. The kelsh and terror hounds were washed out of the Fortress Island by thousands of miniature waterfalls that poured between the impervious wall's crenels and arrow slits.

Lon had expected an influx of seith to appear, intent on rescuing the terror hounds and kelsh from the wall, but none ever appeared. The calahein had left the stragglers to die.

After a final flight around the perimeter, Bromax carried Lon back toward Itorea's keep. Its walls were fifty feet higher than the blade's and also made of indestructible stone. It would effectively protect all human survivors from the flood.

Chapter 51
Foresight

Did you read the queen's mind? Lon asked his sister as he and Bromax approached the keep.

She cut me off before I had a chance.

Then we have to try again. Lon's mind filled with determination. *This isn't the last we'll see of the calahein. If we know the queen's full plan, then we'll know how to defend against it.*

It's too dangerous, Mellai replied, thinking through the simplest explanation of what had happened to her. *The queen dictates every action of the calahein. When I penetrated their telepathy, I became part of that cycle. Even after the queen forced me out, I had no control over my body. I couldn't move for half an hour.*

Then we'll do it together.

But, Lon—

But nothing! If ever there were a time to trust in synergy, this is it.

Mellai's stomach churned at the thought of delving into the calahein's consciousness again, but Lon had a point. If she and her brother could break through the final barrier and read the queen's mind, they'd have a huge advantage.

Alright, Lon. You win.

Not yet, I haven't. I still need to find a living calahein in this mess. I'll meet you at the castle.

* * * * *

"Are you insane?" King Drogan shouted, standing behind Mellai with his two-handed sword drawn. "Why would you bring a living terror hound into the middle of my keep?"

"For once," Tarek added, standing next to the king, "I agree with him. This is dangerous, even for a Beholder."

The combined Beholders' guard, along with Aron and Shalán, had followed the commander and the king down from the wall. They all stood with Mellai and Huirk in a circle around Lon and his imprisoned terror hound.

"Now tell everyone your idiotic plan," Mellai chimed in.

Huirk circled around the group as Lon spoke, glancing between the terror hound and the west wall. Eventually, he spoke to Bromax in their native tongue and the two ghraefs flew up to patrol the skies.

"But what if this doesn't work like you hope?" Tarek said after Lon finished explaining. "What if the calahein take control of your minds?"

"Then you'll have the best brawl of your life," Lon replied, slapping the commander across his face.

"This is serious, Son," Aron interjected. "If we lose you two, even for an hour, then our situation here becomes perilous. Even with the ghraefs' assistance, these Rayders can only hold out for so long."

"I've made up my mind," Lon said, summoning True Sight and reaching his essence through Mellai's protective energy shield that surrounded the hound.

Wait, Mellai spoke to his mind as she grabbed his hand. *Together, remember?*

Lon nodded. *Ready?*

No.

Good. Neither am I.

*　*　*　*　*

Once again, Mellai was the terror hound. She was being held captive, fighting desperately against the restraint.

A strange voice entered her mind, different than the kelsh which usually commanded her. "We're not the calahein," it said. "Listen to me, Mellai."

Mellai? she thought. The name sounded familiar.

"Hey, Little Sis. Snap out of it!"

"Don't call me Little Sis," she shouted back. She hated that name, and now she realized why—she wasn't actually the terror hound. Mellai rejoined her brother as an ethereal third party to the calahein mind. Everything was still visible, but her brother's voice was the only one that reached her ears. And she could feel his hand in her own.

"I thought you were going to bite me," Lon teased.

"Thank you," she answered sincerely. "Ready to dig deeper?"

"No."

"Good."

Mellai pushed into the terror hound's mind, but kept her full senses. She and Lon shot across Itorea's flooded blade and over the Sylbien River. A kelsh stood on the shores of the opposite bank, wondering what had happened to its terror hound. The hound was alive, but it wasn't obeying anymore.

"This is weird," Lon said.

"Just wait," Mellai replied, pushing even deeper.

They flew through the burned section of the Perbeisea Forest, into the same mind of the seith she had previously occupied.

"Are you sure this is the same one?" Lon asked.

"Absolutely. Look at it."

The seith was behaving erratically. Not only had the same foreign mind entered their consciousness again, but she had brought along a companion. These intruders were powerful together. Unstoppable.

"Careful," Lon said, squeezing Mellai's real hand. "You're doing it again."

Mellai withdrew to an observatory stance. "Thanks."

"Don't mention it."

"This is where I was stopped last time. Stay close to me, Lon. Don't let go."

Mellai pushed in once more, whisking away toward Réxura's ruins. She met the same barrier again and it stabbed at her mind.

"Fight back!" Lon shouted.

Mellai flailed at the unknown source, only bringing more pain. "I don't know how to attack!"

"Together, Mel!"

With her brother's hand as a lifeline, Mellai found Lon's consciousness and gripped it.

"Ow!" *he cried.*

"Help me, Lon!"

They battled as one, pressing back against the barrier. Mellai felt her awareness falter, a type of vertigo similar to Huirk's straining aerial maneuvers, then the obstruction shattered. They shot toward the tip of the Vidarien Mountains, but stopped in the center of Réxura's ruins. There they raced straight underground through a network of passages until they finally entered a large cavern many miles below the surface.

Curled up on the floor was the calahein queen. She looked like a kelsh, but bigger than even the largest ghraef in Ursoguia's council and incapable of fitting through the underground passages. Unlike the other fall-colored members of the calahein, the queen was completely hairless. Thin membranous skin stretched over her prostrate form, split open in many places and oozing yellow puss. Her flattened snout was wide open, lips curled back in concentration.

"That's the ugliest thing I've ever seen," *Lon said.* "What's she doing?"

"Let's find out."

Hand in hand, Mellai and Lon prepared to fight into the mind of the calahein overseer. To their surprise, they met zero resistance. The queen had abandoned her mental defenses so that she could focus on another task.

The First Age was repeating itself. Beholders had broken through. Her life was forfeit. They would find her. Kill her. But she would birth a new queen to take her place, just as her mother had done. And the Beholders wouldn't find the egg. She will release one of her children from her control.

It will escape with its new queen. Undetectable.

A colony of kelsh surrounded the queen, massaging her body. Soothing her. Waiting for their new leader.

And the queen sent out one last command for all forces to return. She needed their protection.

"That's how they did it!" Lon shouted.

"Shut up, Lon."

"But we know where she is, Mellai! Let's kill her before she lays that egg!"

✳   ✳   ✳   ✳   ✳

Mellai pulled out of the queen's mind, yanking Lon with her until they were again themselves, kneeling in front of the terror hound. While Lon leaned sideways, recovering from the experience, Mellai screamed at him.

"Are you a complete idiot, Lon? Did you ever think that if we could read the calahein's thoughts, they could do the same to us? Now the queen knows we're coming. We'll never reach her in time!"

"But we know the only path in," Lon argued. "If we hurry, there won't be time for any of them to escape."

"You're thinking exactly like the First Age Beholders, and they failed. Remember how large she was? She's been there for centuries, probably since the First Age, slowly expanding her colony underneath Réxura while the Appernysians carried on with their clueless lives. There must be dozens of ways out of that place."

"Hiding right beneath Réxura," Lon said, cursing as he stood, "the last place we'd ever look for her."

"And now it's too late. Your lack of self-control has ruined our only chance."

Lon paced the ground, deep in thought as he gripped his sheathed falchion. Minutes passed as everyone watched him, long enough for the ghraefs to return, before Lon finally stopped and looked at his sister. His shoulders were slumped, but fervent determination filled his countenance.

"I know what to do."

* * * * *

Lon tried to swallow, but his mouth had gone dry. Everyone was watching him expectantly, but his usual confidence had disappeared. In contrast, the soldiers on top of the wall were celebrating. The skies were clear, free of any threat, but only those circling Lon knew the true reason behind the calahein's retreat. Every living beast was gathering at Réxura to defend their queen.

"Kill the hound," Lon said to Mellai. "We don't need it anymore."

A sharp yelp came from the imprisoned creature as she broke its neck.

Kaylen stood in front of her husband, holding his face between her hands and forcing him to look at her. "What's going on, Lon?"

Lon couldn't look her in the eyes. "We found the queen, buried under Réxura, but she's trying to lay a new queen egg. Once she does, we won't be able to track it. That's how the calahein survived the First Age."

"And she knows we're coming," Mellai said again, standing up and folding her arms.

"There's still a way to solve this," Lon continued, "to ensure that nothing escapes the colony, but we have to leave." He stepped back from Kaylen and climbed onto Bromax's back. "Come on, Mellai. There's no time for delay."

Kaylen was undaunted. She followed after her husband and planted herself in front of him. "I'm going with you."

Lon looked to his sister for assistance, but she just stared back with impatient confusion. Lon shook his head, unable to verbalize a protest. Although reason provided zero logic for bringing Kaylen along, Lon's heart gladly conceded. If ever there were a time that he wanted his bride with him, it was now.

"What's going on here?" Tarek said, stepping between the two Beholders. "What am I missing?"

"We're going to end this battle for good," Lon replied, carefully masking the burning in his throat as he returned the gaze of his best friend. "But we have to go now." He patted Bromax's side. "Please."

As the ghraef spread his wings, Lon searched the faces surrounding him. He saluted his squad and Drogan, thanked Tarek for leading the Rayders into Itorea, then paused at his parents. They stood side by side, Aron's arm wrapped around Shalán in a firm embrace. Shalán's face conveyed motherly concern, but it was Aron's expression that held Lon's attention.

He knows, Lon thought, gratefully perceiving that Mellai was not connected to True Sight to read his thoughts. The tiniest amount of moisture pooled in their father's eyes. Aron nodded at his son with a mixture of heartache and fatherly pride, then held Shalán even tighter.

"I love you," Lon said to them both just before Bromax leaped into the air, Mellai and Huirk right behind them.

As the ghraefs lifted into the sky and flew over the wall bearing up humanity's last defenders, Lon braided his and Kaylen's legs into Bromax's long black hair, then turned to everyone he was leaving behind. He drew his falchion and held it high above his head. "For Appernysia!"

Everyone below joined him, raising their swords in a united, repetitious chorus. "For Appernysia! For Appernysia!"

Chapter 52

My Time Draws Near

Bromax and Huirk pushed themselves to the limits of their strength. They flew west with incredible speed, intending to bypass all ground troops and kill any seith who opposed them. Nearly one hundred and seventy-five miles separated them from the deep burrows hidden under Réxura.

Having been using True Sight to scan the terrain and skies, Mellai quickly connected with her brother. *What was that all about?* she asked in her mind as Huirk flew next to Bromax.

Lon wouldn't look at her. *What?*

Mellai used her essence to turn her brother's head. *We've been sharing each other's emotions since we were born, Big Brother, but I've never seen or felt you act like this—not even in Pree. You're scaring me.*

Lon leaned the side of his face against Kaylen's head and wrapped his arms around her waist. Tears poured from his eyes, wetting the low ponytail securing his wife's blonde hair. *I'm scaring myself.*

Why? We're just going queen hunting, Lon. You've been through worse. It's not like we're doomed to die.

Lon only stared unblinking at his sister, despite the wind that whipped past them.

Mellai's stomach twisted with dread. The way her brother was behaving since they broke into the calahein mind . . . something was wrong. Way wrong.

Mellai called upon her power and acted quickly, before Lon could shut her out. She touched his mind with her essence and immediately discovered the source of his anguish. He was going to sacrifice himself to ensure the calahein's extinction. One massive explosion, just like that Beholder in the Forest of Blight, but with the intent to destroy the entire colony under Réxura.

Just as disconcerting was the fact that Lon just let her probe his mind. Zero resistance. He was fully committed to this solution, even with his new wife sitting right in front of him—who was thankfully too stunned over the mass quantities of water trapped in Itorea to pay much heed to their silent conversation.

Mellai carefully approached the topic, knowing the precariousness of the circumstance. Her brother's life literally hung in the balance of this conversation.

You said no more solo missions, Lon. You promised.

I know, but it's the only way to create an explosion large enough. I have to use myself as a host.

Why not use one of the calahein? Mellai suggested, albeit half-heartedly.

You know it doesn't work like that. Only Beholders can absorb energy—anything else would just die, like I almost did in Pree before I learned to control it.

Then why not let me do it instead? My future was taken from me when Theiss died, but you still have Kaylen. She needs you.

Lon sighed. *You still have a future, Mellai, and you're more powerful than I am. If this doesn't work, Appernysia needs your protection.* He pointed at Huirk's tail crystal, the same King's Cross branded on every Rayder. *You've already done more than me to unite Appernysia, and I've been at it for over a year.*

Mellai raised her hands at Lon. *Will you slow down for a second?*

I've felt this coming, Mellai, since before I left Pree. It's only grown stronger as the months passed. I promised to protect the people you love—at the cost of my own life, if necessary. My time has come. Let me go with honor.

Stop, Lon! Let's think this through together. There has to be another way. Lon shrugged. *Go ahead.*

Have you tried using a dead host before, like a rock or something?

It just shattered the rock and knocked everyone down, Lon replied. *Nothing like the raw power of an energy blast.*

Mellai pounded Huirk's back with her fist, accidentally drawing the ghraef's attention. He turned his head and looked at Mellai with one eye.

"Sorry, Huirk. I'm just frustrated."

The ghraef huffed and resumed scanning his surroundings for danger.

What if we compress the dirt under Réxura? Crush the calahein?

The calahein live underground, Mel, just like ants. I doubt it's possible to simply crush them. They'll just burrow out again. And the queen egg might be extra strong. Packing dirt on top of it might be like a bird sitting in her nest, keeping the egg cozy until it is ready to hatch.

Then let's just rush straight in and find the egg.

Lon shook his head. *You read their mind with me, right? Once the queen lays her replacement egg, we won't know where it is.*

Not if the queen hasn't laid her egg yet. Then I could just kill her instead.

But we don't even know if she has laid the egg, Lon responded.

Then help me find a terror hound so we can find out. Mellai laid against Huirk's back, rubbing it with her hands. "I know you're even more tired than me, but try to fly faster. Our lives depend on it."

Huirk spoke to Bromax, then the ghraefs beat their wings harder to gain altitude and speed. Mellai could feel Huirk's lungs wheezing beneath her, but there was no way she would retract the request, not with everything that was at stake.

✳   ✳   ✳   ✳   ✳

Once the ghraefs passed over the west wall of Itorea, Kaylen broke free from her trance and began talking with Lon. Mellai had used her power to listen in on the conversation, but it was of little importance. Some casual talk, but mostly questions from Kaylen about the battle they had just survived. Who did Lon rescue? How had he done it? Did he have any narrow escapes? Lon freely shared everything with her, except for his intentions when they reached Réxura. That was one point Mellai agreed with. Kaylen shouldn't worry about a death that might not happen.

It wasn't until the Beholders reached the west edge of the charred Perbeisea Forest that they finally encountered the calahein. Mellai couldn't believe how far the beasts had retreated in such a short amount of time. Only forty miles still separated them from the calahein colony below Réxura.

Despite the danger, Mellai coaxed Huirk to dive low so she could grab another terror hound. As the ghraef regained altitude, Mellai delved into the hound's consciousness, not waiting for Lon's help. The control that used to run through the beasts' connected minds had almost entirely disappeared, and Mellai easily located the queen on her own. Every ounce of the queen's concentration was focused on the egg still forming inside her.

She's still laboring, Mellai told Lon. *As long as she's preoccupied with that, I'll be able to breach their connection on my own. You focus on the skies.*

Lon nodded, but his expression still lacked confidence that they would reach Réxura in time. Mellai couldn't deny her own anxiety. Even though hours had passed since the queen went into labor, thirty minutes might as well be thirty days. It was the longest flight Mellai ever experienced.

When they were fifteen miles from Réxura, Mellai grabbed another terror hound from below and pushed into its mind.

Oh, no, Mellai thought, before she could stop herself.

What? Lon answered.

Mellai sighed with defeat. *The egg is fully formed. It's on its way out.* She continued giving Lon every detail when five minutes later—the Beholders were only ten miles from Réxura—the egg was birthed into the arms of an orange-furred kelsh. Mellai used every ounce of her training and willpower to focus on the egg and track its position, but she permanently lost sight of it a minute later. The kelsh carrying the egg became invisible to her perception, and all surrounding calahein in the underground passages were staring at dirt walls to prevent Mellai from seeing its escape route. Shortly after giving birth, the queen recovered her telepathic authority and banished Mellai from their burrow.

Mellai kept the terror hound, begging Lon to help her fight their way back into the calahein mind.

It's pointless, he argued. *Even if we break in, we still won't know where the egg is traveling. And the effort might leave us too weak to destroy it.*

Mellai couldn't refute his logic, but that didn't stop her from yelling at her twin anyway. She used every second to beg and plead with him. Her rational self had given way to absolute desperation. Lon's only response was an increased grip around Kaylen.

"Land here," Lon called to Bromax, eight miles from the center of Réxura.

The ghraefs dove quickly, alighting in an area free of calahein. But they remained alert nonetheless. As with Kaylen, neither Bromax nor Huirk had been informed of Lon's intent.

Lon released his and Kaylen's legs from Bromax's woven hair, then Lon slid off the ghraef and helped Kaylen dismount.

"I'm counting on you, Mel," Lon said, turning to speak with his sister. "Our people can't afford to keep up this civil war."

Mellai had already dismounted. She ran at her brother and pounded on his chest with her fists, barely able to form coherent thought. "I don't care anymore, Lon. Nothing else matters. You can't do this!"

Lon pushed Mellai's hands out of the way and wrapped his arms around her. Mellai barely heard him whisper over her frantic sobs. "I love you, Mellai."

"Don't you do that! You call me Little Sis, not Mellai. This isn't goodbye!"

Kaylen and the ghraefs had been standing aside, confusion written on their faces, but her last sentence must have tied all the mayhem together for Bromax and Huirk. The ghraefs roared and tore at the earth with their paws, tail crystals bashing soil in protest.

"No Beholder should ask this of their ghraef," Lon said, turning to look at Bromax, "but I have no choice. I need your help. I can't do this on my own."

"Can't do what on your own?" Kaylen had moved to stand directly between Lon and Bromax, forcing her husband to look her in the eyes. "What are you planning?"

"I'm so sorry," Lon said, his practiced composure finally shattered. He cried openly, releasing his sister to burying his face in Kaylen's shoulder. "I have no choice."

"What does he mean?" Kaylen asked, her bottom lip quivering.

Mellai wiped the tears from her face, but more just took their place. "We have to destroy the queen's egg, Kaylen. That can only be done if Lon sacrifices himself."

Bromax thumped his obsidian tail crystal again, standing tall on his four legs and pushing out his chest. Mellai tried to smile at the ghraef and the courage he showed by joining Lon, but she couldn't bring herself to do it. She moved to his leg and pressed herself into its thick black hair, oblivious to Lon and Kaylen's interaction. "I don't know what to say, Bromax."

The ghraef lowered his snout and pressed his cheek against Mellai's back, then kindly nudged her back with his leg. As the Beholder moved back, Huirk stepped over the top of her to sit in front of Bromax. Mellai didn't need to understand their language to see that the conversation was difficult for both ghraefs. She turned back to her brother and best friend.

"Without you," Kaylen cried, "there is no reason for me to live." Her face was pale with shock and she leaned into her husband for support.

"What about Mellai and my parents?" Lon whispered. "How about Scut?"

"I married *you*, Lon," Kaylen replied. "*Our* lives are tied together."

"I need to go," Lon said, cupping his left hand against her face while he pulled a glowing diamond from his pocket. He placed the sun crystal in his wife's hand. "Stay here with Mellai."

"No!" Kaylen screamed, tossing the diamond to the ground. "I can't lose you again!"

Lon pulled his wife close as he passionately kissed her, then looked at his sister, his eyes pleading. Mellai nodded with understanding. She grabbed Kaylen with her essence and pulled her away from Lon.

"Let me go!" Kaylen continued, sprinting back toward Bromax, but Lon had already climbed onto his back and the ghraef leaped clear before she could reach him. Kaylen whipped back to Mellai, her eyes frantic. "You bring them back! I can't lose him again!"

Mellai only stared at her best friend, more tears flooding her face.

Kaylen turned toward Lon again, dropping to her knees and screaming at the sky. "Don't do this, Lon! Please come back!"

Mellai felt Lon connect with her mind. His thoughts were as poignant as the pain his heart. *If I come back there, I won't be able to leave again. Please take care of her.*

Of course, Mellai replied, breathing deep to calm herself. *Do you remember where the queen is located?*

It doesn't matter. I'll just punch a hole straight down the middle of Réxura. Now get out of here. I don't know how big this blast will be.

Mellai picked up the sun crystal and grabbed Kaylen by her arm, forcing her to stand and climb onto Huirk's back. A few kelsh had converged on their position, but Mellai easily killed them, tossing them aside as she sat behind her friend and secured their legs. "Head north."

Huirk leaped into the air, but struggled to gain altitude. His exhaustion was finally beginning to overpower him. Mellai used True Sight to lift the ghraef into the air, but Huirk shook his head and resumed gliding toward the open Taejan Plains—the safest place away from calahein troops. Mellai held her sobbing friend as she watched her brother. Lon's voice reached her mind as Bromax rose high into the air.

Appernysia, jewel of light, bolstered by unceasing might, unmatched force and glory strong—

"No longer could your death prolong," Mellai interrupted, speaking both in her thoughts and aloud.

Bromax was circling above Réxura, his own essence losing his luster as Lon gathered energy into himself.

"I free you now from world-bound strife," Mellai continued, *"and wish for you a better life. Release your pain, forget remorse, continue on your ordained course."*

Bromax broke into a steep dive, while a cloud of seith rushed out of their burrow to attack. Their essences were absorbed into Lon as he continued gathering more energy. His glow intensified, sputtering with instability.

Mellai wiped away her tears with her leather vambrace. *"Go and find your resting place, embrace no more this mortal race. Where pain and sorrow took their toll, let joy and peace encase your soul."*

Kaylen turned her head, her face pale as she watched with wide, bloodshot eyes. Although the sun had long since disappeared, sleeping behind the mountains to the west, a new light was growing, captured by her husband and his ghraef—Appernysia's greatest heroes.

Mellai's grip on Kaylen's arm tightened when Lon neared the surface. Bromax's essence had disappeared behind the brilliance of Lon's glow. With a strained voice, Mellai continued. *"I will be watching for the day when my pains, too, are washed away. But 'til that time doth find me here, I bid goodbye. I'll shed no tear."*

Just before Lon disappeared into a hole he had created in the soil, his voice filled Mellai's mind and echoed across the plains.

"Farewell, my friends. My time draws near."

Kaylen gasped and buried her face in her hands. For a brief moment, darkness consumed them, then a burst of light poured out of the ground. Soil and rock erupted violently for miles, tearing through the earth's surface with so much force that it knocked Huirk from the sky. The ghraef barely managed to level out before crashing into the ground.

The women were unhurt, secured to the thick brown hair on Huirk's back, but Mellai leaped down and scanned his body for wounds. Finding nothing beyond light abrasions, she moved in front of Huirk's face and stared into his eyes.

It was the only time Mellai ever saw a ghraef cry.

Epilogue

Months passed. Winter's frost had melted into a wet spring on its transition into one of the hottest summers ever to reach Appernysia. Mellai wiped her forehead as she looked down from Huirk's back, searching for calahein. Those outside the perimeter of Lon's blast had become leaderless and erratic. Many had committed suicide on the spot, clawing at their mindless skulls, but small groups still had to be hunted. Many of these had been discovered in the Kerod Cluster, behind the razed city of Draege where not a soul was left alive.

Toj had been razed, but with no casualties. Kátaea had died of heart failure shortly after Lon and Bromax appeared, leaving Nadjor and Laecha to evacuate the combined residents of Humsco and Toj. They ordered everyone to board the barges the very next day. They had escaped down the Saap River and out to sea, then continued on to the Fortress Island before the calahein ever arrived.

Taeja had been overrun by the calahein, too, but little damage could be done to a city of dirt. Most of Mellai's repairs had been focused on filling holes the kelsh had begun tunneling into the ground. She planned to return at a later time to assist with its full construction before the Taejans returned home, but other pressing matters needed her attention first.

Aside from Itorea, Flagheim had suffered the most damage. Buildings centuries old had been decimated by tooth and claw, as had the few people living there. Mellai found no sign of Bryst's defectors besides a few trails of blood splattered across the ground.

Last of all, and with an anxious heart, Mellai had asked Huirk to carry her to Pree. It was the only village untouched by the cala-hein. When Mellai questioned why, Huirk had pointed southwest toward Ursoguia, reminding her of the village's close proximity to the ghraefs' nest. Much to Mellai's surprise, Delancy and his daughter had survived the winter, both still stubbornly refusing to leave. The rest of Pree's villagers, however, had stayed in Itorea to assist with repairs.

Despite all the damage, a sense of peace was finally settling on the kingdom as August came to a close. Mellai and Huirk had not seen a terror hound, kelsh, or seith for three months.

"Oof," Kaylen muttered, adjusting her spot on Huirk's back. "Maybe this was a bad idea."

"Nonsense," Mellai replied, reaching around her friend to place her hands on Kaylen's round belly. Is my little niece moving?"

"It could be a boy," Kaylen argued, elbowing Mellai in the ribs. "We'll find out in a month."

"How about I just tell you now? We could pick a name and everything."

Kaylen shook her head and lifted her nose, breathing the air deeply. "I love the smell after a heavy rainstorm."

"We needed it, too. The aqueducts were starting to run dry."

"So where are you taking me, anyway?" After Lon's sacrifice, Kaylen had returned to Itorea and spent every waking moment with Aron and Shalán, helping to repair the extensive damage—that is, when she wasn't battling her own pregnancy sickness. She hadn't stepped foot outside of Itorea's walls until now.

"You'll see," Mellai teased.

Huirk dropped low, skimming over the Prime River and carving it with his tail crystal. The protruding javelin heads caught now and then, splashing the water forward onto Mellai.

"Sometimes I wish I never made that thing," Mellai grumbled, wiping water from her neck.

"But it matches your pendant," Kaylen said, pointing at the King's Cross medallion hanging on top of Mellai's clothes.

"And my tattoo," Mellai added quietly, touching her right temple. She had seen Llen only once after the Battle of Itorea, when he had appeared to help with the ceremony. After adding a blue King's Cross to her right temple, signifying a reunited Appernysia, Llen had informed Mellai that it would be his final visit.

"Appernysia is now under your full care," he had said, disappearing before Mellai could ask about her brother. So many questions filled her mind. Was Lon well? Had he become a Jaed, too? Would she ever see her twin brother again?

"But nothing compares to your sun crystal," Mellai said. "I still can't believe Lon stole that."

Kaylen fingered the glowing diamond hanging around her neck, then kissed it and let it hang over her heart by its gold chain. A moment later, she gasped and pointed east, placing her other hand over her mouth. "Is that Lon?"

"And Bromax," Mellai added. She patted Huirk on his side. "Give her a better view, would you?"

Huirk flapped his wings and lifted into the air, gliding over the new lake that had formed in place of Réxura, feeding the Prime and Pearl Rivers. Just west of the lake was a solitary mountain, only it wasn't a mountain anymore. Mellai had been helping the Taejans for months, carving it into a commissioned, granite memorial of Lon and Bromax.

"It's not finished yet. We still need to work on the details." But King Drogan's vision had finally started to show through. Lon was in the middle of the monument, fully dressed for battle and standing more than a mile above the surrounding plains. At his side was a sheathed falchion, its hilt made into a giant sun crystal of diamond that radiated with pure white. Bromax was lying down, scaled down to fit the size of the mountain base. His body wrapped around the

Beholder so tightly that his tail crystal—an obsidian stone nearly as large as the ghraef's head—touched his own snout.

"It's beautiful, Mellai. I don't know what else to say."

Huirk swung around the statue, a tiny spec compared to its enormity, before splashing through the lake-filling waterfall that shot out of Bromax's mouth.

"I told you not to do that anymore!" Mellai shouted, kicking Huirk on his sides before drying their clothes. The ghraef only laughed, his tongue wagging out of his mouth as he followed the river and landed at a camp between the lake and monument.

"She lives!" Tarek said, stepping out of a canvas tent. "Welcome abroad, Kaylen! I've been telling Mellai for months that you needed the fresh air." He stepped on Huirk's leg and planted a wet kiss on the Beholder's lips. "You look about ready to burst, Kay Kay."

"I had to come check on you," Kaylen said. She pointed to his right temple. "That scar looks much better in blue."

Tarek beamed. "A true King's Cross for a true Taejan. Well, at least I'll be once I upgrade Taeja from a city of dirt. Sometimes I wish Lon hadn't promised Omar that he'd finish building it."

"But when are you going to make an honest woman of my best friend? Not after Taeja's built? That will take too long."

"Nah. Just when this is done." He pointed up at the statue. "Mellai and I will be the first to marry when it's complete."

"I haven't said yes yet," Mellai said, wiping Tarek's slobber from her mouth.

"Oh, come on. We all know you can't resist me."

Mellai turned her head when Tarek tried to steal another kiss. "Any updates, my Phoenijan lover?"

"No other Beholders yet, if that's what you're asking." He leaned closer and spoke in a whisper. "But my money's on Wade. We all know he's the best guy here, and I just found out a nifty little secret about him. Want to guess what it is?"

Mellai rolled her eyes. "I hate guessing."

"He's your cousin, my precious little Melly Belly." Tarek reached up to pinch her side.

"Seriously?" Mellai said, swatting away his hand.

Tarek nodded. "Your real grandmother is his grandfather's sister. He doesn't talk about it much, though, for obvious reasons. You know, the whole dishonor-execution thing with your blood grandparents."

"We're related," Mellai repeated, more of a statement than a question.

"But he doesn't know it yet. I thought I'd leave that conversation to you." Tarek stepped down and waved at them. "Now get Kaylen back to Itorea before that baby shoots out by himself."

"*Her*self," Mellai argued.

Tarek laughed and blew a kiss to them as they flew away, then disappeared into his tent again.

"Do you really know if the baby is a girl?" Kaylen asked, her hands investigating her belly.

Mellai smiled. "I'm not telling."

Glossary

Pronunciation Guide:

\ā\ *as* **a** *in ape*	\ər\ *as* **er** *in person*	\th\ *as* **th** *in thin*
\a\ *as* **a** *in apple*	\ī\ *as* **i** *in ice*	\ū\ *as* **u** *in union*
\ä\ *as* **o** *in hop*	\i\ *as* **i** *in hit*	\uh\ *as* **u** *in bug*
\ch\ *as* **ch** *in chip*	\ō\ *as* **o** *in go*	\ü\ *as* **oo** *in loot*
\ē\ *as* **ea** *in easy*	\qu\ *as* **qu** *in quiet*	\ů\ *as* **oo** *in foot*
\e\ *as* **e** *in bet*	\sh\ *as* **sh** *in shop*	\zh\ *as* **si** *in vision*

Abram – (ā´-bram) deceased friend of Reese Arbogast.

Aely Leeran – (ā´-lē | lē´ran) friend of Kaylen Shaw, servant in Itorea's donjon.

Allegna Ovann – (uh-leg´-nuh | ō´-van) wife to Dhargon Ovann; mother of Shalán Marcs.

Appernysia – (a-pər-nē´-zhuh) the kingdom in which this story is set, established at the beginning of the First Age.

Anice Rowley – (a´-nis | rō´-lē) wife to Trev Rowley.

Anton Vetinie – (an´-tuhn | Ve-tē´-nē) chancellor to Queen Cyra.

Aron Marcs – (ā´-ruhn | märks´) husband to Shalán Marcs and father of Lon and Mellai Marcs.

Banty Prates – (ban´-tē | prāts´) birth name of Snoom.

Battle for Taeja – a battle between Rayders and Appernysia for the city, Taeja; during the Second Age; won by the Rayders.

Beholder – a person with True Sight who can manipulate the world's energy.

Beholder's Eye – the tattoo surrounding the left eye of Beholders.

Bors Rayder – (bōrz´ | rā´-dər) a Taejan who led the Phoenijan rebellion against the king and Beholders at the end of the First Age; all Taejans who followed him took the title of Rayder.

Braedr Pulchria – (brā´-dər | půl´-krē-uh) son to Hans and Ine Pulchria; raised in Pree.

Braj – (brazh´) Appernysian soldier and runner.

Bromax – (brō´-maks) ghraef companion to Lon Marcs.

Bryst Grayson – (brist´ | grā´-suhn) Rayder supply wagon overseer.

calahein – (ca´-luh-hīn) ancient enemy of Appernysia; exterminated from their home in Meridina near the end of the First Age; composed of kelsh, seith, and one queen.

Cavalier Crook – the southwestern quadrant of Itorea that houses the city's nobles.

Channer – (chan´-ər) member of Lon's twelve-Rayder tactical squad; cousin to Keene.

Char Gemott – (char´ | ge´-mut) young Appernysian lieutenant; dies in the Briyél Forest.

Ched Trelnap – (ched´ | trel´-nap) previous sergeant of Appernysia and bailiff of the king's council.

Clawed – (clād´) leader of a Rayder uprising; also known as Claude.

Coel – (kōl´) village leatherworker in Pree.

coming of age – an important transition from adolescence to adulthood in Pree, enabling a person to participate in village councils, start their own trade, build their own home, and marry and start a family; age fifteen for girls and age seventeen for boys.

Cortney Baum – (kōrt´-nē | bäm´) young Rayder daughter of Gil and Flora Baum.

Cyra Jagonest – (si´-ruh | ja´-gō-nest) queen of Appernysia; wife of Drogan Jagonest.

Darius – (dār´-ē-uhs) leader of Jaul's survivors after the town's governor was killed.

Dawes – (däz´) Lon Marcs's Rayder horse, previously owned by Gil Baum.

Dax – (Daks´) Wade Arneson's horse.

Delancy Reed – (de-lan´-sē | rēd´) village brewer in Pree; father to Sonela Reed.

Dhargon Ovann – (där´-guhn | ō´-van) husband to Allegna Ovann; father of Shalán Marcs.

donjon – (duhn´-juhn) the central keep of Itorea where the king and queen dwell.

Dovan – (dō´-ven) member of Lon's twelve-Rayder tactical squad.

Draege – (drāzh´) mining city located on the north face of the Kerod Cluster.

Drake – (drāk´) member of Gil Baum's Rayder squad.

Drogan Jagonest – (drō´-gen | ja´-gō-nest) king of Appernysia; husband of Cyra Jagonest.

Duncan Shord – (duhn´-cuhn | shōrd´) previous sentry to the royal chambers of Itorea's donjon; member of Mellai's guard.

Edis Ascennor – (ē´-dis | uh-se´-nōr) deceased wife of Myron Ascennor.

Elie Swasey – (el´-ē | swā´-zē) member of Clawed's Rayder rebellion.

Elja – (el´-zhuh) member of Lon's twelve-Rayder tactical squad.

Elora – (ē-lōr´-uh) village alfalfa farmer in Pree; widow with four sons.

Ernon – (ər´-nuhn) a page to King Drogan.

First Age – the time period which began when Appernysia was first settled; ended after the Rayder revolution and banishment to the Exile; reference Second Age.

Flagheim – (flag´-hīm) fortress city of the Rayders; located in the Exile about thirty miles north of the Dialorine Range.

Flora Baum – (flōr´-uh | bäm´) Rayder widow of Gil Baum; mother of Cortney Baum and two older sons.

Furwen Tree – (fər´-wen) a massive tree with wood as hard as stone, grows over six hundred feet tall; located in the Perbeisea Forest.

Gavin Baum – (ga´-vin | bäm´) oldest son of Flora Baum.

Geila – (gā´-luh) young pureblood Rayder woman executed for fornication with Sévart; gave birth to a child in the wilderness.

Gera – (ge´-ruh) head cook in Itorea's donjon.

ghraef – (grāf´) a large beast with thick, hardened skin that is covered in fur and an armored tail with a unique crystal on its tip; served as companions to Beholders, but disappeared after the end of the First Age.

Gil Baum – (gil´ | bäm´) the deceased Rayder husband to Flora Baum, killed by Lon Marcs.

Gorlon Arbogast – (gōr´-luhn | är´-bō-gast) father to Theiss Arbogast; lives in Roseiri.

Hadon – (hā´-duhn) village farmer of wheat and oats in Pree, along with Landon.

Haedon Reeth – (hā´-duhn | rēth´) advisor to King Drogan.

Hans Pulchria – (hänz´ | pŭl´-krē-uh) village blacksmith in Pree; husband of Ine Pulchria and father of Braedr Pulchria.

Henry – (hen´-rē) personal healer to King Drogan and Queen Cyra.

Huirk – (hyərk´) ghraef companion to Mellai Marcs.

Humsco – (huhm´-scō) a small village located in the Western Valley of Appernysia, eighty miles south of Roseiri and along the West River.

Hykel – (hī´-kl) wife to Nybol.

Ian – (ē´-en) Appernysian soldier and runner.

Ine Pulchria – (īn´ | pŭl´-krē-uh) mother of Braedr Pulchria and wife of Hans Pulchria.

Itorea – (ī-tōr´-ē-uh) the capital of the Kingdom of Appernysia; also known as the Fortress Island or City of the King.

Jaed – (jād´) an ethereal being; regulates the balance of the world's energy; only visible by Beholders.

Jareth – (jer´-eth) soldier in the Appernysian army; member of Mellai's guard.

Jaul – (jäl´) shipping town located on the west shore of Casconni Lake.

Jude – (jüd´) chambermaid in the royal chambers of Itorea's donjon.

Justice – a portable Rayder bridge used to span the Zaga Ravine.

Kamron Astadem – (kam´-ruhn | as´-tuh-dem) general of Appernysia's army; fled during the Battle for Taeja.

Kat Jashfelt – (kat´ | jash´-felt) female spymaster of Appernysia.

Kátaea Ann – (kä´t-ā-uh | an´) village delegate in Toj.

Kaylen Shaw – (kā´-len | shä´) betrothed of Lon Marcs and daughter of Scut Shaw; member of Mellai's guard.

Keene – (kēn´) previous member of Lon's twelve-Rayder tactical squad; cousin to Channer.

kelsh – (kelsh´) the ground troops of the calahein.

Kerod Cluster (ker´-uhd) – a small group of mountains in southeast Appernysia; full of precious metals and covered in endless groves of aspen trees.

King's Court – an entity consisting of the seat of government and the royal household.

King's Cross – branded into the right temple of all Rayders; in the First Age, it was tattooed into the right temple of the Phoenijan from the blue petals of the Lynth Flower.

Kutad Leshim – (kü-täd´ | le´-shim) previous leader of the Appernysian trading caravan; new sergeant of Appernysia; member of Mellai's guard.

Laecha Eddi – (lā´-chuh | ed´-ē) wife to Nadjor Eddi.

Landon – (lan´-duhn) village farmer of wheat and oats in Pree, along with Hadon.

Lars Marsen – (lärz´|mär´-sen) deceased member of Lon's twelve-Rayder tactical squad; oldest member of the squad.

Leland – (lē´-land) soldier of Appernysia who escorted the Rayders through Itorea.

Lia – (lē´-uh) chambermaid in the royal chambers of Itorea's donjon.

Linney Leshim – (lin´-ē) deceased daughter of Kutad; the name Mellai Marcs uses to disguise herself while in Roseiri.

Lio Cope – (lē´o | cōp´) head of Tarek's commander escort.

Llen Drayden – (len´ | drā´-den) a Jaed; appeared to Mellai Marcs.

Lon Marcs – (län´ | märks´) twin brother of Mellai Marcs and son of Aron and Shalán Marcs.

Lon Shaw – (län´ | shä´) nickname used by Lon Marcs to hide his connection to his father, who was a defecting Rayder.

Lynth Flower – (linth´) a rare blue flower that grows only in the center of Itorea's donjon; its petals were used to tattoo Beholders and Phoenijan in the First Age; replicated as a silver pendant that is given to honored soldiers in Appernysia.

Mellai Marcs – (mel-ī′ | märks′) twin sister to Lon Marcs and daughter of Aron and Shalán Marcs; also known as Mel.

Meridina – (mer-i-dē′-nuh) underground city of the calahein; destroyed near the end of the First Age.

Meriwald – (mer′-i-wald) wife to Ramsey.

Myron Ascennor – (mī′-ruhn | uh-se′-nōr) deceased father of Tarek Ascennor and prior village delegate of Pree; died protecting the Marcs family from a Rayder assault in Pree.

Nadjor Eddi – (nad′-jōr | ed′-ē) village delegate in Humsco.

Nellád – (nel-ad′) younger of Flora Baum's two sons.

Netsey D'Lío – (net′-sē | d-lē′-ō) lady of Itorea; daughter of Lord Tyram D'Lío.

Night Stalker – a tactical game created by the Rayders to test their stealth and skill; one team of five men tries to capture a diamond from a separate team of fifteen men without detection.

Nik – (nik′) member of Lon's twelve-Rayder tactical squad.

Nybol – (nī′-bōl) village sheep and goat herder in Pree; husband to Hykel.

Old Trade Route – abandoned trade road in Appernysia that runs from Humsco to Pree before returning to Roseiri; reference Trade Route.

Omar Brickeden – (ō′-mar | bri′-ke-den) respected Rayder scholar; acting Rayder commander after the death of Rayben Goldhawk; personal tutor and confidant of Lon Marcs; raised Aron Marcs.

Pak (pak′) – ghraef in the First Age; died in an explosion in the Forest of Blight.

Pearl River – two rivers (North Pearl River, South Pearl River) connected by Casconni Lake; used to transport shipments between Réxura and Draege.

Perbeisea Forest – (per-bā′-zhuh) sacred woods located west of Itorea; made up of Furwen Trees.

Phoenijan – (fēn´-i-zhan) elite guard of Appernysia in the First Age; composed completely of Taejans and led by Beholder lieutenants; after the Rayder revolt at the end of the First Age, the role of the Phoenijan was dissolved.

Porter – (pōr´-tər)deceased friend of Reese Arbogast.

Pree – (prē´) a small village located in the southwestern corner of the Western Valley in Appernysia, five miles east of the Tamadoras Mountains.

Preton – (pre´-tuhn) previous member of Lon's twelve-Rayder tactical squad.

Quinten Witkowski – (quin´-ten | wit-kow´-skē) cadet to Wade Arneson; branded by Lon Marcs as a Rayder.

Ramsey – (ram´-zē) village farmer of vegetables and fruits in Pree, along with Wellesly; husband to Meriwald and father of Tirk.

Ramik Gunderott – (ra´-mik | guhn´-dər-ät) chamberlain of the king's council; dwells in Itorea's donjon.

Rayben Goldhawk – (rā´-ben) deceased Rayder commander; accepted Lon into the Rayder brotherhood and made him First Lieutenant.

Rayder – (rā´-dər) title acquired when the Phoenijan followed Bors Rayder in a revolution against their king and the Beholders at the end of the First Age.

Rayder Commander – leader of the Rayders; functions similarly to the king of Appernysia.

Rayder Exile – the land north of the Zaga Ravine and the Dialorine Range; where the Rayders were banished at the end of the First Age.

Reese Arbogast – (rēs´| är´-bō-gast) younger sibling of Theiss Arbogast.

Réxura – (rex´-ər-uh) a major trade city located at the eastern tip of the Vidarien Mountains.

Ric Jois – (rik´ | jois´) previous head sentry to the royal chambers of Itorea's donjon; member of Mellai's guard.

Riyen – (rī´-yen) previous member of Lon's twelve-Rayder tactical squad.

Roseiri – (rōs-ēr´-ē) a village located in the Western Valley of Appernysia, twenty miles south of the Vidarien Mountains and along the West River; home to Dhargon and Allegna Ovann.

Ryndee – (rin´-dē) lady-in-waiting to Queen Cyra.

Rypla – (rip´-luh) right-hand man to Kutad in his trading caravan; died just after warning Appernysia that the calahein had destroyed Réxura.

Saap River (säp´) – forms the southern boundary of the kingdom of Appernysia.

Sátta – (sä´-tuh) soldier in the Appernysian army; friend to Aely.

Scut Shaw – (scüt´ | shä´) village dairy farmer in Pree; father of Kaylen Shaw.

Second Age – the current time period in the story which has been in existence for one thousand two hundred years.

seith – (sēth´) flying calahein; great bane of the ghraefs.

Serglo – (sər-glō) villager in Toj.

Sévart – (sā´-värt) young pureblood Rayder man executed for fornication with Geila.

Shalán Marcs – (shuh-län´ | märks´) wife to Aron Marcs and mother of Lon and Mellai Marcs; village healer in Pree.

Snoom – (snüm´) a member of Mellai's guard; see Banty Prates.

Sonela Reed – (suh-ne´-luh | rēd´) daughter of Delancy Reed.

Sylbie – (sil´-bē) large city that handles shipments from Réxura to Itorea; located at the connecting fork of the Sylbien River and Prime River.

Taeja – (tā´-zhuh) ruined city in the Taejan Plains; home to the Taejans and Beholders in the First Age; retaken by the Rayders after the Battle for Taeja.

Taejan – (tā´-zhuhn) title of the Rayders before their revolution at the end of the First Age; from the Taejans came the Phoenijan and Beholders.

Taejan Plains – (tā´-zhuhn) the northwestern region of Appernysia between the Tamadoras Mountains and the Nellis River.

Taie Island – (tī´) island centered in the middle of Casconni Lake; Jaul's residents fled to this island to escape the calahein.

Tarek Ascennor – (ter´-ek | uh-se´-nōr) son of Myron Ascennor; Rayder general; best friend to Lon Marcs.

Tarl – (tärl´) deceased member of Lon's twelve-Rayder tactical squad.

Tayla Leshim – (tā´-luh | le´-shim) deceased wife of Kutad.

Thad – (thad´) member of Lon's twelve-Rayder tactical squad.

Theiss Arbogast – (tīs´ | är´-bō-gast) young man who lives in the village of Roseiri; courting Mellai.

Thennek Racketh – (then´-ek | rack´-eth) Rayder lieutenant responsible for maintaining control of Three Peaks.

Thuan – (thü´-än) baron of the city, Draege.

Thorn – a conical watchtower situated north of the Zaga Ravine.

Three Peaks – solitary watchtower mountain located in the Taejan Plains; Rayders took control of this watchtower just prior to the Battle for Taeja.

Thudly – (thuhd´-lē) sentry in Itorea's donjon.

Tirk – (tərk´) son of Ramsey.

Toj – (täj´) small fishing village at the joining of the West and Saap Rivers.

Trade Route – trade road that extends from Itorea to Pree, then circles around the Western Valley of Appernysia; reference Old Trade Route.

Tragan – (trā´-gen) nine-year-old son of Ramsey.

Trev Rowley – (trev´ | rō´-lē) current village delegate in Pree.

True Sight – the ability of a man to see the world's energy.

Tucker – (tuh´-kər) deceased friend of Reese Arbogast.

Tyram D'Lío – (tir´-uhm | d-lē´-ō) member of the king's council; father to Netsey D'Lío.

Ursoguia – (ər-sä´-gwē-uh) home of the ghraefs; located forty miles southwest of Pree, deep in the Tamadoras Mountains.

Vance Talbot – (vans´ | tal´-buht) deceased captain of the Rayder cavalry.

Verle – (vərl´) previous page to King Drogan.

Wade Arneson – (wād´ | är´-ne-suhn) loyal member of Lon's twelve-Rayder tactical squad; Rayder Lieutenant; Lon's personal protector.

Warley Chatterton – (war´-lē | cha´-tər-tuhn) Rayder lieutenant over siege weapons.

Weeping Forest – a boggy forest of weeping willow trees situated at the northern base of the Dialorine Range.

Wegnas – (weg´-nas) burial grounds south of Itorea.

Wellesly – (wel´-es-lē) village farmer of vegetables and fruits in Pree, along with Ramsey.

Western Valley – the southwestern region of Appernysia between the Tamadoras Mountains and the Pearl River.

Zaga Ravine – (zä´-guh) a deep gorge that extends from the Tamadoras Mountains to the western tip of the Dialorine Range; marks the northern edge of the Kingdom of Appernysia.

Zaxton – (zax´-tuhn) Appernysian scout at the Quint River; killed by Lon's Rayder squad.

About The Author

Born in the wrong age, Terron James continually fantasizes of shining steel, majestic stone architecture, thundering cavalry rushes, and opportunities to prove his honor. Under the direction of his queen, Terron labors diligently in his kingdom, striving to prepare an inheritance worthy of his five heirs.

When he finally graduated from the University of Utah with his English BA, Terron had become besties with most of the English department staff, as well as the employees of Brio, who make a wicked cup of hot chocolate.

Terron currently resides in Tooele, Utah. His dream is to capture every sunset with his wife, fingers interlocked, the reflection of his soul in her brown eyes, and the ocean surf rolling over their bare feet.

Terron is a junior high English teacher at Excelsior Academy and a former Tooele Chapter president of the League of Utah Writers.

Visit www.TerronJames.com